THE SECRETS OF THORNDALE MANOR

THE AUDACIOUS SISTERHOOD OF SMOKE & FIRE
BOOK 2

SYRIE JAMES

ARE YOU SIGNED UP FOR DRAGONBLADE'S BLOG?

You'll get the latest news and information on exclusive giveaways, exclusive excerpts, coming releases, sales, free books, cover reveals and more.

Check out our complete list of authors, too!

No spam, no junk. That's a promise!

Sign Up Here

www.dragonbladepublishing.com

Dearest Reader;

Thank you for your support of a small press. At Dragonblade Publishing, we strive to bring you the highest quality Historical Romance from some of the best authors in the business. Without your support, there is no 'us', so we sincerely hope you adore these stories and find some new favorite authors along the way.

Happy Reading!

CEO, Dragonblade Publishing

I wish to dedicate this novel to the memory of my beloved Aunt Leila and Uncle Neil Handelman, who were devoted to me all my life and such enthusiastic supporters of my work. They are dearly missed.

*"Murder cannot be hid long …
at the length truth will out."*

*William Shakespeare
The Merchant of Venice, Act 2, Scene 2*

CHAPTER ONE

Yorkshire, England
September 1850

S CHOOL HAD ONLY been in session for a month when the maid's body was discovered in the river.

Athena Taylor caught wind of the calamity at the conclusion of the first class of the day when the snowy-haired housekeeper passed by the schoolroom door.

"Mrs. Lloyd!" Athena shivered as she crossed the room and paused in the open doorway. "Why are the fires not lit?"

Laying fresh fires was the duty of Sally Osborn, one of the two housemaids at Thorndale Manor. But upon rising, Athena had noticed that fires had not been lit in any of the customary chambers. Breakfast had been a frigid affair, and the casement windows in the classroom were fogged with moisture from a hard rain that had fallen during the night.

"I'm so sorry, Miss Taylor," replied Mrs. Lloyd, gracefully crossing her arms over her ample midriff. "Sally hasn't come in to work today."

"Hasn't she?" Athena rubbed her hands together in a vain attempt to warm them, an action she had observed the girls performing throughout the class period. "That's unusual, isn't it?"

"It is. Sally's been here nine years, and she's never missed a day of work. She arrives regular as clockwork at seven every morning."

It occurred to Athena that in the five months since she had taken possession of Thorndale Manor, she hadn't had a great deal of interaction with Sally Osborn. Athena and her sister Selena had spent the bulk of that time readying the house for their new enterprise, the Darkmoor Bridge School for Girls.

Sally was an unassuming young woman in her late twenties who quietly went about her work. Unlike the other servants, who lived on the premises, Sally was a day laborer who lived in the nearby village of Darkmoor Bridge with her father and sister.

"As I understand it, when the weather is too awful for Sally to get safely home, she shares Tabitha's room?" Tabitha, the other housemaid, slept on the second floor in the servants' quarters. "Is it possible that Sally spent last night here?'

"No, Miss Taylor. Sally went home yesterday evening before the rain."

"Well, then, I wonder what has happened." Athena heard the rustle of her pupils capping their ink bottles and stowing writing materials in their desks. "Perhaps we should send someone to check on her."

"I would have sent someone to fetch her, but I had no one to spare. Tabitha is in bed with a head cold. Hetty scalded herself when she dropped the coffeepot this morning."

"Oh, no! Is Hetty all right?"

"She is, but she's still cleaning up from breakfast. Then I need her to empty the chamber pots and lay the fires, which Sally would have done. As soon as she's able, I'll have Hetty run over to the village to ask after Sally."

"Oh, let's not bother poor Hetty." The kitchen maid was clearly overtasked already. The students, who had donned their cloaks, began filing past Athena and out of the room. "There must be someone else we can send."

But who? Athena had acquired the minimal staff left by the previous owner. The cook, gardener, and man-of-all-work would be busy with their own duties.

A young voice cried brightly, "I'll go!"

It was Miss Lucy Russell, a precocious girl of eight, and the youngest pupil at the school.

"I know where Sally lives," Miss Russell rushed on. Her long, dark locks were tied back with a white ribbon and her bright-blue eyes, which matched her pin-tucked frock, shone with excitement. "It's the stone cottage two doors down from the village shop. We pass it every Sunday on our way to church."

Athena was surprised that Miss Russell knew this. "Did Sally tell you where she lived?"

"No, miss, I *deduced* it. Which wasn't difficult. Sally said her house had a yellow door, and it's the only house in the village with a yellow door."

"I see." Athena was impressed by the girl's vocabulary and observational skills. "Thank you for the offer, Miss Russell, but I couldn't let you go alone. Besides, the morning exercise period has just begun. You must proceed to the courtyard."

"I'll get *far* more exercise if you let me go," Miss Russell pleaded. "I'll take the shortcut on the river path. I can dash to the village as fast as anything and be back in time for our next lesson."

"I'll go with her," offered Florence Jones, pushing back a lock of ginger hair from her freckled face. Miss Jones was a year older than Miss Russell, and Athena had noticed that over the past month since school had started, the two girls had become fast friends. "She won't be alone."

Athena couldn't suppress a chuckle. "All right, girls. I shall permit it this once. Please ask Sally if she is well and hurry straight back to school to report what she says to me."

"Yes, Miss Taylor!" the girls proclaimed in unison.

"Be careful!" Athena called out as they dashed off. "It rained last night, and the path may be damp!"

"We will, Miss Taylor!" Miss Russell replied before the girls disappeared from view.

Athena joined her sister in the rear courtyard and apprised her of the situation with Sally, while their three other students darted about in the autumn sunshine. As Athena breathed in the fresh morning air, still redolent with the memory of last night's rain, she glanced up at the ancient Elizabethan building looming above them. Its walls of faded stone, Gothic casement windows, and gabled roofs spoke of the wealth of the men who had designed and built it more than two hundred years ago.

Athena knew how lucky she was to own Thorndale Manor. It was an opportunity she was determined to make the most of. However, although Athena usually enjoyed this brief respite before the remaining gauntlet of classes, she couldn't help but sigh.

Selena gave her a curious look. At age twenty-eight, her sister was a year younger than Athena and she had hazel eyes, whereas Athena's eyes were blue. Selena's blonde tresses, which took after their mother's, contrasted with Athena's dark-auburn hair, which they'd been told had come from a paternal grandfather. Their styles of dress were different, too. Selena's rose-pink gown with its embroidered bodice and layered, ruffled skirts was a livelier fashion choice than the tailored, dark-purple skirt and jacket, high-necked white blouse, and pin-striped waistcoat that Athena wore. In facial features, though, they resembled each other as well as their older sister, Diana. All three had the same too-small noses, high cheekbones, and eyes that crinkled when they smiled.

Selena wasn't smiling now. "You're not worried about Sally, are you?"

"Of course I am."

"I'm sure she's fine. Maybe she enjoyed a bit too much ale at the inn last night and overslept."

"She doesn't seem the type to frequent an inn, or drink ale."

"We don't really know Sally, or what she does in her free time. People can surprise you."

"Perhaps. But that's not the only thing that worries me."

"What else?"

"Our dismal enrollment." Athena nodded at the three girls wandering in the damp courtyard amongst the pots of bright red geraniums and flowerbeds that were starting to go to seed. "Despite months of diligent advertising, we only have five pupils. *Five*! It is humiliating."

"The term has only just begun." Selena gave her an encouraging smile. "This is a brand-new venture. Things will get better, you'll see."

"I wish I shared your confidence." Athena shook her head grimly. "We should have paid more attention to the history of the house before the captain bought it."

When the excellent Captain Fallbrook—Diana's new husband, a baronet who refused to be known by anything other than his military rank—had bought the property for them last spring and had put the house in Athena's name, she and Selena had been over the moon. At last, after more than a decade as governesses, a strange, lonely occupation overseeing primarily spoiled, unruly children where their employers had not valued their abilities as teachers, they would own a grand house that was big enough to house a school of their own! Not just any school. A school for girls that would offer not only those accomplishments considered essential for a young lady, such as needlework, art, language, and music, but a far more comprehensive course of study—the same curriculum that was taught to boys. A school that would educate young women as their intellect deserved and prepare them to be strong and independent.

It was a dream that they and Diana had cherished for years. Diana, now the baronetess Lady Fallbrook, lived at Pendowar Hall in Cornwall and had many responsibilities, including running the estate while her husband was away at sea, overseeing the education of her husband's cousin, and preparing for a new baby that was due to arrive in February. But the three sisters were avid correspondents and Diana continued to provide advice from afar.

Meanwhile, Athena and Selena had been so ecstatic at the prospect of the school, they hadn't given much thought to the reputation of Thorndale Manor, or how it might affect their plans.

Everyone in Yorkshire knew the story. That Caroline Vernon, a prior resident of Thorndale Manor, had been convicted nine years ago of poisoning Harold Sinclair, the man to whom she had been engaged, and she had been hanged in front of a jeering crowd in the square at York Prison.

Caroline Vernon's father, Arthur Vernon, apparently mortified by the dreadful act his only daughter had committed, and increasingly shunned by polite society, had sunk into an abyss of alcohol and gambling. Last autumn, he had passed away, leaving an estate so mired in debt that his only son and heir, Ian Vernon, had been obliged to put Thorndale Manor on the market. No offers had come forth, until Athena had told Captain Fallbrook about the available property, and he had scooped it up on sight.

Reflecting upon these circumstances gave Athena a twinge of guilt. It bothered her that she, as the new owner of the estate, had benefitted from the misfortunes of others. *But,* she reminded herself, *the circumstances of the Vernon family were not of my making.* And, whether or not the purchase of Thorndale Manor had been a wise investment was still a matter of debate.

"The previous owner's difficulty in selling the house should have been a warning," Athena remarked testily. "Not to mention the legend about the ghost." It was said that the ghost of the murderess Caroline Vernon haunted the house and neighborhood. "It is so ridiculous!

Selena darted her a glance. "Is it?"

"Of course. There are no such things as ghosts."

"Then what *was that* the first night after we moved in?"

Athena bit her lip, reliving the moment in her mind. She and Selena had been walking down the second-floor hallway of Thorndale Manor when they had heard a sound and had sensed an eerie, unseen presence, even though—and they had checked— no one else had been about.

"I don't know. It was a dark night, and we had heard the legend about a ghost. I think we let our imaginations run away with us."

"And yet, the grocer's wife said, '*You are braver women than I to live in that house.*'"

"Just more gossip for the rumor mill. The grocer, if you recall, rolled his eyes over his wife's proclamation and winked at us."

"True."

"I prefer to stand on facts. That was the one and only time we have ever experienced such a thing. Despite all the rumors and superstitions, over the past five months, we have not seen nor heard the slightest whisper of an apparition at Thorndale Manor, and neither has anyone else."

"Also true."

Athena had hoped that the house's history and the legend about a ghost would simply be seen as intriguing stories. After all, the murder of Harold Sinclair had not occurred at Thorndale Manor, but at a neighboring estate. Caroline Vernon had paid for her crime nine years ago. Thorndale Manor was under new ownership now and it was the ideal setting for a school. Everything would be fine.

The reality, however, had proven to be quite different.

Many parents had been reluctant to send their daughters to a school that was housed in a building with such an infamous past.

"That said," Athena pointed out with a frown, "if we don't find a way to get more students, our school may have to close before it's even had a chance to get started."

Selena took Athena's hand in hers and gave it an affectionate squeeze. "Don't worry. Things will start looking up soon."

"You can't know that."

"But I do. We'll work so hard and teach these girls so brilliantly that our own reputation will grow and supersede the awful events that befell the Vernon family."

Athena couldn't help but smile. At times, Selena's relentless optimism seemed naive. But at this moment, it was exactly what Athena needed to hear. Although Athena was the headmistress of the school, she and her sister had split the teaching duties between them. Selena was one of the smartest, most cheerful people Athena knew, and their pupils had all fallen in love with her. Her proposition was entirely possible. Thorndale Manor was a splendid house and together, she and her sister could … *would* … build this school into something great.

"You're right." Athena nodded. "After all, we have a new music master arriving shortly."

"Thank goodness for that." Selena laughed.

They were prepared to teach all the academic subjects in their curriculum, but music was one of their shortcomings. Neither of them was known for their singing, and their pianoforte-playing abilities had stalled at age ten, when they had become so engrossed in novel reading, they hadn't made time to practice. As governesses, they had gotten by, teaching the basics of music as best they could, but for Darkmoor Bridge School, they wanted a more professional approach.

"Mr. Peter Chapman seems ideal for the position," Athena observed. A music tutor who reputedly sang and played the pianoforte with expertise, Mr. Chapman had, as a young man, been the ward of a wealthy neighbor, Mrs. Hillman, who owned a neighboring estate, Darkmoor Park. They had engaged him by letter. He had been traveling on the Continent all summer and was due to arrive in the village of Darkmoor Bridge in a few days' time to start work.

"Based on Mrs. Hillman's reports, I believe our girls will like him very much." Selena smiled. "And once the word gets out, by spring, I predict we'll have a dozen pupils."

"At least!" Grinning, Athena checked the watch that hung from the chatelaine at her waist. It was 10:30 A.M. Clapping her hands, she called out, "Girls! Time for class!"

The three remaining pupils sped like mad towards the house, as if in competition to see who could reach it first. Athena and Selena turned to follow.

As the girls disappeared into the building, Selena said, "I hope you told Miss Russell and Miss Jones to come straight back without stopping?"

"I did."

At that moment, the two young ladies raced into the yard. Athena frowned. They hadn't been gone long enough to check on Sally and get back, and they were both running—an action strictly reserved for the play yard. *Something must be wrong.*

"Miss Taylor! Miss Selena!" Lucy Russell exclaimed. They both halted in front of them, out of breath.

"It's horrible!" Miss Jones's face was ashen. "Just horrible!"

"What's horrible?" Selena asked.

"Sally Osborn is dead." Miss Russell seemed more intrigued by the circumstance than frightened.

Athena stared at the girl, confounded. "What do you mean, dead?"

"She d-drowned!" Miss Jones exclaimed in a trembling voice. "They found her in the river!"

The shocking, awful news reverberated through Athena's core. "*Who* found her?"

"Her sister, Miss Osborn. We saw Sally's body on the ground."

"On the embankment beneath the bridge." Miss Jones shuddered. "She looked so white and cold."

"Are you quite certain she's dead?" Selena asked gently.

"Yes. The men said so," Miss Russell replied.

"What men?" Athena asked.

"I don't know. We heard them talking, and we turned and ran."

Athena employed the most soothing voice that she could muster. "Girls, I'm so sorry you had to see that. But you may have heard wrong."

Selena took the girls into her arms and hugged them. "Let us hope and pray that Sally will be all right."

"I know this was a shock. You may have some quiet time in your room until luncheon," Athena offered.

"I don't want quiet time," Miss Russell insisted.

"Neither do I," agreed Miss Jones. "Please, may we return to class?"

"Of course you may."

The girls rushed off into the house.

Selena shook her head. "I hope the girls misinterpreted what they saw and heard."

"So do I." Athena's stomach tightened with worry. "Poor Sally. What a horrible thing!" Had she truly drowned? If so, how and when? She felt her sister's eyes on her. "What?"

"You're dying to go down there and find out what happened." It was a statement, not a question.

Athena never could hide anything from Selena. Since childhood, they had been as close as twins. "I am," she admitted.

"Go." Selena made a waving motion with one hand. "I teach the next two class periods, in any case."

"Are you sure you don't mind?"

"You'll be back in plenty of time to help me supervise luncheon, won't you? If not, I only have five pupils to look after. I know you too well, Athena. *Go.* Satisfy your curiosity. You won't be any good to anybody until you do."

CHAPTER TWO

Athena was glad to be wearing her half-boots, for the riverside path was damp with mud from the previous night's rain.

The morning sun sparkled on the dark waters of the slow-moving river. Insects buzzed in the tall grasses, and birdsong filled the air. Scattered oaks and willows, obeying nature's command, were turning golden to celebrate the early days of autumn. The scene was so beautiful and serene, it seemed impossible to believe that anything dire could have happened here—that a young woman might, that very morning, have lost her life.

And yet, as Athena rounded a bend in the path, the truth of the tragedy burst upon her. A small group was gathered on the embankment beneath the bridge that led to the village. Sally Osborn's older sister, Bridget, a plump, young woman in her late twenties, stood weeping beside her grey-faced father. Two horses were tethered to trees nearby.

A ruddy-faced, blond gentleman attired in a green-silk coat and top hat was writing with a pencil in a small notebook. Athena recognized him as Neville Sinclair, the parish constable, a man she guessed to be in his mid-thirties. At his side, the vicar, Mr. Johnson, a tall, awkward gentleman who looked to be about a decade older, stood with his hands behind his back, in what appeared to be deep reflection.

The onlookers included the village shopkeeper, a couple of

men Athena had seen at church, and two barefoot lads in short pants. They were all staring at the unmoving, wet form of a young woman clad in a dark cloak and frock who lay face up on the ground beneath a large oak tree. Her countenance was ghostly white.

It was indeed Sally Osborn.

A sharp pang stabbed Athena in the chest and sudden tears burned her eyes. How sad that the young woman had met such a terrible fate. As Athena fumbled to withdraw her handkerchief from her reticule, the bag slipped and fell to the ground.

Before she could retrieve it, the boughs of a nearby weeping willow tree jostled, and a man emerged. He stood well over six feet tall and looked even taller due to the top hat perched atop his neatly combed, inky-black hair. A tailored grey frock coat and trousers hugged his lean frame, and a black silk tie was knotted at his throat.

Their gazes met. Athena froze. She recognized that strong jaw, the chiseled face, and the piercing, cornflower-blue eyes that matched the morning sky. Although the one time they had been introduced at church, he had avoided her gaze and uttered only four curt words—*How do you do?*—before he had vanished into the crowd, Athena had heard a great deal about him from her housekeeper, Mrs. Lloyd.

His name was Ian Vernon. He was thirty-three years old.

And he had good reason to hate her.

Because Thorndale Manor had been in his family for over two hundred years. It had been his home since birth, and his birthright. Until his father had gambled away the family fortune.

Mr. Vernon retrieved Athena's reticule from the damp ground. "Your bag, Miss Taylor." His voice was low and deep, but so sharply edged that she felt its sting like the blade of knife. In fact, a cold civility seemed to vibrate through his entire being.

She understood why.

Ian Vernon, she had learned, had become a licensed architect in an attempt to support himself and his father, but he hadn't been able to save Thorndale Manor. After his father's death, Mr. Vernon had been obliged to sell the family estate and remove to a small cottage on an adjacent scrap of land.

"Thank you, Mr. Vernon." Athena's heart pounded in confusion as she accepted the muddied article. *How on Earth*, she wondered, *do you tell someone you're sorry they lost their home, when it is the very home that you now own and love? Is there a kind way to accomplish that?*

Perhaps it is better left unsaid.

Dashing away the moisture that had accumulated in her eyes, Athena gestured to the body by the riverbank. "Two pupils at my school told me what had happened."

"Your school? Ah, yes." He regarded her with tense reserve, as if he were straining to behave like the gentleman he had been bred to be. "And how is your school doing?"

"Well, thank you."

"I'm glad to hear it." He didn't sound glad at all.

"This is so awful."

"Indeed. It is a real tragedy. Sally Osborn was a sweet, quiet girl who worked for us for many years at Thorndale Manor."

Athena flinched at his tone and phrasing, which seemed to deliberately emphasize the fact that Sally had once worked for *his* family. He turned as if to walk away.

"Wait. Do you know what happened?" Athena inquired quickly.

He paused. "I do."

She waited.

His features tightened, as if he were conducting an internal debate as to whether or not to continue the conversation. Finally, with obvious reluctance, he said, "I was on my way into the village early this morning when I came upon Miss Osborn weeping in great distress. She'd noticed Sally missing from her bed and, worried, had set out this way to reassure herself that Sally had arrived at work."

"And she found her here." Athena could guess how horrible

that must have been.

"Sally's body had been caught in a pocket of the river, wedged between that fallen tree trunk and a rock." He indicated an area not far from the embankment where the unfortunate young woman's body now lay. "I fished her out, but there was nothing to be done."

"How dreadful." She noticed now that his boots were wet and encrusted with mud and river debris, proof of the awful act he had undertaken. "How do you think she ended up in the river?"

"I don't know. But I believe Mr. Sinclair has drawn his conclusion." Mr. Vernon gestured to Neville Sinclair, the gentleman who was still jotting something in a notebook.

Sinclair was the wealthiest man in the neighborhood and the owner of Woodcroft House, a place Athena had never visited. She had spied Mr. Sinclair and his wife at church and had wished to introduce herself and her sister, but social etiquette required that the Sinclairs take the first step and request a mutual acquaintance to make an introduction, and they had not done so. *No doubt because we are mere school mistresses and beneath their notice.*

There was something else about the surname Sinclair that sounded familiar, but Athena couldn't remember what it was.

"I fetched Sinclair," Mr. Vernon added, "and he came, reluctantly."

"Why 'reluctantly'?" Athena gave him a questioning glance. "Isn't he the parish constable?"

"He is and has been for nearly a decade. But he has just been appointed as the new magistrate for the county of York and is to preside at the next assizes. He is anxious to pass on the duties of parish constable to his successor, Mr. Johnson, who seems to be in training." He pointed to the vicar.

"I see."

Mr. Vernon touched his hat, as if to signal an end to the discussion, but once again, Athena stopped him. "Mr. Vernon." Gathering her courage, she added, "Sir … I wanted to say … I feel bad about the way things worked out for you with regard to Thorndale Manor. I understand that it must have been very hard to sell your home."

He gave her a stony stare. "*Hard* to sell Thorndale Manor? You *understand*, do you?" His words simmered with resentment. "How could you possibly understand?"

Athena felt as if he'd slapped her in the face. "So. You *do* hate me," she muttered under her breath.

"I beg your pardon?" His eyes narrowed.

A sense of the injustice of it all stabbed her in the gut. She wanted to hurl at him, *What right do you have to be angry with me? It wasn't my fault that your father gambled away your birthright. If Captain Fallbrook hadn't bought Thorndale Manor, someone else would have!*

Instead, she replied through gritted teeth, "Nothing."

"Good day, Miss Taylor." He turned and strode away.

Athena watched him go, annoyance dripping through her every vein. *What a rude, insensitive man. If that was how the matter lay, she would just have to make the best of it.* She would do her best to avoid Mr. Vernon in future, which, she guessed, would surely be fine by him.

Athena made her way towards the group assembled beneath the oak tree. She wanted to talk to Neville Sinclair and to express her regrets to Miss Osborn and her father, with whom Athena had become acquainted at church and at a vicar's tea.

As she passed Sally's body, although Athena told herself to hurry by, she couldn't help but pause and take a look.

Sally was sopping wet, her rumpled cloak open and revealing the black frock that encased her slender form. Her feet were encased in low-heeled, blue shoes that were streaked with mud. Her tangled, red hair had been drenched darker by the river water, and her face was as white as stone.

Athena had only been six years old when her mother had died, and she remembered very little about it. She had, however, attended many funerals since then, where the deceased had been on display before burial. Each time, particularly at the funeral for her father, she had felt a sense of pain, sadness, and emptiness, but in time, she had been comforted by the hope that the deceased's soul had departed to a higher place.

This time, however, a new and different sensation accompanied these emotions: puzzlement. Something about the maid's appearance didn't seem right. *Of course something isn't right,* Athena reminded herself. *The poor young woman just drowned.*

Taking a deep breath to compose herself, Athena crossed to where Bridget Osborn and her father stood. Mr. Osborn leaned on his cane with his only hand, the empty sleeve from his missing arm pinned up against his chest. The young woman was still weeping softly.

"Mr. Osborn, Miss Osborn. I'm so very sorry."

"Foolish girl," Mr. Osborn said, his eyes on the ground. "Never did look where she was going."

It seemed a harsh assessment for a daughter who had just lost her life. *The man must be in the throes of shock,* Athena thought. She had heard that the widower had lost his right arm and fractured his hip in an accident some years ago and could no longer work. She knew as well that Miss Osborn, a barmaid at the village pub, was the main support of the family, but Sally's earnings as a housemaid had helped as well.

Bridget Osborn coughed and wiped her eyes on the sleeve of her plaid, cotton dress. "Oh, Miss Taylor! My only sister and now she's gone."

"I can't believe it." Athena's heart went out to the young woman and her father.

"I woke up to find she hadn't slept in her bed, so I came looking for her. And to come upon her like that, face down in the river, after her acting so strange last night! It's a sight I'll never get over as long as I live."

Athena wanted to ask what Miss Osborn meant. In what way had Sally been acting strange last night? But before she could voice the question, two men in rough clothing came marching down the path, carrying an old door between them.

"Bring that over here!" boomed Mr. Sinclair. He directed the men's efforts to lay the door on the ground and lift Sally's body upon it. "All right, then," Sinclair announced when the action was completed, "bring her back to Osborn's house, and be quick about it."

The onlookers made a sad-looking procession as they followed the two men and their unfortunate cargo up the curving path that led to the bridge, leaving Athena alone on the embankment with Mr. Sinclair and the vicar. Mr. Vernon had taken his horse to the river's edge to drink from the flowing waters.

"It's all about asking questions and writing down what you observe," Mr. Sinclair was saying to Mr. Johnson. Athena headed in their direction.

"And forming a conclusion based on the facts," the vicar commented.

"Yes, of course." Mr. Sinclair tugged on his bushy, blond mustache. "I'll show you my report when it's completed. I dare say a few more times and you can handle this on your own, Mr. Johnson."

"Very good, sir."

Athena held out her gloved hand to the vicar. "I'm so sad about Sally Osborn."

"As are we all, Miss Taylor." Mr. Johnson's eyes were sad as he shook her hand. "Do you know Mr. Sinclair?"

"We have never met."

The vicar gestured to the gentleman beside him. "Mr. Sinclair, this is Miss Taylor of Thorndale Manor. Miss Taylor: Neville Sinclair, our parish constable and the newly appointed magistrate for County York."

"Sir." Athena curtseyed. "It is a pleasure to make your acquaintance."

"And yours." Sinclair greeted her with a firm handshake. To the vicar, he said, "We're done here, Johnson, thank you."

"You're welcome, sir. Good morning, Miss Taylor." The

vicar doffed his hat and bowed before striding away.

"Mr. Sinclair, can you tell me what happened?" Athena asked. "How is it that Sally Osborn came to be drowned?"

"It will all be in my report." He headed for his steed, who was tethered to a tree across the way.

"A report I will never see," Athena replied, matching him stride for side. "Please, sir, I was Sally Osborn's employer. I feel a responsibility to her. I should be grateful if you would share your views as to what occurred."

He paused, a sigh escaping his mouth. "You were her employer, you said?" He studied her. "That's right, Johnson said you're the new resident of Thorndale Manor?"

"I'm the *owner* of Thorndale Manor," Athena corrected him. "My sister and I run the Darkmoor Bridge School for Girls."

"Ah, yes. I heard about that. Did I also hear that you haven't been able to drum up more than a handful of pupils?"

Athena's face grew warm. Was it common knowledge that they'd had trouble attracting pupils to their school? "We have only just opened, sir. I'm sure we will have a full complement of students soon."

"If that's your aim, Miss Taylor, I'm sorry to say, you chose the wrong house. But perhaps you weren't aware of its history when you moved in?" He darted a contemptuous look at Mr. Vernon, who was leading his horse back up from the riverbank. "Did you know that *that* man's sister murdered my brother, Harold?"

Athena was briefly stunned into silence. The two men exchanged a look of such deep, unspoken animosity, it seemed to vibrate through the air. Vernon swiftly mounted his steed and trotted away.

"I have heard the story," Athena said, watching Mr. Vernon ride off. But she admitted silently, she'd been so focused on the identity of the criminal, Miss Caroline Vernon, she'd forgotten that the murder victim had been named Harold Sinclair. *This man's brother.*

"Good luck with that school of yours, Miss Taylor. You'll need it."

Athena's hackles went up. "We don't need luck. We shall make our way with hard work and devotion to our pupils' welfare. And, sir, you have still not answered my question. What happened here?"

He shrugged his broad shoulders. "It's obvious, isn't it? The path is damp from last night's rain. Sally Osborn was on her way to work when she slipped and hit her head on one of those rocks. She was knocked unconscious and fell into the water, where she drowned. As I said, it will all be in my report." With that, he headed off towards his waiting horse.

On her way home, Athena reflected on all she'd learned. She couldn't argue with Mr. Sinclair's reasoning. It did indeed appear as though Sally had met with a terrible accident that morning.

And yet, once again, that strange sense came over her, as if something about Sally's body hadn't been right. Had Mr. Sinclair missed something?

If so, what?

"I'M SO SORRY this has happened, girls." Athena surveyed the grave faces of the five pupils seated around her and Selena.

Thorndale Manor's drawing room was painted a restful shade of blue with white trimmings. A fire blazed in the marble fireplace. The elegant furnishings—two sofas and four wingback chairs upholstered in flowered tapestry fabric, a polished sideboard with carved legs, and several mahogany tables of varying heights and sizes—had come with the house at the time of sale, as had most of the furniture on the property.

The shadows on many walls, however, spoke of paintings that had been removed, and the built-in shelves in this room— which she deduced must have also served as the library—were bare, making her wonder what tomes used to reside there.

It was the social hour after dinner, a time when students gathered to read, chat, and do needlework. No one had taken out their books or projects tonight, however. The girls had sat in absorbed silence, listening as Athena had explained what had happened to Sally.

"I regret to say that I did not know Sally Osborn well," Athena continued. "We only met five months ago, when Miss Selena and I came to live here. But I was impressed by her good manners, and her devotion to her work and family. We will all miss her."

For a long moment, the stillness in the room was only punctuated by sniffles from two of the girls. Then a voice cried out.

"I was there!" Miss Jones thrust her shoulders back as she watched the other girls' reactions. "I *saw* her body."

"We know," declared Janet Weaver, a prim, thin-faced girl, who at age twelve was the oldest and tallest student at the school. "You've only told us about a thousand times."

"Miss Jones," Selena admonished gently from her position on a wingback chair. "What happened to Sally is very unfortunate and sad. I am sure it was an upsetting thing to witness. Let us show our respect for the deceased."

With downcast eyes, Miss Jones shrank back onto the sofa.

"Sally was nice," remarked ten-year-old Phoebe Gilbert, wiping her damp eyes with a monogrammed handkerchief.

"She made our beds for us, when we said we didn't want to," added Cecelia Gilbert, Phoebe's nine-year-old sister, dabbing her own eyes. The Gilbert sisters were attired in matching white frocks with crimson piping and sashes, and their brown plaits were tied at the ends with red ribbons. "Will we have to make our own beds now?" Miss Cecelia's pale forehead furrowed.

"I should think so," Athena replied firmly.

Miss Gilbert and Miss Cecelia crossed their arms over their chests and exclaimed in unison, "Oh, bother!"

"How selfish you are, to complain about making your beds,"

Miss Weaver criticized. "Sally just drowned in a tragic accident."

"It wasn't an accident."

All eyes turned to Lucy Russell, who had made this statement.

"What do you mean, Miss Russell?" Athena asked.

Miss Russell replied in a strong, clear voice. "I mean that Sally didn't slip and fall into the river. She was murdered."

CHAPTER THREE

Another hush descended on the room.

Athena swiveled in her seat to face the girl whose startling remark had stopped the conversation. "Miss Russell, why do you say that?"

Miss Russell shrugged her thin shoulders. "Because of her shoes."

Athena exchanged a glance with her sister, whose eyebrows were squished together as if to say, *What on Earth is she talking about?*

"What do you mean, her shoes?" Athena asked.

"Sally *always* wore the same old black, leather boots to work," Miss Russell explained. "She told me she was embarrassed by them because they were so badly scuffed, but she *had* to wear them because she was on her feet all day. She wasn't wearing her boots this morning, Miss Taylor. She had on blue shoes. Very nice slippers that I imagine were her best pair."

Athena stared at the girl, the sharp tingling of recognition rippling through her. When she had seen Sally's body, Athena had felt instinctively that something hadn't been right. She summoned the image of Sally's prone and sodden form into her mind's eye.

Sally had been wearing a cloak and her black maid's dress. She hadn't been wearing a cap or apron, but Athena had noticed that Sally usually hung those items on pegs in the servants' entry hall, to don upon arrival. But Miss Russell was right. Sally's feet *had* been encased, not in boots, but in a pair of blue shoes.

How did that escape my notice? Athena wondered, annoyed with herself. She had always prided herself on her observational skills, but she had missed a detail that an eight-year-old girl had observed.

Before she could say more, Miss Weaver proclaimed, "I don't understand. What do Sally's *shoes* have to do with *murder?*"

"It means that when Sally went down to the river, she wasn't on her way to work at all," Miss Russell replied. "She was going to meet someone."

THAT NIGHT, AS Athena and Selena undressed for bed in the chamber they shared, Miss Russell's assertion still lingered in Athena's mind.

When they had moved to Thorndale Manor, Athena and her sister had given a great deal of thought to the selection of their bedchamber. Growing up, they had always shared a room, and during the years that they had served as governesses, they had missed each other dearly. Even though Thorndale Manor had plenty of bedrooms from which to choose, they were grateful to once again enjoy each other's companionship as chamber mates.

The obvious choice of room would have been the one that had belonged to the former master of the house, the patriarch and widower Arthur Vernon. But that chamber was too dark, and its furnishings were too masculine for their taste.

The bedroom that had been occupied by the son and heir, Ian Vernon, had been stripped bare. The budget to prepare the house for their school had not been large enough to redecorate either chamber, and they hadn't wanted to ask Captain Fallbrook for more.

They had, however, fallen in love at first sight with the room that had once belonged to Caroline Vernon. The idea that a murderess had once slept there *had* been a bit daunting—at first. But the room had apparently been sitting empty for nine years, and its charm and suitability had quickly overcome any objections.

A large bay window, framed by dark-pink satin draperies, overlooked the rear courtyard and gardens. The wallpaper featured pink roses intertwined with trailing leaves and songbirds. The furniture was perfect and not too fussy: a carved mahogany dresser and wardrobe, a small desk and chair, and instead of the usual four-poster bed, two smaller beds separated by a night table. All of Miss Vernon's personal effects had been removed, and the housekeeper had seen to it that the chamber had been cleaned and dusted on a regular basis.

Upon settling in, Athena and Selena had felt at home there from the first moment. And thankfully—as Selena was wont to point out—they had never been visited by Miss Vernon's angry spirit.

"Do you think she's right?" Athena asked as she hung her frock in the wardrobe.

"Do I think who is right?" Selena sat on the edge of her bed, taking off her shoes and stockings.

"Miss Russell. I am still pondering her remarks. Do you think it's possible that Sally Osborn was on her way to meet someone at the riverbank?"

"What I think is that Miss Russell has an overactive imagination."

"Does she? Or is she uncommonly perceptive?"

Selena laughed as she slipped into her white, cotton nightdress. "She reminds me of *us* when we were her age."

"She does." Athena put on her own nightgown and began unpinning her hair. "Only think how much trouble we must have given poor Father." She smiled at the memory, recalling how she, Selena, and their sister, Diana, had looked for mysteries everywhere as children.

It had all stemmed from advice their mother had given them. Although that good woman had departed this life more than twenty-three years ago, when Selena and Athena had been only five and six years of age, they had never forgotten their mother's favorite maxim.

Where there is smoke, there's fire.

"If you hear a rumor or see signs that something is amiss," Mama used to warn them, *"it is probably true."*

Mama had named them all after goddesses, and their brother, Damon, after a Greek legend, insisting that they were each smart, special, and powerful, and that they could achieve whatever they set out to do in life. The sisters had accepted this as a profound truth, for what mother would prevaricate to her own children? Their chosen outlet for these "talents" had been mystery-solving, a pursuit into which they had thrown themselves with fervor, delighting in the possibility of discovering hidden truths in even the most innocuous of circumstances.

Damon hadn't shared their "predilection for detection," as he'd called it. So, they had formed a girls-only society and called it the "Sisterhood of Smoke and Fire."

"Very few of our 'investigations' turned up any great discoveries," Selena reminded her, picking up her brush from the dresser and running it through her long, blonde hair.

"Some did." Athena brushed her own dark-auburn locks. "We found Mrs. Phillips's lost emerald ring, remember? And what about the rector's runaway dog?"

"That's right! We must have visited more than a dozen houses in the neighborhood looking for him. Then I remembered that old Mrs. Fleming had asked for a big bone at the butcher shop, even though she never made soup."

"Very clever of you." Athena gave her sister a grin. "And there the animal was—fat and happy and living with old Mrs. Fleming, who refused to give him up." They shared a laugh.

"We had such fun in those days."

"We did." Athena looked at her. "And it's not over. You

haven't forgotten our promise to Diana, have you?"

"No, but—" Selena began.

"Diana almost died, pursuing hidden truths at Pendowar Hall. We promised to honor her bold quest and fearless disregard for risk, and to follow in her footsteps." Athena paused, hairbrush in hand. "I like the new name we gave ourselves: the *Audacious Sisterhood of Smoke and Fire*. And I meant what we said—that we would seek the truth and never back down."

"I meant it, too." Selena shrugged her shoulders. "But only when there's a truth that needs seeking—or a mystery that needs solving."

"We might have one! The parish constable believes that Sally Osborn was on her way to work this morning when she slipped and fell. But Miss Russell brought up an interesting point. Sally wasn't wearing her work boots."

Selena began braiding her hair. "Maybe Sally decided to wear her best shoes to work for a change."

"Why would she have done that?"

"Miss Russell said that Sally was embarrassed by her boots."

"Yes, but ..." Athena slowly wove her own hair into two long plaits. "It rained last night. Even if Sally did decide to wear her best shoes to work, why would she have taken the river path, knowing that her shoes would be ruined by walking in all that mud? It makes no sense." Athena paused. "Unless ..."

"Unless what?"

"Unless Sally went down to the river path *before* the rain."

"'Before the rain'?" Selena seemed to be mulling this over. "But it rained in the middle of the night. The patter on the windowpanes woke me, and I heard the hall clock strike three o'clock."

"I remember that too." Excitement rose in Athena's chest. "And I've just remembered something else. Miss Osborn told me that when she woke up, she was worried because Sally wasn't in her bed. She said the same thing to Mr. Vernon."

"When did you speak to Mr. Vernon?"

"At the riverbank. He's the one who summoned the parish constable."

"You failed to mention *that* when you told the story."

Athena blew out a frustrated breath. Every time she recalled her conversation with Mr. Vernon, it made her blood boil. "I didn't want to bother you about it."

"Bother me? I don't follow."

"That man has a grudge against me, Selena, for being the new owner of Thorndale Manor. He was intolerably rude to me."

"I'm sorry to hear that." Selena's mouth curved downward. "I suppose that would explain why we have seen so little of him since we moved here. And why he was so curt the day the vicar introduced us."

"Yes." Athena paced back and forth beside her bed. "But to get back to my point. What if we're wrong about the time that Sally went down to the riverbank? What if the reason Sally wasn't in her bed this morning was because she snuck out of the house *last night*, while her father and sister were sleeping?"

Selena climbed into her bed. "As Miss Russell said ... to meet someone?"

"Yes." Athena slid beneath her own counterpane, shivering as the cold, linen sheets came in contact with her bare legs. "Why else would she have put on her best shoes? Unless she wanted to spruce herself up a bit and look less like a working woman, for whomever she was going to meet?"

"I suppose that's possible," Selena conceded. "Maybe she went to meet a friend."

"Maybe. But ..." Athena paused. "Miss Osborn said that Sally was acting strange last night."

"Strange, in what way?"

"I didn't get a chance to ask."

With a happy, little gasp, Selena said dramatically, "What if she had a *secret beau?*"

"Exactly what I was thinking."

At all the great houses where they had been employed, it had been against the rules for a member of the staff to have a beau. When Athena and Selena had become employers, although they had had understood the reasoning behind the directive—servants who had sweethearts generally became distracted and didn't focus on their work—they had decided to be more lenient. How was a young servant to ever hope to marry if they were forbidden to have any relationships of a romantic nature? They had specified, however, that any such connection must be disclosed to both Athena and Selena, and any meetings they had must be strictly reserved for their time off.

"If Sally had formed an attachment under the previous owner, she could never have disclosed it," Athena went on. Her mind darted to the summer she had met Giles Shaw. She'd been twenty-three years old, on holiday with her employer, and she'd been obliged to conduct that affair—what a lesson she had learned there!—in secret.

"After we took over Thorndale Manor, perhaps Sally was too shy or uncomfortable to tell us," Selena mused.

"Or maybe the relationship was too new to share. Sally lived at home, so she could have met with a man at any time after her workday ended. Perhaps she saw him again last night."

"If so, *if* she died last night instead of this morning, then she was in the water a few hours longer than Mr. Sinclair supposed," Selena pointed out.

"Which could well be the case. I saw the body." Athena shuddered at the memory. "She was as white as a ghost."

"You could ask Sally's sister about it. Whether or not Sally had a beau, I mean."

"I will," Athena vowed. "*Something* happened on that riverbank. Did Sally end up in the river by accident? Or did someone hit her on the head and push her in?"

"Wait. Athena." Her sister's voice was tinged now with disbelief. "All this time, I thought we have been discussing an accidental drowning. Are you honestly telling me that you think our housemaid, that plain, quiet young woman, was *murdered?*"

"Where there's smoke, there's fire," Athena charged.

Selena let out a sharp breath. "That only holds true when there *actually is smoke*. You're reading a great deal into a pair of shoes."

"Am I?" Athena blew out the candle on the bedside table and lay back on her pillow. "Perhaps not. And there's one more thing."

"What's that?" Selena's voice, heavy with skepticism, pierced the velvet darkness.

"What prompted Miss Osborn to go out looking for her sister in the first place?"

"She said Sally was missing from her bed. She was worried about her."

"Miss Osborn didn't say that Sally was *missing* from her bed. She said Sally *hadn't slept in her bed*. There's a difference."

"How could Miss Osborn have known if Sally had slept in her bed or not?"

"A good question. But that aside, *why* was it unusual for Sally to be gone from her bed? She must have risen early every morning, six days a week, before she traipsed off to Thorndale Manor."

Selena yawned. "Miss Osborn must have simply woken up earlier than her sister was expected to wake this morning. I think you're grasping at straws, Athena."

"What I think," Athena said, mimicking her sister's earlier phrasing, "is that I need to have another talk with Miss Bridget Osborn."

RAIN POURED DOWN like a lament from the skies during Sally Osborn's funeral. More than a dozen mourners gathered at the graveside service where the vicar extolled the virtues of the deceased.

Athena shivered beneath her umbrella. The freezing dampness seemed to penetrate straight through her black, woolen cloak, hat, and gloves. Although it was a Saturday and school was in session, Selena had offered to teach all the morning classes so that Athena could attend the service and the gathering that followed and pay their respects to the deceased.

"Sally Osborn was a good, quiet young woman who worked hard, loved her family, and never missed a day of church," Mr. Johnson was saying.

Athena had also thought of Sally as "quiet" and had noticed her work ethic. But surely, Sally must have had other defining characteristics. Had she liked to sew? Had she been fond of children or animals? It bothered Athena that she didn't know.

After the service, the small crowd gathered at Mr. Osborn's unpretentious stone cottage, where a traditional wreath of laurel and yew tied with a black ribbon hung on the front door to signal that the household had suffered a death. The doorknob was draped with black crepe and tied with a white ribbon, to indicate that the deceased had been unmarried.

Athena entered the small, dark, crowded front room, hung her wet cloak and hat on a clothes tree, and squeezed her dripping umbrella into one of several buckets. The mingled scents of smoke from the fireplace and hot, damp bodies were nearly overwhelming. The curtains had been drawn. She presumed the veiled object hanging on a wall to be a mirror. Athena thought the superstition—that the deceased's spirit could become trapped in a reflective surface, preventing them from moving on to the afterlife—to be absurd. But after all her years working in households as a governess, she had come to understand that superstitions could help reduce people's anxiety by giving them a sense of control over the unknown.

In the kitchen, platters of sliced ham, boiled potatoes, breads, cakes, and pies, were spread out on a large, wooden table. Athena helped herself to a cup of tea and exchanged solemn greetings with the vicar and other villagers. She offered her condolences to

Mr. Osborn, who thanked her glumly and then disappeared into a back room.

Athena waited until all the other visitors had left to approach Miss Osborn.

"I'm so sorry for your loss." Athena sat down on a chair near the hearth across from the young woman. "I regret that I didn't know Sally well. But I know how hard it is to lose a loved one."

Miss Osborn wiped her eyes with a crumpled handkerchief. "Who did you lose?"

"My parents and my godmother."

"I'm sorry." Miss Osborn coughed deeply. "It's so unfair, isn't it? When the people we love are taken from us?"

"It is." Athena pondered how to best broach her inquiries. "Were you and your sister very close?"

"We were. At least, we used to be. Grew up like two peas in a pod, me and Sally. As children, we did everything together. Always shared the same room."

Athena smiled at that. It reminded her of her own closeness with her sister. "Always?"

"Always, except when she worked at Woodcroft House. When Sally took that job at Thorndale Manor, it was close enough to walk, so she moved back home."

"Sally worked at Woodcroft House?" Athena hadn't realized that. Woodcroft House was Neville Sinclair's home. The home in which Neville's brother, Harold, had been murdered. "When did she work there?"

"Started when she was thirteen as an under housemaid. Sally moved up to chamber maid in two years. I was so proud of her." A smile briefly lit Miss Osborn's face. "If only Papa could have been proud of her, too."

"What do you mean?"

Miss Osborn sighed. "All her life, Sally kept trying to please Papa, but he was always yelling at her about something. Sometimes I think he hated her. Maybe it was because our mother died giving birth to Sally, and he could never forgive her for that? It was even worse after Papa lost his arm. He complained that Sally didn't make enough money as a housemaid. He called her 'the useless daughter' and kept pestering her to work with me at the George and Dragon, but Sally refused." Miss Osborn erupted in another cough. "Forgive me, Miss Taylor. I shouldn't be telling you all this."

"I'm glad you told me. I feel so bad for Sally." Concerned, Athena added, "Are you ill, Miss Osborn?"

Miss Osborn waved the question away. "It's nothing, just a cough."

"It doesn't sound like nothing. Have you seen a doctor?"

"Who can afford a doctor?" Miss Osborn's mouth twisted. "There isn't one in the village, anyway. I saw the apothecary, Mr. Quince, who said I just need some good sea air to clear my lungs. If I move to Scarborough for the winter, he says, I'll be right as rain. Scarborough! For the entire winter! Where's the money going to come from for that?" She let out a huff, which evolved into another coughing fit. "Forgive me," she said again, taking a sip of water from a tumbler.

If Miss Osborn required sea air, Athena worried, her condition might worsen in the coming months, for Yorkshire winters could be harsh. Athena wished she could help this young woman, along with all the people in the parish who were in need. But she was responsible for an entire estate, five students, and a bevy of servants, and other than the modest income from her pupils' tuition and whatever Captain Fallbrook sent her, she didn't have a penny in her pocket.

"I do hope your cough improves," Athena said with feeling.

"Thank you."

Glancing up, Athena noticed that the clock on the mantel read six o'clock, which didn't match the time on the watch hanging from her belt. The reason for this suddenly occurred to her. "Did you stop the clock, Miss Osborn?"

"I did—to mark the time of Sally's death. I had to guess what it might be. The parish constable said it probably happened early yesterday morning." Tears pooled again in Miss Osborn's eyes.

It was the ideal opening for the questions on Athena's mind.

CHAPTER FOUR

THE OSBORNS' COZY front room was silent except for patter of the rain on the roof and windowpanes and the sound of someone snoring—Athena presumed it to be Mr. Osborn—from somewhere at the back of the house.

All the other guests at the funeral gathering had left. As Miss Osborn dried her tears with her handkerchief, Athena seized on the young woman's comment about the parish constable to redirect the conversation, hoping to learn more about the morning Sally had died.

"Miss Osborn," Athena began, folding her hands in her lap, "yesterday, you said that you had awoken to find that Sally hadn't slept in her bed?"

Miss Osborn nodded. "Her bed was still made."

"Was that unusual?"

"Sally *never* made her bed. *Never.* She said she had enough of making beds for others all day long. So I made her bed every morning after she left for work. I didn't mind. I like to keep things tidy. And working at the George and Dragon, it's all cleaning tables and serving pints—I don't have any beds to make. I told Mr. Sinclair that Sally hadn't slept in her bed, but he said I was mistaken, that she had obviously just made her bed before she left that morning."

Athena wondered why Mr. Sinclair had so quickly rejected Miss Osborn's statement. Was he so convinced of his own theory that he couldn't entertain any others? Was he dismissive of women in general? Had he simply been anxious to close the case? Or all of the above? "What do *you* think happened to Sally?"

"Mr. Sinclair said Sally was on her way to work and slipped on the path. She hit her head and fell into the river."

"Yes, but do *you* think that's what happened?"

Miss Osborn's forehead furrowed. "I don't know."

"Did you happen to notice Sally's shoes?"

"What do you mean?"

"When Sally was found, she wasn't wearing her boots. She was wearing a pair of blue shoes."

"That can't be right." Miss Osborn's head jerked in disagreement. "Sally only wore her blue shoes to church and for special occasions. She would never have worn them to work."

"And yet, that was what she was wearing."

"Are you certain?"

"I am."

Miss Osborn frowned and stood. "Let's check."

Athena followed Miss Osborn to the small, neat bedroom that the two women had shared. The young woman opened a pine wardrobe, burrowed beneath the few hanging garments, and brought out a pair of old, leather boots.

"You're right! These are ... They *were* Sally's." Miss Osborn's voice broke on the last three words.

The sight of those boots made Athena's heart twist with sadness. Their owner would have no more need of them. "Can you think of any reason why Sally would have worn her blue shoes yesterday instead of her boots?"

"Maybe they have a hole or a broken lace?"

They studied the boots. They were worn and scuffed, but the laces were intact, and the soles didn't have any holes. "They look fine to me," Miss Osborn observed.

When they had resumed their seats by fire, Miss Osborn let go a cough and a sigh. "I don't understand. Sally would never have gone to work without those boots. And she didn't like walking in mud. After a hard rain, she would be more likely to take the road to Thorndale Manor. It's usually less muddy than the river path."

Interesting. "Did you tell Mr. Sinclair this?"

"No. When I came upon Sally face down in the shallows, everything else flew out of my mind."

"Perhaps Sally wasn't on her way to work at all that morning," Athena suggested. "Perhaps she went out the previous night before it rained?"

"Why would she have done that?"

"To meet a friend?"

"Sally didn't have any friends. Leastways she hadn't for a long time." Miss Osborn stared down at her hands, her voice low and flat. "Except for that maid at Thorndale Manor. Tabitha, I think her name is?"

Athena took that in with a nod. It might prove useful later. "Did Sally have a beau?"

"A beau?" Miss Osborn shook her head emphatically. "*No.* Sally had no beau."

"How can you be so sure?"

"Because she had sworn off men long ago."

Athena hadn't expected that. "Why did Sally swear off men?"

"Too much heartache, I expect." Miss Osborn stared at the fire in the hearth with a sigh. "When she was working at Woodcroft House, Sally told me she was seeing a man in secret and was madly in love. But he vanished one day without a word, and she never heard from him again. I think she decided not to risk her heart again."

Athena's own heart twinged, recalling her unlucky experience with love. In her case, though, it was *she* who had broken up with the gentleman in question. Even so, the pain of that awakening still lingered. "I understand why Sally would have made such a decision all those years ago. But is it possible that she met a man recently and changed her mind?"

Miss Osborn's brow wrinkled. "I suppose. She *was* acting

strange the other night."

"You mentioned that. In what way was Sally acting strange?"

"When she came home from work, she had this faraway look in her eyes, and all through dinner, she jumped whenever I said something. I asked, 'What's wrong?', but she kept saying, 'Nothing.' I'd swear she was hiding something from me."

Athena's pulse quickened. She felt that she was getting somewhere. "Did Sally often keep secrets from you?"

"No! Well, I don't know." Miss Osborn's features softened. "As girls, we used to tell each other everything. Sally was so much fun in those days. She was all happiness and light. She sang and danced and told jokes. We used to swim in the river and walk in the woods and make daisy crowns for our hair. But after she started working at Woodcroft House, we didn't see each other except on her one Sunday off a month. And then, when Sally started working at Thorndale Manor and moved back home, well, she was never the same after that."

"When was this?"

"Nine years ago, I think."

"In what way had she changed?"

"Sally got all quiet. She didn't smile anymore. She came home from work, ate dinner, and read her Bible until bedtime. We used to love to read the Bible out loud together, Miss Taylor. We used to memorize the psalms and quote them to each other. But after Sally moved home, she read the Bible by herself for hours, almost like it was a duty. She was still doing that all these years later. If she got any comfort from it, I couldn't say."

"*Was* she seeking comfort? Had something been troubling her?"

"I asked her, but she wouldn't say."

"Do you think she was still upset about her lost love?" Athena wondered aloud.

"Maybe. If so, it's very sad. That happened so long ago." Miss Osborn sighed. "But that light in her eyes, I never saw it again." She paused, adding, "Except the night before she died, I caught a hint of it."

"What kind of hint?"

"It was like Sally was excited about something. But at the same time, nervous. If that makes any sense."

"It does make sense." Athena's stomach tightened. "This is important testimony, Miss Osborn. You need to tell the parish constable."

"Oh! I wouldn't dare." Miss Osborn shook her head firmly. "He would never listen to anything I say."

"He'll have to," Athena insisted. "It's his job. If Sally met someone on the bridge path that night, they might know what happened to her. Perhaps it was just an accident. Or … perhaps not."

Miss Osborn gave her a blank look. "What are you saying, Miss Taylor?"

"I'm saying, it's possible that Sally didn't slip and fall into the river. Someone might have hit her on the head and pushed her in."

Miss Osborn's eyes widened, and she gasped. "Who would do such a thing?"

"That's what we need to find out."

"No. No! I can't imagine that. No one would have wished to harm my sister. She was too sweet and good."

"But—" Athena began.

Miss Osborn cut her off. "Whether it happened at night or in the morning, what difference does it make? My sister is dead. And nothing's going to bring her back." Fresh tears sprang into Miss Osborn's eyes. She stood. "Forgive me, Miss Taylor. I don't wish to discuss this further. It's been a long and frightful day."

Athena rose, again expressed her deepest sympathy for Miss Osborn's loss, and took her leave.

As she walked home, Athena's heart pounded with every step. Her suspicions about the shoes now seemed very likely. Even if Sally had, uncharacteristically, chosen to wear different shoes to work, she wouldn't have done so knowing she'd have to walk in mud. *Which meant she hadn't been on her way to work. She must* have gone down to the riverbank that night before the rain.

"It was like Sally was excited about something. But at the same time, nervous."

Had she gone there to meet someone? Had Sally had a secret beau? Miss Osborn may not have been privy to the secret, but someone else might have been.

Athena knew exactly whom to ask.

AFTER TEACHING HER science class, Athena turned the girls over to Selena for fifth-period French and made her way to the drawing room.

The late-afternoon sun filtered in softly through the mullioned windows of the corridor, where rectangular shadows on the walls gave testament to paintings that used to hang there. Athena loved art almost as much as books and she wondered what those missing paintings had represented. The artwork that remained, primarily landscapes of the English countryside, was lovely. She was grateful that the former owner had included them when he'd sold the house—at a price, as she understood it, that had been far less than market value.

Former owner. Athena frowned. When she and Selena had moved in to Thorndale Manor, those two words had just been a name without a face. Now she knew more. Mr. Ian Vernon was a bitter man. The house, Athena knew, had taken months to sell. Perhaps his efforts to sell the furnishings had been equally frustrating. Perhaps the pictures he'd left, and the furniture as well, had not been an act of generosity at all, but rather, a means to simply get rid of them. *Well, his loss is our gain.*

A clattering sound reminded Athena of her mission. She entered the drawing room to find Tabitha, a diminutive young woman with light-brown hair and a trim figure, busily dusting.

"Tabitha, may I have word?"

"Yes, Miss Taylor." The housemaid paused in her labors and curtsied.

Athena recalled that Tabitha hadn't been well the other morning. "I hope you are feeling better?"

"Much better, thank you. But there's so much to be done, what with me being the only housemaid now. I wanted to tidy up in here while I could. I hope I won't be in your way?"

"Not at all. I'm sorry so much work has fallen upon your shoulders," Athena told her. "Mrs. Lloyd is looking into a replacement for Sally."

"Oh! Good." The maid's voice went quiet. "Poor Sally. It's so awful what happened to her."

"It is indeed. Horrible. In fact, that's what I'd like you to speak to you about. I'm thinking you might have known Sally better than anyone else on the staff, since you shared a room together?"

"Well, I don't know. Sally didn't sleep here very often. Only when there was a terrible storm, or she was too tired to walk home."

"Still, you worked together for how many years?"

"Sally was here when I got here. So that would make it six years."

"Did you consider Sally to be a friend?"

Tabitha shrugged. "I suppose. Sally was a bit odd, though."

"Odd how?"

"She kept to herself and didn't talk much. Sometimes when we were making up the beds or beating the carpets, we'd have a laugh or two. But everything she did had to be just so. If a bed corner didn't look tight enough, she'd do it over ten times—she said Mr. Vernon had drilled that into her."

"Do you mean Mr. Ian Vernon?"

"Oh, no, miss. *He* is a very nice gentleman. I mean the father, Mr. Arthur Vernon, who passed away last year."

"I see." This was a very different description of Mr. Ian Vernon than Athena would have given, based on their recent meeting. She decided to get right to the point. "Can you think of anyone who may have wished to harm Sally?"

"Harm her?" Tabitha's brows shot skyward. "No."

"Do you know if Sally had a beau?"

Tabitha shook her head firmly. "No. Beaus are not allowed."

"I understand that they were not allowed before, but that rule has changed. You only have to inform myself or my sister of the liaison."

Tabitha chewed on her lip. "I know you both said that, and it was kind of you, but …"

"'But'?"

"Well." Tabitha fiddled with the feather duster in hands. "There's been talk downstairs, and some of us, if we ever *did* step out with someone, we wouldn't feel right telling you about it."

"Why not?"

"For fear that you'd think our work would suffer, or we were planning to leave any minute. Which might not be so at all! We worry that you'd find someone to replace us and let us go."

Athena hadn't considered that. "Thank you for explaining that." She pressed on. "So, you're saying that if anyone on staff *did* have a sweetheart, they probably wouldn't tell us?"

"Probably not. But I don't have one, I swear!"

The young woman sounded so desperately sincere that Athena believed her. "All right, then. But remember, if you ever did, as long as you tell us and continue to do your job, it will not affect your employment here."

"Thank you, Miss Taylor." The maid gave her a nod.

"Now, getting back to Sally. I'm trying to understand what happened to her. You may be honest with me, Tabitha. Anything you say can't harm Sally now. I suspect she may have had a relationship with a man, and I'd be grateful to hear anything you might know about it."

"Sally didn't have a beau, Miss Taylor. Not in all the years I knew her. I can tell you that for certain."

Athena stared at her. "How can you be certain?"

"A woman knows when her friend is up to something like that. And whenever the subject came up, she swore she'd have nothing to do with a man again. Because of some heartache she'd once suffered. Sally kept to herself. She had a horror of breaking rules. On the nights she did spend here, Sally wouldn't blow out the candle. She stayed up reading the Bible. There was one passage I heard her quoting over and over under her breath. It nearly drove me to distraction."

"Which passage was that?"

"'*Even a fool is considered wise if he keeps silent, and discerning when he holds his tongue.*'"

Athena recognized the passage. It was from Proverbs 17:28. "You say she repeated it over and over?"

"Yes. Sometimes in her sleep."

Athena thanked Tabitha and ventured to the study that she shared with Selena, where she sat in deep reflection. If Sally Osborn had not had a beau, why had she gone down to the riverbank the night she'd died?

And what had that Biblical passage meant to her?

"I SAW YOU returning from Sally Osborn's funeral yesterday afternoon," Miss Russell remarked.

Athena and her pupil were standing in the front drive outside the school, as they did every Sunday morning, waiting for the girl's parents to arrive. Mr. and Mrs. Russell ran a haberdashery shop in Thrushcross, about six miles away, close enough that, unlike the other girls at school, Miss Russell was able to go home to visit every Sunday.

"How did you know that I'd gone to the funeral?"

Miss Russell shrugged her shoulders. "You were dressed all in black and wore a black veil."

Once again, Athena was intrigued by this young girl, who

always seemed to have her eyes and ears open. Athena had spent half the night thinking about her conversations with Miss Osborn and Tabitha and had awakened convinced that there was more to Sally's death than Bridget Osborn or the parish constable believed.

However, when Athena had mentioned her concerns to her sister, Selena had insisted, *"I still say it is a long stretch of the imagination to suspect that someone deliberately took Sally Osborn's life, based on the state of her bed and her choice of shoes."*

"You disappoint me," Athena had retorted. *"What happened to the girl who used to see a clue to a mystery in every corner?"*

"She *has* grown up. The likeliest explanation is usually the simplest, you know. Which is that Sally made her own bed and decided to wear different shoes."

"Something tells me that's not what happened."

Selena had pursed her lips and shaken her head. *"I wouldn't go down this road, Athena, if I were you."*

"Why not?"

"Because Thorndale Manor's history is already tainted by a long-ago murder. Do you really want to suggest that another killing has taken place, this time even closer to home? It has been hard enough to get students as it is, Athena. Leave it alone."

"Did you learn anything useful at the funeral?" Miss Russell's inquiry broke into Athena's thoughts. "Anything that might help solve Sally's murder?"

Athena considered her reply. Although she admired the girl's observational skills and sense of curiosity, Athena didn't want her to fixate on an unhealthy subject. "Miss Russell, no one is saying that Sally was murdered. Her death is reported to be an accident. I urge you to put the matter from your mind."

"Even though *you* haven't?"

Athena started. How could Miss Russell know what Athena was thinking? She really was uncanny. "You must focus on your schoolwork, and the lovely day you're about to share with your parents."

Miss Russell lowered her gaze and sighed. "Yes, Miss Taylor."

Moments later, the Russells' carriage pulled into the drive, and its occupants descended.

"Hello there!" boomed Mr. Russell, a portly, bespectacled man whom Athena guessed to be in his mid-forties, and whose light-red hair was streaked with grey. He wore a serviceable brown suit and shoes that looked recently polished. "How's my favorite little girl?" He lifted Miss Russell in his arms and gazed at her with warmth.

Miss Russell giggled. "I'm fine, Papa. But I'm not a little girl anymore. I'm eight years old. You must put me down."

"Your wish is my command." After setting the girl gently on her feet, Mr. Russell removed his derby and gave Athena a polite bow. "Miss Taylor."

"Mr. Russell. Mrs. Russell." Athena dipped a curtsy.

Mrs. Russell, neatly attired in a gown of dark-blue-and-white plaid cotton, her pale hair pinned up beneath a plumed hat, nodded courteously to Athena and then bent down to embrace her daughter. "I have missed you, dearest. How is school?"

"Very interesting," Miss Russell replied matter-of-factly. "Our maid was killed on Friday."

Mrs. Russell's mouth fell open. "*What?*"

Mr. Russell stared. "Did you say 'killed'?"

Athena's chest tightened. Regardless of her own thoughts on the subject, it was clear that her sister had been right. The last thing they needed was for a rumor of this kind to spread. "I'm afraid your daughter misspoke," she said hastily. "One of our maids took a misstep down by the river. Her drowning was an unfortunate accident."

"Even so." Mrs. Russell's brow wrinkled as she rose. "That is disturbing to hear. This house is already associated with a great tragedy. A woman who once lived here committed murder, isn't that right?"

"Oh, stop being hysterical, Ellen," Mr. Russell declared with a sigh. "*That* happened ages ago." To Athena, he added in a stern voice, "However, the river sounds like a dangerous place, Miss

Taylor."

"I hope you don't allow the girls to go down there unaccompanied?" asked Mrs. Russell with a worried frown.

"Of course not," Athena assured the woman, even though she knew it was a lie. She *had* allowed Miss Russell and Miss Jones to do exactly that the other morning. That was a mistake and now she was paying for it. She darted Miss Russell a silent look, hoping to convey her warning not to speak of it.

Miss Russell appeared to have received the unspoken command. "Don't worry, Mama. I would *never* go down to the river *alone.*"

"Well, thank goodness for that," Mrs. Russell responded. "Shall we go, then? Cook is making roast beef and Yorkshire puddings for dinner, your favorite, Lucy. We'll bring her back by seven P.M. as always, Miss Taylor."

Athena voiced her thanks and watched the carriage speed off down the drive. *That was a narrow escape,* she thought. She was still determined to get to the bottom of what had happened to Sally. *But,* she reminded herself, *you will have to proceed quietly and carefully.*

"WHAT TIME DID Mr. Chapman say he was coming?" Selena inquired later that afternoon as she parted the drawing room curtains and gazed out front.

After escorting their four other pupils to church and supervising luncheon, Athena and Selena had released the girls, as per their Sunday tradition, to read or draw, walk in the courtyard, or otherwise occupy themselves on their own until dinner.

"Two o'clock." Athena tidied a stack of magazines on a low table and checked her watch. "Any minute now, in fact. He said in his letter that he would be arriving by coach at Darkmoor Bridge this afternoon."

"Our new music master is a punctual man," Selena declared with a smile. "He is walking up the drive as we speak."

Athena heard some bustle in the front hall and in short order, Tabitha entered the drawing room.

"Mr. Peter Chapman to see you," the housemaid announced, her cheeks unusually bright. She glanced beneath her lashes at the newcomer, who rewarded her with a smile before she hurried from the room.

Athena felt the same unsettled response to the newcomer.

Mr. Chapman was one of the most handsome men she had ever seen.

CHAPTER FIVE

A BROAD-SHOULDERED MAN with a trim physique, Mr. Chapman was elegantly attired in a navy-blue frock coat; a burgundy, silk bow tie; and pale-grey, pin-striped trousers. Athena recalled that he was thirty-five years of age. His high cheekbones and slender nose graced a pleasing countenance that featured the classic look of the Roman statues Athena had admired in pictures.

Selena darted her a covert look that seemed to echo Athena's enthralled assessment.

He swept a bow, removing his hat to reveal a crown of well-styled, dark-brown curls. "Peter Chapman, at your service." His eyes, the color of molten chocolate, radiated friendliness and charm.

Athena found her voice. "Mr. Chapman, how do you do?" She introduced herself and her sister, and they both dipped curtsies.

"I hope your journey was uneventful?" Selena asked.

"It was. I have only just arrived in the village. I had my trunk delivered to Darkmoor Park and stopped to say *hello* to Mrs. Hillman before making my way here."

Athena knew that he would be residing with Mrs. Rose Hillman, his former guardian, who lived about a mile and a half away. "Thank you for coming. We have been looking forward to meeting you."

"And I, you." He glanced about. "What a charming room, and what a marvelous house. You are fortunate to be in possession of such a place."

"We are, indeed," Athena agreed.

"I can only dream of owning a house like this someday."

"It does feel like a dream sometimes," Selena remarked.

"Would you like tea, sir?" Athena asked. "Or a tour?"

"Both, if you please. Tea first. I have had a long journey, and I am parched."

Athena rang for tea. Mrs. Lloyd immediately brought in the tray with the tea service and a plate of biscuits, bread, and butter.

"This looks lovely, thank you," Mr. Chapman said.

The housekeeper's cheeks were rosy as she dipped a curtsy and left the room.

As Athena poured three cups of tea and passed them out, she couldn't help sharing the maid's, housekeeper's, and Selena's wide-eyed response to this newcomer. They'd never had such a handsome or charming visitor at Thorndale Manor. To think that he would be working here! She looked forward to the association.

At the same time, she warned herself, an *attraction* to this man was imprudent. She could not indulge in a flirtation with her staff. She wanted it known to one and all that she took her duties as the headmistress of this institution seriously, and she was determined to remain single—for the good of the school and for herself.

She hadn't always felt that way. As a young woman, Athena had looked forward to one day falling in love and marrying. She'd had little opportunity to meet a man while working as a governess, though, until that summer holiday with her employer's family when Giles Shaw had entered her life. He had been good-looking and attentive. She had been entranced for a time. But then his true nature had revealed itself. Mr. Shaw had been intent on controlling Athena's every move and thought, and he had been a firm believer that women were second-class citizens who should not be educated. He had laughed at her dream of running a school. She'd had a glimpse of her future with him and had realized it could never be.

Over the past decade, she had seen so few examples of happy unions. The men she'd worked for had all shared Mr. Shaw's views and the women had been bored and restless, complaining that marriage felt like a prison, and to relieve the tedium, they had, like their husbands, often indulged in affairs.

It was the status of a married woman that had come to bother Athena the most. A single woman held the same rights as a man. She could own property, assume responsibility for her debts, enter into a contract, and make a will. But the moment a woman took a husband, she lost nearly all those rights. Although she could still legally own her land or house, she could no longer manage it without her husband's consent. *He* immediately took complete control of all her personal property, her earnings, and her children.

Even if Athena ever were to find a man for whom she would be willing to give up all that, she knew she could not have both marriage and a career. Men of her class did not allow their wives to work. For the younger sons who earned their bread by their daily toil, it would be an embarrassment, a sign that the man didn't earn a sufficient income to provide for his family. For those who had inherited their fortune, it would be equally demeaning. Gentlewomen were meant to remain in the background, with no opinions or accomplishments of their own, quietly raising their children and running their homes—not a school.

The Darkmoor Bridge School for Girls might have been in precarious financial waters at present, but she and Selena would fix that. After such a long wait, Athena wasn't about to sacrifice their dreams for anyone. She knew that society looked down on spinsters, but she didn't care. Far better to carry on as she was, single and engaged in an occupation she found important and fulfilling, than to exchange all her rights for a life with a man.

"First off, I want to thank you for hiring me."

Mr. Chapman's voice broke in upon Athena's thoughts.

"After years of private tutoring, I required a change," he went on. "I look forward to teaching music at your school."

"Of all the applicants we considered, you are the most qualified," Athena assured him with a smile.

"In your letter, you said you have experience teaching the pianoforte, singing, and dancing as well?" Selena asked as she sipped her tea.

"I do." He spread jam and cream on a hot scone.

"Mrs. Hillman gave you the most glowing recommendation," Athena put in.

"Did she? It has been many years since I have seen Mrs. Hillman. I am grateful to hear that she thinks so well of me." He bit into his scone and murmured his appreciation. "I feel bad though that I am starting work a month after school has begun. As I believe I explained in my letter, I was obliged to stay with my previous employer during his tour of the Continent, to teach his sons and daughters."

"Yes. Did you enjoy the tour?" Selena asked.

"Every day was remarkable." He leaned forward in his chair. "The sight of the Roman Forum at sunrise, and the art in the Vatican and the Uffizi Gallery in Florence alone are worth the journey. But the highlight for me was the music. We attended the most marvelous concerts." He caught himself and paused. "But I won't bore you with tales of my travels. I am here now and eager to teach. How many pupils do you have, if I may ask?"

Athena set down her teacup. "Five at present. We hope to double that number, in time."

"My last employer had six children." His lips turned up in a grin and his brown eyes sparkled. "Five will be an easy task for me, but give me a dozen and I shall be pleased to teach them all."

They shared a laugh.

After tea, they gave Mr. Chapman a tour.

"Rise and shine is at seven A.M., with breakfast at 7:45 A.M.," Athena explained as they made their way into the dining room, which was paneled in mahogany and featured a crystal chandelier and a long, mahogany dining table surrounded by a dozen chairs upholstered in burgundy velvet. "We take all our meals here. After that, lessons begin in the schoolroom."

They visited the schoolroom next, which featured casement windows overlooking the garden.

"This room, we are told, was formerly the parlor for the lady of the house," Selena told Mr. Chapman.

They had removed the furnishings and painted the room white. A blackboard hung on one wall, a map of Europe on another. "We were fortunate to acquire desks from a school in York, who had more than they needed," Athena explained.

"It is a fine place for learning," Mr. Chapman replied, taking it all in.

"School is in session Monday through Saturday, with Wednesday afternoons off," Athena told him. "We have scheduled times for morning exercise, lunch, and an afternoon break, and six lesson periods per day: reading and writing, arithmetic, history, science, foreign language—we teach French, German, and Latin—and during the last period of the day, we alternate between art and music."

"An admirable curriculum. Do you still intend for me to teach three days per week?"

"Yes. Mondays, Thursdays, and Saturdays, from four-thirty to six P.M., if that suits you?" Athena answered.

"Excellent. May I presume there is a music room?"

"There is." Selena led the way to the pertinent chamber, which was one of Athena's favorite places in the house.

A sizeable room with a high ceiling, its two large, bowed windows flooded the room with light. Floral wallpaper in shades of green, black, and amber complemented the dark-green, velvet draperies and the Persian carpet that covered a section of the polished oak floor. Other than a row of chairs against one wall, the only furnishings were two pianofortes: a grand and an upright.

"I hope this will do for your needs?" Athena asked.

"Admirably! I couldn't ask for more." He gestured towards the grand pianoforte. "May I give it a try?"

Athena smiled. "Of course. If you require music, we found reams of it in the bench."

"That won't be necessary." Mr. Chamber sat down at the instrument, flexed his fingers, and began to play.

Whenever Athena's previous employers had brought in musicians to play at parties, she had hidden in the hall to listen, and she had been privileged to attend a few concerts in town. Although she didn't recognize this song or its composer, Mr. Chapman performed with a passion and verve that was captivating, as if he were pouring his innermost feelings into the music.

The dramatic melody filled the room, crowding out everything else. Selena's captivated expression suggested that she was equally affected. Suddenly, four students burst in through the open doorway and stopped, their eyes wide. Mrs. Lloyd and Tabitha followed. They all watched and listened as if entranced.

Mr. Chapman, barely glancing up at this intrusion, played on gloriously for another few minutes and concluded the piece with a flourish. Everyone burst into applause.

"Bravo!" cried Selena.

"That was wonderful," Athena enthused.

Mr. Chapman stood and faced the girls, a smile lighting his handsome face. "Well, well, and who are these lovely creatures? They look far too grown up and sophisticated to be the girls I'm going to teach."

The students giggled and exchanged furtive whispers.

"Are you our new music master?" blurted Miss Weaver, with hope in her voice.

"He is, indeed," Athena announced. "Girls, may I present Mr. Chapman?"

He gave an illustrious bow and then shook hands with each pupil as Athena introduced them. "Miss Jones? How do you do? Miss Weaver? It's a pleasure to make your acquaintance. Miss Gilbert? And Miss Cecilia Gilbert? Not twins, I think, but as close as twins. I'll bet you tell each other everything, am I right?"

The Gilbert sisters grinned, their eyes shining.

"I was promised five students, but I count only four," Mr. Chapman noted.

"Miss Russell lives in a nearby village, and she goes home every Sunday," Miss Jones explained.

"Ah! I see," replied he.

"Mr. Chapman, may I present our housekeeper, Mrs. Lloyd, and head housemaid, Tabitha?" Athena interjected with a hand flourish.

He strolled up to the two servants and bowed. "It is a pleasure to make your acquaintance. Mrs. Lloyd, please give my compliments to your cook. Tea was delicious."

"Thank you, Mr. Chapman," replied Mrs. Lloyd as she and the maid, with uncharacteristic grins, curtseyed.

Miss Gilbert tugged on Mr. Chapman's sleeve. "Will you play something else?"

"Yes! Play another song!" cried Miss Cecelia.

"I'm happy to. But you'll have to ask your headmistress."

"Please, Miss Taylor! Please!" cried the girls, jumping up and down.

"Mr. Chapman doesn't start work until tomorrow," Athena pointed out.

But the girls continued their pleas and Selena whispered in Athena's ear, "We have nothing else going on at the moment."

"Very well. Mr. Chapman, if you wish—play on."

He resumed his seat and encouraged everyone to gather around the pianoforte. "What shall it be? Perhaps something you all know so you can sing along?"

The students peppered him with suggestions. He chose "Greensleeves" and began playing. Mr. Chapman's clear, confident, and expressive tenor led the way as everyone in the room exuberantly sang along. Athena was delighted by the jolly atmosphere that pervaded the room. When the song was finished, everyone clapped loudly, including the player.

"What a splendid choir. I can see that I shall have very little to do when it comes to teaching you girls to sing."

The students shouted with laughter. It took an unusual amount of persuading before Athena and Selena succeeded in ushering the girls and the servants out of the room to return to their previous activities.

When all was quiet once more, Athena thanked Mr. Chapman and said, "This has been our school's most enjoyable Sunday on record."

"An unremarkable achievement, considering that school has only been in session for a month," noted he with a wink.

Athena and her sister laughed. They agreed that he would arrive the following day a half hour before his class began. When they reached the front hall, he paused.

"I almost forgot. I have an invitation for you from Mrs. Hillman." He removed a letter from his coat pocket. "It's addressed to you both."

"I'll take it." Selena opened the missive and read it with a smile. "Mrs. Hillman has invited us to tea at Darkmoor Park on Wednesday at three o'clock."

"How kind," Athena said. She and Selena had enjoyed tea at Darkmoor Park once before, several months ago. "But one of us must stay here. Selena, you may feel free to go."

"I thought school is not in session on Wednesday afternoons?" Mr. Chapman inquired.

"It's not. But someone must still watch over the girls," Athena explained.

"How about if I come on Wednesday?" Mr. Chapman offered. "I could roll up the carpet and give dancing lessons. We'll have a jolly time, and you can both go to tea."

Selena's breath caught. "Are you serious?"

"It's a generous offer, Mr. Chapman," said Athena. "But I'm afraid we couldn't pay you for the extra time."

"I wouldn't accept, even if you did." Mr. Chapman studied her. "I see you silently deliberating, Miss Taylor. You're thinking,

As headmistress, the school is my responsibility. But everyone deserves a little time off now and then."

Athena hesitated. She did feel that if she accepted, she would be shirking her duty. But the idea of an afternoon off *was* tempting.

"I assure you that your students will be in safe hands," said Mr. Chapman. "You'll be back in time for dinner, and I'll be on my way."

Athena turned to her sister. "What do you think?"

"I think we should accept with alacrity."

Athena smiled. "You heard my sister. Wait a moment, and I'll dash off a note of acceptance to Mrs. Hillman."

After the front door closed behind Mr. Chapman, Selena gave a happy sigh. "What a pleasure it will be to look at *that* man's face three afternoons a week."

"I wonder if he dances as well as he plays and sings?"

"If only we could be here on Wednesday to find out."

"We'll have plenty of other opportunities to see him perform," Athena remarked.

"Yes, we will. How wonderful is that?" They couldn't help but laugh.

MR. CHAPMAN'S PIANOFORTE class on Monday went smoothly. Athena sat quietly in a corner, observing. He put the two instruments to good use, giving each girl time to practice. Although the pupils had varying degrees of experience and skill, he conducted an instructive and engaging lesson that left all the girls smiling. Athena came away very pleased with their new music teacher, and with herself for hiring him.

After the girls had retired for the evening, Selena hemmed sheets, and Athena tackled some paperwork in their study.

Everything is proceeding smoothly, Athena congratulated herself.

Her students were getting along. Athena was having a marvelous time teaching science, art, reading, and writing. Even after only a month of instruction, she was delighted to see the progress her pupils were making, and to hear the excitement in their voices when they came to understand a new concept. Selena was equally enthralled, having reported that their students were faring well in mathematics, foreign languages, and history.

However, as she reviewed Mrs. Lloyd's planned menus for next week and paid several bills, her thoughts kept drifting two other subjects that had been haunting her for days. One: their too-small enrollment. How she was going to fix that remained a mystery.

And two: *Sally Osborn.*

Athena wouldn't feel satisfied until she knew what had happened to that unfortunate young woman. Taking out a fresh piece of paper, she dipped her pen in the inkwell and summarized everything that she had learned so far.

1. Sally was found dead in the river, with an injury to the back of her head.
2. She was wearing her best shoes instead of her work boots.
3. Either Sally had made her bed, or she hadn't slept in it.
4. Sally apparently hadn't had a beau, nor any friends but Tabitha.
5. The night before she died, Sally's mind had been elsewhere. She had seemed excited and nervous.
6. Sally was fond of quoting scripture, in particular Proverbs 17:28.
7. Sally had a secret romance years ago while she worked at Woodcroft House.
8. Sally left Woodcroft House nine years ago and started working at Thorndale Manor.
9. After that, she swore off men and was "never the same."

What did it all mean?

Athena reread the list, and when she came to the eighth item, she paused, her pulse beating faster. *Nine years ago.*

Nine years ago, Caroline Vernon had been hanged for murdering Harold Sinclair.

Athena knew very little about that murder, except that the victim had apparently been poisoned. Had Sally Osborn been working at Woodcroft House when Harold Sinclair had been killed? If so, could it have had anything to do with Sally's reason for leaving that job, and her change in behavior afterwards?

Proverbs 17:28 echoed in Athena's mind. *"'Even a fool is considered wise if he keeps silent, and discerning when he holds his tongue.'"*

What if, Athena suddenly wondered, *it wasn't Caroline Vernon who murdered Harold Sinclair, but someone else entirely?*

Had Sally Osborn seen something the night Harold Sinclair had been killed? What if she had been a witness to the murder itself—and knew it hadn't been Caroline Vernon—and yet had held her tongue all these years? If so, had someone just learned what she'd known and killed her for it?

Sally's decision to wear her best shoes still suggested that she'd gone down to the riverbank to meet someone special, perhaps a beau. And yet, a new idea came to Athena's mind. Might Sally have set up a meeting at the riverbank to blackmail the true murderer of Harold Sinclair? It would explain her excitement and nervousness, for such an endeavor would have involved a change of thinking, and she must have known it could prove dangerous. Perhaps it had. Perhaps the meeting had gone wrong, and Sally had paid for it with her life.

Selena's warnings came back to her.

"It is a long stretch of the imagination to suspect that someone deliberately took Sally Osborn's life, based on the state of her bed and her choice of shoes."

Was Selena right? Was Athena mad to be conjecturing such things? She longed for counsel from her older sister, Diana—and she owed her a letter.

Withdrawing a fresh sheet of paper from her desk, Athena wrote a long letter to Diana, bringing her up to date on all that had happened over the past few days. She informed her of Sally's death and everything she had learned so far, and she had just begun writing about her suspicions when a light knock sounded on the open door. Mrs. Lloyd was standing in the doorway.

"Miss Taylor, may I have a word?"

"Certainly. Come in." Athena covered her letter with a blotter. The housekeeper's visit, she realized, was opportune. Mrs. Lloyd had worked here for decades and must have known a great deal about its former occupants.

"I've found a suitable young woman for the maid's position," Mrs. Lloyd announced without preamble, stopping before Athena's desk. "Her name is Laura. She is employed as a maid of all work for a tradesman's family, and she jumped at the chance to work at Thorndale Manor. She can start in a week and will live on the premises."

"Thank you so much, Mrs. Lloyd. I trust your judgment as always and look forward to meeting Laura."

Mrs. Lloyd nodded. "You are most welcome, Miss Taylor."

"Before you go, do you have a few minutes?" Athena gestured to the chair before her desk. Mrs. Lloyd sat down. Athena leaned forward and clasped her hands. "Mrs. Lloyd, the other day you mentioned that Sally Osborn had worked at Thorndale Manor for nine years. How did you remember that number so specifically?"

The housekeeper hesitated. "Well, miss. I remember because we were all in a fog of grief at the time. It was just after Miss Vernon had been taken away to York Prison."

Athena's insides fluttered. She'd been right. Sally Osborn had left Woodcroft House just after the murder of Harold Sinclair. "What else do you remember about that time?"

"I remember that one of our maids had just left to get married." Mrs. Lloyd grimaced as if she'd just tasted a sour grape. "I was glad to see the back of that one—and grateful when Sally showed up at the door, asking about the position."

The housekeeper, Athena noted, had clearly disliked the maid in question. Athena wondered why but dismissed the notion for now as perhaps irrelevant.

"I've heard about Miss Vernon's conviction, but I know very little about the crime itself. Mrs. Lloyd, can you tell me what happened?"

Mrs. Lloyd crossed her arms over her full bosom. "What happened is, Harold Sinclair was poisoned. They blamed Miss Vernon. And she paid for it … with her life. End of story."

"A tragic story," Athena acknowledged gently. "I imagine you must have known Miss Vernon well?"

The housekeeper's face remained impassive. "I did. I was here the day she was born. I was a chambermaid at the time. She was the master's only daughter."

"Were you fond of her?"

"Very. Miss Vernon was the prettiest and sweetest little girl you ever saw. In my eyes, she could do no wrong."

Athena took that in, wondering, *Did that include murder?*

She leaned forward in her chair. "What else can you tell me about her, Mrs. Lloyd?"

CHAPTER SIX

ATHENA STARED ACROSS her desk at Mrs. Lloyd, whose arms were still folded across her chest, almost as if she were hugging some unseen person or object.

"What else do you want to know about Miss Vernon?" the housekeeper asked quietly.

"Anything you can tell me," Athena replied, just as quietly. She was anxious to know everything she could about the young woman who had lived in this house, who had slept in the same room where Athena and her sister now slept—and who had been convicted of a horrific crime.

Mrs. Lloyd hesitated, as if searching for the right words. "She was a good child. So was the young master."

"You're referring to Mr. Ian Vernon?"

Mrs. Lloyd nodded, her expression softening. "Everyone on staff loved them. Their mother adored them as well. It was a shame she died so young."

"How old were the children when Mrs. Vernon passed away?"

Mrs. Lloyd stared down at her hands. "Miss Vernon was only two. Master Ian was eight."

"How sad." A heaviness descended on Athena's chest. She had only been six years old when her own mother had died, an absence that still cut her to the core and had been deeply felt by everyone in her family. Her sister Diana, at the tender age of seven, had stepped in to fill that void, managing the household as best she could, for many years doing more to raise Athena and her sister and brother than their father had been able to manage. "It is a difficult thing, to be raised without a mother's love."

"It is indeed, Miss Taylor." If Mrs. Lloyd sensed Athena's personal experience with the matter, she didn't remark upon it. "But they didn't go without affection. Our neighbor Mrs. Hillman went out of her way to befriend those children."

"Mrs. Hillman?" When Athena and Selena had met her, the woman hadn't mentioned a connection to the Vernon children. But then, their get-together had been so brief, and the conversation had focused primarily on the attributes of Mrs. Hillman's former ward, Mr. Chapman.

"Mrs. Hillman never had any children of her own, you see. She took Miss Vernon and Master Ian under her wing, invited them to Darkmoor Park twice a month, and sometimes more, for tea parties and lawn games and such. They always came back with new toys and stacks of books to read."

"How kind of her." Athena felt a rising respect for Mrs. Hillman and looked forward to getting to know her better.

"The children, I believe, loved that good woman equally in return. They keenly anticipated every visit. And they did kindnesses for her as well. One time, I'll never forget it, Master Ian was home on his summer holidays. I think he was thirteen or so and Miss Vernon was just a wee thing of seven. They asked me to help them prepare a gift for Mrs. Hillman."

"What kind of gift?"

"They wanted to bring her a wheelbarrow full of roses in honor of her birthday. We had plenty of roses in the garden, so I found two pairs of shears and told them to help themselves. But half an hour later, back they came with the wheelbarrow full of buckets of roses and the longest faces you've ever seen. Master Ian said they couldn't deliver the flowers to Mrs. Hillman that way. She had a great fear of thorns, he said, and he'd forgotten that roses had so many. I offered to help them. Master Ian insisted that we remove every thorn from every stem. The task took the better part of the afternoon. But we got it done and the children delivered those flowers and told me they were a great success."

"What a delightful story." It surprised Athena to hear about this act of thoughtfulness on the part of a young Ian Vernon. It seemed such a contrast to the angry man to whom she had spoken on the riverbank the other day. "What about their father, Mr. Arthur Vernon? Was he a caring man?"

Mrs. Lloyd paused. "He was, for a time. At least he *seemed* to be in the early days when things went his way."

Athena looked at her. "What do you mean?"

"It isn't for me to say, Miss Taylor. I don't wish to speak ill of the dead."

"I understand." Athena wasn't about to let it go at that, however. "But what about the *early days*? Surely, you can speak of them?"

Mrs. Lloyd conceded with a frown. "Mr. Vernon was decent to those children when they were young. He made sure Master Ian got a good education at Eton and Oxford. Miss Vernon was like a doll to him. He bought her a pony and then a horse, had the prettiest dresses and riding costumes made for her, and took her out riding all the time. When she turned eighteen, he gave her a coming-out ball. People said it was the grandest coming-out ball in the history of the county and Miss Vernon was the prettiest debutante they'd ever seen. But then ..."

"Then?" Athena prodded.

"Six months later, Mr. Harold Sinclair asked for permission to marry her, and Mr. Vernon snapped him up just like that."

"But Miss Vernon didn't want to marry him?"

"I should say not. She despised the man. And with good reason."

"What reason, Mrs. Lloyd?"

"*That* is not for me to say," the housekeeper said again. She clamped her mouth shut, then opened it and went on heatedly. "But Mr. Arthur Vernon had long been infatuated with the

Sinclairs and with Woodcroft House. He saw it as a feather in his cap for their two families to be joined. Overnight, Miss Vernon found herself affianced to that horrible man. She told her father that she wouldn't go through with it. But he had always claimed he had a weak heart, and he used that to pressure her into giving in, insisting that it would kill him if she didn't marry Mr. Sinclair. She wept all day and cried herself to sleep every night. It nearly broke *my* heart to see it. The two men agreed to wait until she'd turned nineteen years of age to marry, and they set a date in June. But a week before the wedding, Mr. Sinclair ..." She withdrew a handkerchief from her pocket and dabbed her eyes.

"I know Mr. Sinclair was poisoned," Athena prodded gently. "But where did it happen? And how?"

Mrs. Lloyd swallowed hard, as if to collect herself. "It was at a garden party at Woodcroft House. He keeled over dead right in front of my eyes. They found rat poison in his glass of punch."

Athena's hand went to her mouth. "And Miss Vernon was convicted of the crime and hanged for it?"

The housekeeper nodded. "But she didn't kill that man!" The words shot from her mouth as if from a loaded cannon. "She wouldn't have even hurt a fly. Miss Vernon was the sweetest, kindest girl who ever drew breath. What happened to *her* was the crime!"

Athena wanted to offer some soothing or sympathetic words, but before she could speak, Mrs. Lloyd stood abruptly.

"Forgive me, Miss Taylor." Her voice broke. "I have work to do." So saying, she quit the room.

Athena sat in silence for a long moment and then added a few more paragraphs to her letter to Diana. She had learned a great many things from this conversation but latched on to the item she considered to be the most important.

Mrs. Lloyd's assertions fit with Athena's latest theory: that Caroline Vernon might be innocent of the crime of which she'd been convicted. The crime for which she had paid with her life.

"SELENA," ATHENA REMARKED on their way to Darkmoor Park for tea on Wednesday afternoon, "I have some new thoughts about Sally Osborn."

"Are you still worrying about that?"

"I am." The sky was bright blue, and a breeze fluttered their bonnet ribbons. Cow parsley grew in the ditches on the side of the road, and sheep *baaed* and grazed on the distant moors. "Miss Osborn insisted that Sally had become a changed person after she quit her job at Woodcroft House. A post she left *nine years ago*."

"Nine years ago. Hmm. Apparently, you believe the timing to be significant. Ah. Isn't that when the infamous murder took place? The one that has cast such a shadow over Thorndale Manor?"

"Precisely. I asked Mrs. Lloyd about it the other night. She confirmed that Sally Osborn came to work at Thorndale Manor right after Harold Sinclair was murdered."

"Interesting. Go on."

As they continued down the road, Athena went over everything Mrs. Lloyd had revealed from the childhood of the Vernon siblings and Miss Vernon's enforced betrothal to Harold Sinclair's poisoning at a garden party at Woodcroft House. "He died on the spot."

"Dear lord." Selena's nose wrinkled.

"But Mrs. Lloyd insisted that Caroline Vernon couldn't have possibly murdered him."

Selena flapped a dismissive hand. "Of course she did."

"What do you mean?"

"Remind me, how long has Mrs. Lloyd worked at Thorndale Manor?"

"As I recall, she's been here forty years."

"Forty years! That is dedication. And from what you said, she was very fond of Miss Vernon."

"Apparently, the entire staff adored both her and her brother."

"*That* is a red flag, Selena."

"In what respect?" Although Athena could guess the answer.

"If Mrs. Lloyd loved Miss Vernon, of course she would rush to her defense. She would find it difficult, if not impossible, to believe that Miss Vernon could do something so heinous as to commit murder."

Athena nodded. "You could be right. It's a natural instinct to protect the people we love. However, we mustn't simply accept that Caroline Vernon was guilty. People are wrongly convicted every day. We ought to keep our minds open on the subject."

"It sounds as if your mind is already made up." Selena glanced her way. "You still think there's a connection between Mr. Sinclair's death all those years ago, and Sally's death last Friday?"

"I'm just saying it's a possibility. Sally was a housemaid at Woodcroft House when Harold Sinclair died. She might have seen the person who poisoned Sinclair's drink. What if it wasn't Caroline Vernon?"

Selena paused, as if taking that in. "Who else would have had a motive to kill Harold Sinclair?"

"A good question. And one I intend to look into."

"*If* Sally saw someone else poison Mr. Sinclair's drink, why didn't she say anything?"

"Maybe she was too frightened to come forward. Miss Osborn said that Sally's personality changed after she left Woodcroft House. That could be due to her failed romance. But what if it wasn't about a lost love at all? What if the killer threatened her life if she spoke up? That could explain why she was fixated on that particular proverb in the Bible, about *keeping silent* and *holding one's tongue.*"

Selena seemed to turn that over in her mind. "If all that is true, why did this 'killer' wait so long to do away with Sally? Why not kill her nine years ago?"

"I've been asking myself the same thing. I have a possible

answer."

"Which is?"

"Sally's sister, Bridget, is ill. The apothecary told Miss Osborn that she needs to spend the winter at the seaside, but they don't have the funds. What if Sally, desperate to help her sister, decided to raise the money the only way she knew how: by blackmailing the murderer of Harold Sinclair?"

Selena's eyebrows shot up. "Athena. Are you sure you're not getting carried away here?"

"It's a theory worth considering."

"Are you doing this because of what happened to Diana?"

The charge took Athena aback. "Diana?"

"Our sister nearly lost her life, in her determination to solve a mystery at Pendowar Hall. We both admire her for it, and all that she accomplished there. But this isn't a competition, Athena. You don't need to solve a mystery yourself to be Diana's equal."

"I'm not trying to be Diana's equal." The accusation, however, was unsettling. Athena had, when they were children, felt less clever than their older sister, and she had tried over and over again to prove her own worth by working harder at things. Surely, though, that wasn't what was driving her now? "But I do share Diana's sense of curiosity and desire for justice," she insisted. "I thought you did, too."

"I do. When it's warranted. I'm just not convinced it is, in this case."

"Well, we're about to have tea with Mrs. Hillman, who also, apparently, knew Miss Vernon very well. Let's see what she has to say about the matter."

THE IRON GATES on the perimeter of the Darkmoor Park estate were open and welcoming.

Athena's and Selena's half-boots crunched along the gravel

drive as they wended their way down an avenue of immense oaks, all showing off their early-autumn canopies of gold, orange, and red. The manor house soon came into view. Although they had been here once before, the sight of the noble, old building filled Athena with a renewed sense of awe.

The elegant structure, built of grey stone, stood three stories high. A multitude of tall casement windows marched across the front of the house and its roofline was peppered with gables and an assortment of chimneys.

When the sisters reached the stone pathway that bisected the front lawn, a strange unease settled in Athena's stomach. The rows of windows high above seemed like pairs of dark eyes, taking measure of their approach, as if to decide whether or not they were worthy of entry. An inexplicable shiver rippled down her spine.

"What is it?"

"Nothing." Athena didn't want to hear yet another reproach from her sister.

They mounted the front steps, which led to a roofed porch topped by a row of carved stone cherubs. Fluted stone columns supported the portico's roof and flanked the ancient, wooden, double front doors, which were studded like something from a castle.

Selena pulled the bell cord, and they were soon admitted by a straight-backed, dark-haired butler in a black tailcoat. The huge entrance hall featured an old-fashioned exhibition of weaponry— the traditional place to store weapons so that they would be ready to hand in times of trouble—a display that dwarfed the one in the entry hall at Thorndale Manor.

The butler led them through the wood-paneled great hall, which—with its high ceiling, immense marble fireplace, and mahogany sideboards covered with gold, silver, and pewter objects—seemed to have been created to showcase the house's history and status. Athena took it all in with wonder. Thorndale Manor's front hall was plenty large and yet seemed a mere speck in comparison.

"None of the homes where I served as a governess were this magnificent," murmured Selena.

"Neither were mine."

They were brought to a drawing room at the back of the house, where they had met with their hostess on their previous visit. The chamber was as splendid as the great hall but in a completely different way.

An ornate, suspended, gilded bronze-and-crystal chandelier presided over the spacious room, whose sage-green walls were hung with ancestral portraits and landscapes in gilded frames. Casement windows, the size of double doors, overlooked acres of verdant lawn, back gardens, and the distant moors. Multi-colored Turkish carpets covered the polished, oak floor, and a variety of sofas and chairs upholstered in soft shades of blue, green, and gold faced each other and the carved marble fireplace. Floral arrangements topped the mahogany end tables, imbuing the room with their fragrance.

It was, Athena thought, a space designed for elegance and comfort. She was impressed by the wealth and good taste of the owner, who called out to them from a silk damask chair.

"Miss Taylor, Miss Selena, I'm so glad you could come." Mrs. Hillman used a gold-handled cane to rise to her feet. A diminutive woman whom Athena guessed to be in her early sixties, her friendly eyes, warm smile, and gently wrinkled face seemed to reflect both intelligence and kindness.

"It is so good of you to have us," Athena replied as she and Selena dipped a curtsy.

Mrs. Hillman's upswept, dark-brown hair was generously threaded with grey and made a fine accompaniment to her fashionable gown of shimmering, copper satin. "Please, have a seat." She waved towards the sofa across from her, separated by a low table.

After they had all sat down, the older woman resumed with a self-effacing smile. "I have been wanting to invite you ladies again for some time now, but I have been occupied with work on the estate, and my knees have been troubling me of late. Oh good, here is tea," she added as the stern, grey-haired housekeeper and a pretty, young housemaid entered with the tea service.

Mrs. Hillman efficiently poured out tea into delicate bone china cups, while on the low table between them, the servants arranged a tasty-looking array that included finger sandwiches, scones, jam, cream, and two kinds of cake.

Selena grinned. "This looks amazing, thank you."

The servants withdrew. As Athena and her sister helped themselves to the delicacies on offer, Selena remarked, "Darkmoor Park is such a beautiful house, Mrs. Hillman. I should love to know its history."

"That is an interesting story." Mrs. Hillman took a sip of tea. "It began as a Cistercian abbey around 1170. In the late sixteenth century, it was acquired by the Third Earl of Slatesbury, who converted the monastic buildings into a smaller version of this house. Over the centuries, his descendants added new wings and outbuildings. The estate was not entailed, and in 1743, it was inherited by a daughter of the earl who married a commoner, George Hillman."

Athena took a bite of lemon cake, savoring the tangy blend of sweet and sour. She could see where this tale was heading. "And George Hillman was ...?"

"My husband's grandfather," Mrs. Hillman confirmed with a nod. "The earldom eventually became extinct and in 1817, I met Roger Hillman at a ball while on holiday in Bath." Mrs. Hillman's eyes went misty, and her lips curved in a smile. "I was just a clergyman's daughter, teaching at a small girls' school at the time."

"You taught school?" Selena sounded delighted.

"I did. It was a very traditional school that focused on needlework, etiquette, and deportment, with only the most rudimentary training in reading and writing. But as you both know, a young lady without means is obliged to earn a living, and

I enjoyed the work. I was already on the shelf at age thirty when I met Roger, but he didn't mind. We fell in love and were married, and he brought me home to Darkmoor Park. We wanted children desperately, but alas, that was not to be. We were very happy together until my Roger died in a horseback riding accident. And so, the estate passed to me."

Athena's smile evaporated. "I am so sorry to hear about your husband."

"What a tragedy, Mrs. Hillman." Selena sounded stricken with empathy.

"It was. Roger loved Darkmoor Park. I have done my best to take care of the estate as I feel he might have done. It was quite a different house when I came here as a bride, dark and stuffy and hopelessly out of date. I have spent the past thirty-three years renovating one room at a time—all except the great hall, which he didn't want to change. This room was all my design, and it was a labor of love."

"You have done a remarkable job," Athena said. "It is so stylish and refined."

"Yet despite its grand size, it is also cozy," Selena agreed.

"Thank you." Mrs. Hillman picked up her fork and took a dainty bite of cake. "Now enough about the past. Tell me: how is Peter doing? Is he a good teacher?"

"Mr. Chapman is a marvel." Athena smiled.

"We so appreciate you recommending him," Selena said.

As they enjoyed the tea and treats on offer, Athena related what had occurred on Sunday when Mr. Chapman had arrived at the school. "The girls took to him like ducks to water. It is only because of him that we are both able to be here this afternoon."

"He is holding a musical entertainment," Selena explained with a grin.

"I am glad he is proving worthy. I have not spent as much time in that young man's company as perhaps I should have." Mrs. Hillman let out a sigh. "Did I tell you? Before Peter came to me, he was the ward of my sister, Daisy. She raised him as if he were her own son."

"You did not mention that," Athena replied.

"How I loved Daisy." Mrs. Hillman paused as if lost in thought. "She was three years younger than me and committed the unpardonable sin of falling in love with a soldier stationed at a garrison in York."

"How was that a sin?" Selena asked.

Athena was curious about that as well. "You said your father was a clergyman? Surely, it wouldn't have been a great step down for his daughter to have married a soldier?"

Mrs. Hillman hesitated again. Her gaze sought her lap, and her cheeks grew rosy. "Perhaps he and my mother would have approved Daisy's choice, had the man in question not already been married, with a newborn child."

"Oh," Selena blurted out.

"Yes, Daisy ran off with a married man. It was quite a scandal at the time. And then, both her soldier and his forsaken wife died of typhoid within days of each other. When Daisy learned that her lover's son was now an impoverished orphan, it broke her heart. Although as a single woman, she couldn't formally adopt him, she passed herself off as a distant relative to get permission to take him and raise him herself."

Athena's heart went out to all the participants in this trage-dy—the couple who had risked everything for love, the poor wife and mother who had been abandoned by her husband, and the child, Peter Chapman, who had been the innocent victim of it all. "It was kind of your sister to take the child in. I don't imagine it was easy for her."

"It wasn't. Especially since Daisy never married. But some-how, she raised that boy on her own until ..." Mrs. Hillman paused to take a long breath. "When Peter was thirteen years old, my sister passed away."

"I'm so sorry," Selena remarked softly.

"Thank you." Mrs. Hillman gave a sad shrug. "It was a long time ago, but I still miss her and think of her often. Anyway, I suddenly and unexpectedly found myself the boy's guardian. I sent him to the best schools. I'm pleased to see that he has become an accomplished young man."

"He is quite the musician," Athena agreed. "And very charming."

The sound of the doorbell pierced the air. Mrs. Hillman's brow furrowed. "Who can that be? I'm not expecting anyone else today."

The butler entered and spoke into Mrs. Hillman's ear.

"But I thought he wasn't due until tomorrow," Mrs. Hillman replied. "I suppose I must have written the wrong date in my diary. Please, show him in."

Moments later, the butler returned with the visitor.

Athena nearly dropped her teacup as Mr. Ian Vernon strode into the room.

CHAPTER SEVEN

"MRS. HILLMAN. HOW are—?" Mr. Vernon stopped short, his smile fleeing as he caught sight of Athena and Selena.

An awkwardness filled the air. Athena's insides tightened as she and her sister stood to mark his entrance.

He was attired in a well-cut black suit and blue cravat, his inky-black hair perfectly combed back from a face that was even more good-looking than Athena had remembered. But looks did not make a man a gentleman, Athena reminded herself. She couldn't forget his ill-mannered behavior the last time they'd spoken.

He fiddled with the strap of a large, leather satchel that hung from one of his shoulders, and then with a bow, he told their hostess, "Forgive me. I thought our appointment was for three-thirty. I must have been mistaken."

"You must forgive *me*," Mrs. Hillman replied. "I recall the time of our appointment perfectly, but I thought it was for tomorrow."

"Ah," said he.

"I'm sure you know Miss Taylor and Miss Selena?" Mrs. Hillman gestured to them with a friendly smile.

"We have met." Mr. Vernon gave them each a polite nod, his gaze meeting Athena's for only the briefest of seconds. "It is a pleasure to see you again." His tone was flat, belying the statement.

"And you, Mr. Vernon," Selena answered.

"Sir," was all Athena said. Irritation prickled down her spine. This man seemed to have only one attitude: hostility. If he and Mrs. Hillman shared a connection dating back to his childhood, Athena wondered what had necessitated, as he had put it, "an appointment." And what was in that oversized satchel of his?

As if in answer to her unspoken questions, Mrs. Hillman explained, "Ian has been working up plans to renovate my dower house. These are the final revisions, I believe?"

"Yes. Subject to your approval, of course."

"That's right! You're an architect, aren't you, Mr. Vernon?" Selena asked.

"I am." To Mrs. Hillman, he added, "I don't wish to intrude, ma'am. I shall take my leave and return tomorrow."

"Nonsense, Ian. You are never an intrusion, my dear. You must stay to tea."

"We could go," Athena offered hastily. "You have business to conduct, and my sister and I can return another day."

"Don't be silly. You must all stay." Mrs. Hillman waved Mr. Vernon towards the unoccupied chair beside her. "Please, sit down, everyone."

Mr. Vernon complied, setting his satchel on the floor beside his chair. Athena and Selena resumed their seats.

Mrs. Hillman clapped her hands, and the housekeeper—apparently having anticipated her employer's unspoken request—reappeared with another teacup and plate for the new arrival, and then silently vanished.

As Mrs. Hillman poured tea for Mr. Vernon, Athena sighed inwardly. It was going to be a long and uncomfortable afternoon now. She would just have to make the best of it. "You said you are renovating your dower house?" she inquired of Mrs. Hillman. Athena wondered why. A dower house was a less pretentious residence intended for the use of a widow, when the eldest son inherited and moved into the manor house. But Mrs. Hillman had no children.

"You will say it's silly of me, that I have no need of the dower house, and it is so far removed from the main house. But I have finished all the renovations at Darkmoor Park and require a new endeavor." Darting an affectionate look towards Mr. Vernon, Mrs. Hillman added, "Besides, it gives me an excuse to see one of my favorite people on a regular basis."

"I hope that is not your primary reason behind this project," Mr. Vernon said, frowning as he helped himself to a slice of cake.

"Of course not. The dower house is a piece of Darkmoor Park's history. It has a charm of its own and I hate to see it crumbling to ruins."

"There are a few changes I should like to make at Thorndale Manor, if we can ever afford it," Selena said, her tone wistful.

Mr. Vernon froze, his fork halfway to his mouth. "What would you change?"

Athena's throat constricted. She and her sister *had* discussed future hopes for the house, but it felt unwise to speak about such things in front of Mr. Vernon, the acrimonious former owner.

Selena blushed, as if aware of her mistake. "Forgive me, sir. I shouldn't have mentioned that. They are idle dreams at best. At present, we can't even afford new pencils."

"The house is wonderful," Athena said quickly. "We have no complaints."

"And yet Miss Selena is not satisfied," he insisted. "Again, I ask: what would you change?"

Selena darted Athena an almost desperate look as if to say, *I'm sorry*. Hesitantly, she said, "Well, for example, we gather with our pupils in the drawing room every evening. It would be nice to enlarge it to accommodate more students in the future."

"That would be impossible," Mr. Vernon shot back.

"Why?" Athena asked.

"Most of the walls in the drawing room are structural and cannot be moved. Even if that were not the case, there is no way to enlarge that room without taking away much-needed space from the adjoining chambers."

"Oh." Selena's face fell. "That's a shame."

Although this was interesting insight, which Athena valued, she didn't appreciate Mr. Vernon's manner or tone. Were his opinions simply based on experience—or tainted by personal grievances? "Thank you for your advice," she stated, her jaw tight.

"I would take care before attempting any major renovations at Thorndale Manor, lest you affect the integrity of the entire building," he warned.

Mrs. Hillman's gaze traveled from Athena to Mr. Vernon's disgruntled face and back again. She clicked her tongue. "Ladies: you must forgive Mr. Vernon if he sounds like a grumpy, old bear. It broke his heart to let Thorndale Manor go." To Mr. Vernon, she added, "But we have been over this at length, my dear. You had no choice."

Mr. Vernon stared down at his teacup. "Leave it, Mrs. Hillman. Please."

Mrs. Hillman ignored his plea. "You were fortunate to find a buyer when you did, Ian. And from what I hear, these ladies are doing something marvelous with the place."

Mr. Vernon sat rigidly in his seat. He opened his mouth, then shut it again. His face colored slightly. "As you say, ma'am. What's done is done. We must make the best of it."

Athena sensed Mr. Vernon's discomfort and embarrassment and despite herself, she once again felt bad for him. Who was to say how she might react, if forced to give up her beloved home and birthright to another? She was searching her mind for an appropriate comment when Mrs. Hillman, seeming to warm to her subject, turned to Athena and Selena.

"Now, Miss Taylor and Miss Selena, you must tell us all about your school. What subjects do you teach?"

As they drank a second cup of tea and finished the delicacies on their plates, Selena expounded for some minutes on the matter, and Athena interjected her own observations and hopes.

Mrs. Hillman was delighted by all that she heard. "What a wonderful and worthwhile undertaking. Don't you agree, Ian?"

Mr. Vernon, who had been silent during this part of the conversation, set down his teacup and said quietly, "I have long believed that girls deserved a far better education than has been afforded them. It sounds as if your pupils are in very good hands, Miss Taylor and Miss Selena. I hope your enterprise will inspire the foundation of many more similar educational institutions for young ladies."

His comment took Athena by surprise. It was the first positive remark he had made about her or about the school. "Thank you, Mr. Vernon."

Mrs. Hillman gave a deep sigh. "Ian's sister, Caroline, would have loved to attend such a place. She was so curious about the world."

Mr. Vernon went still. He made no comment, but as he carefully replaced his teacup in its saucer, a haunted look came into his blue eyes.

Athena could guess at the reason behind his response. He must have suffered greatly when his sister had died on the gallows all those years ago. Athena's thoughts darted to Mrs. Lloyd's pronouncement—that, in *her* opinion, Miss Vernon had been wrongly judged. Athena wanted to know Mrs. Hillman's thoughts on the matter, and it seemed to be the perfect time to find out.

"We've heard about what happened to Miss Vernon," Athena said softly. "And we are so sorry about it."

"As are we all." Mrs. Hillman's voice was also hushed.

"My housekeeper told me that you and Miss Vernon were very close?" Athena prompted.

The older woman nodded her head. "Caroline was the like the daughter I never had. Just as this gentleman was—and still is—as dear to me as my own son." She gave Mr. Vernon a smile, which he returned, his eyes still sad. "They were such handsome children. You can see them there." She pointed to a portrait in oils hanging on a nearby wall. "I think Caroline was five years old when I had that commissioned. Ian, I believe you were eleven?"

The room was so filled with artwork, Athena hadn't paid it much notice. She now directed her gaze to the youthful portrait. It featured a lovely girl, dressed in a pale-pink frock with a white sash, and a handsome boy in a finely tailored suit and embroidered waistcoat. The resemblance between the two was unmistakable. Both had the same raven-black hair and identical, cornflower-blue eyes. Athena could see in the young boy's face the precursor of the man he was to become.

"How sweet they are," Selena murmured.

Athena had to agree.

"And there is Caroline at age eighteen, just before she came out." Mrs. Hillman gestured to a large painting hanging over the mantelpiece.

Athena turned her attention to the second portrait and drew in a breath of wonder. A breathtakingly beautiful young woman had been preserved forever by the magic of art and paint.

The subject wore a white, satin gown, with matching rosettes at her bodice and atop her short, cap sleeves. Her black hair was swept up in a style that had become popular more than a decade ago and was still fashionable, with a coronet of braids and ringlets framing her pale face. Her facial features echoed those of her brother. Her expression and the look in her eyes conveyed intelligence, warmth, and kindness.

Athena sensed, just by looking at her, that this was a young woman with a big heart, someone you would want to befriend. In her gloved hands, Caroline Vernon carried not the usual nosegay or fan, but a book—a symbol, perhaps, of the young lady's love of reading.

"She was beautiful," Athena murmured.

"Yes." Mrs. Hillman's voice caught.

Mr. Vernon said nothing, but he stared at the carpet and cleared his throat, as if suppressing some deeply felt emotion.

Athena's own throat seemed to close. It struck her as unbelievably sad that this young woman had been snatched from life only a year after the portrait had been painted. Had she really committed that murder? Or had she been wrongly convicted, as Mrs. Lloyd had insisted? Athena longed to know more. "How is it, Mrs. Hillman, that you became acquainted with the Vernon children?"

"Caroline and Ian's mother, Penelope, and I were bosom friends since childhood, even though she was five years younger than me. When Penelope married Arthur Vernon, I knew it was a love match. But I teased her that she only took him because she knew that by living at Thorndale Manor, she would only be a mile-and-a-half walk away from me."

Athena and Selena chuckled.

"Oh! What a lovely time we had in those early years." Mrs. Hillman's smile faded, and her voice grew serious. "And then Penelope became ill. After she died, I was distraught, but my heart went out to those poor, motherless children. Arthur Vernon was wrapped in his own grief, so I ..." She gave Mr. Vernon a questioning look. "I hope you didn't mind, Ian? All those lunches and tea parties and outings to the river to sail your boats? All the long walks in my gardens when we 'hunted' for lions and tigers? I know your sister enjoyed it, but you were a growing boy. It wasn't too much, was it?"

"I treasure every memory, Mrs. Hillman," was his earnest reply.

Their hostess lay a hand over her heart. "A welcome thing for a lonely, old woman to hear."

"You are hardly old, ma'am, and I hope you are not lonely," he said quietly. "You have me. You have friends in the village." He gestured to Athena and Selena. "And two new friends."

Athena didn't know what to make of this. She wanted to hate Mr. Vernon, whom she felt certain hated her. But he wasn't exhibiting the same animosity that he had that day on the riverbank. This was a much softer side.

"My sister and I are honored to have made your acquaintance, Mrs. Hillman," Selena assured her.

The older woman's eyes crinkled. "The feeling is mutual. It is a shame that you couldn't have met Caroline. I think you would have gotten along well together."

Athena seized on the comment. "Do I take it, from her portrait, that Miss Vernon was fond of books?"

"Oh, yes. Caroline read everything she could get her hands on. She used to read aloud to me—poetry and the works of Shakespeare and all our favorite novels. Oh! I do so enjoy hearing a book read aloud. It is one of my favorite things. Caroline had the most calming and expressive voice. When she read, it was as if the rest of the world didn't exist, and all my problems went away." Moisture gathered in Mrs. Hillman's pale eyes. "What happened to her is such a tragedy. I imagine you know the story?"

"Just bits and pieces," Athena admitted.

Mr. Vernon darted Mrs. Hillman a warning look. "It is all ancient history. We needn't get into it."

"Why not?" Mrs. Hillman replied. "In my mind, it can't be talked about often enough."

Mr. Vernon's mouth tightened. Athena sensed his frustration and thought, *Perhaps it was insensitive of me to pursue a topic that might bring him pain.* Before she could think of a way to redirect the conversation, Mrs. Hillman went on.

"When Caroline was eighteen, she fell in love with a sailor."

"A sailor?" Selena echoed.

"Edward Ackroyd is a seaman in the Royal Navy, and the son of a coal miner. He and Caroline were mad about each other, but he didn't have a penny to his name. Her father wouldn't allow the marriage. A common sailor, Mr. Vernon said, was not fit to shine his daughter's shoes. Instead, he accepted an offer from Harold Sinclair, the richest man in the neighborhood, and one of the vilest human beings I have ever met. Although it is a lady's right to end an engagement, her father wouldn't allow it. I tried to get him to see reason, but his mind was set on the union. He threatened Caroline, using his weak heart as an excuse to force her into acquiescence."

Mr. Vernon cleared his throat and insisted sternly, "Let us stop there. I'm sure Miss Taylor and Miss Selena have heard the rest."

"Have you?" Mrs. Hillman's featured hardened. "Have you heard how Caroline suffered, knowing she could never marry the man she loved and would be forever tied to a man she despised? A week before the wedding, at the annual garden party at Woodcroft House, Caroline begged Harold Sinclair to agree to call off the union. He refused. I wasn't there—I couldn't stomach the idea of attending one of that man's parties. But as I understand it, all the neighborhood was in attendance, high and low, and everyone heard them arguing. Isn't that so, Ian?"

Mr. Vernon's lips were pressed together, and tension seemed to radiate from his body. "I only know what I've been told. I wasn't there, either. I was in London at the time."

"They say that Mr. Sinclair collapsed and died at the party in full view of everyone," Mrs. Hillman snapped. "They found arsenic in his glass of punch. Caroline swore she'd had nothing to do with it. But at the assizes trial in York, a maid at Thorndale Manor said she'd found rat poison in Caroline's bedroom."

"What maid?" Athena's mind went to Sally Osborn, but that was wrong—Sally hadn't started working at Thorndale Manor until *after* Caroline Vernon had been convicted and sentenced for murder.

"I don't recall her name," Mrs. Hillman replied with a dismissive wave of her hand. "I think she left Thorndale Manor shortly after that."

Athena recalled Mrs. Lloyd mentioning, with distaste, a maid who'd left at the time to get married. Sally had filled her place.

"That woman was obviously lying," Mrs. Hillman went on vehemently. "As if Caroline could have ever poisoned anybody! She was all goodness and light. But Neville Sinclair had taken over his brother's place as parish constable, and he needed someone to pay for the crime. It was a miscarriage of justice!

That girl should never have been accused, much less convicted!"

Mr. Vernon shot to his feet. "Ma'am, you must stop this now." His tone was troubled, and his eyes seemed to flash a warning. "Remember what the doctor said. You *must not over agitate yourself* or you could have another stroke."

Athena felt guilty now. She should have foreseen that the story might discompose both their hostess and Mr. Vernon. "I'm so sorry. It was a terrible thing. We won't speak of it further."

Mr. Vernon knelt down on one knee at Mrs. Hillman's feet and took her hands in his. "Pray, calm yourself. We both know Caroline could never have done that dreadful deed. But we have Caroline's memory to console us."

Mrs. Hillman nodded slowly, wordlessly, as their gazes met.

Athena was moved by Mr. Vernon's concern and by the obvious affection between the two. Once again, it presented a side to him that Athena had not seen before. She wished there were some way that she could undo the tension that had arisen and ease the older woman's anxiety. Perhaps a distraction was in order?

Athena spied a book on a nearby end table. She crossed to it and picked it up. "Mrs. Hillman, you have excellent taste in reading."

Mrs. Hillman dabbed her eyes, breathing easier now. "Do I?"

"What book is that?" Selena asked.

"*The Wind Pirate* by Pryor Corbett."

"One of our favorites!" Selena cried.

"Have you already read this?" Athena asked Mrs. Hillman.

Mrs. Hillman hesitated. "Yes, some time ago. I took it out to read again."

"Mr. Vernon, are you familiar with Pryor Corbett's work?" Athena asked.

Mr. Vernon's arched brow seemed to imply that he was aware of what she was attempting to do and thought kindly of it. Resuming his seat, he said simply, "I have heard the name."

"Pryor Corbett is an excellent writer," Selena enthused. "*The*

Wind Pirate is the first of his seven novels."

"His stories always keep us on the edge of our seats," Athena agreed. "This one is an adventure story about a young woman who, to avoid marriage to a man she dislikes, disguises herself as a boy and escapes to sea on a ship run by pirates."

"Her father and brothers taught her many masculine skills, including the art of sword fighting, so she fits in with the pirate crew," Selena added.

"She admires their goals, for these are good pirates," Mrs. Hillman put in, her eyes twinkling. "They only steal from other pirates and return the spoils to their former owners or the crown."

"Tension is high, for the heroine must take pains every moment to avoid discovery, and at the same time, fight her attraction to the handsome, young pirate captain." Athena smiled.

"It sounds interesting," Mr. Vernon pronounced. "But I'm afraid pirate tales are not my cup of tea. I know Mrs. Hillman is fond of them."

"Indeed I am. This book is one of my favorites, too. I was hoping to read it again. But my eyes tire so easily these days."

An idea suddenly came to Athena. Their hostess had just mentioned how much she enjoyed hearing books read aloud.

Athena's mother used to read to her and her siblings when they'd been young. Upon that dear woman's death, Athena's sister Diana had taken on that task and read aloud to them from the trove of books in their mother's library, beginning with simple stories and progressing to more complicated works. In time, they had all taken turns reading aloud to each other. Throughout their years as governesses, Athena and her sisters had continued the practice. By now, Athena had read aloud from so many hundreds of books, the occupation felt to her as natural as breathing.

"Would you like me to read a couple of chapters of the book aloud to you?" Athena offered.

"Oh! Would you?"

"It would be my honor. Although perhaps I should wait until you and Mr. Vernon have gone over his drawings?" Athena checked the time. It was just after four o'clock. "Or I could return another day. My sister and I must be home before six in time for dinner."

"No, no, go ahead and read now," Mr. Vernon insisted. "My drawings can wait until you've finished. And I admit, I should like to hear something by this author you're all so keen about."

"Very well, then." Athena sat back down, opened the book, and began to read. "It was a blustery day in mid-November when Lydia Penrose decided to become a pirate …"

As she read *The Wind Pirate*, Athena did her best to narrate with enthusiasm and to imbue each character with their own distinct personality and voice. As usual, she got so caught up in the story, she was barely aware of the other people in the room.

When she'd finished the second chapter and raised her gaze from the pages, she was pleased to see that Mrs. Hillman was smiling. Selena's features were suffused with pride and affection. For some reason, it was suddenly important to Athena that Mr. Vernon should approve. She turned to face him—and her heart seemed to skip a beat.

He was sitting forward in his chair, his eyes glossy and bright. And he broke into applause. "Bravo, Miss Taylor."

"Yes, bravo!" Mrs. Hillman clapped along. "That was the finest reading I have heard in years."

"Thank you, but all the credit goes to the novelist. I merely brought his words to life."

"Nonsense!" Mrs. Hillman insisted. "You performed those words with great skill! Why, I believe you could go on the stage, Miss Taylor."

"I have tried reading to her myself, to no avail," Mr. Vernon admitted.

"Ian is a master when it comes to architecture and design but ask him to read aloud and he'll put you straight to sleep. *You*, on the other hand, have talent. It is a rare gift to be able to read aloud like that." Mrs. Hillman paused as if thinking and then said, "Miss Taylor. I have a proposal to make."

"'A proposal'?" Athena repeated.

"I believe your school to be a worthy endeavor. I gather that funds might be scarce at present. I should like to help by making an endowment to the institution of a hundred pounds."

"A hundred pounds!" It was princely sum.

"Mrs. Hillman! That is very generous of you," Selena cried. "And very appreciated."

"I do have one *little* request to make," Mrs. Hillman added with a smile.

"There's always a little request," noted Mr. Vernon, his lips twitching.

Mrs. Hillman eyed Athena directly. "I should like you, Miss Taylor, to read aloud to me. Twice a week, here at Darkmoor Park, for one or two hours at a time."

"Twice a week?" Athena replied uncertainly.

"That is my hope and wish. My donation stands whether or not you accept my request. However, I should be grateful if you could indulge an old woman on this matter."

Athena pondered this unexpected and very substantial offer. That money would make such a difference. She could pay their servants' salaries, and the salary for their new music master, for many months, without depending on Captain Fallbrook. She would be able to afford much-needed school supplies. Most importantly, it would enable them to keep the school running for quite a while until they found more pupils. However …

Athena sighed with regret. "Mrs. Hillman. I can't thank you enough for your kind offer. You say the endowment would be unencumbered and I appreciate that. But I would feel guilty accepting your contribution without rendering the service you request. It is such a small thing you ask of me. I would so enjoy reading to you here on a regular basis. Indeed, I should be happy to do so free of charge if I could. Sadly, though, I cannot."

"May I ask why not?" Mrs. Hillman inquired.

"I am the headmistress of our school. I have many responsibilities. I couldn't possibly be gone twice a week, for several hours."

"I see." Mrs. Hillman frowned. "I wish I could come to you …but my knees, you see. I am not as mobile as I once was."

"*Athena!*" Selena gave her a firm look that seemed to say, *We need that money.* "We have a half day of instruction on Wednesdays, and the girls have Sunday afternoons at leisure after church. Perhaps you could read to Mrs. Hillman then? Would that work for you, Mrs. Hillman?"

A smile took over Mrs. Hillman's face. "It would."

Athena deliberated. She'd found her free afternoons to be valuable for making lesson plans and keeping up with school business and the management of the estate. Suddenly, a solution occurred to her. "Selena, what if we split the duties? I could read to Mrs. Hillman on Wednesdays, and you could do Sundays."

"I would be happy to." Selena glanced tentatively at their hostess. "*If* that would be agreeable to Mrs. Hillman?"

"I promise you, my sister is a far better reader than I am," Athena quickly assured Mrs. Hillman. "Whenever the girls at school want a tale read aloud, they always clamor for Miss Selena, not me."

"Do they, indeed?" Mrs. Hillman quirked a brow.

Selena's cheeks reddened and she gave their hostess an affirming shrug. "I suppose there is no accounting for taste."

"And I suppose I have just discovered a gold mine." Mrs. Hillman chuckled. "Is it settled then, ladies? Wednesday and Sunday afternoons? Shall we say two o'clock? And if the weather is bad, I'll send my carriage to fetch you?"

Athena and Selena accepted the terms. Selena agreed to start first, on the upcoming Sunday. Mrs. Hillman explained that she would write a cheque for the promised donation and have it delivered to Thorndale Manor the following day.

A few minutes later, Athena and Selena expressed their deepest thanks to Mrs. Hillman, and everyone said their farewells.

When Mr. Vernon said *goodbye*, his blue eyes were warm, and his voice was free of rancor. "Thank you for helping to calm and entertain Mrs. Hillman," he said quietly.

Athena nodded in reply. "It was my pleasure."

As she and Selena began their walk homeward, Athena's thoughts drifted back to the gentleman they had just left, and the alteration in his manner over the course of their visit.

She was reminded, suddenly, of the lemon cake she had tasted that afternoon. Its sour flavor had been mitigated by a delectable hint of sweetness.

Perhaps Mr. Vernon had a sweet side to him, after all.

CHAPTER EIGHT

"THE ARRANGEMENT OF veins in a leaf is called 'venation,'" Athena explained.

It was Friday afternoon, and the late-September weather was so delightful that she had moved their botany lesson outdoors. For the past hour, she and her students had been observing the way plants grew in the wild. They were now seated on a blanket beneath a giant, oak tree on the far edge of the estate, surrounded by a carpet of fallen autumn leaves.

"Take a look at the intricate structure of this leaf," Athena went on, holding up a large, golden oak leaf as an example. "Do you see all these veins? They are closed off and dry now because the leaf has fallen from the tree. But when this leaf was green and new, every one of these veins moved water, nutrients, and sugars."

"Are the veins in a leaf similar to the ones in our bodies?" asked Miss Russell.

"Indeed! They are both vessels of transport." Athena was delighted by the girl's observation. "Can you think of another way in which a leaf's anatomy can be compared to the human body?"

Miss Russell squinted as if deep in thought. Then, studying her hand, she said, "Well, both have an outside layer, don't they? In our case, we have skin?"

"Exactly right! Does anyone know what the protective outer

layer of a leaf is called?"

Miss Weaver shyly raised her hand.

"Yes, Miss Weaver?"

"It is called its *epidermis*, which is derived through Latin from the Ancient Greek word for 'skin.'"

"Girls," Athena said, impressed, "I suspect we may have a couple of future doctors in our midst."

Miss Weaver and Miss Russell shrugged modestly, but their bright eyes conveyed their pleasure in the compliment.

Miss Jones shook her head. "Doctors? Women can't be doctors."

"Yes, we can," Athena responded. "Last year, Miss Elizabeth Blackwell earned her medical degree from a college in New York state—the first woman in America to do so. We may not have women doctors in England yet, but if Miss Blackwell could do it, so can you!"

Misses Weaver, Russell, and Jones grinned at this suggestion.

The Gilbert sisters, however, who had been whispering during this exchange, began giggling.

"Miss Gilbert, Miss Cecelia. What is it about our discussion that you find so funny?" Athena asked.

Miss Cecelia bit her lip. "Nothing, Miss Taylor." She and her sister exchanged a glance and burst out laughing again.

"It is clearly *something*," Athena pointed out. "Please share. We always appreciate a laugh."

"All right," Miss Gilbert replied reluctantly. "It's about ..." She blushed and covered her eyes with her hands. "Mr. Chapman!"

All the girls broke into laughter now, their cheeks growing rosy.

"Oh, Miss Taylor, you should have been here on Wednesday!" cried Miss Weaver.

"Mr. Chapman played the pianoforte for *an entire hour*," added Miss Jones. "And we all danced and danced and danced."

"It was heaven!" exclaimed Miss Cecelia.

"Yes, so you have all said." Athena was pleased by their enthusiasm.

"And yesterday's music lesson was such fun!" declared Miss Gilbert.

The girls proceeded to argue about who had gotten the longest time at the pianoforte and which one of them had earned the highest praise from their new music master.

"All right, that's enough. I'm glad you are enjoying your music lessons and I'm sure Mr. Chapman gave you all equal time at the pianoforte and equal praise."

She was about to bring the lesson to a close, when Miss Gilbert gave a little gasp, and said, "Miss Taylor, who is that?"

Athena followed the direction of the girl's stare. Mr. Vernon was climbing over the stile in the fence that separated his property from hers.

Athena started. *Why was he walking this way?* In the past, whenever she and her sister had noticed him on his side of the fence, he had quickly vanished, as if intent on avoiding an encounter.

"It's Mr. Vernon," announced Miss Russell.

Miss Jones said, "Isn't he the brother of Caroline Vernon, *the murderess?*"

The students all squealed in horrified delight.

"Girls, hush. We don't know that Miss Vernon was actually guilty of murder," Athena heard herself saying, and she immediately wished she could retract the words.

"What do you mean, Miss Taylor?" Miss Gilbert's lips parted. "Are you saying that she didn't do it?"

"That is not a question for this class to ponder," Athena replied quickly. Over the past two days, Miss Vernon's awful fate had never been far from Athena's mind, but she didn't want to open the matter for discussion with her pupils. It was apparently too late, however; the cat was out of the bag.

"Caroline Vernon's ghost haunts Thorndale Manor," Miss Russell proclaimed, with hooded eyes and a mysterious cast to her voice. *"Everyone knows that."*

"We know no such thing," Athena insisted.

"The ghost of Caroline Vernon murdered our maid, Sally!" cried Miss Jones, a remark that provoked nervous shrieks and laughter from the other girls.

Just then, Mr. Vernon came striding up. Athena worried that he might have heard this ridiculous comment, but if so, his expression gave no evidence of it.

"Good afternoon, Miss Taylor. Ladies." He smiled tersely and bowed.

"Mr. Vernon. Good afternoon." Athena stood and dipped a quick curtsy. The girls were all staring at him frozen and wide-eyed. "Ladies, where are your manners? Stand up, please! And say good afternoon to Mr. Vernon."

The girls scrambled to their feet and said in unison, "Good afternoon, Mr. Vernon."

He nodded and turned to Athena. "Pray forgive me for interrupting. I saw you out here and was hoping I could have a word with you when your lesson is finished."

He was being so cordial. As he had been at the end of their tea at Darkmoor Park. But she still hadn't forgotten his rude manner at their previous meeting.

"You are not interrupting, sir. Our lesson is finished." She echoed his polite tone. To the girls, she instructed, "Please return to the house for period five." Selena would be waiting for them in the schoolroom. "Miss Weaver, as you are the oldest, I'm putting you in charge of getting the girls back safely and quickly."

"Yes, Miss Taylor. Let's go girls." Miss Weaver, with her shoulders thrown back and her head held high, shooed off her classmates, who, with occasional backwards glances at Mr. Vernon, began traipsing back to the manor house.

"You wished to speak to me, sir?" Athena asked.

"Yes. Your sister said something at Darkmoor Park about a lack of new pencils. I had an extra box that I should like to give you." From his coat pocket, he produced a small, cardboard box imprinted with the familiar Cumberland Pencils trademark and offered it to her.

Athena accepted the box with surprise and gratitude.

"How kind of you." And how thoughtful that he'd remembered a remark Selena had made in passing. Athena was beginning to think that her first impressions of Mr. Vernon might not have been the most accurate representation of the man. "I made a list for the stationer's, but I was obliged to pay the grocer's bill instead. Mrs. Hillman's endowment, when it arrives, will make things easier, but—this is very timely and much appreciated. Thank you."

"You're most welcome." He cleared his throat. "Miss Taylor. There is something I have been wanting to say to you for some days now. I wish to apologize for that morning last week at the riverbank."

"Oh. Sir, there is no need—"

"There is," he insisted abruptly. "It was a terrible moment, but that is no excuse for the way I behaved." He looked her in the eye. "I heard what you said under your breath. Just to be clear: I do not hate you."

Athena flushed as she recalled that awful morning, and the observation she had muttered to herself. She hadn't realized he had heard it.

"If I'm completely honest, I admit to feeling a bit jealous because you and your sister have had the good fortune to acquire Thorndale Manor," he added. "But I realize that is not fair or rational."

"And yet it is completely understandable," Athena conceded. "I would probably hate me if I were you."

"As I said, I do not hate you. The blame for what occurred with my family home lies entirely at my departed father's feet. I transferred my ire to you and for that, I should like to offer my abject apologies. I hope you will forgive me?"

It was a very fine apology. And the look of appeal in his blue eyes was impossible to resist. Athena's ire melted away as rapidly as an ice chip in the summer sun. "I appreciate what you have said, Mr. Vernon, and I do forgive you."

His dark brows raised in inquiry as he held out a hand to her. "Friends?"

Athena hesitated. She felt she must maintain a sense of propriety and reserve with him. After all, she still owned his former home, and no matter how magnanimous he was being, it had to irk him. And yet to turn down an offer of friendship would be rude.

"Friends," she repeated as they exchanged a firm handshake. At his touch, a little shiver raced up her arm. *What was that about?*

"Thank you." He took a breath. "And there is something else for which I'd to thank you."

"Oh?"

"I appreciated you reading to Mrs. Hillman yesterday—it was a clever diversion. It is not healthy for her to get upset. And I'm glad you and your sister are going to read to her on a weekly basis. I know it will mean the world to her."

"We shall see about that," Athena replied, trying not to speculate on the cause of that shiver. "Once Mrs. Hillman hears Selena read aloud, I doubt she'll want me to come anymore."

"Ha!" He shook his head, his lips twitching. "You are too modest. You are very talented."

"Well, thank you. I was glad to do it." With regret, Athena added, "I wish I could continue our conversation, sir, but I must return to the house. I have a class to prepare for."

"May I accompany you? I used to take daily walks this way, and I miss them."

"Of course. And please feel free to walk these grounds anytime you like. We are neighbors, after all."

"Thank you."

As they strode in the direction of Thorndale Manor, the twitter of birds rang out from the canopies of the trees, which were flinging gold and orange leaves onto the breeze. Athena felt Mr. Vernon's eyes on her and when she glanced his way, he smiled, and she sensed he'd been studying her. His expression was so unexpectedly warm and softly appraising that it caused a fluttering in her stomach. *What,* she wondered, *is going on with me?*

She searched for something to say. "Did I hear you correctly yesterday?" Athena asked, picking up the thread of their conversation. "Did you say Mrs. Hillman suffered a stroke?"

"She did. Last year. She was treated by a doctor in York. She has suffered no lasting ill effects, thank goodness, but the doctor and I are worried about her. When she starts in about my sister, she works herself up into such a frenzy."

"I'm so sorry about what happened to your sister."

"As am I." His features tensed again, and he shoved his hands into his pockets, staring at the ground as they walked.

"I take it you agree with Mrs. Hillman. That your sister was innocent?"

"I do."

"Mrs. Lloyd said the same thing."

"Anyone who knew my sister would have agreed." He heaved a soft sigh. "To harm another human being, it simply wasn't in Caroline's nature."

"And yet she was convicted of such a terrible crime. How?"

"The law does not always seek the truth in such matters, Miss Taylor. It just wants someone to pay."

Athena considered what little she knew about the crime. "Mrs. Hillman said the whole neighborhood was at the garden party where Harold Sinclair died?"

"So I heard."

"And you think someone else poisoned his drink?"

"They must have. But the evidence was stacked against my sister. Caroline was in love with another man. She was desperate to end her forced engagement to Harold Sinclair. She argued with him at that party, in view and earshot of everyone. Most damning of all, a box of the same poison that killed him was found in Caroline's bedchamber."

Athena frowned. "It does sound very grim."

"Her trial at the assizes only lasted an hour. To make things even more unfair, the victim's brother had just become our parish constable. She didn't stand a chance." He frowned. "The events that ended my poor sister's life were also the ruin of mine, not to mention my father's. Our reputations were destroyed. We were shunned by society. My father slowly drank himself to death, while gambling away our every penny. But what happened … happened, and there's nothing I can do about it now."

Athena bit her lip. "Perhaps there is."

He looked at her. "I beg your pardon?"

"If you're right … if your sister didn't kill Harold Sinclair … perhaps it could be proven. And if so—"

"Do you think I didn't try?" He cut her off, his voice heavy with frustration. "From the moment Caroline was arrested, I did everything I could to discover the true perpetrator. My father threatened to disinherit me for looking into it—he believed Caroline had killed his friend and he couldn't forgive her. I investigated, anyway. I spent months questioning every member of the staff at Woodcroft House, and every villager, miner, mill worker, and farmer in the neighborhood. Did they see or hear anything suspicious at that party, or afterwards? Did they see anyone handle Sinclair's drink? Could they think of anyone who might have wished to harm Harold Sinclair?"

"And what did you learn?"

"*Nothing*. Nobody had much liked the man. Some people had wild notions about who else might have wanted him gone, but they were all nonsense that led to dead ends." He gave a bitter laugh. "*Dead ends*. An appropriate metaphor. Considering Caroline's fate."

Athena thought of that young woman being hanged and shuddered. "I'm so sorry," she said again. "I'm sorry for Miss Vernon and I can't imagine how difficult all this must have been for you. But … Mr. Vernon, I have been thinking about this and would like to share a new perspective on the matter."

He arched a brow. "What new perspective?"

"I believe the murder of Harold Sinclair may be connected to the death of Sally Osborn."

"Sally Osborn?" He glanced at her askance. "How on Earth did you come up with that?"

Athena told him about the inconsistencies in that young woman's demise—Sally's choice of shoes, her unslept-in bed, her behavior the evening before she'd died—and the fact that Sally had been working at Woodcroft House when Harold Sinclair had died. "According to her sister, Sally was forever after a changed person. I wonder if Sally knew who really poisoned Mr. Sinclair but kept quiet all this time. Now her sister is ill. Sally may have decided to blackmail the killer and was murdered for it. If we do a little digging, we can find the truth and solve both crimes."

They had reached the manor house by now, and they stopped by one of the back doors. He shook his head, frowning. "That is quite a theory, Miss Taylor. But I'm afraid I don't believe a word of it."

"Sir—"

"Sally Osborn's death was an unfortunate accident. It has nothing to do with my sister, who paid for her 'crime' long ago. And I'll thank you not to pry into it."

"But, Mr. Vernon," Athena tried again. "If what happened to your sister was a miscarriage of justice—"

"It was."

"Then if we find Harold Sinclair's true killer, it will clear your sister's name."

"'We'?" He fixed Athena with his stern gaze. "*We?*" All the good will that had begun their conversation had evaporated, leaving his voice suffused with anger. "Miss Taylor. You are talking nonsense, and I want no part of it. It has taken me nine long years to forge a new business and attempt to rebuild my reputation. I am only just now getting my head above water. The last thing I want is to dig up that old story. I imagine that doing so would not be good for your school, either. You have far better things to do with your time. Please stay out of things that don't concern you and give up this foolish notion."

With that, he headed back in the direction from which they had come.

Athena's heart felt leaden as she entered the house. If Mr. Vernon, who had dearly loved his sister, didn't believe Athena and didn't want to pursue this, what hope did she have of convincing anyone else?

OVER THE NEXT two days, whenever Athena wasn't occupied by teaching or lesson planning, she found her mind returning to the admonitions Mr. Vernon had made.

"You are talking nonsense … The last thing I want is to dig up that old story. And I imagine that doing so would not be good for your school, either."

Her own sister had accused Athena of "getting carried away."

"You don't need to solve a mystery yourself to be Diana's equal."

Athena didn't *feel the need* to solve a mystery. This was not a competition with her older sister. She was merely reacting to things she had seen and heard, things that didn't feel right to her. But were her ideas truly nonsense?

The question invaded her thoughts by day and caused fitful sleep at night.

Athena rose on Monday morning with a new conviction. *"You have far better things to do with your time,"* Mr. Vernon had said. He was right.

Although she still questioned everything that had been bothering her, she had a school to run. She had students who depended on her to set an educational course that could perhaps affect their whole lives. She ought to devote all her time and attention to that endeavor and stop worrying about things that, as Mr. Vernon had insisted, did not "concern her."

This conclusion, however, was completely turned on its head later that day with the arrival of the afternoon post, when she received a letter from her sister Diana.

CHAPTER NINE

Pendowar Hall
Portwithys, Cornwall

My dearest Athena and Selena,

Thank you so much for your letters. Please forgive me for being such a poor correspondent of late. I seem to be running a mile a minute all day long, with no time to myself, and after the sun sets, I am often too tired to pick up a pen. The doctor says this weariness is normal for a woman in my condition, but it is new to me.

Speaking of which, I felt the baby move for the first time yesterday! It was like the wiggle of a minnow or a fluttering of tiny wings. Such a thrilling sensation! To know that a new life is growing inside my womb is absolutely thrilling. I look forward to motherhood. February seems a very long time to wait. I have just begun choosing new wallpaper and furnishings for the nursery in anticipation of the babe's arrival.

My only regret is that William cannot be here for the child's birth. His ship does not return to England until next June—which means he will have been away at sea for more than a year. I promise I will not bore you in every letter with the woes of being a sea captain's wife. But, oh, how I miss him! William is the reason for every beat of my heart, and for every breath I take. I love him, I think, beyond explanation.

If not for his letters, I think I should go mad. They don't come nearly as often as I should like. A month went by without a single word, and then the other day, I received four missives at once. He is enjoying good health—his injured leg is very nearly back to normal—and he is pleased to be back on board ship and in command of a good crew.

The new steward whom William and I hired to help run the estate, Mr. Matson, has proved to be invaluable. Last week, one of the tenants had a drainage issue. Mr. Matson not only took care of it with aplomb, but he took me with him and educated me on the subject so that I might be able to handle such things one day if need be.

Our weather has been delightful. Lovely, warm days, perfect for walking in the gardens and on the beach. Emma and I spent yesterday afternoon collecting shells for her collection. Don't be angry with me, but the other day, we darted for a moment into Smuggler's Cave. I have stayed away from that place ever since ... you know. But something compelled me to see it again. To my surprise, it didn't frighten me at all. It was just a cavernous, sandy space with a bubbling stream. Yes, I know the potential power of that stream—how can I ever forget it? And I promise to be wary of it in the future.

Emma is doing well. I know she is William's cousin, and therefore my cousin too, but we have become so close that I often think of her as my 'other sister.' At times, she seems much older than her sixteen years, and yet at other times, she can appear to be a girl of ten—a wonderful dichotomy. Emma is so bright, I sometimes feel as though she is the teacher, instead of me! It is still hard for me to believe that just a year ago, Emma didn't know how to read or write. She has made steady progress in those areas. I allowed her to select our next book to read together, giving her two choices from among our favorites: Jane Eyre *and* A Lady's Ransom. *What do you think she picked? The Pryor Corbett novel! No surprise, I suppose—who can resist adventure on the high seas?*

Before I forget—I have another idea I have been meaning to mention for your school. I have discovered that Emma learns more quickly and retains what she has learned more fully when I conduct our lessons outdoors. This is not necessary for all classes, of course, and only works in fine weather, but you might find it a useful tool, particularly when teaching the sciences.

And now I must change to another subject that has been on my mind ever since your letter arrived, Athena. I am so sorry to hear about the death of your maid, Sally. It is a tragedy whenever a young person dies, and how awful that it happened in such a way. You shared your thoughts about the manner and timing of Sally's death, and I understand why it concerns you—and why you are concerned that the parish constable may have come to the wrong conclusion.

As you know, I was faced by a similar situation when I first arrived at Pendowar Hall. The parish constable's callous disregard for his 'case' seemed incredible to me. At first, I had nothing to go on but a few random facts and a hunch. And yet, even if our dear Mrs. Phillips had not made me promise to investigate, I believe that I wouldn't have been able to help myself from looking into it.

It is in our nature to question things, isn't it? We three all seem to see inconsistencies that are invisible to everyone else, as well as a compulsion to explore what lurks beneath.

From what you wrote, Sally's behavior the night before she drowned, and her choice of shoes and unslept-in bed, all sound out of character to me. Anyone who thinks otherwise is not paying attention. I, too, am intrigued by that long-ago murder, which has so negatively affected the reputation of Thorndale Manor. How interesting that your housekeeper swears the supposed perpetrator, Caroline Vernon, was innocent! To know that the man was killed at a party, with so many people in attendance—it opens the door to a great many suspects. And! The fact that Sally left her post at Woodcroft House a much-changed person—it cannot be a coincidence.

As Mama said, where there's smoke, there's fire.

Athena, you once told me when I was facing a similar dilemma: Do not doubt yourself!

I offer you the same advice. Investigate. Do it for Sally Osborn and Caroline Vernon, who perished long before their time, and perhaps through no fault of their own. Do it for yourself. Do it for your school. Because Thorndale Manor's fine, old reputation needs to be restored to its former glory. You may be the only person who can discover the truth and set things right.

But at the same time, please, please be careful. I learned the hard way: once a person has killed, they will not hesitate to do so again. Keep your eyes and ears open. Do not believe every-thing you are told. Trust no one. And protect yourself.

With all my love, your sister,
Diana

Diana's words stayed on Athena's mind all day long and well into the evening. She was particularly gratified by one thing in Diana's letter—the recommendation to take classwork outside. Athena had done exactly that with her recent botany lesson, to great effect, and it had been all her own idea. Perhaps, when it came to teaching, she was Diana's equal, after all?

Diana's other contentions, however, were more unsettling. As Athena got ready for bed, it began to rain, a pattering that turned into a full-blown storm. The wail of the wind and the pounding of the deluge seemed to echo the turmoil inside her brain.

"What are you thinking?" Selena asked as she climbed into bed.

Athena finished braiding her hair and climbed into her own bed by the window, which was being bashed by the relentless rain. "I'm thinking about Caroline Vernon," she admitted. "And about Sally Osborn. And Diana's letter."

"So am I." Selena sounded discomposed.

Athena sat upright in bed, twiddling her hands. "Do you think Diana's right?"

"About what?"

"About following my hunch about Sally and Miss Vernon. Am I onto something? Or are my ideas merely nonsense?"

"I don't know." Selena heaved a long breath that resounded with uncertainty.

Athena gave an echoing sigh. "If I do investigate further, will I be betraying Mr. Vernon? He implied that prying into the murder of Harold Sinclair would be like opening an old wound. And he said the same thing you did—that 'digging up the story' might be damaging to our school."

"It might," Selena acceded.

"But how could it be wrong to do so, if the result might clear his sister's name and restore the reputation of this very house?" Athena pointed out.

"There's no guarantee that will happen."

"True. It's a conundrum." Athena groaned with frustration and dropped back upon her pillow. They lay in silence in the flickering candlelight for a while.

Selena's voice broke the stillness. "It is odd when you think about it. That this was *her* room."

"Yes." Athena glanced about the chamber. "It's strange to think that Caroline Vernon slept here almost her entire life."

"Do you think this furniture was hers? That maybe even … one of these beds was hers?"

Athena hadn't considered that before. "I don't know." The idea sent an eerie shiver down Athena's spine. "Ever since our tea at Darkmoor Park, whenever I close my eyes at night, I see Caroline Vernon's portrait in my mind."

"Me too. That raven-haired young beauty in shimmering, white satin." Selena paused, and her voice grew grim. "I read somewhere that the bodies of convicted murderers are not allowed to be buried. They're given instead to medical science for dissection and study."

"I have read that, too." Athena shook her head. "I understand the need for human bodies for medical research. But it means that Caroline Vernon's body, no doubt, was desecrated. And never laid to rest."

"It's *so awful.*"

"I know." Athena blew out the candle. Rain battered the windows. "Do you think, after a person dies, that their essence remains?"

"I thought you don't believe in ghosts?"

"I don't. Not a ghost as people traditionally *think* of ghosts—creatures that haunt with malice and wreak havoc. But rather ... a spirit that infuses a place where they once lived, and ... lingers."

"We did feel a *presence* on our first night in this house."

"But never again since."

"No, but what could have accounted for it? Was it Caroline Vernon's spirit studying us, the new tenants of her home? Perhaps she liked what she saw, and that's why she went quiet?"

"Perhaps," Athena replied as they both gave in to tiredness and said goodnight.

Sleep didn't come easily for Athena, however. The rain continued its ceaseless beat. The wind howled. For several hours, she tossed and turned, and when she finally did drift off, she dreamt of Caroline Vernon.

In the dream, Athena was walking on the Thorndale Manor grounds. She was alone. The sun painted the sky a vivid blue, but she could not feel its warmth. Not a bee was buzzing, and not a bird was singing.

A young woman burst forth from the hedgerows, running with all her might. It was Caroline Vernon, attired as she had been in the portrait hanging above Mrs. Hillman's fireplace. Except that her black hair was loose, her white gown was spattered with blood, and her blue eyes were wide with fright.

"Help me!" Miss Vernon raced up to Athena. "Help me!"

"How can I help you?" Athena cried.

"Find the truth." Miss Vernon's voice was a desperate plea. "Find out who murdered Harold Sinclair. It wasn't me. *It wasn't me.*"

Athena awoke, gasping and bathed in perspiration, her heart beating so hard, it seemed to be forcing its way out of her chest.

"Athena!" It was Selena's voice. "Are you all right?"

"Yes," Athena whispered. The soft glow from the embers in the hearth pierced the darkness.

"You were talking in your sleep."

"What did I say?"

"You said, 'How can I help you?'"

Athena lay in bed, gripping the covers. "I had a bad dream."

"What was it about?"

Athena told her.

"How disturbing." Selena's voice was no louder than a whisper.

Athena was about to reply when a loud crash rent the air. They both leapt from their beds. "What was that?"

"It came from somewhere above us," Selena noted.

They lit candles and dashed into the corridor. Miss Russell and Miss Weaver emerged shivering from their chambers, their hair in rag curls. At the same time, the door to the servants' stairs opened and Tabitha appeared, a candlestick in hand.

"What happened?" Miss Russell exclaimed.

"I heard a loud thud above my room," Tabitha said.

Determined to restore order, Athena announced, "I'm sure it's nothing to worry about. Girls, go back to bed. Tabitha, please retire as well."

The girls and maid did as they'd been ordered. Athena returned to her room and put a warm dress over her night-rail. "I'm going to find out what happened. Stay here, Selena. There's no reason we should both get wet."

Downstairs, Athena grabbed her cloak, boots, and an umbrella. She lit a lantern and, bracing herself, ventured out into the stormy night. The wind-driven rain blew down and sideways, pelting her with such force that despite her protections, she was soon drenched. Worse yet, it was pitch black and impossible to see anything that wasn't within direct range of her lantern's beam.

She had just determined that her mission had been a folly when she came upon the probable answer to the riddle. An immense branch from one of the ancient oak trees lay in the rear courtyard, just a few yards from the house. It must have broken off in the storm and had perhaps fallen onto the roof before dropping to the ground.

Athena returned to her room and, drying herself and her hair, told Selena what she had discovered. After hanging her wet clothes by the hearth, adding new wood from the basket, and stirring the fire back to life, she gratefully climbed back into bed.

"We're lucky it happened at night, and no one was injured."

"Indeed, we are." Athena lay shivering beneath the covers. "It feels ominous that such a huge branch fell on our roof, immediately after I had that disturbing dream." The dream had felt so real.

"I am no interpreter of dreams." Selena paused, her voice hushed. "But as I understand it, they reflect the dreamer's experiences, fears, and beliefs, rather than being a mysterious message or portent."

"What do you mean?"

Selena hesitated again. "Do *you* think Caroline Vernon killed Harold Sinclair?"

"No," Athena answered, surprised by the conviction in her voice. But now that she'd voiced it aloud, she realized it expressed her true belief. "Three people who knew Miss Vernon well swore she couldn't have killed him or anyone. When I saw her portrait, I felt the same way."

"So did I," Selena said.

"You did?"

"Yes. It was as if goodness itself were somehow captured on that canvas."

"And yet all the evidence pointed to Caroline Vernon, and so she was hanged."

"Which is a travesty." The concern on Selena's face was visible even in the dimly lit room. "I think your dream was a message from your soul, Athena. It was your conscience trying to tell you something. Begging you to *find the truth*. The same message, I think, that Diana was trying to deliver in her letter. Perhaps we ought to listen."

Athena sat up in bed, her pulse hammering a newfound, insistent beat. "*We?*"

Selena nodded. "I know I've been the naysayer in all of this, but there *might* be something in what you say. Sally's death might have been an accident, or it might be connected to Harold Sinclair's murder. Either way, Caroline Vernon may indeed have been wrongly convicted. If we can find the real perpetrator and prove it—then we will not only achieve justice for that poor woman but also restore the reputation of Thorndale Manor."

"And save our school!"

"Yes."

Athena paused. "What about Diana's warning?"

"To be careful?"

"Yes. Look what happened to her at Pendowar Hall."

"We'll do what she said. We'll keep our eyes and ears open. Remember our other favorite saying."

Athena felt herself smile. "Fortune favors the bold."

"Whatever happens next, sister dear, I am on board."

THEY AGREED THAT their first course of action should be to speak to the parish constable, Neville Sinclair, to try to persuade him to reopen his brother's murder case. Athena decided to do it since she and Neville Sinclair had already met.

After sending a note requesting an appointment, she sought out Mrs. Lloyd to ask for directions. "I plan to go on Wednesday after reading to Mrs. Hillman," Athena told the housekeeper, whom she found sitting on a high stool in the pantry, polishing the silver. "What's the best way to get to Woodcroft House from Darkmoor Park?"

"It's an easy walk, no more than two miles if you take the shortcut." Mrs. Lloyd gave detailed instructions that involved crossing a field and entering the estate through a back gate that led to the rear grounds. "But why do you wish to go there?"

"I want to speak to Neville Sinclair."

"I wouldn't go near that man with a ten-foot pole." Mrs. Lloyd vigorously scrubbed a knife. "*He's* the reason our Caroline was sent to prison for that horrible crime."

"I know. But I'd like to learn more about Caroline Vernon's case." Athena paused. She didn't think it appropriate to share her suspicions with the housekeeper, but perhaps the woman could fill her in on a few facts. "Mrs. Hillman told me that Caroline's conviction was heavily influenced by a statement from a maid who worked here—she claimed she'd found a box of rat poison in Miss Vernon's room. Do you recall the maid's name?"

"Ethel Leighton." Mrs. Lloyd's mouth twisted. "It was a pack of lies! Every word of it!"

"Do you know where Ethel lives now?"

"No idea. Ethel only worked here a few months. After Miss Vernon's trial, Ethel disappeared. She said she was getting married, to whom, I don't know." Mrs. Lloyd poured more polishing cream on her rag and attacked a large serving spoon. "I never should have hired that girl. She was nothing but trouble. One morning, I caught her stealing a silver brooch from Miss Vernon's jewelry box. She had the gall to lie to my face about it, insisted she was just going to polish it. Polish it, my eye!" She let out an incredulous huff. "That wasn't even her job! It was the butler's duty back then—when we *had* a butler. Now it's my job, of course," she added matter-of-factly. "In any case, I gave her one more chance, and that was a mistake. A few weeks later, a hundred pounds went missing from the cash box in the master's study. I'll swear on twenty Bibles that Ethel took it, but I couldn't prove it."

"I see. Thank you for sharing that, Mrs. Lloyd."

Athena realized she needed to learn more about Ethel Leighton. If she was truly a thief, then she might have been the type of person whom a villain could have paid to lie on the witness stand. It was another point to bring up with Neville Sinclair.

First, however, she was due to visit Darkmoor Park. When Athena arrived, Mr. Chapman greeted her in the front hall.

"So good of you to come today to read to Mrs. Hillman," he said, smiling.

"I was honored to be asked—and grateful for her support for the school. Indeed, it is Mrs. Hillman's generosity that helps me to afford your salary."

Mr. Chapman chuckled. "Do you know, Miss Taylor, I've only been here a short time, but I already feel more at home at your school, working with your students, and working with *you*—than anywhere I have ever taught before."

His brown eyes were filled with warmth and sincerity. She sensed a depth of interest there, as though she were special in his eyes. She couldn't deny it—her students and housekeeper and housemaid were not the only ones who found Mr. Chapman irresistible. If Athena had half a mind to, she could easily fall prey to charms. But that was *not* going to happen.

She cleared her throat. "I'm happy to hear you say so, Mr. Chapman. Will you stay to hear me read from *The Wind Pirate?*"

"I wish I could." His features softened, as if with deep regret. "But you must forgive me. I have a music lesson to prepare for."

They said their goodbyes and he disappeared to another part of the house. Athena found Mrs. Hillman in the drawing room, where she read aloud several chapters of the Pryor Corbett novel, picking up where Selena had left off the Sunday before.

Mrs. Hillman listened with her eyes closed and a beatific smile on her face, letting out many happy sighs and laughing at all the appropriate moments.

"I love the tension in that last scene, the way Lydia must keep all her feelings for John Brandon in check," Mrs. Hillman said, when Athena had finished.

"It is such fun," Athena agreed. "Miss Penrose is practically dying to tell Brandon how she feels, and yet doing so would give away her true gender and mean that she'd be cast off the ship."

"At least, that is what Lydia fears at *this* early point in the story." Mrs. Hillman gave Athena a mischievous look.

Athena laughed. "There is something wonderful about re-

reading a book that you have enjoyed many times, don't you think?"

"I do. The characters and dialog and situations are so beloved and familiar that you can anticipate them with delight, and laugh and cry and be overwhelmed with emotion all over again."

"I think reading is a bit like music. Every paragraph is a new measure. Every sentence is a new beat. Every word is a note. And the whole piece paints a magical picture in your mind."

Mrs. Hillman smiled. "I've never heard a book described in musical terms before. I suppose it explains why I love music almost as much as reading." She paused. "Speaking of which. Have you heard there's to be a concert at the village hall a little over three weeks from now?"

"I heard something about it. Who is performing again?"

"The celebrated soprano Mrs. Augustus from Edinburgh. It's not often that a singer comes to our small community. She'll be en route to London and has agreed to appear in Darkmoor Bridge for one night only. I've heard her several times and she's divine."

"I wish I could go, but I'm afraid that expense is not in the cards." Athena rose. "And now do forgive me, ma'am, but I must be on my way."

"I'm so grateful to you for doing this," Mrs. Hillman said. "You were right, though, about one thing."

"Right about what?"

"About your sister. Miss Selena is not only every bit as good a reader as you are, but she may be the *tiniest* bit better." Mrs. Hillman's eyes sparkled. "Last Sunday, she was precisely the tonic I needed."

"Selena has many talents," Athena replied proudly, and with a laugh. "I knew you would appreciate her. Perhaps you would rather have her read to you exclusively from now on?"

"Oh, no. I enjoy the diversity. I look forward to your visit next week."

After taking her leave, Athena made her way to Woodcroft House. As she crossed a field dotted with bleating sheep, she pondered her upcoming conversation with Mr. Sinclair.

She didn't want a repeat of her earlier, disastrous altercation with Mr. Vernon. Somehow, she had to get Mr. Sinclair on her side. It would be best, she decided, to begin by questioning him about the garden party where Harold Sinclair had died and learn all she could about that event before sharing her theories.

Athena soon entered through the rear gate of the Woodcroft House estate, which led to the outlying grounds. Seemingly endless acres of woods and green lawns sloped down gracefully between herds of grazing deer towards the mansion house in the distance. A grand, rectangular structure built in the baroque style, it was a tribute to the wealth and prominence of its owner.

Beyond the stables, Athena passed the kennel, a sturdy-looking, red-brick structure inside a fenced-in yard. Dozens of hounds erupted into frenzied barking from behind a series of grated windows. In an outdoor pen, two enormous mastiffs snarled and hurled themselves against the iron bars.

Athena shuddered and picked up her pace. She understood the need for guard dogs. Poaching was a common problem on many estates, especially those with a deer park. But having been bitten by a neighbor's mastiff as a child, she feared such animals. As for hunting dogs—although her father had been fond of hunting, Athena did not comprehend how anyone could derive pleasure from such a sport.

A series of formal gardens followed. Athena circled to the front entrance of the house, where she applied for admittance. A dignified butler in a tailcoat took her card and bade her to wait in the entrance hall. Athena's breath caught as she took in the elegant, high-ceilinged chamber with its black-and-white-checkered marble floor and walls hung with a display of ancient weaponry that rivalled the one at Darkmoor Park.

The butler returned and showed her to an adjacent parlor, where Neville Sinclair sat writing at an immense desk covered in piles of paperwork. The room was clearly a gentleman's domain, the walls covered by paintings of horses, hunting dogs, and hunting scenes.

"Miss Taylor to see you, sir," the butler announced before withdrawing.

"Thank you, Miles." Mr. Sinclair set down his pen and studied the card in his hand. His brow furrowed, and he rubbed his chin. "Ah," he said at last. "Miss Taylor. I believe we met on that unfortunate morning down at the river?"

"We did, sir."

"Please have a seat." He gestured to the chair facing his desk. "How may I help you?"

Athena had discovered, after working many years for men, that the best way to gain their favor was to appeal to their vanity.

"Thank you for seeing me, Mr. Sinclair. That morning you spoke of—when you mentioned it being difficult to get students for my school—you were right. It has been a struggle to find parents willing to send their daughters to study at Thorndale Manor."

"I wish it weren't so." He nodded slowly, his lips pursed in a slight frown. "But that house has a bad reputation now and such things are hard to ignore."

"Which is why I have come to you. I am new in Darkmoor Bridge. I would like to know more about the history of my house and how it came to have its, as you say, bad reputation. I should think, as one of the leaders of this community, you would know more about it than anyone."

"I wouldn't say that. But I'm happy to tell you all I know." Neville Sinclair fingered his blond mustache as he regarded Athena across his desk. "There was nothing wrong with that place for centuries, you know. Not in the same league as Woodcroft House or Darkmoor Park, but it had its merits and the Vernons appeared to be a fine, upstanding family. That is, until Caroline Vernon came along and changed everything."

"All the blame for the house's and the family's tattered reputation, then, goes to Miss Vernon?"

"She was just the evidence of it. It was bad blood that infected that girl. Her father, Arthur Vernon, was no gem, mind you. My father and my brother befriended the man, but I never did. Just look at his decline into debauchery and sin. I suppose I can understand it, though, after learning the truth about his daughter. Miss Vernon was as pretty as you please on the outside, just like an angel, but all the while hiding the temperament of the Devil. She murdered my brother in cold blood and then went home as if it were a day just like any other."

Athena cringed inwardly at the lack of empathy in his words. "I should like to ask you about that day, Mr. Sinclair. I have only heard the merest mention of it and yet as you say, it changed everything. As I understand it, your brother perished here at a party?"

Mr. Sinclair nodded. "It was a long time ago, but I remember it as if it were yesterday."

"And can you say with absolute certainty that Caroline Vernon was the one who killed him?"

He lowered his gaze, picked up a pen, and fiddled with it. "I can. I do."

Something in the man's tone and expression suggested that he was being less than truthful.

"Please go on." Athena sat forward in her chair, determined to draw the truth out of him.

CHAPTER TEN

"IT WAS THE annual Woodcroft House garden party." Neville Sinclair, still worrying a pen between his fingertips, gazed at Athena across the desk in his study.

The sun filtered in through the tall casement windows that overlooked Woodcroft House's expansive grounds. Athena was eager to hear what Mr. Sinclair had to say but reminded herself that his brother had been the victim of the murder in question, which may have clouded his judgment.

"My parents had been hosting the party for decades on the third Saturday in July," Mr. Sinclair continued. "Harold hated the thing and had wanted to give it up after he'd inherited the estate. But the vicar had persuaded Harold to continue the tradition."

"Who was invited to the party?"

"There were no invitations. It was open to everyone in the neighborhood, from the farmers and tradesmen and their wives to the most prominent families. Anyone except children could come, and most did."

"Were you in attendance that day?"

"Yes. I was living in London at the time—I had completed my study of law at Inns of Court and had just been called to the bar. But I knew how much the locals looked forward to the party all year, and I thought it my duty to help host it." He set down his pen in the inkstand. "It was the usual set-up out on the back lawn. Tea, punch, biscuits, pies, cakes. Harold and Arthur Vernon had both spiked their punch with a shot of whiskey and were chumming around with each other, as always." Mr. Sinclair seemed to warm to his subject as he went on. "It was about an hour or so into the party and people were swarming the place when Miss Vernon made her appearance. Arthur Vernon was furious. She wasn't supposed to be there. I'm told he'd been keeping her at home under lock and key."

"Her father locked her up?" Athena's entire body seemed to tense at this vile notion.

"Apparently, to make sure she wouldn't run away before the wedding, which was in a week's time." Mr. Sinclair made a face. "I told you the man was no gem. Anyway, she got out. She was dressed all in white. Like I said, like an angel—an avenging angel, as it turned out. She asked to speak to Harold privately, but he was a bit in his cups and told her to go home and leave him be. Then they started arguing."

"Did you hear what they were arguing about?"

"Every word. I remember it as if it were yesterday. Dozens of others heard it as well and they all said the same at the assizes. Miss Vernon said, 'I don't love you. And you don't love me. You just want to possess me.' She said she was terrified that if she ended their engagement, it might literally kill her father, who had a weak heart. She begged Harold to break it off instead. 'Say that you changed your mind—say that you hate me, I don't care,' she told him, 'but please don't make me go through with this.' Harold refused. He insisted that he had made a deal in good faith with her father. If *she* wanted to call off the wedding, so be it, that was her prerogative, but *he* would not go back on his word. Which was just as it should be." Mr. Sinclair nodded, his lips pressed tightly together. "A gentleman *never* breaks his word, Miss Taylor."

Athena took this in with a frown. "What happened next?"

"Harold put down his drink and stormed away. I caught up with him and he ordered Miles, our butler, to call the carriage to take Miss Vernon home. He asked me to see her out. By now, her father had gotten wind of what had happened, and he insisted on going with—to keep an eye on her, I suppose. After the carriage came around and they were safely off, I returned to the party and saw Harold finishing his drink. A few minutes later, he was coughing like mad and struggling to breathe. Then he fell down dead."

Athena winced. "How awful."

"It wasn't pleasant to witness, I'll give you that." Mr. Sinclair's tone was curiously matter-of-fact, and devoid of emotion. "When our apothecary, Mr. Quince, tested Harold's glass, he found *arsenic*. Harold wouldn't end their engagement, so Caroline Vernon poisoned his drink to get free of him."

Athena looked at him. *"Did she?"*

He tipped his head to one side. "I beg your pardon?"

"The situation you described raises several interesting points, don't you think? First: how can you be sure the poison was intended for your brother? I presume there were a great many glasses in use at the party?"

"Harold had his own custom-made whiskey glass. Cut crystal, with his initials inscribed on it in gold. It was the only one like it." He crossed his arms over his chest. "Whoever poisoned that glass knew he would drink from it."

"I see. But you said your brother put down his drink when he went off to find your butler. Where did he put his glass?"

"On a table."

"Which means his glass was left unattended for an interval. Isn't that so?"

"Exactly. That's how Miss Vernon got to it."

"Did anyone actually see her add poison to your brother's drink?"

He paused, blinking rapidly. He opened his mouth as if to speak, then shut it again. Finally, reluctantly, he said, "No."

Aha, Athena thought. "Didn't everyone at the party have the same access to that glass?"

"Perhaps." He leaned back in his chair with a frown. "But

Miss Vernon was standing right beside his glass when he left it. She had the perfect opportunity."

"As I understand it, you were the parish constable at the time? This was your case?"

"I inherited the position when my brother died."

"Wasn't that a conflict of interest?"

"I beg your pardon?" he said again.

"Might you have been a bit prejudiced, being in charge of an investigation into your own brother's death?"

He fixed his gaze on some point on the other side of the desk. "Not at all. The whole thing was completely aboveboard."

Athena wasn't so sure about that. "Did you investigate any other possible suspects, other than Miss Vernon?"

He dismissed her notion with a wave of his hand. "Didn't need to. We had all heard Miss Vernon arguing with my brother. Her motive was clear. And then a maid at Thorndale Manor found rat poison in Miss Vernon's room. The key ingredient in rat poison is arsenic. I didn't need to look further."

"So, you think Miss Vernon brought rat poison with her to the party? With the intention of poisoning Harold Sinclair if he didn't end their engagement?"

"I do."

"How do you imagine she brought the poison with her?"

He picked up a pencil now and began tapping it on the desktop. "In her handbag, I suppose. For all I know, she had it in her pocket. I don't really care. Look, here—"

"You must acknowledge, sir, the possibility that someone else might have had a motive to kill your brother," Athena challenged. "*Anyone* at that party could have tampered with his glass. Rat poison is a very common substance. It can no doubt be found in every home in England."

"*Not in a lady's bedchamber,*" he returned sharply.

"If Miss Vernon had truly killed Harold Sinclair, why would she have kept the damning evidence in her own room? That would have been folly."

He moved restlessly in his chair. "She was probably waiting for the perfect moment to dispose of it, but the maid got there first."

Athena paused. What would it take to get this man to open his mind? "All the people who knew Miss Vernon best insist that she could never have killed anyone."

"Who are all these people?" He made a scoffing sound. "Her brother? Her dearest friends?"

Athena realized that this line of thinking wouldn't help her. "Sir, even if poison *was* found in Caroline Vernon's room, it doesn't prove that she did it. And what proof did you have that poison was actually found there? The maid who gave that testimony, Ethel Leighton, might have been lying."

"Why would she have lied?"

"My housekeeper, Mrs. Lloyd, said that Ethel Leighton was a troublemaker. She may have stolen a hundred pounds from Arthur Vernon's cash box. She quit the region immediately after Miss Vernon's trial. Perhaps Ethel was paid to lie on the witness stand, to protect the real murderer."

Mr. Sinclair shook his head, his eyes blazing with irritation now. "Miss Taylor, you are wasting my time with these outrageous theories. Miss Vernon died nine years ago. What is your aim here? Do you have some fantasy that if you could clear her name, it might somehow restore Thorndale Manor's reputation to its former glory?"

Athena felt blood rush to her cheeks. He had seen through her. But honesty, she had found, was always the best policy. "Yes, sir, but … *what if Caroline Vernon was innocent*? What if her killer is still free? If you would consider reopening the case—"

"*Reopen it*? Are you mad?"

"By doing so, you could learn the truth and achieve justice for your bother."

Mr. Sinclair slapped the desk with his hand. "I *did* learn the truth!" he thundered. "I did achieve justice for my brother! Miss Vernon hanged for the crime and it's over and done with."

Athena swallowed her disappointment as Mr. Sinclair leaned forward across the desk and looked her in the eye.

"It's a shame Harold had to die so young—but I won't pretend to be crushed by it. In fact—and this is no secret—I despised my brother."

Athena was so surprised by this admission, it took her a moment to respond. "Why?"

"Harold was three years older than me and always taller and broader. He decided early on that it was his job to terrify and torture me. Our nursery maid said he used to poke me with pins when I lay in my cradle." He heaved a long sigh. "From the time I could walk, there wasn't a stick on the grounds that Harold didn't beat me with. He was always kicking me under the table or jumping out at me from around corners and mercilessly pummeling me. Reminding me that he was the heir, and I was only the spare, a nobody who would never inherit or be worth the money my father was obliged to spend to educate me."

Athena had witnessed bullying in her years as a governess but had never seen anything this severe. "I'm so sorry. Did you tell your parents?"

"I did, but they either didn't believe me or didn't care. My mother worshipped the ground Harold walked on. He was her first born and could do no wrong. My father said I needed to 'act like a man and fight back.' Not an easy matter when your tormentor is older and so much stronger."

"I'm sorry," Athena said again.

"It's ancient history now. My brother's gone. And for the rest of us, life goes on."

As Athena gathered her thoughts, a knock sounded at the open door. A diminutive, blonde woman attired in a violet, silk dress entered the study. Athena recognized her from sightings at church as Mr. Sinclair's wife.

"Neville? Dearest, have you forgotten? Mr. Hastings will be here at any moment to go over the details for next week's hunt. We have over thirty people attending and a great deal to discuss."

"Thank you, Lily, for the reminder." Mr. Sinclair's features were still tense as he gestured from his wife to Athena. "Lily, this is Miss Taylor, the schoolmistress from Thorndale Manor. She had a few questions for me."

Mrs. Sinclair gave Athena an unsmiling, dismissive nod. "How do you do, Miss Taylor? Miles will escort you out."

It was Athena's cue to leave. She rose and dipped a curtsy. "Thank you again for seeing me, sir. I bid you good day."

The butler showed Athena to the door. As she crossed the estate's vast grounds, Athena was steeped in frustration. She had a great deal of new information about what had occurred at that garden party—albeit from Neville Sinclair's point of view—but she hadn't gotten a chance to share her theories about Sally Osborn. Even if she had, however, the exercise would have probably been pointless.

Mr. Sinclair would no doubt think it ludicrous to connect his brother's long-ago murder to Sally's recent death, for one of two reasons: because he was absolutely convinced that Caroline Vernon had murdered his brother ... or, for a different reason entirely ... a possibility that was setting off alarm bells in Athena's head.

Neville Sinclair had despised his brother Harold, who had mercilessly tortured him since birth.

Was it possible that *Neville Sinclair* had murdered his brother in revenge?

ATHENA REACHED THORNDALE Manor just as the sun sank beneath the horizon. She found Selena in the conservatory, where the last rays of the fading day illuminated the glassed-in chamber overlooking the back gardens.

"There you are!" Athena flung herself onto a wicker chair surrounded by potted plants and stretched out her weary legs.

Selena, seated in the chair opposite, looked up from a mathematics book. "How did it go?"

"The reading, or the consultation?"

"Both."

"Mrs. Hillman loved the chapters I read. But she pronounced you to be the superior reader. No surprise there."

Selena bit her lip. "Sorry." With teasing eyes, she added, "I'll try to be less entertaining next time."

"Don't! Give the woman her money's worth. We're lucky to have this extra work thrown our way. I offered to withdraw and let you take both weekly sessions, but she said she appreciated the variety."

Selena grinned. "She is a kind soul. I have enjoyed every moment in her company. She reminds me of our godmother, Mrs. Phillips, may she rest in peace—and what our own mother might have been like, had she lived to such an age."

"I find myself thinking of Mrs. Hillman like a dear, old aunt—even though we never had an aunt to speak of."

They exchanged a smile as Selena closed the book in her lap. "Now tell me about your visit to Mr. Sinclair."

"It proved both illuminating and frustrating." Athena filled her sister in on everything that she and Mr. Sinclair had discussed.

When she'd finished, Selena sat up straighter in her chair. "Are you thinking what I'm thinking?"

"I'll bet I am."

"Neville Sinclair was a second son, obliged to work as a barrister. With his brother out of the way, Neville became the owner of Woodcroft House, one of the most prestigious properties in the county."

Athena nodded. "He's an important citizen, the parish constable—and now the newly appointed magistrate at York. When he is not so occupied, he is a man of leisure who can hunt with hounds every day of the week if he chooses."

"How much did he covet that estate, and the life the goes with it?"

"What might he have done to acquire it?"

"It would have been a simple matter for him to poison his brother's drink."

"And how clever to do it at a party, where plenty of others had that opportunity," Athena pointed out excitedly. "He could have had a packet of arsenic in his pocket and just waited for the right moment."

"But didn't he say he walked away with Harold, to find the butler to summon the carriage?"

"Yes, but we only have his word for that. Even if it's true, he could have poisoned the drink when he went back to fetch Miss Vernon."

"And then—he could have deliberately framed her by paying off the maid, Ethel, to lie about the poison."

"Yes!" Athena replied excitedly. "If Neville Sinclair *were* the killer, it would explain his determination to close the case quickly and not reexamine it now. And it would help explain why Mr. Vernon wasn't able to find evidence pointing to any other suspects. Who would suspect the parish constable of murder?"

Selena bit her lip. "On the other hand ... if he's guilty, it would be unwise of him to admit to his hatred of his brother."

"Good point." Athena considered that. "Perhaps it was a deliberate act of misdirection? A clever tactic to throw me off the scent?"

"I suppose it could have been." A thoughtful expression crossed Selena's face. "Do you remember what Mama used to say about first instincts?"

"Yes. She said, '*Your first instinct is usually the right one.*'" Athena hesitated. "Although my first instinct about Mr. Vernon doesn't seem to have been correct."

Selena's forehead furrowed. "Oh?"

"When we first met, I thought him hateful. Now I'm not so sure. Mr. Vernon actually apologized and asked if we could be friends."

"Did he? That day at tea, I thought he was nice."

Athena felt her sister's eyes on her, as if studying her. Unaccountably, Athena realized she was blushing. "Yes, well. Anyway. Back to Neville Sinclair. If he murdered his brother, it won't be easy to prove. He is the magistrate now. We'd have to go above his head—but to whom?"

"Let's not get ahead of ourselves. Right now, all we have is a theory. We should ask someone who has lived in the neighborhood a long time and who knows Neville Sinclair really well to see if we're on the right track."

"I can't ask Mr. Vernon. He made it clear that he doesn't want me looking into this."

"What about Mrs. Hillman?"

"Oh, I couldn't. When the subject came up that day at tea, she became so upset."

"That's because she is incensed over what happened to Caroline Vernon. If Mrs. Hillman knew that we are trying to find justice for Miss Vernon, she might feel differently. I think she'd be glad."

Athena considered that. "All right. I'll talk to her."

ATHENA WAS TRYING to find a free moment to run over to Darkmoor Park, when the following afternoon, the very woman she wanted to see made a surprise visit to the school.

"I was at the dressmaker's," Mrs. Hillman explained as she slowly entered the drawing room, leaning on her cane. "I have been curious to see Thorndale Manor again now that you're running a school here and I thought as long as I was out, I might as well stop by and see what you do."

"I'm so pleased you came, Mrs. Hillman," Athena told her.

Their visitor sat in on the last three classes of the day, quietly watching the whole time from the back of the room and giving an occasional nod or smile of approval. The girls seemed uncharacteristically shy in the presence of this stranger and were on their best behavior, giving their attention to the classwork, dutifully raising their hands before answering questions from their teachers and participating in their singing lessons with fewer giggles than usual.

"What a wonderful opportunity these girls are getting under your instruction," Mrs. Hillman told Selena, Athena, and Mr. Chapman as the girls filed out of the music room, chattering amongst themselves. "I'm glad to see my money is being put to good use."

"Thank you," Athena said with a smile. "We're so pleased that you were able to see it firsthand."

"Mr. Chapman is supping with us this evening, and we'd be happy to have you join us, Mrs. Hillman," Selena offered.

"Thank you," that good lady replied. "But I gave my cook special orders for tonight's meal, and I wouldn't want her to have gone to all that work for nothing."

As Mr. Chapman and Selena ushered the girls out to the rear courtyard for a break before dinner, Athena asked Mrs. Hillman if they might have a private word. The two women retired to the study, where Athena could be assured of privacy.

Once they were seated, Mrs. Hillman said, "You have such a serious expression on your face, Miss Taylor. What is it you wish to speak to me about?"

"It's a delicate matter, my dear Mrs. Hillman. I hesitate to bring it up because the last time we spoke on the subject, you became upset."

Mrs. Hillman took that in and nodded slowly. "I imagine you wish to talk about Caroline?"

"Yes. However, I don't wish to cause you further pain. If you'd rather we end this discussion here and now, I will completely understand—you have only to say the word."

"I am in a calm frame of mind today, my dear. Whatever you wish to say, I am happy to hear it."

"All right." Athena took a breath. "I'd like to share a theory that my sister and I have, about a person who may have been responsible for Harold Sinclair's death."

A look of keen interest took over Mrs. Hillman's face. "Go on."

Athena gave Mrs. Hillman an overview of all that had been happening from Sally Osborn's death to the present day, culminating with her suspicions regarding Neville Sinclair. "He had motive and opportunity, and as the parish constable, he had the means to bring the case to a rapid conclusion. But other than a few brief meetings, I don't know the man—and I'm guessing you do. Do you think it possible that Neville Sinclair could have done it? If so, how shall I proceed? I am eager to know your thoughts."

Mrs. Hillman had listened to all this in silence, while worrying her hands in her lap. After some hesitation, she gave her reply.

"Miss Taylor, I have long dreamt of finding justice for my darling Caroline. If the true perpetrator of that crime could be discovered and apprehended, it would right a terrible wrong. But I must say, you are barking up the wrong tree."

"Why do you say so?"

"Because I have known Neville all his life, and his brother as well. Harold was violent even as a child. But Neville was different. Neville was the quiet, intelligent, studious one. He could be hardheaded at times, but as a boy, he used to rescue birds who'd fallen out of their nests. He grew up to be a worthy man who takes his duties seriously—a pillar of the community." Mrs. Hillman sat forward in her chair. "I may not share other people's admiration of the man today—indeed, I despise Neville Sinclair for rushing to judgement about Caroline and assuring her conviction. He may very well have hated his brother. But that doesn't make him a murderer."

Athena wasn't ready to give up. "And yet, it's *possible*, isn't it? People can often surprise us. They appear to be one thing when deep down, they are really another."

Mrs. Hillman shook her head. "Not Neville Sinclair. The man is as honest as the day is long. I don't believe him capable of killing anyone."

"I see."

"Miss Taylor, I am touched that you have been thinking about this. But if your hope, as you say, is to reopen that murder case—your effort is a vain one." Mrs. Hillman tapped her cane agitatedly on the floor. "Neville Sinclair is now the magistrate for York. His word is law. Even if you were to find new information, I doubt he would change his opinion on a ruling that was made nine years ago, based on evidence that *he* presented in court."

"I see what you mean. It would make him look foolish."

"Exactly." Tears pooled in Mrs. Hillman's pale eyes. "I fear that any attempt to redeem Caroline is a lost cause. Oh! Just thinking about it gives me such a terrible headache. Forgive me, I must go."

Athena escorted Mrs. Hillman from the house and watched, in low spirits, as she took her leave. Perhaps Athena was, as Mrs. Hillman had said, "barking up the wrong tree." But if Neville Sinclair was not their perpetrator, then … who could it be?

"DID YOU *REALLY* like my song?" Miss Weaver asked Mr. Chapman at dinner.

"You have a charming voice," Mr. Chapman assured the young lady as he carved into his slice of mutton. "And your song was delightful."

"Thank you!" Miss Weaver gazed at him rapturously across the table.

Athena noticed the other girls picking at their food with tight lips. It reminded her of the sisterly rivalry that had existed when she had been a girl, over an amiable art tutor who had seemed to show a preference for Selena. "This is not a contest, girls," she reminded them. "You all have very sweet voices."

As the girls chattered on, Athena's mind returned to the conversation she'd just had with Mrs. Hillman. Neville Sinclair had seemed like the perfect solution to the mystery, but Mrs. Hillman's arguments had been very convincing.

She'd only had the briefest moment to quietly inform Selena of what she'd learned before they had trooped in to dinner with their students. Selena, as if attuned to Athena's disappointment, had squeezed her hand and whispered in her ear, *"Don't fret. That was just our first suspect. There must be other homicidal fish in the sea."*

Athena's lips twitched at the memory. Her sister did have a way of cheering her up in difficult times. Their quest might be more difficult because Neville Sinclair was now the magistrate in charge. And Athena knew that she could not speak to Mrs. Hillman about the matter again—it agitated the older woman too much. But that didn't mean this was over.

Athena turned her attention back to the discussion at the table.

"I'm going to be an opera singer when I grow up," announced Miss Gilbert.

"Oh?" Mr. Chapman chuckled. "I shouldn't think your mother and father would approve of that."

"Why not?"

"Opera singers have terrible reputations," he answered with a grin. "As do actresses. They are known to receive a great many gentlemen callers."

Cecelia Gilbert covered her mouth with one hand. "Oh! Then Mama and Papa would *definitely* disapprove."

"I don't care what they think," Miss Gilbert insisted with a toss of her head. "I'll do what I want."

"I want to be a *writer* when I grow up," Miss Russell declared as she buttered a slice of bread.

Athena smiled at that. "What will you write?"

"Novels. They will all be Gothic tales and feature a heroine in grave danger."

"Oooh," enthused Miss Weaver through a mouthful of potatoes. "I love those kinds of stories."

"What's your favorite novel, Mr. Chapman?" Miss Russell asked.

"Me? I don't read books. I prefer notes on the page—*musical* notes, that is."

"Music and reading are both enjoyable occupations," Athena pointed out.

"You are missing out, though, if you don't read novels, sir," Selena insisted.

Miss Russell's fork tumbled to the floor. As she crouched down beneath the table to retrieve it, she exclaimed, "What is this, Miss Taylor?"

"What is what, Miss Russell?"

"There are initials carved on the underside of the table. It says *EA*."

"Who is *EA*?" Miss Jones wondered.

"It's a mystery," Selena answered in a stealthy tone, which made everyone laugh.

Athena seemed to recall someone mentioning a person with those initials but couldn't remember who or when. "This table belonged to the former owners of Thorndale Manor. Those initials might have been carved a century ago, or more."

The rest of the meal was devoted to a discussion about the merits of reading versus music. Although reading took the lead for quite a while, by the time the pudding had been consumed, the joys of singing, playing the pianoforte, listening to a concert, and dancing seemed to have won the argument.

After dinner, as everyone funneled out of the dining room, Mr. Chapman asked Athena, "May I borrow you for a moment, Miss Taylor? I'd like to go over my planned curriculum for the coming weeks."

"Certainly." Selena took the girls to the drawing room for their study hour, and Athena accompanied Mr. Chapman to the music room. They spent half an hour selecting vocal and pianoforte pieces from among his own collection.

"All fine choices," Mr. Chapman said. "You have good taste."

"You are an excellent guide."

"I'd like your opinion about one more piece if I may. It's a duet."

He showed her the sheet music. Athena recognized the song. "Do you think it's too difficult for the girls?"

"Shall we find out? Will you play it with me?"

Athena hesitated. It had been many years since she had played this piece, and Mr. Chapman was a far superior musician. "I can try," she said finally.

He placed the sheet music on the pianoforte's music stand. "You can play the melody, as it's a bit easier, and I'll play the secondo. Sound good?"

She nodded and sat down beside him on the bench. They began. At first, Athena's fingers seemed to stumble over the keys, and it was all she could do to keep up with Mr. Chapman.

"You're doing fine," he said kindly, darting her a smile.

About halfway through the piece, Athena started to feel more confident, and as they breezed through the final stanzas, she almost felt as if her fingers were flying. They finished with a flourish, and Athena exhaled with relief and delight. She had almost forgotten the freedom and sense of joy that came with playing the pianoforte.

"Well done!" he exclaimed. "You'll be taking my place as music master yet."

Athena laughed. "That will never happen. And the girls would never forgive me if you were to leave. I think they are all infatuated with you."

He leaned closer, his lips curving upwards as he gave her an admiring glance. "I should rather that their *teacher* were infatuated with me," he said softly.

Athena felt a ripple of sparks fly through the air between them and suddenly became aware of how close they were sitting to each other on the piano bench. She quickly stood, her cheeks growing hot. "Mr. Chapman. Please don't say such things. You work for me."

"I know. But a man can dream, can't he?"

Despite herself, Athena was flattered by the keen and yet respectful look in his eyes. She silently censured herself. This flirting was inappropriate. "Sir," she began, but he cut her off.

"I am only teasing." He rose from the bench and returned the music sheets to his leather case. "Or only half-teasing," he admitted. "I deem myself grateful for your friendship, Miss Taylor."

"As I do yours," Athena returned.

Mr. Chapman gestured to the window. Although it was still light out, the moon was visible in the early-evening sky. "Would you do me the honor of joining me for a turn about the garden, Miss Taylor? It's a lovely evening."

"I should return to the drawing room for social hour."

"The girls are being looked after by Miss Selena, are they not? You can't work every minute of the day. You deserve a little time for yourself."

Athena hesitated. She hadn't had a chance to walk in the garden all day, and the idea was appealing. "Very well, Mr. Chapman. But for only half an hour and no more."

CHAPTER ELEVEN

"TELL ME ABOUT yourself, Miss Taylor," Mr. Chapman said as they made their way through the rear courtyard towards the gardens in the fading light of day.

"I should rather hear about you." Athena recalled what little she had learned about his infamous introduction to the world. Worried that it might be too sensitive a subject, she said, "As I understand it, Mrs. Hillman was your guardian?"

"Yes. She took over my care after my mother passed away. But we are not blood relations because … my mother wasn't my natural mother." He glanced at her. "But perhaps you are acquainted with the story?"

"Mrs. Hillman did tell me that her sister, Daisy, fell in love with your father—and that he was married at the time?"

"What a scandal, eh?" His eyes were teasing. "But you can't plan with whom you're going to fall in love, can you? After my parents both died of typhoid, I was sent to an orphanage. Daisy—although unmarried and with no obligation to me whatsoever—passed herself off as a distant relation and got permission to take me in. She moved to Lancashire, where she was unknown, and brought me up."

Athena was touched by his honesty and courage in admitting this. "How difficult that must have been for her, to raise a child alone."

"It was. Mrs. Hillman kindly sent money on a regular basis to help us out, but my mother—I always thought of Daisy as my mother—was proud and determined. She worked as a laundress to support us until I was thirteen. She sadly died about the same time that Mr. Hillman passed away. I became Mrs. Hillman's ward, and she financed my education. For that, I shall always be grateful."

"Did you enjoy school?"

He made a face. "Not at all."

"Why not?"

"Boys' schools in England are a place of torture, Miss Taylor."

"I have heard such stories." Athena thought of Neville Sinclair's tale of his brother's bullying—and *that* had been at home. "I wish something could be done to protect young boys."

"Our institutions are ingrained in the tradition, I'm afraid." He quirked a dark-brown eyebrow at her. "I trust nothing so untoward would ever go on at a girls' school?"

"Perish the thought!"

"What made you decide to open a school like this?"

"My sisters and I have been dreaming of such a venture ever since we were girls." She told him about Diana, who now lived in Cornwall and was married to a Royal Navy captain and baronet. "It is only through his generosity that we are in possession of Thorndale Manor."

"How wonderful for you."

"We are very fortunate. Although …" Athena broke off.

"'Although'?" he prodded.

"Oh, let's not go there. I don't wish to share my troubles with you, Mr. Chapman."

"Why not? We are friends now, aren't we? And friends share their troubles, don't they?"

Athena let out a light laugh. "I suppose they do."

"Well, then?"

She gave in to his questioning look. "This school is an expensive place to run. And, as you have seen, our enrollment is very small. It has been difficult to get students."

"Why is that? I've been wondering."

They had reached the hedgerows now, and Athena idly plucked a tiny stem from a bush and inhaled its spicy fragrance.

"The ghost of Caroline Vernon casts a long shadow over Thorndale Manor."

He took that in and nodded. "Ah. Yes. I know the story."

Athena frowned. "Many people, it turns out, don't want their children to live in a building that—reputedly—used to house a convicted murderess."

"What nonsense." He shook his head. "That happened so long ago."

"But it's a problem, and one we didn't realize we'd be facing until we began advertising for students. We can easily accommodate more than a dozen pupils, Mr. Chapman, yet as you know, we have only five."

"There must be something you can do about it."

A breeze began to stir, and a chill invaded the air. Athena noticed that dark clouds were gathering in the sky. "Perhaps there is. I have a plan."

"What kind of plan?"

"I'd rather not say. It may be impossible."

"Even so, I should love to hear it."

Athena hesitated, and then thought, *Why not?* Mrs. Hillman and Mr. Vernon had both expressed opposition to her quest. Maybe Mr. Chapman would have a more open mind. "Promise you won't laugh?"

"I swear to keep a straight face, no matter what you say."

"I don't believe Caroline Vernon committed the murder of which she was accused."

"You don't?"

"No. I hope to prove her innocence and in so doing, restore the reputation of Thorndale Manor."

His eyes widened, and then he smiled. "Well, bravo! An admirable goal, if perhaps a bit difficult to attain." He paused. "I met Miss Vernon, you know, several times."

"Did you?" Athena envied him, wishing that she could have known Miss Vernon herself. "When?"

"I first met her when I came to visit Mrs. Hillman on a school holiday. Miss Vernon was just a child then, but I saw her several more times over the years. She came to Darkmoor Park frequently. The last time I was here, Miss Vernon was engaged to Harold Sinclair."

"What was Miss Vernon like?"

"She was a sweet little girl, but as a woman, I thought, perhaps a bit … unstable."

"'Unstable'? How?" The wind picked up and Athena wrapped her shawl more tightly around her.

"She was always weeping in deep despair over her impending marriage."

"Perhaps she was in despair due to her lack of power over her own life," Athena replied testily. "She was in love with someone else, a sailor, affianced against her will, and locked up at home by her own father."

"'Locked up'? Dear Lord, I'd forgotten that. I'll never forget what happened to Harold Sinclair, though. Poisoned at his own garden party! And Miss Vernon accused and convicted. What a horrific state of affairs. Mrs. Hillman has never gotten over it."

"I know." Athena sighed. "Were you there? At the party?"

"No. I had left Darkmoor Bridge a month or so before that party and only heard about what happened later. I have always just accepted that Miss Vernon was guilty, despite Mrs. Hillman's protestations to the contrary." He paused. "If Miss Vernon was innocent, it won't be easy to prove at this point."

"I realize that. But I'm determined to try."

"Perhaps I can help."

Athena looked at him. This man was so different from Mr. Vernon, who had derided all her ideas and told her to leave it be. "You would help? How?"

"I don't know. Do you have any leads?"

"None. I did have one idea, but Mrs. Hillman immediately

dismissed it." She told him her theory about Neville Sinclair.

"Neville Sinclair?" He rubbed his chin with one hand. "I can see why you might suspect him. He did gain a great deal from his brother's death, and he convicted Miss Vernon very quickly. But it sounds like he had viable evidence to support that conviction."

"Evidence that might have been manufactured."

"Perhaps." He shrugged. "But I still agree with Mrs. Hillman's assessment of him."

"Why?"

"I haven't seen Neville Sinclair in years, but I've known him since I was a boy, when I first came to see Mrs. Hillman at Darkmoor Park. I remember hiding with Neville in the woods one afternoon so he could escape his brother's wrath. We talked for hours. He told me that he wanted to become a clergyman when he grew up, to help people and do some good in the world. But his father insisted on something bigger and better for Neville—that he must go into the law. Neville was deeply disappointed. I think he was—and probably still is—a good soul. I can't see him murdering anyone, much less his own brother, no matter how much he hated the man."

Athena nodded as she processed this information. "Thank you for sharing that."

"However," Mr. Chapman put in, "Harold Sinclair was a completely different story. Someone else may have wished to do him in."

"But who?"

Mr. Chapman appeared to be mulling that over. "You said everyone in the neighborhood was at that party?"

"Practically everyone, I'm told, except Mrs. Hillman and Mr. Vernon."

He paused. "There is someone else you might consider."

"Who?"

"The sailor."

Athena blinked in surprise. "Miss Vernon's sailor?"

"Yes. I never met him, but love can lead people to do foolish things."

Athena pondered that. "Interesting idea."

"What was his name again?"

Athena thought back to the story Mrs. Hillman had told her. "I think he was called Edward Ackroyd?"

"That sounds about right."

They were almost back to the house and drops of rain splashed Athena's face. "Oh, no. It's about to storm."

"Let's make a run for it!"

They raced to a back door and entered through the conservatory just in time, for two seconds later, the heavens unleashed a thunderous downpour.

"That was close," Athena observed.

Mr. Chapman glanced at his pocket watch. "Thirty minutes on the dot Miss Taylor, as promised."

"Thank you for getting me back so promptly." Athena laughed. Picking up their conversation, she added, "What were you thinking just now? That Edward Ackroyd may have murdered Harold Sinclair to prevent him from marrying the woman he loved?"

"Perhaps. But it all went wrong. And Miss Vernon ended up being accused of the crime."

"If he loved her, wouldn't he have come forward and admitted the truth?"

"Maybe by the time she was arrested, he was away at sea."

Athena's heart seemed to skip a beat. "Maybe. I wonder where Edward Ackroyd is now?"

"Halfway around the world on a Royal Navy ship, I expect." He bowed. "I have enjoyed our conversation, Miss Taylor. I wish you the best of luck in your pursuit. And do let me know if I can be of any help."

"I will."

After Mr. Chapman had departed, Athena hummed to herself. She had a new suspect to investigate.

Edward Ackroyd.

"You and Mr. Chapman were gone quite a while this evening," Selena observed.

Athena had just called "Lights out" to the girls, and she and Selena had retreated to their study. A hard rain battered the windowpanes and the fire in the hearth did little to combat the chill in the room.

"Not so very long." Athena sat down at her desk. "We just walked and talked. He's a charming man."

Selena looked up from her own desk across the cozy room. "And you're not immune to Mr. Chapman's charms, I think? *Or* those of Mr. Vernon?"

Athena's pulse went pitter-pat. Why was she blushing? "What are you talking about?"

"There's been something different about you, ever since the afternoon we had tea at Darkmoor Park."

"Selena!"

"You said Mr. Vernon wants to be friends. But I got the impression that Mr. Vernon likes you as *more* than just a friend. I suspect you feel the same way."

"Don't be daft!" Athena sputtered.

Selena's lips twitched as she shot Athena a penetrating glance. "I think you also enjoyed that walk and talk with Mr. Chapman."

"Selena, Mr. Chapman works for the school! We are merely friends in a *professional capacity*. It can never be anything more."

"Can't it? There's no law that I know of against a single woman becoming involved with her employee, or of her being attracted to two unattached men at the same time."

"Stop it!" Athena huffed out an exasperated breath. "I am not interested in either of those men. At least not in the way you're implying." She wasn't! Was she? Then why did she suddenly feel so red in the face?

"I know what you've said in the *past*. That you have no wish to hand over your personal freedoms and the control of this property to a man, in exchange for a ring on your finger. But do you still feel that way?"

"Absolutely," Athena insisted.

Selena threw up her hands. "Fine. Perhaps I'm reading something into this that isn't there."

"You are." Athena busied herself arranging the pile of papers on her desktop. "Let's talk of something else. I'm dying to tell you what Mr. Chapman and I spoke about. I assure you there's nothing remotely romantic about it."

"Go on, then."

Athena launched into a detailed account of her conversation with Mr. Chapman. Selena listened to every word with interest.

When Athena had finished, Selena tapped a pen on her desk pensively. "Hmm. That's two people who have ruled out Neville Sinclair. I suppose we should listen."

"Agreed. Perhaps you were right—he does seem an unlikely candidate, since he openly admitted to hating his brother."

"What do we know about Edward Ackroyd?"

"Only that he was a poor sailor in the Royal Navy, the son of a coal miner, and Miss Vernon's father wouldn't allow the marriage."

"We need to learn more. I wonder what ship he's serving on?"

"I could ask Mrs. Lloyd," Athena suggested.

"Excellent."

They went to bed. An hour ticked by. Rain battered the windows. Although she could hear Selena's even breathing across their room, Athena once again found it impossible to sleep. Her mind was going a mile a minute, reviewing all that she had learned the past few days, from the events at the Woodcroft House garden party to Mr. Chapman's intriguing suggestion about Edward Ackroyd.

These musings were suddenly interrupted by a voice in her head, echoing Selena's unexpected charge that evening.

"You're not immune to Mr. Chapman's charms, I suspect? Or those of Mr. Vernon?"

Ridiculous! *Selena couldn't be more wrong,* Athena told herself. Yes, Mr. Vernon had warmed up since their frosty introduction, and he had made a handsome apology for his behavior at the riverbank. And, if she were being honest, she *had* felt a fluttering in her stomach while in his presence last week. Which went so much against her nature and defied her wishes for herself. But all that had been overridden by his angry reaction, when she had shared her suspicions about the deaths of Harold Sinclair and Sally Osborn.

As for Mr. Chapman, *he* was a charmer. He had not only admired Athena's quest but had offered his help. But even though, earlier this evening, she had felt sparks fly between them, that—she told herself—was simply because they'd been sitting too close together on the piano bench. She had no wish to pursue a relationship with him or with any man. Did she? No!

Why on Earth was she even thinking about this? Why did she even care?

The clock in the hall struck midnight. Fed up with this unwelcome introspection, Athena threw on her slippers and white, silk dressing gown, lit a candle, and slipped from the room to clear her mind.

The storm still howled in the eaves and smacked against the windowpanes. Athena shivered as she strolled the second-floor hallway to its farthest end and then strode back. It occurred to her that the house was eerily silent. Normally, while on nighttime patrol, she heard an occasional cough from one of the girls, or intermittent snoring. But tonight, she heard nothing. *Why?*

Suspicious, Athena opened the door of the room occupied by the Gilbert sisters and peeked in. The chamber was dark as pitch, but the light from her candle confirmed her fears. Their beds were empty.

Athena's shoulders tensed. She checked the rooms where Miss Russell, Miss Jones, and Miss Weaver slept—but there was no sleeping going on at present. All five girls were missing.

What are they up to?

A childhood memory returned, of a time when Athena and her sisters had wanted an adventure on a similarly dark and stormy night, so they had met in a place where they'd known their father would never look for them.

The attic.

Instinct told Athena that it was as likely a place as any for five wayward pupils to congregate.

She and Selena had only visited the attic at Thorndale Manor a few times, soon after moving in. With determined steps, she took the fastest route there, heading up the narrow servants' stairwell to the ancient, wooden door that opened to the topmost floor beneath the roof.

Athena paused just inside the doorway, adjusting to the blackness and the dank, musty smell. Although the attic was an immense space that ran the entire length and breadth of the building, it felt cramped due to its steeply sloped ceilings, and the vast number of *things* stored there.

Mr. Vernon had claimed to not want anything up here and had not bothered to clear it out. Athena and Selena had, apparently, inherited centuries of that family's old possessions, none of which had seemed useful for the school. The idea of cleaning it all up had been so daunting that they had put it off for a future day.

Was anyone up here?

With her candle raised, Athena looked about and listened. But the drumbeat of the rain on the roof drowned out the possibility of catching any clandestine conversations, and the darkness and clutter made it impossible to see more than a few yards ahead.

A sudden wail rent the air. *What was that?* A shiver ran down Athena's spine as she recalled the local superstition about Thorndale Manor. *Could that have been a ghost?* The wail occurred again, and she realized, with a dash of embarrassment, that it was only the wind moaning in the eaves.

Don't fall prey to foolish nonsense, Athena reprimanded herself as she cautiously made her way forward. Her candle flame cast a pale glow on the old, grooved, wooden floor, several brick chimney stacks, mountains of boxes and trunks, and discarded, ancient furniture that was all coated in a thick layer of dust. At length, she heard low voices. Muted laughter. A girlish warning: "Shh!"

Aha. I was right.

Athena rounded a rack of old clothing and found the errant quintet seated cross-legged in a circle on the floor near a small, gabled window, their candlesticks on the floor between them. At Athena's approach, all five girls gasped and let out piercing screams.

"It's her ghost!" shrieked Miss Gilbert.

"She's come to kill us!" cried Miss Jones.

"Go away, horrible specter!" exclaimed Miss Russell.

Miss Weaver and Miss Cecelia just gawked at Athena in petrified silence.

"Girls," announced Athena calmly, "it's Miss Taylor."

"Oh! You frightened us to death, Miss Taylor!" Miss Gilbert confessed.

"We thought you were the ghost of Caroline Vernon!" Miss Russell heaved a relieved sigh.

"There are no such things as ghosts. What are you doing up here at this hour?" Athena demanded.

The girls, seeming to recover from their shock, blushed and lowered their gazes.

"We're telling ghost stories," Miss Russell admitted.

"Terribly *frightening* ones," Miss Weaver remarked.

"It was Lucy's idea!" proclaimed Miss Cecilia.

"She told one about a headless Caroline Vernon!" cried Miss Gilbert.

"She marched through the dining room, holding her own head on a platter!" exclaimed Miss Jones.

The girls all shrieked again and then broke into nervous giggles.

"And you felt the need to tell these stories *in the attic?*" Athena did her best to sound authoritative and disapproving, even though she hadn't forgotten her own similar youthful antics and was close to laughing herself. *"In the middle of the night?"*

"An attic is the best place to tell ghost stories," Miss Russell explained. "We couldn't very well do so in our rooms, could we? You would have heard us and said, *'Lights out!'"*

"Yes I would have. This is unacceptable behavior, girls."

"It was all just for fun, Miss Taylor," Miss Weaver insisted.

"It would cease to be fun if one of you were injured. I have not inspected the attic. It may not be safe. Now get your candles and stand up." Once they had done so, Athena continued. "You have a bedtime for a reason. You must keep to your rooms as instructed. Promise me you will never venture up here again or meet clandestinely anywhere else. Do I have your word?"

"Yes, Miss Taylor," the girls chorused.

"You won't punish us, will you?" Miss Cecilia pleaded.

"I'll think about it and let you know in the morning. Now let's go. I want you all downstairs and in bed at once."

As the girls filed past her, Athena spied a wet patch on the rough, wooden floor nearby, a few feet in from the exterior wall. Had the girls spilled something? Athena directed her candle to investigate the area. She discovered beads of water clinging to the underside of the low, sloping roof.

Oh, bother, Athena thought. The roof was leaking. She wondered if this had anything to do with the branch that had fallen in the previous storm. As she watched, a drop of water plinked down onto the wet patch below and disappeared—probably, she realized, dripping down onto the ceiling of one of the servants' rooms below.

To whom could she apply for advice about a leaking roof? Athena only knew one person in the building trade. Mr. Vernon.

CHAPTER TWELVE

"MR. VERNON IS indeed the best man for the job, miss," Mrs. Lloyd confirmed, when Athena told her about the leaking roof the next morning.

As Athena had feared, Tabitha had been obliged to place a bucket in her bedroom to collect the water dripping from the ceiling the previous night.

"All the years that he was growing up, Mr. Vernon liked building and fixing things," Mrs. Lloyd explained with a proud smile. "Every summer when he was home from school, he helped the construction crews in the area, just for the love of the work and to learn. It was his idea to add on our conservatory. He couldn't have been more than seventeen years old. He wanted to bring the outdoors inside, he said. He drew up the plans himself, convinced his father, and worked right alongside the builders as they put the thing up."

The mental image of a young Ian Vernon, shirtless and hammering away on a building site, caused an annoying quiver to dart through Athena's stomach. She blinked hard to make it go away. "But Mr. Vernon is an architect now."

"Yes, but he still does construction work from time to time. There are other men in the trade in town, but they're nowhere near as skilled. Mr. Vernon grew up here and knows Thorndale Manor better than anyone. I'd ask him straightaway and wouldn't think twice about it."

Athena didn't relish the idea of approaching Mr. Vernon. Their last conversation had ended so badly—and this wasn't his house anymore. Would he even be interested in helping her? Athena doubted it. But it sounded like he was her best option.

She decided she would stop by his cottage the following day. She was about to ask Mrs. Lloyd about the other topic on her mind, Edward Ackroyd, when the housekeeper was called away to see to a problem with the laundry.

During the exercise period in the rear courtyard, Miss Russell tugged on Athena's cloak.

"Please don't blame the other girls about last night." Miss Russell held a leatherbound notebook close to her chest. "The ghost story meeting was my idea. If you must punish someone, punish me."

Athena was touched by the girl's willingness to accept full responsibility, come what may. "I shall take that into consideration. But tell me: why are you so interested in ghosts?"

"Because I've seen one."

"Oh?" Athena struggled to keep her face impassive as they fell in step together. "When?"

"When I was a little girl."

"How little?"

"I don't know. Three or four. It was a hot summer night and Mama had left the window open. I was awakened by a sound outside. I looked out and that's when I saw the ghost."

"What did the ghost look like?"

"She was all white and glowing. I said, 'Mama! Come look!', but when I turned back, the ghost was gone."

"What did your mother say when you told her?"

"She said I had dreamt it."

"You are a very smart girl, Miss Russell," Athena said gently. "You must know there are no such things as ghosts."

Miss Russell pursed her lips and stamped her foot. "But *I saw her.*"

Athena sensed that any further attempts to persuade the girl on the matter would be futile. Changing the subject, she asked, "Have you been writing in your notebook?" Athena had approved the notebook that the girl had brought from home but didn't know what she used it for.

"I write in it every day. It's where I record my most important thoughts. And all the stories that the servants and people in the neighborhood have been telling me about ghosts."

"When have you had time to speak to people in the neighborhood about ghosts?" Athena was beginning to feel concerned.

"On Sunday, after church."

"Miss Russell," Athena scolded. "You have no business discussing such things with the villagers."

"Why not?" Miss Russell's blue eyes sparkled, and her voice grew increasingly animated as she spoke. "Last Sunday, Miss Quince, the apothecary's daughter, told me that she once saw a woman in white *float through her back garden* just after midnight. And Tabitha said she once heard something in the attic above her room." The girl paused and let out a long, disappointed sigh. "But Mrs. Lloyd checked, and it was just a pigeon that had gotten in through an open window."

Athena thought back to her first night at Thorndale Manor, when she and Selena had sensed a mysterious presence. She shook her head. "Don't you see? There is no foundation for either of those stories. They were figments of the women's imaginations, fed by local legends."

"Tabitha might have imagined it, but the ghosts that Miss Quince and I saw were *real*," the girl insisted.

It was time to change the subject again. "What else have you been writing about in your journal?"

"Well." Miss Russell hesitated again. "If you must know, I have been writing about Caroline Vernon."

Athena's pulsed quickened. "Why?"

"The other day, during our science lesson, you said something that got me thinking."

"What did I say?"

"You said Miss Vernon *may not have committed murder at all.*"

"Oh. I shouldn't have—" Athena began, but the girl hurried on.

"You forbade me from investigating Sally Osborn's drowning, but you didn't say anything about Miss Vernon. She's another woman from this house *who was involved in murder.* You can't object to me looking into *her;* it happened so long ago, before I was even born."

"I do object, Miss Russell. I—"

"I asked Mrs. Lloyd what happened back then," Miss Russell continued, as if Athena had not spoken. "But she refused to talk about it. Miss Quince got upset when I brought up the subject. Which is interesting, don't you think? I wonder if she is hiding something?"

"Miss Russell!" Athena exclaimed. "This line of thinking is not healthy for you. This is a school, not a place for flights of fancy. You must devote your time and energy to studying and learning."

The girl's shoulders sagged. "Mama and Papa said the same thing. They say I am too smart for my own good. But I finish all my assignments early. What else am I supposed to do?"

Athena frowned. Although Miss Russell was the youngest pupil in the school, she had indeed made a habit of turning in her work ahead of schedule, and it was almost always brilliantly done. Athena needed to find some productive way for this girl to spend her time. An idea suddenly occurred to her. "Miss Russell. You said you want to be a novelist some day?"

"Yes?"

"Why not begin now?"

"Now?"

"This will be your own personal assignment. I want you to take all the extra time on your hands and write a book."

"*A book?*" Miss Russell's mouth fell open. "I don't know how to write a book."

"I suppose you'll have to figure it out, then."

"How would I even start?"

"I imagine you'll want to plot out a story."

"About what?"

"Anything you like."

"Can it be about a ghost?"

Athena was about to protest but then thought better of it. Let the girl write about whatever interested her. "If you wish."

"Come in, girls!" Selena was clapping her hands. "It's time for period two."

As the other pupils crossed the courtyard towards the house, Miss Russell looked up at Athena with worry in her blue eyes. "Miss Taylor?"

"Yes?"

"You haven't said what my punishment will be. For our meeting in the attic."

Athena smiled down at her. "I'm not going to punish you for that, Miss Russell."

"You're not?" Miss Russell exclaimed with apparent relief.

"It was a girlish caper. You all had your fun and have promised never to do it again. Am I right?"

"Yes! Thank you, Miss Taylor." Miss Russell paused. "One more thing. What if I can't do it? Write a book, I mean?"

"I have faith in you, Miss Russell," Athena assured her. "It all starts with the first page."

THE SKIES WERE grey and overcast as Athena crossed the lawns and fields to Thorndale Cottage, reputedly the former bailiff's house, where Mr. Vernon lived. She had never been there.

For some reason, she had felt compelled that morning to don one of her nicest day gowns, a two-piece ensemble in forest-green linen that featured a dome-shaped skirt, a white lace collar, and tight-fitting sleeves with embroidered cuffs. She had taken extra care with her hair as well, pinning it up neatly above her nape and making sure that not a hair was out of place. Why she had gone to such effort, she couldn't say. This was just a short visit to Mr. Vernon, to seek advice about the leak in her attic, nothing more.

A new, wooden fence separated her property from his. After she climbed over the stile, it was a short walk across a narrow garden to the cottage. The one-story building, fashioned of grey stone, was charming and looked very well-maintained. It had a sloped roof, several good-sized sash windows, and a green front door beneath an arched trellis of old climbing roses that still featured a few fading blooms.

Studying the cottage, Athena was filled with a sense of nostalgia, for it reminded her of the cozy, old country house where she had grown up. And yet she couldn't help wondering if the former owner of Thorndale Manor considered this to be a step down in life.

She knocked. After a moment, the front door was opened by a grey-haired woman wearing a servant's cap and an apron that was dusted with flour. "May I help you?"

"I'm Athena Taylor. I sent a note yesterday, to arrange a meeting with Mr. Vernon?"

"You're the one what lives at the manor house now? Runs that school?"

"Yes, I am."

"Wait here." The woman disappeared, leaving the door ajar. Athena heard her say, "Mr. Vernon, Miss Taylor is here to see you."

"Please show her in, Mrs. Elliston," was Mr. Vernon's muted reply.

The woman ushered Athena inside and shut the door. The house was filled with the aroma of simmering meat and potatoes mingled with the fragrance of baking bread. The entryway and corridor were paved in stone and the walls looked like they had been recently whitewashed.

Mr. Vernon appeared from a room just off the hall. "Miss Taylor. I received your note. To what do I owe the pleasure of this call?"

He wasn't smiling, but Athena detected no rancor in his tone, which came as a relief. She would have to be careful, though, to avoid the topic that had so displeased him the last time they had spoken. "Sir, I would be grateful for a moment of your time. I have a problem at the manor house. Mrs. Lloyd insists that you're the only one who can help me."

He nodded politely. "Well, then, I had best try if I can."

The servant took Athena's cloak, hung it on a clothes tree by the door, and vanished to the back of the house. Mr. Vernon gestured for Athena to precede him to the room he had just vacated.

Athena paused to take in the chamber. A fire blazed in the stone hearth, adding warmth and light to the cozy room, which apparently served as both the dining room and library. Built-in bookshelves lined almost every wall and they were absolutely crammed with books, some of which looked to be two or three books deep. Piles of books covered the end tables, and numerous boxes marked *BOOKS* were stacked in the corners.

"Oh!" Athena cried, delighted. "You kept them."

"I beg your pardon?"

"I presumed you'd sold all the books from the library at Thorndale Manor. But … correct me if I'm wrong … I'm guessing these are some of them?"

"Yes. The rest are in boxes in my attic."

"It does my heart good to know that you kept them."

He shrugged. "I couldn't bear to part with them."

This evidence of Mr. Vernon's love of books raised him several more notches in Athena's estimation. For how could you dislike a man who appreciated a good library?

The furniture in the room, in contrast to the rustic exterior of the house, was elegant and looked expensive. Athena guessed, with a pang, that these were the few pieces Mr. Vernon had been able to keep for himself. On a small, mahogany dining table, she noticed unrolled architectural drawings and she stopped to study them. They included a floor plan, an elevation, and a sketch of a house and surrounding vegetation. All were skillfully done, labeled DARKMOOR PARK DOWER HOUSE, and signed *Ian Vernon*.

"What beautiful work."

"Thank you."

"Where is the dower house at Darkmoor Park? I didn't notice it on either of my visits."

"It's about a half mile from the main house. The man who built it centuries ago apparently wanted to put as much space as possible between himself and his widowed mother."

Athena smiled. "I hope he built her a pleasant house?"

"It was fine in its day. It will be even finer, I hope, when I'm finished improving it."

A watercolor portrait that hung above the mantel now caught Athena's attention—and drew her like a beacon. It was, unmistakably, Caroline Vernon, perhaps painted a year or two before the one in Mrs. Hillman's drawing room. In this bust view, Miss Vernon was smiling radiantly with a teasing look in her blue eyes. To Athena's surprise, the painting had the same signature as the architectural drawings.

"That's your sister, isn't it?" The question was out before Athena could stop it. *Fool! Why did you mention her? Will it upset Mr. Vernon?*

But he only nodded, and said, "Yes."

"It's lovely." Athena was filled once more with a longing to meet the young woman in the portrait. *If only that were possible. How tragic that it is not.* "You're a talented artist."

"Thank you," he said again. "It's not a perfect likeness—I'm not a portraitist, and I don't often work in oils. But it pleased me to paint it, and it comforts me to see her there." He fell briefly silent, as if shaking off a memory, and then he gestured to two wingback chairs upholstered in blue satin that faced each other before the fireplace. "Please, take a seat."

As Athena sat down in the chair across from him, Mr. Vernon leaned forward with clasped hands and went on. "Now about

Thorndale Manor. What seems to be the trouble?"

Without preamble, Athena replied, "The roof is leaking."

"Where?"

Athena described the location. "I discovered a wet patch on the floor the night before last, during that rainstorm. Water was dripping down from the ceiling."

"I see." His eyes narrowed. "What were you doing in the attic at night during a storm?"

Athena smiled. "Looking for my missing students. They were holding a secret meeting."

"Were they telling ghost stories?"

"How did you guess?"

"My friends and I loved to tell ghost stories when we were at school. Our dormitory had a fantastic attic."

"Were you never caught?"

"Of course we were. Many times." He fixed his gaze on her and lowered his voice to a dramatic pitch. "And we were summarily punished. Bed without supper, rapped knuckles, the occasional beating with a cane."

A shudder swept through Athena's body. "Oh, no!"

He shrugged and gave his first hint of a smile. "We didn't care. It was the danger of discovery that made it such a thrill and worth the risk." He paused. "How did you punish your girls?"

"I didn't. Unless you call asking their leader to write a novel a punishment."

"'Write a novel'? Some people might find that very difficult, indeed. How old is this girl?"

"Eight."

"Eight years old!" His eyes widened and he gave a short gasp. "Do you expect her to make good on the assignment?"

"I do. She has a prodigious mind—and too much time on her hands. I promise you, something wonderful will come of this."

"I hope you're right." His former reserve was gone now, replaced by a warm grin. "I think I like your teaching methods. Meanwhile, back to the matter at hand—your roof?"

"Yes. I wonder if the leak has anything to do with a branch that fell the other night, during an earlier storm?" She told him about the incident.

"It could be. You said Mrs. Lloyd recommended me? Did she try anyone else?"

"No," Athena admitted. "I was reluctant to come. I know you're an architect and you're busy with a job for Mrs. Hillman, and who knows how many others. But Mrs. Lloyd said that you also do building work."

"I do, now and then."

"She insisted that you know the house better than anyone and that you're the best man for this job."

"That's kind of her. I will always find time for Thorndale Manor." He stood. "Would you like me to take a look at it now?"

Surprised, Athena rose from her chair. "Now would be wonderful. Thank you."

He grabbed his overcoat, hat, and an umbrella and helped Athena into her cloak. A few minutes later, they were on the Thorndale Manor grounds and strolling back towards the house.

"I don't trust that sky," said he, gazing up at the grey heavens, which were again full of threatening clouds.

"It wasn't nearly so gloomy when I set out."

"If we're lucky, we'll make it back to Thorndale Manor before the rain begins." They weren't that lucky. Two minutes later, the skies opened up. Mr. Vernon held his big, black umbrella over them both. "Take my arm."

Athena complied. Rain poured down as they strode across the field, through the rear gardens, and down the path through the hedgerows. Athena couldn't remember the last time she had been this close to a man. The scent of the damp wool of Mr. Vernon's coat filled her senses, punctuated by the fragrance of his cologne, which seemed to have notes of orange blossom and sage. The feel of his body against hers made her pulse beat double time, as if in cadence with the drumbeat of the rain.

They walked arm in arm and didn't exchange another word.

Athena told herself that it was the roar of the downpour that made it difficult to talk, but in truth, it was because her breath had caught in her throat, making speech impossible. She heard a hitch in Mr. Vernon's own throat and wondered if he felt the same sensations that coursed through her body.

She hadn't bargained on *this*. It had been so much easier when she'd thought Mr. Vernon hated her and she had found him irritating in return. Could it really be just over a week ago that they had exchanged a handshake and had agreed to be friends? And now her heart was racing at his nearness and the fragrance of his cologne.

She swallowed hard and sternly willed the sensations to go away.

As they approached the rear of the house, the deluge intensified. They began to run. By the time the pair had reached the glassed-in conservatory and hastened inside to catch their collective breath, the bottom half of Athena's cloak was sopping wet and streaked with mud. They hung their wet, outer garments on a coat rack. Athena struggled to quiet the thumping of her heart and dared a glance at Mr. Vernon. She caught him looking at her with a strange heat in his eyes. He quickly averted his gaze and the bloom in his cheeks seemed to deepen.

Clearing his throat, Mr. Vernon closed his wet umbrella and propped it against a potted tree fern. "Nice day for a stroll," he quipped.

She laughed, and he joined in. She felt the tension between them easing. "Forgive me for bringing you here in such dreadful weather."

"It was my idea to come today. And what better time to investigate a roof leak?"

Athena patted her hair, glad to see that it had not escaped its pins. "Mrs. Lloyd told me that you designed and helped to build this conservatory?"

He nodded. "A youthful project. I'm fortunate that my father approved it."

"It's my favorite room in the house. My sister and I often come out here to read or do paperwork, and we sometimes hold drawing and sketching classes here—the light is very good."

A relaxed smile crossed his face. "Thank you for telling me that. I'm glad the conservatory is being used and enjoyed. This was the first thing I designed that was actually built and I was proud of the way it turned out."

"You should be," she said.

The pleased look on his face made Athena feel all lit up inside. To her relief, her pulse had begun to resume its natural pace.

"Shall we check out that roof?" he asked.

Athena grabbed two lanterns, and they lit the candles inside. When they reached the attic, a dim light filtered in through the small, rain-battered windows, but it did little to illuminate the space. Mr. Vernon paused just inside the doorway and Athena nearly bumped into him. Her heart skittered again as she ground to a halt.

His expression changed, almost as if he were reluctant to enter. "This attic is old and not particularly safe." His voice seemed to have an odd note to it. "The floor is not sound in places."

"I didn't encounter any problems when I was up here," Athena noted.

"You were fortunate. So were your pupils. I wouldn't advise coming up here again on your own. Allow me to lead the way."

Mr. Vernon cautiously advanced through the long, cluttered space until Athena pointed out the problem area. He spent a few minutes studying it, paying close attention to the section of sloping roof where water was intermittently seeping in.

She couldn't decipher his mood. His former warmth and jolly attitude were gone, replaced by taut features and a distracted air. Was he was preoccupied by the same thoughts that still resounded in her own brain—the recollection of the interval they had shared beneath the umbrella? She hoped not. Their friendship was brand new. She didn't want to complicate it with anything messy and romantic that could never lead anywhere.

"Did you see water anywhere else?" Mr. Vernon asked.

Ah, Athena realized, embarrassed by her mental ramblings. *He's distracted because he's concentrating on the problem at hand, and nothing more.* "I didn't look beyond this spot."

"Stay where you are. I'll check farther on." He disappeared for a few minutes and then returned. "As far as I can see, this is the only place that's leaking."

"Thank goodness."

"I think you're right about the tree branch. This roof is made of Westmoreland green slate. I suspect that when that branch fell, it broke a slate. It could be cracked or might have even fallen off, causing water to seep in through the gap."

"Can you fix it?"

"I can. You're lucky that you caught this so early. There hasn't been a chance for wood rot to set in, so none of the timbers need to be replaced. I'll have to wait for a dry day to climb up on the roof and check for certain, but if I'm right, I know a merchant who has the slate we need. I'll find another man or two to assist with the repair. I should be able to get to this in about a week."

"Thank you so much. What do you think it will cost?"

He quoted a number that sounded very modest. "That should cover the materials and any men I hire. I won't charge for my time."

"Oh! Sir." She gasped and shook her head, unable to stop herself from smiling at this show of generosity. "I won't hear of that. I *must* pay you for your time."

"Miss Taylor, I am aware that you're on a tight budget. I don't want to add to that burden. Besides, I would prefer to do the work myself than to allow someone else to get it wrong."

"Well." Athena gave in with a shrug. "This is very kind of you, Mr. Vernon. I can't tell you how much I appreciate it."

They headed downstairs and when they reached the rear entry hall, he asked, "Do you mind if I take a look around? I haven't been back home since … that is, back in the house since April."

It touched her that he wanted to see the house again. It felt like a giant leap forward from his prickly position when they'd first met.

"Please, feel free, Mr. Vernon. Would you care to go on your own? Or shall I accompany you?"

"I'd be pleased to have your company."

His smile was truly beguiling and once again, despite herself, it caused a fluttering in Athena's stomach. *No fluttering,* she reminded herself.

CHAPTER THIRTEEN

"WE CAN GO anywhere except the schoolroom," Athena informed Mr. Vernon. "Selena is teaching a class there at present."

"And the schoolroom is … where?"

"I believe it was formerly called 'the ladies' parlor'?"

"Ah. Understood."

As she and Mr. Vernon wandered through the rooms and halls on the ground floor, his eyes were everywhere, taking it all in with undisguised fondness. He made occasional comments, interested in the small changes that Athena and her sister had made—a new rug here, a different paint color there, a picture that had been moved. Athena sensed that he knew and loved Thorndale Manor on a profound level that she could never hope to match, even if she were to live here her entire life.

They entered the dining room, where he stood with his hands behind his back, as if lost in thought. *Is he thinking of the thousands of meals he enjoyed in this room?* He had no doubt dined at this very table.

"Mr. Vernon," Athena said quietly, "I've never had a chance to thank you for agreeing to leave so much of the furniture when we bought the house."

He replied in a rueful tone, "I couldn't very well have fit it all into the cottage."

"You could have sold the furniture to someone else, I expect, at a greater profit."

He shrugged. "Perhaps. But it has been here so long, I felt that it should stay with the house. And I hoped it might prove useful to you if I left it."

How kind, she thought. "It has been a godsend. My sister and I could never have afforded to furnish Thorndale Manor otherwise. Every single piece has been a boon for the school. Take this dining table, for example—it is not only beautiful, but the ideal size for our purposes. Has it been in your family a long time?"

"I imagine so. It was here when I was a boy."

A thought suddenly occurred to her. "I wonder if you could solve a mystery for me. It involves this very table."

His eyebrows raised. "What mystery?"

"There are some initials carved into its underside." Athena crouched down beside the table. "One of my students found these recently. Do you have any idea to whom they belong?"

He bent down and studied the carving on the table's under-side, then let out a light laugh. "I never noticed this before. This could only have been carved by Edward Ackroyd—the rascal."

Edward Ackroyd. Athena's pulse jumped. Here was her chance to learn more about Ackroyd, to find out if he was capable—and culpable—of murder. "He was the sailor who was in love with your sister?"

"Yes," he said as they rose to their feet. "It wouldn't surprise me if he had carved that as a child."

"A child? How long did he and your sister know each other?"

"Oh, for years. They met at a fête, as I recall, on the grounds of Darkmoor Park. Mrs. Hillman used to hold them annually for all the children in the neighborhood. She liked Edward and sometimes invited him when my sister and I went over to Darkmoor Park. I was six years older, but Edward and Caroline were the same age and got along like a house on fire. Every now and then, he was allowed to visit here at Thorndale Manor. My father didn't approve of their friendship—Ackroyd was the son of a coal miner—but that didn't matter to Caroline. She used to beg and plead and harangue until she wore my father down."

"When did Mr. Ackroyd join the Royal Navy?"

"At age twelve." Mr. Vernon leaned up against the sideboard, his arms crossed against his chest. "Ackroyd's father said it was time for the boy to start working in the coal mine. Ackroyd refused, ran away, and went to sea. He and Caroline wrote to each other for years, and he visited us whenever he came home on leave."

Athena took in this information with great interest. "Mrs. Hillman said they had hoped to marry?"

"Yes. It might have been a difficult life for Carolyn to be married to a man who was away at sea so much of the time, but they were head over heels for each other."

"My sister Diana married a captain in the Royal Navy. They've only been wed about six months, but they are madly in love as well. I know she can't imagine her life without him."

"It was the same for *my* sister. I think she and Ackroyd would have been happy together. If only ..." He drew an invisible design in the carpet with the toe of his boot. "When Caroline turned eighteen, she confessed to me that they had been secretly engaged for four years. My father got wind of her plans and put an end to them."

Athena remembered this part of the story. "He gave her a coming-out ball."

"The likes of which this county had never seen. He invited young men from all the best families in Yorkshire. Caroline received at least half a dozen offers of marriage, all excellent prospects. She turned them all down. Father was furious and affianced her behind her back to the man *he* had wanted from the start."

"Harold Sinclair."

Mr. Vernon nodded. "Sinclair was ten years older than Caroline, and they had nothing in common. Caroline told me she hated him. My father used to arrange small meetings alone between them, completely against propriety, hoping my sister would warm to him, I suppose. But it didn't work. Worse yet, during these unchaperoned intervals, I suspected that he was hurting her—physically, I mean—but she always denied it and I could never prove it. I think she was worried I might retaliate and get injured myself."

Athena recalled Neville Sinclair's description of the older brother who had bullied him. "It's such a sad story."

"The whole thing not only broke my sister's heart, but Ackroyd's as well."

Mr. Vernon had made Edward Ackroyd out to be such an agreeable individual. But who knew to what lengths a man might be driven to protect the woman he loved? "Was Mr. Ackroyd home the summer your sister was due to be married?"

"Yes."

Athena's pulse jumped at this news. "Did he attend the garden party at Woodcroft House where Sinclair was poisoned?"

"I don't know. I was in London at the time."

But Edward Ackroyd might have been there. All the neighborhood was said to have been invited.

"What did Mr. Ackroyd do when Miss Vernon was arrested?"

"He wasn't here. As I understand it, the day after that party, he had to return to his ship. A few days later, Caroline was sent to York prison. After her joke of a trial and the hanging, I wrote to give Ackroyd the news. He was so devasted, he stayed away at sea for years."

It was just as Athena had theorized. Edward Ackroyd could have killed Harold Sinclair and kissed Caroline Vernon goodbye, hoping to marry her the next time he got leave, having no clue that his love would be sentenced and hanged for the crime.

"I am so sorry for your sister and for Mr. Ackroyd. I wish I could have met them."

"Well." Mr. Vernon looked at her. "As it happens, you can meet *him*."

Athena stared at him. "How?"

"Ackroyd is home on leave at present from the Navy."

"Home? Now?" She breathed in sharply. "How do you know?"

"We've kept up a correspondence all these years. He returned about a fortnight ago. He visited a friend for a few days, but I believe he is back home at his parents' house again. If he's at church tomorrow, I'd be happy to introduce you."

Athena couldn't believe her luck. She thanked Mr. Vernon and walked him to the door, where they agreed that he would return to confirm his suspicions about the roof after the weather cleared. No sooner had he gone than Athena heard the school-room door open and the chatter of girls hurrying to the dining room for luncheon. Athena's mind was in a whirl as she made her way to join them.

Edward Ackroyd had not only been in the neighborhood when Harold Sinclair had been killed ... he had also been here two weeks ago, when Sally Osborn had died.

Was it just a coincidence?

Athena didn't believe in coincidences.

AT SERVICES ON Sunday morning, as she sat with Selena and their pupils, Athena stole glances at the congregation, wondering if Edward Ackroyd was there.

The small church was nearly full. Athena caught Mr. Vernon's eye. He nodded and touched his hat. Mrs. Hillman, elegantly attired in a frock of lavender silk, sat in her allocated pew across from the section reserved for the Sinclair family, where Athena spotted Neville Sinclair, his wife, and their two young children. Mr. Quince, the silver-haired apothecary, sat with his unmarried daughter, Margaret, a broad-shouldered blonde who looked to be in her late thirties. Farther back, Athena caught sight of Bridget Osborn and her father.

After the service, while the congregation milled out front and their students played tag on the scrubby lawn, Athena spoke with Selena in the churchyard. "I didn't see anyone new."

"Neither did I."

They had gone over everything Athena had learned about Edward Ackroyd the evening before. "It is so frustrating. I know in my bones that Caroline Vernon did *not* kill Harold Sinclair. Whoever did it got off scot-free, and they may have murdered Sally Osborn as well. I'm not going to rest until I find out the truth."

Selena shot Athena a warning look, just as a ragged cough resounded. Bridget Osborn and her father were standing just a yard or two away. Athena realized her mistake and blushed. Had the Osborns overheard what she'd said? She hoped not. Athena crossed to them, with Selena at her heels.

"Good morning, Miss Osborn, Mr. Osborn." Athena greeted them with a smile.

"How are you?" Selena asked.

"As best as can be expected, for a man with one arm," grumbled Mr. Osborn.

"We miss Sally something fierce." Miss Osborn was racked by a cough.

"Miss Osborn, is there anything we can do for you?" Selena asked softly.

"I don't expect so, Miss Selena."

"She's fine," Mr. Osborn insisted gruffly. "Let's go, Bridget."

They said their goodbyes and the Osborns strode away. Selena gestured silently towards a yew across the churchyard. When she and Athena had moved beneath the tree, Selena said quietly, "You really must be more discreet, Athena, where and when you talk about …you know."

"You're right." Athena also kept her voice low. "I'm sorry. I'm just annoyed that Edward Ackroyd isn't here. I should so like to talk to him."

"Me, too. I can't help thinking, *if* Mr. Ackroyd did the deed, perhaps he stayed away at sea for years not only due to heartbreak, but out of guilt."

"It would also explain why Sally Osborn waited so long to confront him. How could she have done so if he hadn't even been here?"

"Two weeks ago, when Mr. Ackroyd returned, Sally recognized him and either grew a conscience—or a desire to blackmail him."

Athena felt a sudden rush of energy. "She met Mr. Ackroyd at the riverbank, and he killed her."

"We may have figured it out, Athena."

"If only we could find a way to prove it."

Just then, Mr. Vernon strode up. Athena's pulse quickened. He looked so dapper in his charcoal-grey suit and a tie that matched his cornflower-blue eyes. The memory of their race through the rain echoed in her mind. *Stop that*, she reprimanded herself. *You are friends, nothing more.*

"Miss Taylor, you said that you'd like to meet Edward Ackroyd?"

"I would."

"He's here."

Athena inhaled sharply. "Where?"

"He's outside the cemetery gates, visiting Caroline's grave marker."

"Outside the cemetery?" Athena repeated in surprise.

He colored slightly and seemed to be searching for words.

"Oh, yes, I see." It hadn't occurred to Athena before, but convicted murderers weren't allowed to be buried in a churchyard. Their bodies were given to medical science to dissect and study. The very idea made Athena want to weep.

Selena's face was full of understanding and sympathy. "I can't imagine how difficult this must be for you, sir."

Mr. Vernon nodded grimly. "It's not something I like to contemplate. In any case … the vicar kindly allowed me to place a grave marker for Caroline just outside the cemetery wall. There's no body there, of course. But Ackroyd is there now, paying his respects. If you'd like, I could introduce you both?"

"That would be very nice, Mr. Vernon," Athena said.

Just then, Mrs. Hillman trudged up. "Good morning, Miss Taylor, Miss Selena." She gave Selena a particular smile. "I cannot wait to hear the next chapter of *The Wind Pirate*. I'll see you this afternoon?"

Selena smiled in return. "Yes. I look forward to it."

"Ian, I need to leave this instant," Mrs. Hillman told him. "I'm tired and I require a nap after Sunday dinner, before Miss Selena arrives. Would you assist me to my carriage please?"

"Yes, ma'am." He turned back to Athena and Selena. "I'm so sorry. I won't be able to make that introduction today, after all."

"That's quite all right," Athena assured him.

They exchanged goodbyes and Mr. Vernon escorted Mrs. Hillman away.

"I'll round up the girls and bring them home," Selena told Athena. "You should find Mr. Ackroyd and introduce yourself."

"You don't mind?"

"Of course not. Go!" Selena hurried off.

Athena scurried around the church to a grassy space outside the cemetery's wrought-iron fence, where she found a man kneeling before a marble gravestone.

She recalled Mr. Vernon saying that Edward Ackroyd was Caroline's age, which would have now made him twenty-eight or twenty-nine years old, although this man's clean-shaven face was so browned and weather-beaten, he looked a decade older. He was broad-shouldered and wiry, with muscular upper arms that seemed to be straining to burst free from his rough, brown jacket. His hair, the color of dried straw, was cut short and he held a sailor's cap in his hands.

"Mr. Ackroyd?" Athena said quietly.

He glanced up at her approach. He had a strong jaw, a slim nose, and sad, green eyes. "Yes?" He squinted, as if trying to place her.

"Forgive me for disturbing you. I am Miss Athena Taylor."

"Do I know you?"

"You do not. Mr. Ian Vernon said that I would find you here. I'm the headmistress of a girls' school at Thorndale Manor."

"Oh." He frowned, rose, and brushed off the knees of his faded pants. "How do you do, Miss Taylor?" he said politely.

She guessed him to be about five-foot-ten, a few inches taller than her. "I am well. I was hoping to have a word with you. I know that you were the sweetheart of Miss Caroline Vernon, who lived at Thorndale Manor."

His expression grew even grimmer. "I was."

"Mr. Vernon said that you knew her since you were a child."

"I did."

Athena knew it was quite bold of her to be asking this, but she couldn't help herself. She needed to know. "And you loved her?"

His forehead furrowed over eyes that looked haunted. "I loved her more than life. But why are you asking this?"

"Allow me to explain." She noticed a stone bench nearby and motioned to it. "Would you be so good as to sit with me for a moment?"

Mr. Ackroyd hesitated, but then with a small shrug, he accompanied her to the bench, and they sat down.

"First, I wish to express my condolences, Mr. Ackroyd. I know that Miss Vernon perished some nine years ago. I have lost several people who were dear to me and the pain never quite leaves you, does it?"

"No, miss, it does not." He stared down at the cap in his hands.

"Today, I live in the same house where your Miss Vernon lived. I dine at the same table where she dined. I sleep in the same room where she slept. And now she haunts my dreams. I long to know more about her, sir. Will you tell me?"

His sandy brows rose as he looked at her. "What do you wish to know?"

"Anything. Everything."

He sighed. "She was the kindest, smartest, and most gentle young lady I have ever met. She was funny, too. She could make you laugh at the drop of a hat." He smiled as if in memory, and his eyes glowed with affection as he spoke. "She was always reading a book. Got me into reading from a young age. I always bring a trunk full of books with me whenever I go to sea. We used to write to each other and discuss what we were reading."

This scenario touched Athena. He spoke so sincerely, she felt herself drawn into the picture he was describing. *But*, she reminded herself, *this man might be a killer.* "Having such a strong attachment to the young lady, it must have been difficult for you to enlist in the Royal Navy."

"It was. But what choice did I have? It was that or spend the rest of my life buried alive in a coal mine. I need to see the sun every day, Miss Taylor. I need the breeze in my face and the sky above. And I was itching to see the world. Caroline understood. After a few years, I was made an able seaman, but I wanted a better living for my wife. We agreed to wait until I had advanced to the rank of a petty officer or until we had both turned twenty-one, whichever came first, and then we would marry."

"But fate had something else in store."

His face grew hard, and he kicked at a pebble with his scuffed boot. "You know what happened, I expect? That she was betrothed against her will to a man she despised? And as if that weren't bad enough, she was accused of killing him?"

"Yes," Athena said softly. "Harold Sinclair." She waited.

His upper lip curled. "Oh, how I hated that man."

"Why?"

"Because he was going to have her, even though he didn't deserve her!" The words escaped him in a rush. He paused and seemed to be struggling to collect himself. "But it wasn't just that. He wasn't kind. And he didn't respect her. Caroline wrote me all about it. She said Sinclair just wanted a pretty face to run his house and bear his children. He didn't care to hear her ideas or opinions—he said *he* would tell her what to think and how to act."

The scenario was all too familiar. It reminded her of Giles Shaw.

Mr. Ackroyd went on, his nostrils flaring. "Worst of all, he hurt her. Physically, I mean."

So, Mr. Vernon was right. "How?"

"She said her father permitted him to make unchaperoned visits now and then. When she refused to kiss him, he grabbed her by the wrists and her hair and forced her to submit. Once he slapped her face so hard, she had a red mark on her cheek for a week. She was glad her brother was away at the time. She made me promise not to write to him about the abuse, for fear he would do something rash and come to harm himself."

"Oh, Mr. Ackroyd." Athena's heart went out to Miss Vernon. No woman should ever suffer such treatment. And yet, Athena had read in the papers about men who did far worse.

"And that was *before* they were married. It drove me mad to think of how he might mistreat her after they were wed. Sometimes, I feared for her life, Miss Taylor."

Athena's throat constricted and she shuddered. She wondered suddenly if *she* might have been subjected to similar treatment had she married Giles Shaw, who, like Harold Sinclair, had not respected women. She wondered, as well, what Mr. Ackroyd might have done to protect the woman he loved from such a fate. Athena hesitated, searching for the right words. "Did you ever think of trying to … stop Mr. Sinclair?"

"I did, plenty of times." He seemed to go somewhere else in his mind for a moment. The fingers on his right hand tightened into a fist. "I wanted to kill him."

There it is. Quietly, Athena asked, "And did you?"

He blinked twice. His lips twitched and his brow creased, as if he were taking time to consider his response. "No!" he said at last. "I was away at sea while all this was going on. I managed to get a fortnight's leave, though, and rushed home, hoping to rescue Caroline before that animal could marry her. We planned to elope to Scotland. But the minute her father found out I was here he locked her up and wouldn't let her leave the house. I never even got to see her. Somehow, she escaped and made it to that party at Woodcroft House."

"Did you attend the party?"

He hesitated again and lowered his eyes, as if avoiding Athena's gaze. "No. I hated the man's guts. Why would I go to one of his stupid parties? Especially when I thought Caroline couldn't be there?"

"Where were you that night?"

He toyed with the cap in his hands. "What difference does it make?"

"You said Harold Sinclair was a violent man. He was about to marry the woman you loved. I just thought you might have gone to the party, to … stop him from hurting Miss Vernon anymore."

His blond brows drew together. He turned to stare at her. "Wait, what is this? Did you corner me here to try to get me to incriminate myself in that crime?"

"Of course not," Athena replied quickly, but she could see that he didn't believe her.

He leapt to his feet, his eyes flashing. "I won't lie. My hat is off to whoever sent Harold Sinclair to Hades. But it wasn't me. I wasn't at that party. It was my last night on shore, and they wouldn't let me see Caroline, so I went to the pub. The next morning, I heard Harold Sinclair had been killed. I didn't even get to say goodbye to Caroline—I had to return to my ship. By the time I'd learned she had been hanged for his murder, I was halfway across the seven seas." He replaced his cap on his head, gave Athena a cold, hard stare, and walked away.

Athena sat there for a long while in deep reflection. On the one hand, her heart went out to Mr. Ackroyd for having lost the woman he loved. On the other hand, she sensed in her gut that he had been lying about something. *But what?*

CHAPTER FOURTEEN

"How did your reading with Mrs. Hillman go?" Athena asked from her seat by the drawing room hearth, when Selena returned to Thorndale Manor later that afternoon.

"Very well." Selena warmed her hands by the fire.

"You are her favorite, you know." Athena put down the papers she was grading. "Mrs. Hillman told me that you are 'just the tonic she needs.'"

Selena laughed as she sat down across from Athena. "The feeling is mutual. But I'm dying to know! Did you speak to Edward Ackroyd?"

"I did."

"What did he say? Do you think he did it?"

"One question at a time." Athena gave her sister an overview of their conversation.

Selena frowned. "You make him sound very sympathetic."

"He was. I felt sorry for him. I think he adored Miss Vernon and worried for her safety at the hands of that brute she was going to marry. Mr. Ackroyd admitted that he *wanted* to kill him."

"But he wasn't at the garden party?"

"That's what he *said*. But he couldn't look me in the eye." Athena stood and paced before the hearth. "I think he lied. I think he *was* at that party."

"Mama taught us to trust our gut. Diana said the same thing."

"I need to check his alibi. Someone might remember seeing

him at the party, or at the pub."

"What can I do to help?"

"You are already helping by teaching our girls brilliantly and acting as my sounding board."

"I'd like to do more."

"I'll let you know if I think of something. Meanwhile, I'm not going to sit and twiddle my thumbs. Mr. Ackroyd is a viable suspect, but there may be others. There's one avenue I haven't yet explored."

"What's that?"

"The maid who said she found rat poison in Caroline Vernon's room."

"That's right! Ethel Leighton."

"Mrs. Lloyd doesn't know Ethel's married name or where she lives now. I'm going to ask around in the village. I think I'll start at the apothecary shop."

"The apothecary? Why?"

"I want to buy a cough remedy for Miss Osborn. And while I'm there—Mr. Quince and his daughter have lived in Darkmoor Bridge forever. They might know something about Ethel Leighton."

Quince's Apothecary Shop, according to the gilded sign above the front door, had been established in 1784.

Athena entered to find the place crowded with customers. Two walls were covered in rows of mahogany drawers and shelves that housed a seemingly endless number of bottles labeled with mysterious Latin names. She spotted Neville Sinclair chatting with the vicar beside a table that advertised various items for sale, including spices, candles, salad oil, and tobacco.

Behind the counter, Mr. Quince, a gentleman of medium height with a florid face and bushy, silver sideburns, was mixing something with a mortar and pestle. Miss Quince, an attractive blonde who was as tall and sturdily built as her father, was attending the first in a long line of customers. Athena joined the queue.

The bell on the shop door rang and Mr. Osborn hobbled in with his cane, his expression dour beneath his faded cap.

"Mr. Osborn, how do you do?" Athena greeted him cheerfully.

"Still this side of the grave." He stopped behind her and didn't return her smile.

"What brings you in today?" she inquired.

"I need something for the pain." He rubbed his shoulder above the empty jacket sleeve that was pinned across his chest. "My arm might be gone, but it throbs like it's still there. And my hip still troubles me something fierce."

"I'm sorry. I hope Mr. Quince can help you. And I hope to pick up a remedy for Miss Osborn's cough."

"Don't waste your money." He scoffed. "The stuff he gave Bridget last time made her too sleepy to work."

His lack of empathy took Athena aback. "But surely, you would rather have your daughter rest than work, if she is ill?"

"Bridget's fine. I can't have her lazing about the house. Not if we want to eat."

"I see." Recalling something Selena had said the day before, Athena redirected the conversation. "Sir. I believe you've lived in the neighborhood many years, isn't that so?"

His eyes narrowed, as if surprised by this change of topic. "Since I was sixteen. Got a job here working on a building crew and never left. Why?"

"I am hoping you can answer a question for me, about local history."

"I can try."

"I'm interested in the fate of one of the former residents of my house—Miss Caroline Vernon."

He glanced down quickly at his boots. It was a moment before he spoke. "She was a dark one."

"Was she?"

"She killed Harold Sinclair."

Athena struggled to keep her expression passive. "Perhaps so. After all, a witness at Miss Vernon's trial, Ethel Leighton, claimed to have found rat poison in the young lady's bedchamber."

"So they said."

"Did you know Ethel Leighton?"

"Never met her."

Before Athena could respond, the woman in line before her turned around and said, "I remember Ethel."

"You do?" Athena recognized the speaker as Mrs. Powell, the village seamstress. They had been introduced at church. A petite woman with a coronet of light-brown braids, Mrs. Powell was attired in a beautifully tailored grey frock that Athena guessed had been copied from a Parisian fashion plate.

"I made a wedding dress for Ethel." Mrs. Powell scowled. "She skipped town to get married and never paid me for it."

"Oh, no!" Athena bit her lip in sympathy.

"Put one over on you, did she, eh, Mrs. Powell?" Mr. Osborn let out a loud, scornful breath.

"Yes, and the fabric and lace trim for that gown cost me a great deal," Mrs. Powell told him, still frowning.

"Doesn't surprise me." He shook his head. "People never seem to pay their debts these days."

"Mrs. Powell," Athena cut in, "do you know whom Ethel married? Or where she lives now?"

"I have no idea. If I did, I'd be the first to call on her and demand that money."

Athena nodded, struggling to hide her disappointment. "May I ask you something else, ma'am? It may seem out of the blue, but it's related to that same time period."

"Yes?"

"Did you attend the garden party at Woodcroft House, the one where Harold Sinclair … met his unfortunate end?"

Mrs. Powell tilted her head, and her forehead puckered. "Yes, I believe I did."

"Do you remember if Mr. Edward Ackroyd was at the party?"

"Mr. Edward Ackroyd? Oh! You mean that sailor who was in love with Caroline Vernon?" Mrs. Powell's eyes narrowed. "I don't recall. It was so long ago. Nearly everyone in the village was there, though." She turned away just as the shop bell rang again.

Well, Athena thought, she had learned one useful thing from this conversation: Ethel Leighton had left town without paying for an expensive wedding dress—which substantiated both the notion that she'd left to get married, and her reputation as a thief.

Just then, Mr. Chapman strode in, his face lighting up when he saw Athena. "Miss Taylor! Good morning." He took his place in line and lifted his hat to Mr. Osborn. "Sir."

Osborn grunted in reply.

Athena gave Mr. Chapman a concerned smile. "I hope you aren't here because you're unwell?"

"Not at all. I'm here for Mrs. Hillman. She gets anxious at night and asked me to get her something to help her sleep."

"I see." Athena recalled how anxious the woman had gotten every time they'd spoken about Caroline Vernon. She was resolved to never bring up the subject with Mrs. Hillman again. "So. Are you all prepared for your music lesson this afternoon?"

"I am. I'll see you promptly at four as usual."

Mrs. Powell cut in. "Sir, did I hear correctly? Do you teach music?"

"I do."

Athena introduced them. "Sir, allow me to present Mrs. Cora Powell, the talented seamstress who runs the millinery shop in the village? And ma'am, may I present Mr. Peter Chapman, an extraordinary musician who now teaches music, singing, and dancing at the Darkmoor Bridge School for Girls?"

"A pleasure to make your acquaintance, Mrs. Powell," said Mr. Chapman with a bow.

Mrs. Powell returned the compliment with a curtsy, adding, "I wonder, Mr. Chapman, if you could teach my daughter to play? I have been looking for a pianoforte teacher."

"I would be happy to stop by and discuss the matter, ma'am." Mr. Chapman quickly went over the details with Mrs. Powell.

When their tête-à-tête had concluded, Mrs. Powell turned to Athena. "I've been meaning to ask, how is your school faring? Is it true that you only have five students?"

Athena wanted to scream with frustration but forced herself to smile. "Yes, ma'am, but we're new. Enrollment will pick up in time."

"It will, without a doubt," insisted Mr. Chapman, coming to Athena's rescue. "The Darkmoor Bridge School for Girls is, Mrs. Powell, one of the finest educational institutions in all of Yorkshire."

Mrs. Powell's brows rose, and her tone conveyed skepticism. "Is it?"

"Yes, ma'am. I am privileged to work there. If you are looking for a school for your daughter, you can do no better. Why, its teachers have such a sterling reputation that the venerable Mrs. Rose Hillman is a patron. She made a very generous endowment to the school."

A keen look now lit Mrs. Powell's eyes. "Did she, indeed?"

"Mrs. Hillman is so impressed with the talents of Miss Taylor and Miss Selena that she has employed them to give private readings to her at Darkmoor Park two afternoons a week. I believe Miss Taylor goes every Wednesday and Miss Selena every Sunday, isn't that right?"

Athena, both embarrassed and flattered by his praise, admitted, "Yes. But really, I'm sure no one is interested in that."

"I'm interested." It was Miss Quince speaking now from behind the counter. "I'm glad to hear of anything that makes Mrs. Hillman happy. She is one of our best customers."

Athena smiled at that. But her smile vanished a second later when the customer ahead of Mrs. Powell finished paying and turned around.

It was Edward Ackroyd.

Athena's heart pounded with mortification. Just moments earlier, she had asked Mrs. Powell if she remembered Edward Ackroyd being at that garden party. He gave Athena a silent glare that was as sharp as cut glass then brushed past her and left the shop.

Had he overheard her discussion with Mrs. Powell? Was he still offended by her line of questioning the day before? Or both? Either way, did it point to his guilt or innocence? There was no way to know.

Mrs. Powell paid for her medicine, said goodbye, and quit the shop, leaving Athena at the head of the line. She placed her order for a cough remedy, requesting one that wouldn't make the patient sleepy.

Miss Quince discussed the matter with Mr. Quince and returned. "My father says he'll make a mild tincture of laudanum. It will just take a few minutes."

While they waited, Athena commented in what she hoped was a casual tone, "It's nice to see Mr. Ackroyd back in the neighborhood."

Miss Quince shrugged. "It's been so long since he's been in, I'd forgotten what he looked like."

"He's been away at sea for nine years, I think?" Athena gave Miss Quince a meaningful look. "Ever since …?"

Miss Quince brushed back a blonde curl from her forehead, returning Athena's stare. "You mean … ever since Harold Sinclair was murdered?"

Athena nodded.

"I guess Mr. Ackroyd didn't have the heart to come home, after he'd heard what *Caroline Vernon* had done."

Miss Quince had emphasized the woman's name with undisguised disgust, which Athena found intriguing. Athena lowered her voice confidentially. "Do you think Miss Vernon really did it?"

"She was convicted, wasn't she?"

"A conviction doesn't guarantee guilt."

"Oh, she did it, all right." Miss Quince's lips curled. "Caroline Vernon was a pathetic creature. She had everything a woman could want and didn't appreciate any of it. To murder a man in cold blood like that! Good riddance to her, is what I say."

The remark was so unexpected and uttered with such venom, it took Athena a moment to respond. It was time to ask the questions she'd come in for. "Miss Quince, do you remember the maid who gave evidence at Miss Vernon's trial? Miss Ethel Leighton?"

"I read about her in the papers."

Mr. Quince placed a small bottle on the counter and withdrew. Miss Quince announced the price for the medicine.

Athena asked, "What is Ethel Leighton's married name?"

"I have no idea. She did everybody a favor, though, so justice could be done."

"But *was* justice done?" Athena persisted.

"Enough chitchat!" complained Mr. Osborn impatiently from behind her. "Pay for the bloody thing and move on!"

Athena paid the bill, turned, and gave the medicine to Mr. Osborn. "Sir, would you do me a favor and please give this to your daughter?"

He gave vent to an annoyed huff. "I told you not to buy her any."

"Well, I did. And I am hoping it will do her some good."

Mr. Osborn frowned, stuffed the bottle in a pocket without a *thank you*, and took his place at the counter.

"I'll see you at school," Athena told Mr. Chapman, who returned the friendly farewell.

She left the shop, still embarrassed by the look Mr. Ackroyd had given her and disappointed that her conversation with Miss Quince had come to such an abrupt end. The woman's remarks were mystifying.

"Pathetic creature. She had everything a woman could want and didn't appreciate any of it … Good riddance to her, is what I say."

What had been behind Miss Quince's spiteful outburst? It was a matter that needed looking into.

OVER THE NEXT two days, Athena's time was so consumed by teaching, lesson planning, and grading papers, she barely had a minute to spare. Miss Weaver continued to show unusual prowess in both science and mathematics, and to foster those interests, Athena was compiling a reading list and a research project just for her.

Early one chilly morning, Mr. Vernon stopped by to inspect the roof, bringing a burly, bearded, blond man named James Carson to assist. They had lashed two tall, wooden ladders together, creating a ladder long enough to reach the eaves of the roof at the gutter line.

Athena stole a few minutes to watch the end of the proceedings, her heart in her throat the whole time. Mr. Carson held the ladder at the base while Mr. Vernon worked at a precarious height using a device he had called a roof crawler, which had been fitted into the guttering to support it up the pitched side of the roof.

"One of the slates is indeed broken and there's a piece missing," Mr. Vernon told Athena and Mr. Carson when, to her relief, he returned to the ground to safety. "That's what's causing the leak."

"Nothing we can't fix," Mr. Carson remarked cheerfully. Athena guessed him to be in his early fifties. He was barrel-chested with beefy arms and looked very fit.

"Thank you both so much for looking into this," Athena said.

Mr. Carson smiled and touched his cap before heading back to the long cart they had brought. Athena crossed her arms over her chest in an attempt to warm herself. She hadn't thought to bring her cape.

Mr. Vernon's concerned gaze found hers. "You're cold. You didn't need to come out to watch. Would you like my jacket?"

"Thank you, I'm fine," she said hastily, not wanting him to be without the added protection. "When do you think you can make the repair?"

"I'll bring Carson and another crewman on Thursday morning. Do you mind if I leave the ladders in place?"

"That's fine. Thank you again, sir."

"Glad to help. See you Thursday."

"See you then."

He nodded goodbye. His parting smile reached his eyes, crinkling the corners, a smile that warmed up Athena's insides and made her feel aglow for the rest of the day and far into the night. *Just friends*, she reminded herself. *Just friends*.

On Wednesday afternoon, she read aloud from *The Wind Pirate* to Mrs. Hillman, a pleasant experience, as always.

As she walked home from Darkmoor Park, Athena inhaled the crisp, autumn air, redolent with the scents of cow parsley and grass in the ditches at the roadside. It was one of her first free moments in days and she was delighted by the peace and quiet.

The late-afternoon sun had painted the sky bluish-grey. Clouds drifted overhead, as puffy and white as the *baaaing* sheep in the nearby meadows. The only other sounds that caught Athena's ears were the stirring of leaves in the trees and the fluttering of her cape and bonnet ribbons in the wind.

Suddenly, there was a new sound. A carriage was approaching from behind. Athena glanced back and noted that the vehicle, which was black and pulled by two horses, was headed her way at a rapid pace. She moved to the side of the road. When she glanced back again, to her dismay, the carriage driver was leaning forward in his seat, his hat pulled low as he urged the horses to go even faster.

Athena's pulse pounded in alarm. The vehicle seemed to be heading directly towards her.

Why is the driver in such a hurry?

A rush of anxiety shot through her system. Athena moved as close as she could to the edge of the road, which dropped off sharply into a deep ditch. But the carriage was bearing down on her as if in deliberate pursuit.

In a few seconds, it will hit me. I'm about to be run over!

The ditch was terrifyingly deep. If she jumped, she might break her neck. But she had no choice. *Do it!* she told herself.

But before she could make the leap, Athena stumbled and fell down onto the road. Directly into the path of the oncoming vehicle.

CHAPTER FIFTEEN

Pain seared through Athena's face and shoulder as she smashed into the road. Although stunned, she didn't have a second to lose. Using all her might, she rolled off the edge of the embankment into empty space.

In an ear-splitting roar of wheels and jangling harnesses, the hurtling carriage passed by with barely an inch to spare. Athena tumbled into the ditch, hitting the ground with a jarring jolt. She lay there for a long moment in the damp grass and cow parsley, breathing hard and too dazed to move.

If that carriage had run me over, I would have probably died.

Athena waited until the sounds of the vehicle had disappeared into the distance, and her pulse and respiration had resumed something close to their natural pace, before sitting up to take measure of her status. A sharp pain spasmed in her upper cheek. She flexed all her fingers, then tested her arms and legs to make sure that nothing was broken. Thankfully, other than an aching shoulder, she still seemed to be in one piece.

She stood up, wincing at a tenderness in her right ankle and miscellaneous other aches and pains. She did her best to wipe off the patches of loose soil from her dress and cape before climbing back up onto the roadside. As she resumed the walk home, favoring her good ankle, her mind buzzed with confusion.

It had felt for all the world as if that carriage had deliberately tried to run her down.

But that was a mad idea. Wasn't it?

ATHENA ARRIVED AT Thorndale Manor to find Selena and Miss Russell seated on a bench in the rear courtyard, deep in conversation. At Athena's approach, they both leapt to their feet, causing the notebook on Selena's lap to tumble to the ground.

"Athena!" exclaimed Selena. "What happened?"

Athena struggled to keep her face expressionless as she made her way over to them. "I fell in the road on my way home from Darkmoor Park." She couldn't announce that she'd nearly been hit by a runaway carriage. What would their pupils' parents make of that if it got back to them?

Selena hurried up to her. "Did you walk all that way on a twisted ankle?"

"It's not twisted, just twinging a little. I'm sure it'll be fine."

"Your cheek is all *purple* and the skin around your right eye is *yellow*," observed Miss Russell, gawking at her. "Is your eye going to fall out?"

"I hope not," Athena answered, amused and determined to change the subject. "What have you two been up to?"

"Miss Russell asked for advice about the book she's writing. I've been reviewing the first chapters. She didn't want you to see it until it was further along."

"What are you writing about, Miss Russell?"

"A girl who makes friends with a ghost."

Athena smiled. "I look forward to reading it."

"Miss Russell, we'll continue this at another time. You have three-quarters of an hour until dinner. Feel free to spend it however you like."

"Yes, Miss Selena. Miss Taylor, I hope your ankle feels better," the girl said before taking her notebook back and dashing off.

Selena offered her arm to Athena as they headed back to the house. "Now, tell me what *really* happened," Selena insisted in a low tone.

It was annoying the way her sister could always see straight through her. Softly, Athena replied, "A carriage nearly ran me down."

"*What?*" Selena froze briefly and stared at her. "Did you try to get out of its way?"

"Yes. But it was traveling at full speed. I had to fling myself into a ditch to avoid it."

"Dear lord. No wonder you're so banged up. You could have been killed."

They retreated to the drawing room. Athena lay on the sofa while Selena fetched Mrs. Lloyd, who brought rags and a bowl of cold water containing chips of ice.

"It's almost the last of the ice in the icehouse," the housekeeper fretted as she placed one wet cloth against Athena's cheek and wrapped the other around her ankle. "You must rest this evening. Don't walk on that ankle any more than you have to."

"Yes, ma'am."

After Mrs. Lloyd had left, Selena sank down on the carpet beside the sofa and took one of Athena's hands in hers. "To think that I could have lost you today." Selena's voice caught.

"It *was* terrifying." Now that she was home and safe, Athena contemplated her brush with death and fought back sudden tears.

"Did you recognize the coach or the driver?"

"No. It was a black brougham with no special markings. I couldn't see the driver's face. His head was dipped low and obscured by a large hat."

"He must not have seen you."

"Perhaps."

Selena tilted her head. "What do you mean, 'perhaps'?"

"I mean, perhaps he was hiding his face for a reason."

"What are you saying?" Selena let go of Athena's hand. "You think the driver came at you deliberately?"

"That's what if felt like." Now that she had said the words aloud, Athena dismissed them. "But that's ridiculous, isn't it?"

Selena went quiet for a moment. "Maybe not. Do you remember what you said in the churchyard on Sunday?"

"What did I say?"

"You announced your intention to find the true killer of Harold Sinclair."

Athena felt herself flush. "Oh. *That.* Yes, that was foolish of me. If I could take those words back, I would." Athena turned on the sofa and glanced at her sister, anxiety brewing in her stomach. "What are you thinking? That the killer overheard and wants me out of the way? So, he hired a carriage and came after me?"

"Or he paid someone else to drive the carriage."

"What a terrifying idea." A newfound worry sprang to Athena's mind. "*If* that's true, have I put *you* in danger as well?"

"I doubt it. I shook my head at you severely on Sunday. I don't think anyone is worried about me. But you may have put yourself in danger by speaking out like that."

Athena frowned. "Wait. If this was a planned attack, whoever was behind it would have had to have known I'd be walking home from Darkmoor Park this afternoon."

"True. Who knew that?"

Athena inhaled a sudden, sharp breath. "A *lot* of people."

"How so?"

"When I was at the apothecary shop two days ago, Mr. Chapman mentioned that I read to Mrs. Hillman every Wednesday afternoon."

"Who else was there?"

"Quite a crowd." Athena tried to think back. "Mrs. Powell. Mr. Osborn. *And* Edward Ackroyd. I told you about the withering glare he sent me."

"Yes."

"I saw Neville Sinclair taking to Mr. Johnson. Mr. Quince and Miss Quince were behind the counter. There were several other people I didn't recognize. I didn't take note of everyone."

A silence fell between them.

"Of course, this whole idea might be utter nonsense," Athena went on.

"It might be," Selena agreed.

"We could be overreacting."

"And letting our imaginations run away with us."

"Like that time, when we were children, and we were absolutely positive that the butcher had murdered his wife?"

Athena's lips twitched, recalling that long-ago event. "And it turned out she had just been away for a month visiting her sick mother?"

Selena nodded and gave what seemed to be a dismissive smile. "This may have simply been a runaway carriage."

"The driver was in a great hurry to get somewhere, and he wasn't paying attention."

"His hat was pulled low, obscuring his vision."

"If he *had* noticed you, he would surely have turned the carriage around at once and come back to make sure you were uninjured."

"Absolutely right. That makes perfect sense." Athena caught her sister's eye. "Shall we put all this behind us and forget about it?"

"Yes."

"Good." Athena let out a sigh. "Going forward, I promise to be more discreet about what I say and to whom."

"I should hope so." Selena stood up. "Now. What is your next step?"

"To be honest, I don't know. And it will have to wait in any case. Tomorrow, we are getting our roof repaired."

"THAT DOESN'T LOOK safe." Miss Cecilia frowned.

"I hope they don't fall." Miss Weaver wrung her hands.

Athena's nerves were once again on edge as she, Selena, and their students watched Mr. Vernon and his crew working on the roof high atop Thorndale Manor.

It was a clear morning with not a single cloud in the bright-blue sky and temperate enough to require only a lightweight jacket. Mr. Vernon had arrived early with his two men and a long cart loaded with boxes of tools, green slate, and other materials. Athena had only had a brief chance to greet them before she'd had to start teaching.

Mr. Vernon had paused, brows furrowing, and taken a second look when he'd caught sight of Athena's face, which sported an ugly, purple bruise on one cheek and a sallow black eye. She simply told him she had fallen. He had introduced his third worker, a shy, slender fellow named Adams. They had gotten straight to work, and Athena had returned to the classroom.

It was now the morning exercise period, but instead of the usual running about, all five pupils were standing in the rear courtyard, as riveted by the scene above as were Athena and Selena.

Mr. Vernon was partway up the roof crawler, which lay atop the roof at the side of the broken slate. Athena couldn't take her eyes off him. He was working in his shirt sleeves, and his dark-grey trousers hugged his long, lean legs and sculpted form, a sight that did strange things to her insides.

Mr. Vernon called out something to Mr. Adams, who stood at the top of the main ladder at the guttering, presiding over a bucket of tools and other materials. Adams leaned forward with an outstretched arm to hand a tool to Mr. Vernon, but the connection missed. Athena and her group all gasped in unison as the tool slid down the roof, landing with a clatter in the gutter.

"Oh!" observed Miss Russell, her blue eyes wide with dismay. "If Mr. Vernon had slipped instead of the tool, he would have fallen *all the way to the ground.*"

"He would have *died,*" Miss Gilbert agreed breathlessly.

"Hush, girls," Athena commanded. "These men are professionals. They know what they're doing. They're perfectly safe." She couldn't be certain that last statement was true, and their observations spread terror in Athena's heart.

As they watched, Mr. Vernon finally got a hold of the necessary tool and used it to work on the broken slate. At length, he managed to free the loose slate from its slot in the roof and carefully let it slide down to the man at the gutter, who in turn threw the broken bits to the ground safely away from Mr. Carson, who held the main ladder below.

Athena and all the watchers applauded.

"Now what?" asked Miss Cecilia.

"They have to put in a new piece of slate." Mr. Vernon had explained the repair process to Athena in advance.

"I expect that will be a big job, which we sadly won't be able to watch," Selena added. "Time for period two, girls."

The students groaned as they dutifully fell in line behind Selena and returned to the house.

Athena stayed on, anxious about the two men working high above. It was indeed a time-consuming job that involved removing more bits of slate and meticulously hammering in narrow strips of lead to hold the new piece of slate before installing it.

When the project was successfully completed, and the men came down from the ladders, Athena heaved a sigh of relief and set up coffee and a plate of chocolate biscuits on a small table.

Athena thanked Mr. Adams and Mr. Carson when they picked up their steaming cups and helped themselves to the treats. Mr. Adams made no reply, but Mr. Carson was more talkative.

"It was our pleasure, miss, and all in a day's work." Mr. Carson sank down on a bench by the refreshments table and removed his cap, revealing a riot of golden-blond curls.

"Have you been doing this kind of work a long time?" Athena asked.

"Since I were a lad," Mr. Carson replied. "Some jobs are

harder than others. This weren't too bad, though. Vernon's a good man. Pays fair and doesn't shirk. I'd work for him anytime."

Athena found herself pleased by this comment but wasn't sure why.

It wasn't until the two crewmen had gone off to start loading supplies onto the cart that Mr. Vernon finally joined Athena.

He sat on the same bench Mr. Carson had just vacated and threaded his fingers through his black hair, forcing it back off his forehead. "That went well. I think." He closed his eyes and took a long deep breath, as if seeking to restore his energy.

Athena took a moment to stare at him while he wasn't aware of her scrutiny. He was so very nice to look at. His handsome face glowed with perspiration. His long-sleeved white shirt, equally damp, clung to his muscular chest, revealing a glimpse of the dark, curly hairs that lay beneath. The sight made Athena feel like a stick of butter on the verge of melting.

"I had a tense moment there when one of the last pieces of broken slate refused to give way," Mr. Vernon went on. "Those copper nails were designed to last ten centuries. But I finally managed to rip them out and everything else worked like a charm."

"I can't thank you enough." Athena reluctantly tore her gaze away. "Coffee, Mr. Vernon?"

He opened his eyes. "Thank you." As she poured him a cup, he added, "We can't know for certain that the new slate is absolutely watertight until the next time it rains. I'll have to go up to the attic and check at that time."

"I can do that."

"I'd rather you didn't. As I said, it's not that safe up there."

"All right." Athena offered him the cup of steaming brew. As Mr. Vernon accepted it, their hands briefly touched, causing a tingle to spread up Athena's arm that seemed to light a fire within her. She found herself longing, suddenly, for him to touch her again, and not just her hand. She wanted to feel his hand on other parts of her body. But more than that, she realized she wanted to get to know him better—to spend more time in his company—to learn everything she could about him.

Their eyes met and held. In his gaze, she once again saw the heated look she'd glimpsed that morning in the conservatory, when they'd rushed in from the rain.

This will never do, she warned herself. It was one thing for her to be fighting an attraction to Mr. Vernon—*that* was something she could manage, couldn't she? It would be far more complicated, however, if *he* were attracted to *her.* Athena resolved to nip these inconvenient feelings in the bud and to keep things friendly between them.

She poured herself a cup of coffee and rather than sitting with him on the bench, she stood beside it.

"Now about your cheek and your eye." He looked up at her again as he sipped his brew. "What *really* happened?"

Athena's free hand went self-consciously to her face. Could he read her thoughts the way her sister could? She didn't want to lie to him. "I had an incident on the road yesterday."

His dark eyebrows drew together. "What kind of incident?"

"I had to jump into a ditch to avoid a runaway carriage. The driver apparently didn't see me."

His mouth gaped. "Good lord. I'm so sorry. Are you all right?"

"Other than a black eye and a bruised ego, I'm fine. My shoulder and ankle were a bit testy yesterday, but they're better now."

"I'm relieved you weren't injured more seriously."

"And *I'm* relieved that you and your men weren't injured today," she replied, deliberately redirecting the discussion. "The entire time you were up there, I was so worried, I found it hard to breathe."

"I'm sorry you were worried." He ducked his head and his voice went quiet. "You needn't have been."

"That was dangerous work, Mr. Vernon."

He paused and then acceded with a nod. "You're right. It *can* be dangerous. I know men who've suffered grave injuries from this kind of employment. George Osborn, for example. It's how he damaged his hip and lost his arm. But if you want something done right, sometimes you have to do it yourself. The key is to move slowly and precisely."

"Well, I'm glad the job is done. Speaking of which. How is the renovation going at Mrs. Hillman's dower house?"

"Very well." He bit into a biscuit.

"I'd love to see what you're doing."

"I'm there most days with one crew or another. The next time you're at Darkmoor Park, I'd be happy to give you a tour of our work in progress."

"I'd love that. Is the dower house anything like Thorndale Cottage?"

He chuckled. "No. Darkmoor Park's dower house is much larger than Thorndale Cottage, and a great deal more impressive."

"Your cottage is charming. It reminds me of the house where I grew up."

"Does it?" He looked at her with interest. "Where did you live?"

"Near Millcoate Hill, in Derbyshire."

"I know it. A lovely spot."

"It was quite idyllic. We lived on the edge of a moor, much like this." Athena gestured to the distant moors and the mist-covered hills beyond. "My father was a gentleman. Riding and hunting were his favorite pastimes. But sadly, when I was seventeen years old, he lost his fortune in a bad investment."

Mr. Vernon frowned. "That's a shame."

"We survived. My brother became a clergyman. My sisters and I worked as governesses to support ourselves."

He fell silent for a moment, then took another sip of coffee. "My father wasn't good with money, either—as you know. Although he gambled away the family fortune, rather than making a bad investment, the result is much the same. Like you and your siblings, I had to start over and reinvent myself."

"You studied to become an architect."

"An occupation that I had been dreaming of since I was a boy and find very fulfilling." He glanced at her. "*You* were obliged to become a governess, which was a kind of training ground for what you do now, running your own school."

"I suppose that's true."

"Who knows if we would have attained these goals, had we not been forced to by fate and the mismanagement of our fathers?"

"What an interesting way to look at it."

"People often say, 'All things happen for a reason.' I don't believe that. But I *have* come to believe that when the unexpected occurs and derails our intentions, it is up to us to adapt and change. To accept what is, forge a new path, and find happiness in a new direction."

"I couldn't agree more, Mr. Vernon."

He stared up at the manor house behind them with what appeared to be affection. "It does my heart good to see Thorndale Manor in your capable hands, Miss Taylor, and to know that the property is being put to such excellent use."

"Thank you, Mr. Vernon. It is magnanimous of you to say so."

He turned back to her with a look that was so warm and endearing, it made Athena feel weak in the knees. She swallowed hard, telling herself that she should end this discussion, but he did it first.

"I must help the men clean up." He set down his empty cup. "Thank you for the refreshments. They were much appreciated."

"It was nothing. I appreciate your hard work and that of your crew. Please send me your bill."

"Don't worry, I will."

They shared a laugh and said goodbye.

As Athena watched Mr. Vernon walk away, she found herself wondering when she would see him again and, despite herself, hoping it would happen soon.

CHAPTER SIXTEEN

LATER THAT AFTERNOON, while Selena was teaching period five French, Athena was seated on her favorite wicker chair in the conservatory, taking notes from a biology book, when Mr. Chapman strode in, early for his music lesson.

"Good afternoon." His smile evaporated when he took in her face. "Miss Taylor! What happened?"

Athena, tired of the subject, lightly replied, "I had an unforeseen meeting with a ditch."

"Where was this?"

"On the road, coming home from Darkmoor Park." She hoped that would be the end of it, but Mr. Chapman's features crinkled.

"That's a fairly wide road. And yet you fell into a ditch? Why?"

Athena sighed. It was easier to admit the truth than to invent some story. She told him about the runaway carriage. "It was just a bizarre incident. I'm fine, really."

"I'm glad you're fine—all evidence to the contrary." Mr. Chapman gestured to the chair beside her. "May I sit with you for a minute?"

"Of course."

He sat. After some hesitation, in a deeply serious tone he asked, "Are you certain the carriage driver didn't see you walking in the road?"

Athena was uncomfortable now and wished she hadn't told him. "He couldn't have seen me. Otherwise …" She couldn't bring herself to complete the thought.

"Otherwise, it might mean that he was deliberately trying to run you down."

The concept sent a chill shuddering down Athena's spine. She and Selena had considered the same thing before dismissing it. "Why would you even think that, Mr. Chapman?"

"I've been worried about you, Miss Taylor, ever since last Sunday when you said something in the churchyard …" He broke off, as if similarly uncomfortable about finishing his statement.

"I think I know the comment to which you refer," Athena replied, frowning.

"Do you think it's prudent to announce your suspicions about the death of Harold Sinclair in a public place?"

"I wasn't thinking. I should have known better."

"If I overheard you, someone else may have as well. They may not have taken kindly to the idea of you snooping around in that affair. Carriages and drivers can be hired, you know. Even ones capable of foul deeds, for a price."

"I thought of that." Athena's stomach tightened. "I told myself it was an absurd fancy."

"Where there's smoke, there's fire, Miss Taylor."

Athena stared at him. "What did you say?"

"*Where there's smoke, there's fire.* It's an old saying. It means—"

"I know what it means! My mother always quoted that to me and my sisters." It felt like a sign—that she and Selena *had* been on the right track in the first place about that carriage.

"It seems highly unusual to me that a carriage would *accidentally* run you off the road. But how could they have known that you would be on the road that very day, at that hour?" His eyes widened, and he gasped. "Oh, no! It's my fault. At the apothecary shop on Monday—I may have mentioned your visiting schedule at Darkmoor Park?"

"Don't blame yourself. How could you have known?"

"The shop was full." He shook his head and clicked his tongue. "Anyone could have overheard."

"You could be wrong about all this."

"I could be," he acknowledged. "Just in case, I would like to look into it for you."

"How?"

"I can make inquiries in villages and towns within a ten-mile radius to see if anyone hired a carriage that day. What did the carriage look like?"

"It was a black brougham pulled by two horses."

"Did it have any special markings?"

"None that I noticed." Off his nod, she added, "Thank you for offering to do this, Mr. Chapman. I don't have time to conduct a widespread search like that."

"It will be my pleasure." He stood with a smile. "Now I'd best go prepare for my lesson." He started away and then paused. "Do you know, it's happened again. I almost walked off without giving you a message from Mrs. Hillman." From his coat pocket, he pulled out a cream-colored envelope. "It's another invitation to tea at Darkmoor Park. This Sunday afternoon. But it's not just for you and your sister. This time, it's to include all of your pupils as well."

Athena's heart swelled as she stood and accepted the missive. "Oh! The girls will love that. If I write a note of acceptance, will you take it home to Mrs. Hillman after your class?"

"Of course. However, I have a request in return."

"What is that?"

His voice was filled with concern. "Whatever I may find out about that carriage ... we should keep to ourselves. This mission of yours is unwise, Miss Taylor. It may open you to unseen dangers. I should have warned you to drop it when you first mentioned it to me. And now I implore you. Please, give it up."

Athena pressed her lips together tightly and then shook her head. "I can't give it up. I have too much at stake, Mr. Chapman. The very reputation of my house is on the line, and with it, the future of my school."

He let go a long sigh. "Well, then, please be careful."

She'd heard that before, from her sister Diana. "I will," Athena promised as he quit the room.

"THIS IS THE most beautiful dining room I've ever seen," enthused Miss Weaver on Sunday afternoon as she took in that elegant chamber at Darkmoor Park.

It is indeed a remarkable chamber, Athena thought, *with its carved ceiling, glittering gilt brass chandelier, gold-flecked wallpaper, and gilded moldings.* Mrs. Hillman, at the head of the table, smiled with a satisfied and proprietary air at her assembled guests, who included Mr. Chapman, Athena, Selena, and their five pupils.

The girls, who had not stopped *oohing* and *aahing* from the moment they'd entered the house, seemed to be equally agog at the splendor of the table, which was elegantly set with bone china dishes, gleaming silverware, etched crystal glasses, and embroidered linen napkins. An artful centerpiece fashioned of sprays of dried wheat, flax, millet, pheasant feathers, and autumn leaves was surrounded by tiered trays and platters laden with a veritable feast that included several kinds of cakes, biscuits, scones, finger sandwiches, and dishes of cream and jam. Two maids stood at attention by the sideboard, ready to refill teacups from several tea pots.

"Thank you, Miss Weaver," Mrs. Hillman said. "I put a lot of thought into the decoration of this room. I'm delighted that you appreciate it."

"I wish I could live at your house," Miss Jones said breathlessly.

"Will Darkmoor Park be *yours* one day, Mr. Chapman?" asked Miss Russell as she turned to that gentleman.

Mr. Chapman's face colored slightly. "That is not something I think about, Miss Russell. The matter lies entirely in the hands of

Mrs. Hillman."

"But Mrs. Hillman has no children, does she?" asked Miss Weaver as she bit into a watercress sandwich.

"And isn't Mr. Chapman your nephew?" Miss Russell persisted.

"He is not," answered Mrs. Hillman. "I may think of Peter as such, but we are not blood relatives. In fact, I have no close relations."

"None at all?" Miss Russell sounded appalled.

"None at all. Nor any natural heirs."

"Miss Russell!" reprimanded Athena, feeling the awkwardness of the moment. "This is not a polite subject to discuss at tea."

"Why not?" Miss Russell said. "Grownups talk about such things all the time."

"You are not yet grown up," Selena pointed out.

"Miss Taylor is right," instructed Mrs. Hillman. "There are three subjects which one must never discuss at social gatherings: religion, politics, and money. This house is worth a great deal of money, and therefore, it is improper to mention who might inherit it. Particularly when I—the current owner—am still living and sitting at the table with you."

Miss Russell blushed. "I do beg your forgiveness."

"Granted," replied Mrs. Hillman with a firm nod, adding, "You are young and still learning how to behave in company— this is a good lesson for you." She leaned forward and lowered her voice dramatically. "However, I will break the rule just this once and satisfy your curiosity."

The room fell silent. Athena sensed that everyone was holding their breath as they turned their attention to their hostess.

"When my late husband passed away, he left Darkmoor Park to me to do with as I pleased. It is not subject to a male-only entail. I have not yet decided to whom I shall leave it." Sitting up straight again, she added, "And now let us talk of other things. Are you enjoying school, Miss Russell?"

"Yes, ma'am," the little girl replied.

The twosome began chatting amiably. Athena regarded them with interest. Mrs. Hillman seemed to be particularly drawn to Miss Russell. Athena recalled that after their outdoor botany lesson, Mr. Vernon had reacted similarly. She could see why. Although their youngest pupil, Miss Russell was one of the brightest and most charming.

"What is your favorite subject, dear?" Mrs. Hillman asked.

"Reading and writing," Miss Russell responded immediately.

"Oh? What are you reading at present?"

"Lots of things. *The Tell-Tale Heart* by Edgar Allan Poe, for one. It's a short story in an old issue of *The Pioneer,* an American magazine. It's about a man who committed a murder and then goes nearly insane with guilt."

Mrs. Hillman cast a glance at Athena. "Is that proper reading material for an eight-year-old girl?"

"It's not in our curriculum," Athena explained. "Miss Russell brought the magazine from home, but Mr. Poe is a fascinating writer. In class, we are reading Miss Austen's *Northanger Abbey.*"

"Ah! One of my favorites." Mrs. Hillman bobbed her head in approval. "Are you acquainted with the novel, Peter?"

"I've never heard of it," he admitted.

Miss Cecilia retrieved another scone. "The second half of the book takes place at an old house that used to be an abbey, just like this one."

"Perhaps that is one reason I like it so much." Mrs. Hillman motioned to the maid to refill her cup of tea.

"I *love* the hero, Henry Tilney." Miss Jones clasped her hands with a sigh.

"I adore Catherine Morland," insisted Miss Russell. "She is bold and brave. She believes there is danger lurking behind the walls of Northanger Abbey *and* a long-ago murder and she is unafraid to go searching for it."

"And yet she's completely wrong!" cried Miss Weaver, laughing.

Miss Russell's smile turned upside down. "What do you

mean?"

"Haven't you finished the book?" Miss Weaver asked.

Miss Russell shook her head. "No. I'm still waiting for my turn with the copy."

"Wait." Mrs. Hillman's forehead furrowed. "Are you saying that you only have one copy of *Northanger Abbey* to share among the entire class?"

"We each get to borrow it one day a week," explained Miss Gilbert. "And Miss Taylor reads it aloud to us on Saturday afternoons."

"That is not a proper way to conduct a class," Mrs. Hillman insisted, pursing her lips tightly. "Every girl ought to have her own book."

"I wish it were so, Mrs. Hillman." Athena set down her tea-cup, her cheeks flushing. "But books are expensive, so we make do with what we have."

"What happened to the endowment I gave you?"

"A portion of it went to pay for the recent roof repair. I need to conserve the remainder to cover servants' salaries and other school and household expenses."

"Miss Selena, are you facing a similar shortage of books in the subjects you teach?" Miss Hillman asked.

"Yes, ma'am, but we are managing."

Bristling, Mrs. Hillman announced, "I have an account at an excellent bookseller in York. Miss Taylor, I shall tell him that you will be calling on him presently. I want you to place an order for as many books as you think appropriate for the needs of your school, and I will pay for them."

"Mrs. Hillman!" Athena blinked rapidly, struggling for a re-ply. At last, she shook her head emphatically. "That is very kind, but I couldn't possibly accept."

"You have already made such a generous contribution to the school," Selena agreed.

"But not enough, apparently. I will not take *no* for answer."

Athena exchanged a look with Selena, whose shrug seemed

to convey her unspoken acceptance. Athena expressed her astonished thanks, which Mrs. Hillman waved away, saying, "Now, girls, if you could have a copy of any book in the world, what would it be?"

A lively conversation ensued in which a great many titles were batted around, including Dickens's *The Pickwick Papers*, Alexandre Dumas's *The Three Musketeers*, Jane Austen's *Pride and Prejudice*, Charlotte Brontë's *Jane Eyre*, Frederick Marryat's *The Children of the New Forest*, and The Cousin Lucy series by Rev. Jacob Abbott.

Athena was enthralled by the girls' enthusiasm, and all seemed sorry to leave when the tea party concluded.

They expressed their thanks to Mrs. Hillman for such a lovely afternoon, after which Mr. Chapman escorted the group out of the house. They all paused outside the front door and were about to say goodbye when Mr. Vernon came striding up the walkway.

Athena's heart caught at the sight of him. She hadn't seen Mr. Vernon since he'd fixed her roof three days before. But in spite of her desire to just be friends, she hadn't stopped thinking about him—and not in a purely friendly way. The memory of him that day, clad in a clinging, white shirt, and the warm, admiring look in his eyes as he'd gazed at her, still made her heart go pitter-pat every time she'd thought of it.

And he was looking at her that same way now as he removed his hat. "Miss Taylor," he said with a bow. "Miss Selena. Mr. Chapman. Girls."

"Hello. Girls, you remember Mr. Vernon?" Athena asked.

"Yes, miss," replied Miss Gilbert. All five young ladies dipped in polite curtsies.

"We just had tea with Mrs. Hillman," announced Miss Russell.

"So I understand." Mr. Vernon smiled down at the little girl and patted her dark head. "I hope you all enjoyed yourselves?"

"We did!" Miss Jones cried. "There were three kinds of cake and ever so many biscuits and sandwiches."

"And Mrs. Hillman is going to buy us new books!" added Miss Russell.

"Is she, indeed? How nice of her." Mr. Vernon turned to Mr. Chapman and the two shook hands. "Congratulations on the success of your music program, Chapman. I'm hearing only good things."

"The credit goes to my students. They are very gifted," Mr. Chapman replied with a grin. As the girls giggled with delight, he added, "Speaking of which, duty calls. I have lessons to plan. I pray you will excuse me." Tipping his hat to one and all, Mr. Chapman bowed and returned to the house.

Mr. Vernon turned to Athena. "Mrs. Hillman told me you would be here today. I hoped to catch you before you left. You had expressed an interest in seeing what we're doing at the dower house?"

"Yes."

"My crew is finished for the day, and I'd be happy to give you a tour if you like."

"Oh! I wish I could," Athena replied with regret. "But—" She gestured towards her students.

Mr. Vernon addressed the girls directly. "You won't mind if I steal your headmistress away for a little while, would you?"

"Can we come too?" asked Miss Russell, bouncing from foot to foot.

Mr. Vernon bent lower, one hand over his heart as he regarded her with serious eyes. "Forgive me, but … another time, perhaps. The dower house is undergoing construction and isn't safe for young ladies like yourselves at the moment."

Miss Russell's face fell, but she nodded solemnly. "All right."

"I'm happy to walk the girls home," Selena offered, her lips twitching as if to hold back a smile as she darted a clandestine look at Athena.

Athena blushed, her sister's earlier words flashing into her mind. *I got the impression that Mr. Vernon likes you as more than just a friend. I suspect you feel the same way.*

Athena couldn't deny it. The thought of spending a few hours in Mr. Vernon's company was very appealing. "Thank you, Selena."

"Take all the time you want," Selena insisted. "There's no need to rush home."

Selena hurried the girls down the path, leaving Athena alone with Mr. Vernon.

Mr. Vernon gave her a winning smile. "Shall we?"

As THEY WALKED to the dower house, Athena reveled in the pleasant scents of growing things and the sight of the trees around them, sporting all the colors of autumn.

"I imagine these gardens are even more beautiful in spring and summer?" Athena remarked.

"They are quite a sight to behold."

They passed the kitchen gardens, where skeletal pear trees were splayed on trellises along the stone walls and beds of scraggly vegetables and wilting herbs were ending their season of growth.

"My sister and I used to have our own vegetable plots here when we were young," Mr. Vernon added.

"Mrs. Hillman is obviously very fond of you."

"She spoiled us. Sometimes I think of Mrs. Hillman as my second mother. My own mother died a few years after my sister was born."

"I know how that feels. I was six years old when my mother passed away."

He glanced at her, one lip between his teeth. "Forgive me. Here I am feeling sorry for myself, when you and your sisters went through the very same thing. I think you mentioned a brother as well?"

"Yes, Damon. He's three years older than I am. I believe the loss of our mother was even harder on him because he'd gotten to know our mother better."

Mr. Vernon nodded as if in sympathy and recognition. "You said Damon is a clergyman?"

"For a poor parish in London."

"Important work."

"He is devoted to it. Sometimes, though, it is soul-crushing work. There are so many people in need, and so little funds to help them—if and when they are willing to accept help. I write to Damon, but I rarely hear back from him."

"Is he married?"

"Not yet. He says he is too busy to marry. I hope he will find a bride one day."

Mr. Vernon glanced at her. "How is it that a woman like you is yet unmarried, Miss Taylor?" His blue eyes sparkled with warmth and interest, causing her stomach to do a little flip.

Did he really want to hear the truth? She supposed not. "Perhaps because I spent all of my prime years hidden away as a governess," she responded lightly.

"Your *prime years* are hardly over," he argued.

"In society's eyes, they are. I'm twenty-nine years old. Hardly an ingenue."

"Society has strange ideas in that regard. I believe that people improve with age."

"Like a fine wine?"

"Precisely."

They shared a laugh.

"Did you never meet anyone whom you might have wished to wed?" he asked.

She clasped her hands as they walked. *I might as well be honest.* "I thought I did, years ago, but it turned out we weren't right for each other."

"May I ask, in what way were you not right for each other? Or would you rather not talk about it?"

"I can talk about it." Athena hadn't spoken about this in years, except with Selena, but somehow, she didn't mind sharing this piece of her past with Mr. Vernon. "His name was Giles Shaw. He was a gentleman's oldest son. We were both on holiday at Scarborough—I was there with the family for whom I was employed. Mr. Shaw and I talked every morning while the children I cared for made sandcastles on the beach. I snuck away to see him whenever I had a free moment. He was clever and he made me laugh. I had known him less than a month when he proposed. I asked for time to think about it and almost said *yes*, but I had seen red flags that had worried me."

"What kinds of red flags?"

"He was always telling me what to do and how to think. 'Don't speak your mind in public; it is unseemly for a woman.' 'My opinions will be your opinions.' 'Don't read that book; it will put dangerous ideas in your head.' When we were married, he said, I would get one new dress per year, and a new bonnet every three years, and he would choose the styles and colors. He had all the names picked out for his six future children, who were to be my primary occupation, along with managing his house. He didn't understand or approve of my desire to open a school for girls with an expanded curriculum. 'Girls can get their education perfectly well from a nanny or governess,' he'd insisted. And 'No wife of mine will work.'"

"Ah," Mr. Vernon said.

"When I broke things off with him, he was shocked—but I was relieved. Since then, I have come to appreciate my lucky escape—and my freedom."

"Your freedom?" He studied her. "Are you saying you don't wish to marry?"

"I do not." Notwithstanding her attraction to this man, Athena's feelings on the subject hadn't changed. "I have come to realize that the institution is not advantageous for some women."

"I know a lot of men who share your Mr. Shaw's attitudes and beliefs—but not all men."

"Even so. A married woman gives up all her rights. She becomes a man's property, bound to his will." They entered a long, formal garden surrounded by high, stone walls. Athena gestured to them. "She is forever trapped, as if enclosed within these four walls. She has no power over herself or even over her own children."

He seemed to ponder that. "I have always thought the system to be wrong. But if you met a man who felt as you do? Who allowed you to keep your *freedoms*, as you call them?"

Had Mr. Vernon, perhaps unintentionally, given a hint of his own beliefs with that phrase?

"Even if there were such man as that in England," Athena said with a smile, "he could not change the law." She glanced at him. "What about you? I should think that *you* would have married long ago." It might have been a brazen thing to say, but *he* had brought up the subject.

He went quiet for a moment. "I would have liked to marry, yes. But I haven't had the opportunity. Ever since my sister..." He didn't finish the statement, and his eyes seemed to be dimmed by regret.

Athena considered all that he had been through over the past nine years—his sister's death, his father's betrayal, the loss of his ancestral home—and her heart went out to him. "I'm so sorry about everything, but especially about what happened to your sister."

"So am I," he replied abruptly. "But don't feel sorry for me. I'm out here, strolling in a beautiful garden on a sunny afternoon with a lovely companion, allowed to live my life. Caroline's life was taken from her."

"It is so unfair," Athena said feelingly.

They continued in silence past autumnal flowerbeds and a verdant lawn and then passed through a gate into another walled garden. Athena realized there was a matter that she had wanted to discuss with him. "Mr. Vernon, may I ask you something?"

"Of course."

"I hope it is not insensitive of me to bring this up. It has to do with your sister."

"Go on."

"Last week, I was at the apothecary shop when Miss Quince said something odd."

"What did she say?"

Athena hesitated to repeat the woman's exact words—Miss Quince had called Caroline Vernon *a pathetic creature.* "She didn't seem to like your sister. She said Miss Vernon had everything a woman could want and didn't appreciate any of it."

He nodded grimly. "That doesn't surprise me."

"Doesn't it? Everyone with whom I have spoken until now adored your sister."

"Margaret Quince had good reason to dislike Caroline."

"Why?"

Mr. Vernon shoved his hands in his pockets and glanced away. "I don't like to tell tales out of school, but I suppose it's no secret. Miss Quince was … How shall I put it? For many years, she was involved in *a relationship* with Harold Sinclair."

"With Harold Sinclair?" Athena repeated, briefly stopping in mid-stride.

He nodded, his features impassive as they continued on. "Sinclair apparently thought Miss Quince too far beneath him to acknowledge, so he saw her on the sly," Mr. Vernon explained. "But everyone in the village knew about it. I felt sorry for her at the time. Sinclair was never going to marry an apothecary's daughter. She seemed to keep on hoping. And then he and Caroline became engaged, and he dropped Miss Quince like a hot potato."

"Ouch." Athena let this new information rattle around in her brain. *Miss Quince was Harold Sinclair's jilted lover. Interesting.* "I understand now. Miss Quince resented your sister for stealing away the man she loved."

"Yes. Except that Caroline didn't steal anyone. She was horri-fied to find herself betrothed to Harold Sinclair."

A new scenario began to form in Athena's mind—and with it,

another possible suspect in the murder of Harold Sinclair. But before she could examine it further, she and Mr. Vernon emerged from the second walled garden and she caught sight of a lovely two-story house ahead, with diamond leadlight windows and a clay tile roof.

"That," said Mr. Vernon, "is the dower house."

It suddenly occurred to Athena that she was about to enter an empty house with an unmarried gentleman, without the benefit of any other person or chaperone.

It wasn't a seemly thing to do. Had she been out of her mind to agree to this? Perhaps.

Boldly, she said, "Lead on."

CHAPTER SEVENTEEN

T HE DOWER HOUSE was a construction zone that Athena and Mr. Vernon had to pick their way through.

"Mrs. Hillman wanted a larger drawing room," he explained as he showed Athena the newly expanded front parlor, which had been opened to include the chamber beside it. "I remember your sister mentioning that she wished you could do something similar at Thorndale Manor. Fortunately, one of these walls was non-supporting and could be removed."

"What a wonderful, spacious room." Athena couldn't help but be impressed by Mr. Vernon's vision, and his expertise in carrying it out. "This fits Mrs. Hillman's sensibilities so perfectly. Do you think she plans to move in here some day?"

"I don't know. I have heard her mention that she may prefer to live in a smaller house and let a younger generation enjoy the comforts of Darkmoor Park."

"A younger generation? But who?" It would be poetic justice, Athena thought, if Mrs. Hillman left Darkmoor Park to Mr. Vernon. He had long been a favorite of hers and doing so might help to make up for his loss of Thorndale Manor. It didn't feel right to say so aloud, however.

"I presume she'll leave it to Chapman. He's her ward and the closest thing she has to a blood relative. I expect he'll marry someday and be very grateful."

That made sense, Athena supposed. She idly wondered what

sort of woman Mr. Chapman might marry. An image appeared in her brain of herself sitting across the dinner table from Mr. Chapman at Darkmoor Park. It wasn't an unpleasant notion, and yet she suddenly realized that she didn't feel *that way* about Mr. Chapman. She considered him more as a friend or a brother.

Her gaze fell on Mr. Vernon's broad-shouldered back and trim waist as he headed across the room. Her pulse picked up speed as another mental image presented itself. She was sitting beside Mr. Vernon on a sofa, holding hands and intimately conversing by candlelight. He pulled her to her feet, and they retreated upstairs to their bedchamber to …

"Be careful where you step." Mr. Vernon's warning brought Athena to a halt, her heart hammering. She had almost walked into a sawhorse. Her face flamed. Why had she been thinking about holding hands with Mr. Vernon? And about bedchambers?

"The old, wooden floors have been refinished so many times, they were paper thin, so we had to rip them out," Mr. Vernon was explaining. "But we can't finish the floors until we plaster the walls."

Athena struggled to rein in her wayward thoughts as they navigated an expanse of rough subflooring, past piles of wooden boards that were waiting to be installed.

In the kitchen, a new iron ranger cooker stood beneath a sizeable iron hood. "I expect Mrs. Hillman has never stepped inside a kitchen in her life, but she wants her cook to be happy," Mr. Vernon said with a grin.

He took Athena upstairs, where the floors were being similarly replaced. The vestibule on the first floor was so large, it felt like its own room. Mr. Vernon's architectural drawings lay open on a makeshift table that had been created by a door on top of two sawhorses.

Athena deliberately stopped to study the drawings, to give her traitorous heart a chance to slow its rapid pace. They were the same drawings she had seen at his cottage, and this time, she couldn't help but marvel at the way his ink lines had been translated into improvements in the real world. On closer inspection, though, she noticed a feature on the drawing of the vestibule that didn't seem to exist in the room itself. "What is this?" she asked.

Mr. Vernon leaned in close and studied the drawing over her shoulder. "That is a very old feature of the house. A secret staircase that leads to the cellar."

His cheek was inches away from Athena's ear, and his breath was warm and sweet as it caressed her neck. Her heart began to thunder in hear ears. "Why did they need a secret staircase?"

"I suppose whoever lived here wanted a way to leave the house and return without anyone else noticing," he said quietly.

His proximity was making it difficult for Athena to think. She glanced at the corner of the room where the stairs were supposed to be but saw only a wall covered in faded wallpaper and wainscoting. "I don't see an entrance to a staircase." Was that really her voice? Why was it no louder than a whisper?

"You don't see it because it's a *secret*," he whispered in return.

His hand rose to the side of her neck and gently brushed aside several tendrils of hair that had gathered there. The act caused an electric shock to sizzle through Athena's entire being. She was struck by an overwhelming sense of want for him to run his hands over other parts of her body. Now, this instant.

"There *is* a door there." He lowered his head so that his mouth almost touched her neck. "It opens by a spring mechanism. But it's practically seamless—and nearly invisible."

"Oh," Athena said breathlessly, but the word came out sounding more like a moan. *You shouldn't be here*, she told herself, *alone with him in this empty house*. She'd known it was inadvisable and yet she had come, anyway.

Athena's pulse was now as out of control as the runaway carriage that had nearly run her down. If she turned her head the slightest bit, her mouth would be inches away from his. Would he kiss her?

Did she want him to kiss her?

Yes, she did.

Athena rotated to face him, scarcely able to breathe. For a long moment, they simply stared at each other. The desire in his eyes was almost palpable and matched her own feelings.

"I have half a mind to kiss you right now," he said softly.

"Why don't you?" she heard herself whisper. Had she really said that aloud? *How brazen!* What must he think of her?

His eyebrows raised slightly. "I thought, with your beliefs about freedom, you might not welcome a kiss from me," he said quietly.

"I would not welcome a kiss from just *any* man. But I think you are different. I think you understand me."

"Do I?"

He lifted one hand to her cheek and cupped it gently. The touch of his fingers felt almost as intimate as a kiss. Did he mean to stop there? Athena couldn't help herself—she leaned forward until her mouth was almost touching his, inviting him to kiss her.

And so he did.

It had been so long since she'd been kissed; Athena had almost forgotten what it felt like. *Oh, the joys of being kissed!* His lips moved against hers as softly and tenderly as a feather. And then they pressed more warmly and eagerly, a sensation that sent hot spirals quivering through her to her very core.

Athena closed her eyes, savoring his caress and returning it, a kiss so wondrous that she never wanted it to stop.

But it did, all too soon. He broke the contact and gazed down into her eyes. "Don't worry." His voice was huskier than usual. "You're still a free woman. It was just a kiss."

Unaccountably, disappointment rang through her. Was it because the kiss was over? Or because of what he'd just said? *It was just a kiss.* "Yes. It was," she answered quickly, surprised by the tremor in her voice.

He released her and stepped back. "I suppose it's time for this tour to come to an end. I have some work to do here, but I'm happy to escort you back to the manor house?"

He sounded so matter-of-fact. Athena struggled to recover her sense of decorum.

"That won't be necessary. I remember the way. Thank you for the tour, Mr. Vernon. I bid you good day."

He returned the sentiment and Athena promptly departed. As she hurried back through the gardens, her mind reeled with confusion. What was she to make of her behavior just now? She had wanted that kiss, had invited it. She had enjoyed every minute of it and had been sorry when it had been over. Mr. Vernon seemed to have enjoyed it, too. It had been evident in every touch of his lips, every hitch of his breath, and by the heated look in his eyes when they had met hers.

And yet when it had ended, he had been so cavalier—as if it had meant nothing. *"It was just a kiss."*

A kiss between a man and woman often led to a marriage proposal. After sharing a stolen embrace with Giles Shaw, *he* had asked for her hand. But clearly, Mr. Vernon didn't see it that way. On the one hand, it was a relief. She was certainly *not* interested in an offer of marriage. On the other hand, it was insulting. Did he think she went about kissing men willy-nilly? That couldn't be further from the truth! But then, Athena thought as her cheeks flamed, what on Earth had possessed her to kiss him?

Athena couldn't believe that, for a moment, she had actually *envisioned herself married to Mr. Vernon. And in bed together!* The *in bed* part didn't shock her—that was an act she'd always thought would be wonderful, *if* she ever married. But she had determined so firmly to never wed.

How was she to reconcile that promise to herself with the way she had acted just now, and with the bundle of emotions still coursing through her?

As she marched towards the manor house, Athena made a new promise to herself. That kiss had been an aberration. She liked Mr. Vernon. Very much. So much so that she had lost control for a moment. But that moment was over.

She would put it behind her and hope that he did as well.

"YOU ARE VERY quiet," Selena said that night as she and Athena prepared for bed.

Athena always told her sister everything. But she didn't want to tell her about the kiss she had shared with Mr. Vernon. The feel of his lips on hers was forever burned in her memory. Despite herself, Athena tingled every time she thought about it, and she had thought of little else all evening.

It felt too private to discuss with anyone, though, even with Selena, her favorite person in the world. Selena was an eternal optimist. If Selena knew what had occurred, she would see hope and possibility. But Athena knew better. The kiss had meant nothing to Mr. Vernon. *"Don't worry. You're still a free woman. It was just a kiss."* It was better this way. That kiss had been a one-time event, and it would never happen again.

"You said very little through dinner or during social hour," Selena persisted. "What have you been thinking about?"

Selena was far too perceptive. Athena had to tell her *something*. "I've been thinking about something Mr. Vernon told me."

"Something he *told you*? Is that all?" Selena's face fell as if with disappointment. "I know you were alone together at the dower house."

"That was just a tour," Athena insisted quickly. "It took almost no time at all. But on the way there, he gave me new information that I think pertains to our case. It's about Miss Quince."

"The apothecary's daughter?"

"Yes. He said Miss Quince was Harold Sinclair's lover for years."

Selena paused in surprise, her hairbrush in mid-air. "His lover? Is that common knowledge?"

"Apparently. She expected Sinclair to marry her. But he jilted her when he became engaged to Miss Vernon."

"Oh! Poor Miss Quince. Or perhaps, with what we now know about Harold Sinclair, we should say *lucky Miss Quince*, for having escaped a life tied to that man."

"I agree. But I doubt she feels that way. I think I told you what Miss Quince said about Caroline Vernon?"

"You said she called her a pathetic creature who got what she deserved. Now it makes sense. Miss Quince was jealous of Miss Vernon."

"Yes, but I'm wondering if there's more to it than that," Athena said as they both climbed into bed. "What if Miss Quince was so furious with Harold Sinclair for abandoning her that she killed him to make sure he couldn't marry anyone else?"

Selena's hand went to her mouth. "And framed Caroline Vernon for it?"

"Yes!"

"It could be." Selena lay back on her pillow. "They say the most common motives for murder are love, hate, and money. This would fall into the first two categories."

Athena was about to blow out the candle when her sister suddenly gasped and sat up in bed again. "I just realized. Miss Quince is the *apothecary's* daughter."

"So?"

"Harold Sinclair was *poisoned!*"

Athena caught on. "Working in the apothecary shop, Miss Quince must know all about poisons."

They exchanged an excited look across the room. "Could she have been the driver of the runaway carriage?"

Athena considered that. "It's possible. I couldn't tell if it was a man or a woman. If not, she could have paid someone to do it."

"True."

"And even if we're totally wrong about the carriage, Miss Quince had a motive to murder Harold Sinclair."

"Was she at that garden party?"

"I don't know. I think it's time to talk to her again."

"I'll do it," Selena offered.

Athena shook her head. "No. You must promise to stay out of this. I don't want another carriage accident, with you as the intended victim."

Selena grimaced. "I have the same fears, Athena, on your behalf."

"Miss Quince already knows that I question Caroline Vernon's culpability. It won't be news to her if I bring it up again."

"Even so. Will you be careful of what you say to her?"

"I will. But only because if I hope to get a confession out of her, it will take a bit of finesse."

ON HER WAY to the apothecary, Athena ran a few errands at the grocer's shop, the bakery, and the haberdashery, where she asked if anyone knew anything about Ethel Leighton. Everyone remembered hearing about the maid who had given incriminating testimony at Caroline Vernon's trial, but no one had any idea what had happened to the woman since.

Athena slipped inside the apothecary shop at five minutes before closing and waited until the last customer had left. She went up to the counter, where Miss Quince had just placed a heavy-looking box that she began to tie with string.

"Miss Quince, I'm glad I caught you before you closed. I need a dozen candles, please."

"Tallow or beeswax?" Miss Quince replied matter-of-factly.

"Tallow. I prefer beeswax—they're far less smoky and smell so much better—but I need to economize."

"Don't we all?"

As Miss Quince fetched the box, Athena remarked casually, "I visited Woodcroft House recently. I suppose *they* use only beeswax candles."

Miss Quince frowned. "*They* can afford it." She stated the

price of the candles.

As Athena paid for them, she launched into her prepared speech. "Speaking of Woodcroft House, I hope you won't think it impertinent of me to mention this, Miss Quince. But I just learned that you were meant to be the mistress of that great house."

Miss Quince looked at Athena sharply. "Who said so?"

"My housekeeper, Mrs. Lloyd. She had the most wonderful things to say about you. How thoughtful you are, how promptly you have always filled every order she has ever placed, and how devoted you are to your father." Mrs. Lloyd had never said any such thing. But Athena told herself that flattery was an acceptable kind of white lie, and it seemed to hit its mark.

"Did she really?" Miss Quince stood taller and lifted her chin. "Mrs. Lloyd and I have so rarely spoken. I had no idea she ever thought of me at all."

"Yes, and the other day, Mrs. Lloyd mentioned that years ago, she and everyone in the village dearly hoped that you and Harold Sinclair would marry."

Miss Quince's eyes grew wide. "Is that so?"

"I don't know what happened between you and Mr. Sinclair, but … my sister Diana was once engaged to a man who dropped her to marry someone with a larger fortune. It nearly broke her heart."

Miss Quince hesitated, as if debating whether—or how—to reply. At length, she said, "That's exactly what happened to me."

"Oh?"

Miss Quince toyed with a piece of string. "Harry and I went together for four years. We were everything to each other. He always said that we would marry. He used to call me his 'princess.'" Her lips pressed tightly together, and her eyes flashed. "Then all at once, he cut me off without a word. Refused to see me. He wouldn't even reply to my letters. That was when I learned he had offered his hand to *Caroline Vernon*." She infused the last two words with bitterness.

"I can't imagine how hard that must have been for you."

"It was mortifying. I'd been with Harry so long that my reputation was ruined, even though I had done nothing to deserve it. But Harry didn't care." Miss Quince's nostrils flared, and her mouth curled with distaste. "And Caroline Vernon was just a pretty face. She didn't understand what she had."

Athena continued fishing. "You were at the garden party the night that Mr. Sinclair died, I believe?"

"I was. I put on my best dress, and I went to that party hoping I could change Harry's mind."

"Did you talk to him?"

Miss Quince paused and glanced away. She continued twisting the string in her hands. "No. He was always surrounded by people. I couldn't get near him."

Athena, sensing that Miss Quince was being less than truthful, leaned forward on the counter and lowered her voice confidentially. "It must have been so awful, to watch Miss Vernon beg him to break off their engagement and to hear his refusal."

"That's when I learned what kind of man he was," Miss Quince said coldly. "He tossed me aside like yesterday's rubbish."

Athena's pulse skittered. "I thought you said you couldn't get near Mr. Sinclair?"

Miss Quince started. "I beg your pardon?"

"You said he was always surrounded by people. So how did you hear what he and Miss Vernon said to each other?"

That seemed to take Miss Quince aback. She hesitated again and then her eyes grew hard. "They were talking that loud—*anyone* could hear," she said quickly. "It's late, Miss Taylor. I must lock up."

At that moment, the curtain separating the shop from the back room was thrust aside and Mr. Quince strode out. He set a glass bottle on the counter.

"This tonic is for George Osborn," he announced brusquely. "See to it that he gets it at once, Margaret."

"Papa, the delivery boy has already left for the day."

"Then deliver it yourself, girl. And be quick about it!"

Miss Quince's face fell. "But, Papa. I must reconcile the books and clean up in back. Can't this wait until tomorrow?"

"No, it can't. I promised Mr. Osborn that I'd deliver it this evening. He's at the pub waiting for it."

"I'd be happy to deliver the tonic to Mr. Osborn," Athena volunteered. "The pub is on my way home."

"I don't think—" Miss Quince began.

"Did anyone ask what *you* think, Margaret?" Mr. Quince turned to Athena. "Thank you, Miss Taylor." To his daughter, he snapped in a condescending tone, "Go clean the back room. Now! Take the books with you. And don't dawdle! Maybe for once in your life, you'll get my dinner on the table before eight o'clock."

Before Athena could think of a comment, Miss Quince hurried out with cheeks burning.

Mr. Quince slid the medicine bottle across the counter. "If you're looking for the truth about Harold Sinclair," he said, looking Athena directly in the eye, "don't waste your time talking to my daughter. She was an idiot, ruining herself with that man, but she's not a killer. Talk to George Osborn."

Athena was so surprised by this unexpected remark, she was nearly at a loss for words. "George Osborn?"

"If anyone hated Harold Sinclair, it was Osborn," Mr. Quince told her before disappearing to the back room.

Athena left the shop with the medicine bottle in hand, struggling to digest what she had just observed and heard. First off, Miss Quince. She had clearly come to hate Harold Sinclair. But had she stooped to murder? Mr. Quince obviously didn't think so, but fathers didn't always know what their daughters were up to.

And what about Mr. Quince's last charge?

"If anyone hated Harold Sinclair, it was Osborn."

Why?

Athena was determined to find out.

CHAPTER EIGHTEEN

Athena had never visited the George and Dragon, which sat on the corner of Main Street at the south end of the village, a seventeenth-century building so covered in creeping ivy that it almost entirely obscured the grey stone beneath.

Pubs were generally considered to be a space for men only, other than some of the staff, but nothing could have kept Athena out of the place this evening. She entered to find a good-sized room with rough, plank flooring and whitewashed walls, a stone hearth emitting the welcome warmth of a blazing fire, and a handful of patrons at the long, oak bar. Athena studied the roomful of customers and spotted Mr. Osborn at a table in back, drinking beer with Mr. Carson, one of the crewmen who had worked on her roof.

Athena began by approaching the bar, where Miss Osborn was wiping down the counter. "How are you?" she asked the barmaid.

The young lady's eyes narrowed as if confused to see Athena there. "Well enough. Forgive me, Miss Taylor. I've been meaning to write to thank you for the medicine you sent. It didn't cure my cough, but it's helped to control it quite a bit."

"I'm so glad." It bothered Athena to think that Miss Osborn's own father hadn't been willing to pay for a medicine that had apparently done her some good. And that Sally Osborn might have died needlessly, if she had indeed tried to blackmail someone to get money to help her sister.

"Can I help *you* with something?" Miss Osborn asked.

"I'm here to deliver this tonic to your father." Athena showed Miss Osborn the bottle and explained that the apothecary shop's boy had left for the day.

"Papa's sitting in the back with Mr. Carson, his best friend."

"I saw that. I'd like to order a beer."

Miss Osborn grinned. "Well, aren't you the bold one. Dark or light?"

"Dark, if you please. And would you be so kind as to bring it to the table where your father and Mr. Carson are sitting?"

"Yes, miss." The barmaid chuckled. "A glass of our finest stout coming right up, as soon as I can pump it from the keg. And it's on the house."

Athena thanked her kindly and crossed to her quarry.

"Mr. Osborn. Mr. Carson. Pray, excuse me."

Both men glanced up. Mr. Carson quickly rose to his feet and doffed his cap. Mr. Osborn gave her an incredulous stare. He grabbed his cane and was about to stand, but Athena stopped him with a raised hand.

"Please, sir, don't get up. I'm here because your order was ready at Quince's Apothecary. I offered to bring it to you on my way home." She handed him the medicine.

"Appreciate it," he grumbled as he accepted the bottle and shoved it in a pocket.

"You're most welcome. Would you mind if I joined you? I ordered a beer."

Mr. Osborn's jaw dropped, and he seemed to be struggling for a reply.

Mr. Carson scratched his curly, blond head and then pulled out the third chair at the table. "We'd welcome your company, miss."

"Thank you." Athena sat.

Mr. Carson resumed his own seat. Miss Osborn appeared with a glass of dark, creamy stout and placed it on the table before Athena. "Enjoy," she said before retreating.

"What's the medicine for, Osborn?" Mr. Carson asked. "Your ghost arm or your hip?"

"Both."

"Does it help?"

"Sometimes," Mr. Osborn muttered as he raised his beer. "Drink is better."

Athena and Mr. Carson laughed, and they all took a sip from their respective glasses.

Athena enjoyed the beer, which had a creamy head and a refreshing, robust flavor. She reminded herself to sip slowly so she could keep a clear head and focus on her task. Somehow, she had to get Mr. Osborn to talk about his relationship with the late Harold Sinclair.

Turning to Mr. Carson, she said, "I cannot thank you enough, sir, for the masterful work you did on my roof."

"I can't say how masterful it was until it rains again," Mr. Carson admitted with a shrug. "But it was an honor and a pleasure to work at Thorndale Manor again. An old house like that always needs some kind of repair."

"Best job we ever did was when we added on that conservatory," Mr. Osborn reflected moodily, taking a drink of beer.

"Did you help build that room, Mr. Osborn?" Athena asked.

"I did. Back when I had two good arms and two good legs."

Mr. Carson wiped foam from his upper lip with the back of his sleeve. "You were always the best man on any crew, Osborn."

"I'd still be if I hadn't taken that fall," Mr. Osborn insisted. "Correction: if that scoundrel Sinclair had only been a gentleman."

Athena's pulse leapt. Here was her opening. "To which Mr. Sinclair are you referring? Harold or Neville? Or their father, perhaps?"

"Harold, of course. The father had died some years before." Mr. Osborn's mouth tightened. "Harold Sinclair wasn't worth the ground he walked on."

"What was your complaint against him?" Athena asked.

"My *complaint?*" Mr. Osborn let go a loud, scornful breath. "Nothing much, just a lame hip and the loss of my right arm."

Mr. Carson interjected. "It was Harold Sinclair's fault."

"How so?"

"We were putting a new roof on the stables at Woodcroft House," Mr. Carson explained.

"I was on top of the ladder with the tool bucket when my hammer slipped from my hand," Mr. Osborn put in.

The men shared the details in tandem in such a rapid manner, Athena guessed it was a subject they had discussed many times before.

"Harold Sinclair and I were standing below," Mr. Carson added. "I was going to bring the hammer up to Osborn, but Sinclair was impatient and grabbed it first."

"Sinclair tossed the hammer up to me. But in trying to catch it, I lost my footing and fell to the ground."

"Oh, no." Athena could envision the scene, having so recently witnessed the dangers of roof repair.

"The stables are only one story high; otherwise, Osborn would have broken his neck."

"They had to carry me home. I begged Sinclair to summon a doctor from York, but would he?" Mr. Osborn slammed his fist against the table. "No! The penny-pincher called Mr. Quince."

"Osborn's hip grew back all wrong and his arm festered." Mr. Carson made a face.

"What a terrible thing." Athena's heart went out to Mr. Osborn. "I take it that is what occasioned the amputation?"

Mr. Osborn nodded. "An operation which *Quince* performed. I'm lucky it didn't kill me. And what's worse, Miss Taylor? Harold Sinclair refused to pay the bill."

Athena couldn't disguise her shock. "That is unacceptable."

"I got up a collection plate in the village." Mr. Carson's eyes were stormy with anger. "We all gave what we could. But Osborn had to pay the rest out of his own pocket."

"Took me over a year to pay Quince back. The money had to come from my daughters' wages, for I was out of work and have been ever since." A vein pulsed in Mr. Osborn's forehead. "We were working on Harold Sinclair's property. He had all the money in the world. Yet he left me maimed for life and holding the bag. I'll never forgive him for that. *Never.*"

"I'm so very sorry that happened to you," Athena said.

"Sinclair was never sorry." Mr. Osborn's face was beet red now. "He didn't even have the decency to visit me when I was laid up."

"Dying was too good for that bastard," sneered Mr. Carson, who raised his glass as if in a toast. "May Harold Sinclair rot in hell."

An odd look passed between the two men. It seemed to indicate a sense of silent satisfaction—or was it collaboration?

"May Harold Sinclair rot in hell," Mr. Osborn echoed.

Both men drained their glasses.

"And on that note, I'm off for home." Mr. Osborn shoved his chair back, retrieved his cane, and lumbered awkwardly to his feet. "Bridget always leaves me a meat pie in the larder and it's better than anything the George and Dragon serves."

Mr. Carson also stood. "It was a pleasure chatting with you," he told Athena.

"And you, sirs," she said, rising, and sorry that the conversation was over.

"Thank you for dropping off the tonic," Mr. Osborn said in a low, grudging tone.

"You're welcome. Good evening, gentlemen."

The men left. Athena took one more sip of her beer, savoring its freshness and wishing she could enjoy a bit more—but she had been gone far longer than she had intended and was already starting to feel mild effects from the drink. It would be inexcusable for her to return to school lightheaded.

A few minutes later, Athena was heading down the river path towards home, her body gently buzzing and her thoughts in a whirl.

She now understood what Mr. Quince had meant. It was no wonder that George Osborn had hated Harold Sinclair, the man Osborn blamed for leaving him maimed and unable to work.

Had that hatred led Mr. Osborn to commit a heinous act? Had he murdered Harold Sinclair? It was entirely possible.

But then again, the culprit might have been Margaret Quince.

Or Edward Ackroyd.

All three had hated the man.

As she passed the spot on the riverbank where Sally Osborn's body had been discovered, Athena tripped over an unseen tree root and nearly fell. She caught herself just in time and stood for a long moment, hands on her knees, catching her breath, her heart pounding with fright. She should have been more careful! If she had been a couple of feet closer to the river's edge, she might have tumbled into the churning waters.

She suddenly wondered—could Neville Sinclair have been right, after all? Had Sally Osborn similarly tripped and drowned?

But no, no. There was the matter of the blue shoes and the unslept-in bed. The maid had come down here to meet someone, and she'd been murdered—Athena knew it in her bones.

But who had killed her? And why?

A shiver coursed through Athena's body as and she hurried on. Was Sally's death indeed connected to the murder of Harold Sinclair? That connection seemed unlikely if George Osborn had murdered Sinclair, for what man would murder his own daughter? But all at once, Athena remembered something that turned that idea on its head.

Something Bridget Osborn had told her the day of Sally's funeral.

George Osborn had never loved Sally. His wife had died in childbirth and apparently, he had always blamed the child.

BY THE TIME Athena had gotten home, the dinner hour was over. The cook brought her a quick, cold meal. Athena requested a cup of hot coffee to clear her head and then joined her sister and their pupils for their evening activities. Selena kept giving Athena questioning looks, as if dying to know why she had returned so late.

It wasn't until they had retreated to the privacy of their study that Athena could share what she had learned. It had begun to rain, a quiet pattering that danced against the windowpanes. Athena added another log to the fire, but the room was still chilly, so they huddled on chairs before the hearth, wrapped in woolen blankets.

First, they talked about Miss Quince. Everything they had theorized about her still seemed perfectly sound. Next, they discussed their newest and most unexpected suspect: George Osborn.

"He had a solid motive to kill Harold Sinclair," Athena declared.

"Even with only one arm, he could have easily poisoned Sinclair's drink. But surely, he wouldn't have killed Sally?"

"We can't be sure the two deaths are connected," Athena pointed out. "But if they are—Miss Osborn told me that her father had no love for Sally, remember?"

"That's right! He blamed her for his wife's death."

"He called Sally 'the useless daughter.'"

"What a horrible thing to say." Selena shook her head, her eyes downcast.

"All her life, Sally kept trying to please him, to no avail."

Selena considered that. "If George Osborn killed Harold Sinclair, and Sally knew it, it would explain why she didn't tell the authorities at the time."

Athena nodded. "But her conscience had plagued her. I'll bet that's why she read the Bible daily. And all that time, her father, the man she'd been protecting, continued to criticize and demean her. Maybe, she finally cracked and decided to talk, her father found out about it, and he silenced her to save his own neck."

"But what about Sally's unslept-in bed, and the blue shoes?"

Athena bit her lip uncertainly. "There's a reason for that. We just haven't hit upon it yet. Something tells me that when we figure *that* out, we'll know everything."

"We now have three suspects." Selena crossed to her desk and took out a sheet of paper and a pen. "I'm going to write this down."

LIST OF SUSPECTS

- Edward Ackroyd: Did he murder Harold Sinclair to prevent him from marrying his true love, Caroline Vernon?

- Margaret Quince: Did she murder her lover when he jilted her to marry Caroline Vernon?
- George Osborn: Did he murder the man who caused him to lose his arm and his livelihood?

All three of these individuals, they agreed, had a clear motive. All three could have also done away with Sally Osborn. And any one of them could have been behind the runaway carriage that had almost run Athena down.

Selena brought the list to Athena, who studied it with a frown. "Wait. What about Ethel Leighton? How does she figure into this?"

Selena hesitated as she sat down again by the fire. "Good question."

"Miss Quinn and Mr. Osborn might have paid Ethel to lie about finding arsenic in Miss Vernon's room, to divert suspicion from themselves. But Edward would never have done so—and besides, he was apparently back at sea by that point."

"So he said, at least." Selena blew out a frustrated breath. "Something about the whole Ethel Leighton angle doesn't add up. Maybe we're wrong about her."

"Maybe." A sudden thought occurred to Athena. "What if

Ethel wasn't paid to lie about the arsenic at all? What if *she* killed Harold Sinclair and framed Caroline Vernon, and that's why she disappeared?"

Selena's eyes widened. "It's possible! But how on Earth can we prove that? We know so little about her."

Athena crossed her arms. "I need someone to talk to about this, if only to get advice. But I can't ask Neville Sinclair—he already made his opinion perfectly clear."

"Isn't Mr. Johnson in training to be the next parish constable?"

"Yes. But all we have are theories, Selena. Without proof, he'll just laugh at us."

"What can I do?"

"You can continue to teach with your usual skill and help keep this school running, as you have been doing."

"But I want to help with the case."

"I told you, after that carriage business, I need you to stay out of this." Athena sighed. "If only I could ask Mrs. Hillman—but I can't risk her having another stroke."

Selena lowered her gaze and said quietly, "Why don't you talk to Mr. Vernon?"

At the mention of his name, Athena's heart seemed to skip a beat. Was it really only a day ago that she and Mr. Vernon had exchanged that kiss? "No. I can't talk to him."

"Why not?"

"Because I brought up the subject with him once before. He considered it to be a wild goose chase."

"But we have more information now."

"True." Athena hesitated. Something else was true as well. She admired Mr. Vernon. She felt she could trust him. He had lived in Darkmoor Bridge all his life and knew all the parties involved. Perhaps Selena was right. Perhaps now that Athena had some solid theories to share, he would have a more open mind.

But after that kiss, how could she even approach him?

"'CORDELIA TOOK A deep breath and slowly entered the chamber. It was dark and cold. She heard someone breathing. Who could it be? Was the villain hiding there?'"

Miss Russell paused dramatically. She was reading aloud in the schoolroom from a chapter of her book in progress, *The Ghost of Tembry Hall*. The other four pupils leaned forward in their seats, hanging on every word.

"'A cold breeze rushed by Cordelia's face. But no window was open. It couldn't have been the wind. Suddenly, a bright-white figure appeared before her eyes. It was a ghost! The ghost of a woman with long, dark flowing hair! And she said—'" Miss Russell paused again, her blue eyes shining as she added in a tone filled with mystery, "To be continued tomorrow."

The students groaned in unison. "Keep reading, please!" cried Miss Cecelia.

"We want to know what happens!" exclaimed Miss Jones.

"Just one more chapter!" pleaded Miss Weaver.

Athena stood with a firm smile. "Sorry, girls, that's all we have time for this morning. Thank you, Miss Russell, that was most engaging." She glanced out the window. Although it had rained lightly throughout the night, the sky was clear now. "Class dismissed. Don't forget your essays are due tomorrow. Please proceed to the yard now for morning exercise. It's cold out, so be sure to wear your cloaks and beware of puddles."

As the girls filed out of the schoolroom, chattering, Athena gave Miss Russell a smile. The girl certainly had a talent for storytelling, and she knew how to keep her audience engaged and wanting more. Thankfully, these readings had appeared to fulfill the other pupils' need for scary stories, for as far as Athena could tell, there had been no more secret midnight meetings in the attic of Thorndale Manor.

Later, while Selena was teaching the next two classes, Mrs.

Lloyd announced an unexpected visitor. Mr. Vernon.

Athena met him in the entryway, where she struggled to rein in her errant heartbeat. His raven-black hair was combed back sleekly above his handsome face, and his smile and bright-blue eyes were full of warmth. His boots were wet and muddy, and she recognized his damp overcoat on the coat rack and his umbrella in the stand.

"Good morning," he said with a bow. "I've come to take advantage of the break in the rain, to see if our handiwork fixed the leak in the roof."

Only two days had passed since their kiss at the dower house, but it had felt much longer. Athena couldn't count how many times her thoughts had drifted back to that moment. *Is he thinking of it as well? Does he hope it would happen again?* If so, she must put an end to that kind of thinking immediately.

At the same time, she was glad he was here. It was the perfect opportunity to seek his advice about what she had learned in the matter of Harold Sinclair's demise—*if* she could drum up the nerve to broach the subject, which might annoy him.

"Very well, sir." She met his bow with a curtsy. "Feel free to make your inspection."

When he returned from the attic, Athena was waiting for him at the base of the stairs. "How does it look?"

"Shipshape. Replacing those broken pieces of slate seems to have done the trick."

"I'm so glad." Athena's insides quivered a bit as she steeled herself to speak. "Sir, may I have a word? I would like your advice on a particular matter, privately."

One of his eyebrows quirked. "'Privately'?"

"Yes," she replied hastily, blushing at how that word might be misconstrued. "I mean away from the eyes and ears of my pupils." *Arrgh. That didn't help.*

"Of course. Lead the way."

They retreated to the conservatory at the other end of the house.

"How may I help you?" he asked as they sat down across from each other on wicker chairs.

The damp air was imbued with the fragrance of the potted plants and trees that filled the glassed-in chamber. Athena fiddled with her hands. Adopting her most business-like manner, she began. "First, sir, I need to set something straight with you. It's about the other day at the dower house. When we … kissed."

"Yes?" His eyes twinkled.

"It was a lapse of decorum on my part. It can never happen again."

"I see." The light in his eyes dimmed.

"It is my hope that we can continue our friendship without the burden of any romantic entanglement."

"'Romantic entanglement'?"

"Yes. We agreed to be friends, and we must leave it at that."

After a brief pause, he said, "As you wish, Miss Taylor."

She detected regret in his voice and yet it seemed to be devoid of censure. "Thank you."

"Is there anything else?"

"Yes. It's a subject I have broached before. I remember your thoughts at the time but beg you to keep an open mind."

His forehead creased. "What subject?"

"The murder of Harold Sinclair."

He sighed. "Miss Taylor—"

"Please, hear me out. I have information that may cast new light on the case."

"'Case'? There is no *case*. I understand that you want to restore the reputation of Thorndale Manor, but this is not the way to go about it."

"Mr. Vernon, I seek the truth about this matter not only to redeem the good name of my house, but also to avenge your sister's death. Is not that truth a most valuable commodity and worth seeking at any price?"

He paused. "Not always."

She didn't know what to make of that. "Sir, you're one of the only people I can trust. I don't intend to disrupt your life. But in my quiet way, I am resolved to learn what really happened."

He pinched his lips together and looked away. Finally, he said, "Go ahead. I'm listening."

She told him everything. It took some time and to his credit, he listened without further protest, taking it all in. When she had finished, he said curtly, "May I speak now?"

"Please."

"First of all, you can strike Edward Ackroyd off your list. You said he wasn't even at that garden party."

"He may have been lying."

"Even if he was, Ackroyd adored my sister. If he had really killed Harold Sinclair, he would never have let Caroline hang for the crime."

"But he was already away at sea when she was arrested and convicted," Athena argued. "You told me he didn't hear about it until it was too late."

Mr. Vernon hesitated. "Still, if he'd done it, I can't see him letting Caroline's memory be forever tainted by the crime. Knowing him, he would have returned the moment he was able and turned himself in to the authorities."

Athena wished she could believe that. But who would admit to a long-ago crime for which they would most certainly be hanged, to redeem the reputation of a woman already long dead?

"I find it equally incredible that Margaret Quince could have killed Harold Sinclair," he went on. "I fully understand if she was angry or felt humiliated by the insensitive way he treated her. I could even believe in a spur of the moment crime of passion. But to imagine that Miss Quince could have deliberately plotted his murder—that she could have taken poison to that party and deposited it in his drink ... no. Extremely unlikely."

"And yet possible," Athena remarked.

"Perhaps," he conceded. "But I still don't believe it. And as for George Osborn—he couldn't have killed Harold Sinclair."

"Why not?"

"Because he fell from the stables's roof at Woodcroft House two weeks before Sinclair died. The man broke his arm and his pelvis and was in bed for months. He couldn't have attended that garden party."

Athena frowned. She hadn't had a chance to ask Mr. Osborn if he had attended that party—she'd just presumed he had. "It's awful, what happened to Mr. Osborn. I didn't realize the accident had happened just before that party." She suddenly remembered the odd look that had passed between Mr. Osborn and Mr. Carson at the pub. "Wait. Mr. Carson seemed equally upset by what had happened to his friend. He could have done the deed for him."

Mr. Vernon's brows raised. "Carson? I've worked with him for years. He would never murder a man, even one as despicable as Harold Sinclair."

"You can't be certain of that."

"Look, I know you have good intentions. But as I told you, I questioned everyone who was at that garden party. Nobody witnessed anyone poisoning Sinclair's drink."

"Did you ask Sally Osborn?"

He blew out a frustrated breath. "*Yes.* Sally Osborn had nothing illuminating to say."

"What about Ethel Leighton?" Athena reminded him. "Why did she lie on the witness stand? Was she blackmailed, or might *she* be the perpetrator behind all of this?"

"Now you're really stretching, Miss Taylor." He shook his head. "All this happened so long ago. Let it lie."

"I wish I could. But even if I'm wrong about these suspects, it doesn't change the fact that *you believe your sister was innocent.* How can we sit back and do nothing? Especially since the true perpetrator may have just attempted to kill *me.*"

"Attempted to kill *you?* What do you mean?"

Athena hadn't meant to bring that up. But there was no stuffing the cat back in the bag now. "Last week when I told you that a carriage nearly ran me over … it's possible that it wasn't an accident."

"What?" He stared at her. "You're saying that someone may have deliberately tried to run you down?" Off Athena's nod, he continued, "Why on Earth would they do that?"

Athena told him what she had said in the churchyard and what had happened at the apothecary's shop. "Mr. Chapman is making inquiries to see who might have hired that carriage."

Mr. Vernon's features tensed. "If you truly believe that might be the case, then confound it, Miss Taylor! Why do you still persist with this line of inquiry? Why haven't you given it up?"

"Because the thought of what Miss Vernon went through preys on my mind and keeps me up at night!" Athena cried.

"It keeps *you* up at night?" Mr. Vernon leapt to his feet. "You speak of the *thought* of what my sister went through. But you cannot know how truly bad it was. Pray, allow me to inform you."

CHAPTER NINETEEN

I N THE YARD beyond, Athena heard the chatter of their pupils as Selena led them back into the house for their next lesson. But inside the conservatory, all was silent.

Athena sat forward in her wicker chair, waiting, as Mr. Vernon began pacing the floor of the glassed-in chamber beside the potted plants and ferns.

"Caroline was dragged from our home, taken in irons to York Castle, and incarcerated in the Female Prison," he said at last. "I bribed my way in to visit her a few times." He let out a bark of disgust. "Debtors, I'm told, had more 'comfortable' rooms on the upper floor. But women felons were housed on the ground floor, where the food and living conditions weren't fit for an animal, much less a human being. Caroline slept on a pile of straw. They shaved her head, withheld water, and only removed her waste once a week. Her tiny cell was situated in the interior of the building without a single window or other means of admitting air or light. She sat in darkness day and night, encaged by moldy walls like a rat in a trap."

"Dear lord." A shudder swept through her. "Didn't they let prisoners take fresh air in a yard?"

"No." He ran an agitated hand through his hair. "By the time of Caroline's incarceration, York Prison had adopted a new style they called 'the separate system,' where prisoners were kept apart from each other at all times. Even prison chapels have dividers in them now to keep prisoners from talking to each other."

Athena was profoundly disturbed. "How long was she at York Prison?"

"Nearly three months. The assizes in York are held four times a year. Caroline had just missed one trial and hanging cycle and had to wait for the next. Many prisoners in the felons' wing got so ill, they didn't live long enough to see their trials. My sister might not have survived even those three months if I hadn't stepped in."

"What did you do?"

"Because she was a gentlewoman, I was able to *persuade* the governor of the prison"—he rubbed his fingers together to indicate that said persuasion had required a financial outlay—"to give Caroline better food and more water, and to allow her to work in the laundry. It was grueling labor, but my sister begged me to arrange it, for it got her out of that dark cell for a few hours a day. Although she wasn't supposed to talk to anyone, she befriended another prisoner, a woman named Harriet who also worked in the laundry." He ceased pacing and stopped a few feet away from her. "Harriet was serving a life sentence for stealing a leg of mutton to feed her starving family. She had gone to prison a healthy young woman, but two years later, she was so ill with consumption, she could hardly breathe."

"Oh! How horrible." Athena stood, her stomach churning. She couldn't bear to think of what these women and others like them had gone through. "I'm so sorry, Mr. Vernon. York Prison sounds like Hell on Earth."

"It was."

"What happened to Harriet?"

Mr. Vernon stared at the ground. "She died. And Caroline ..." He seemed unable to finish the sentence. Pain suffused his features, but it was soon replaced by resolution. "Miss Taylor. You asked for my advice. Well, here it is: the past is past. We cannot alter it, no matter how much we might wish to. I respect your desire to find out who was behind the criminal act of which my sister was convicted, but at this late date, it is a puzzle that cannot be solved. And as I said, I don't want that matter dragged out into public view again." He crossed to her and took both of her hands in his. "How many times must I say it? Please, *stop looking.*"

His expression was so imploring, and so filled with concern, that Athena's breath caught in her throat. Despite the gravity of the moment, the touch of his hands on hers caused sparks to ignite throughout her body. At the same time, her spirits flagged. He had dismissed every theory she had presented. "But, Mr. Vernon," she began.

"Please, no *buts.* I beg you to direct your efforts to something more productive: your students and your school." With that, he left the room.

Athena stood there, struggling to recover from the sensations still coursing through her. Why did she have to respond this way, every time this man touched her? Sudden tears burned behind her eyes.

Were they tears of frustration at the downtrodden state of her quest? Or tears of pain and sorrow for Caroline Vernon and other women like her who may have been unjustly incarcerated and hanged at York Prison? She couldn't be certain.

FROM HER HARD, wooden bench in the train's third-class compartment, Athena gazed out the window at passing fields and farms. She was on her way to York to visit the bookseller Mrs. Hillman had recommended. Riding the train was a relatively new experience, and Athena marveled at this technological and engineering feat that made it possible to travel at the whirlwind speed of thirty-five miles per hour.

It was a challenge to focus on the scenery, however, for her thoughts were occupied by her conversation with Mr. Vernon the previous morning, and his plea for her to *stop looking.*

If only she could. But having learned how much Caroline Vernon had suffered had made Athena even more determined to solve the mystery. She wouldn't seek Mr. Vernon's advice anymore. But she wouldn't give up. She would find a way to clear Miss Vernon's name, which would not only restore Thorndale Manor's tattered reputation, but Mr. Vernon's as well.

He may be against this at the moment, she told herself, *but when all is said and done, he'll be glad I stayed the course. And then …*

The memory of their kiss invaded Athena's thoughts. She ordered it to go away. She had made it clear that she was *not* interested in a romantic relationship with him. She would not waver in that intention, or in her plan to find the truth and set things right.

Athena found Hardwick Booksellers on a busy shopping street a few blocks from the York Minster. The moment Athena stepped inside the long, narrow shop lined with endless rows of books and inhaled the pleasing scent of old paper and bindings, she felt at home.

She spent a good hour and a half with the shop's proprietor, going over a list of books that she deemed suitable for a young girl's education and entertainment. Mr. Biggs was only too happy to charge the volumes to Mrs. Hillman's account. He promised to order any books they didn't have from their sister shop in London and to have the whole shipment delivered to Thorndale Manor within a week or two.

Athena left the shop feeling satisfied. How wonderful it would be, going forward, for each of her pupils to have her own copy of the textbook or novel they were studying! She was grateful to Mrs. Hillman for making this possible. *I shall happily read aloud to that good woman every week for the rest of my life, if she should wish it.*

Athena was about to hail a cab back to the train station, when a road sign caught her eye, indicating the way to Clifford's Tower. On a previous visit to York, she'd had a glimpse of the famous ruined keep of the medieval Norman castle. She recalled that it stood directly adjacent to York Prison, which was only a fifteen-minute walk from where she stood.

After hearing Mr. Vernon's account of Caroline Vernon's horrific experience at that prison, Athena felt a sudden need to see the place. Before she knew it, her footsteps were leading in that direction.

She soon arrived at Clifford's Tower, the semi-ruin of an immense, two-story, stone fortress that had been designed like a four-leaf clover and stood high atop a humanmade mound. The tower was situated within the perimeter of stone walls that enclosed York Castle, where the new prison had been constructed twenty-five years ago.

Athena continued along the boundary wall to the York Prison gatehouse, a crenellated stone fortress that resembled a small castle itself. Athena paused by a massive, wrought-iron gate and peeked in through the railings.

Within, she could see the castle courtyard, where she'd heard that the hangings took place. A wide-open area of scrubby lawn was surrounded by a series of imposing-looking buildings. The two most elegant were erected of sandstone and fronted by Ionic columns and pilasters. One of them, she presumed, must be the Assize Court. Which of the others housed debtors and felons? Which building was the Female Prison?

How many prisoners had been, and were still, unjustly incarcerated in this place?

Athena shuddered at the thought. She hungered to go inside those gates, and to stand in that empty courtyard where Miss Vernon had met her awful fate. But she knew that was impossible. The gates were locked, and she had no good reason to be here.

"Shiny, red apples," called out a high-pitched, reedy voice. "One for a penny."

A snowy-haired, withered-looking woman was seated on a stool outside the wall, beside a large basket of apples. Athena's stomach rumbled, reminding her that it had been many hours since she had eaten. She approached the woman and offered her a coin.

"Here ye go, missy." The old woman shined an apple against one sleeve of her faded dress before offering it to Athena.

"Thank you." Athena accepted the apple, her attention still focused on the imposing sites beyond those wrought-iron gates.

"Here to see a prisoner, are ye?" the old woman asked.

"More to … honor the memory of one," Athena replied distantly.

"Oh? I expect he were hanged?"

"Sadly, yes. And it was *a she.*"

The woman clucked her tongue. "Been selling apples here for nigh on forty years. I've seen far too many a felon hanged in that castle courtyard."

Athena looked at the elderly woman with renewed interest. "Do you happen to remember a hanging that took place nine years ago? A woman by the name of Caroline Vernon?"

The old woman pursed her lips and seemed to be lost in thought for a moment. "I should do. Not nearly so many women are hanged as men. Nine year ago, ye say? That would be 1841? What was her name again?"

"Caroline Vernon. She was accused of murdering the man to whom she'd been betrothed."

The woman's bushy, white brows quirked upwards, and she bobbed her head. "Aye, now I remember the one ye're speaking of. She were a lady, weren't she? Not the usual common filth?"

"She was a gentlewoman, yes." Athena's heart pattered rapidly. This woman had actually been here the day that Caroline Vernon had died. Athena wondered suddenly if Mr. Vernon had witnessed the hanging. *How dreadful that must have been.* "What can you remember about that day?"

"I'd say a good five thousand people turned out for that one. They'd put up posters all over York. 'Tis not often ye get to see a woman prisoner take the short drop, much less a woman of her class. Skinny, pale young thing, as I recall. Might have used to be pretty, but who could tell with that shaved head and sickly complexion? She held her head high, though, when they marched her up to the platform, I remember that. But ..." The old woman scratched her chest and let go a sigh. "The people who come to see a hanging are wicked, miss. They booed and shouted at her and cheered when the thing were over."

"How horrible." Tears pricked at Athena's eyes. "She was innocent, you know. She didn't commit the murder of which she'd been convicted."

The woman snickered. "That's what they all say, dearie. Most of them what get hanged here deserve what's coming to them."

Athena's heart felt as though it had begun to bleed. Incapable of further speech, she managed a small "Thank you" and, after giving the woman several more coins from her bag, she walked away.

At the railway station, Athena—her stomach too tightly wound to eat—gave the apple to a hungry-looking young lad selling newspapers. During the train ride to Darkmoor Bridge, she barely noticed the passing landscape, so deep was she in unhappy contemplation about all that she had seen and heard.

Miss Vernon, Athena vowed silently as she wiped away tears, *I swear I will find out who did this to you. I will avenge your death.*

And I hope it will help you to rest in peace.

ATHENA'S DREAMS THAT night were haunted by what she'd seen and heard at York. She found herself walking the endless halls of a prison, past cells housing starved, bald, wailing women prisoners who shoved their thin arms through the bars and pleaded with Athena to get them out.

The dream's tortuous route reached the end of a hall. Athena stopped short at the sight of the prisoner who stared out at her from behind the bars. She was rail thin, her head had been shaved, and her features were hollow—but Caroline Vernon's cornflower-blue eyes were recognizable, as vivid as those in the portrait Athena had seen, yet now haunted with fear and misery.

"Find Ethel Leighton!" Miss Vernon whispered. "Find her and free me!"

"Ethel Leighton?" Athena repeated.

"She lied on the witness stand. I don't know why. Perhaps someone told her to do it. Promise me that you will find her!"

"I will, I promise!" Athena replied before awakening with a gasp.

Their new maid, Laura, a sweet, quiet woman in her mid-twenties whose dark-brown hair was neatly pinned up beneath her white cap, was opening the curtains. Athena lay in bed, crumpling the edge of her coverlet with dismay.

"What's wrong?" Selena was at the basin, washing her face.

"I had an awful dream." Athena told her sister about it and sighed. "If only I could make good on that promise. If only I could find Ethel Leighton and learn why she lied. Did she have a motive to kill Harold Sinclair? Was she blackmailed? Either way, if I could get her to admit to her part in this, it would help disprove Caroline Vernon's guilt."

"But to find her, we need to know her married name and uncover some clue as to where she lives now," Selena said as she dried her face.

"I've asked so many people about it," Athena replied. "Nobody has been able to help."

"Pardon me, Miss Taylor." Laura glanced up tentatively from the hearth, where she was laying a new fire. "Did you say you're looking for an Ethel Leighton?"

"We are. She briefly worked here nine years ago."

Laura rose and wiped her hands on her apron, her eyes directed at the floor as she spoke. "There is a groundskeeper at Woodcroft House named Mr. Leighton. He used to let me play on the grounds as a girl."

Athena sat up abruptly. "Is this man any relation to Ethel Leighton?"

"I don't know."

Athena pulled back her covers and stood, newfound hope pouring through her veins. "Thank you, Laura."

As soon as her classes were finished that morning, Athena hurried to Woodcroft House, where she found the groundskeeper, Mr. Leighton, a sturdy, weathered-looking man, weeding the hedgerows.

Athena explained her errand. He nodded and informed her that Ethel was his cousin.

"I haven't seen her in many a year, miss. But we exchange letters now and then. Her married name is Hunt. She lives at Goose Down Cottage in Duxley-on-Green."

Athena was almost too excited to speak. "Thank you, sir."

Athena discovered that Duxley-on-Green was a small village just twenty-five miles distant, and accessible by the train to York. She wanted to call on Ethel Hunt without delay.

"What will you say?" Selena asked, when Athena had described her plans. "If she's truly guilty—if she stole money from the Vernons and lied on the witness stand—I doubt she'll be willing to share her misdeeds with you."

"I have to try." It was a long way to travel, however, without a guarantee of an audience.

Athena quickly wrote the woman a letter.

Thorndale Manor
Darkmoor Bridge, Yorkshire

Dear Mrs. Hunt,

Pray excuse my boldness in writing to you. My name is Athena Taylor. I am the headmistress at the Darkmoor Bridge School for Girls. I am acquainted with your cousin Mr. Albert Leighton, who speaks so very highly of you! He said you were a valued member of the staff at Thorndale Manor some years ago.

I will be in your neighborhood this Sunday afternoon. I should so like to meet you! Would it be convenient for me to call on you then? Many thanks and I look forward to hearing from you.

Best regards,
Athena Taylor

A reply came swiftly. It was brief and to the point.

Goose Down Cottage
Duxley-on-Green, Yorkshire

Dear Miss Taylor,

I will be at home this Sunday afternoon. My time is short, as I have six children and a great many responsibilities, but I should be pleased to meet you.

Best wishes,
Mrs. Ethel Hunt

After church on Sunday, Athena took the train to the stop a few miles before York, and from there walked the two miles to Duxley-on-Green. The village was small and quaint, and after asking directions, she found Goose Down Cottage, which stood on a side street in a row of tiny, identical, grey stone cottages. The patch of grass in front needed mowing, and the black paint was peeling on the front door.

A frazzled-looking servant in a plain, grey dress and white apron showed Athena to the front parlor, a small room with fraying furniture, where a plump woman in a yellow gown paraded back and forth, bouncing a wailing infant in her arms. Five children who looked to range from ages two to eight darted noisily about or played on the floor at her feet.

"Miss Taylor to see you," the serving woman announced. The children stopped carousing and crying and stared wide-eyed at Athena.

Athena smiled at the youngsters. "Hello. How are you all today?" The oldest two, a rosy-cheeked boy and girl, giggled.

The woman called out loudly, "Mary! Take the baby and all the children upstairs." After the servant and children had left, the woman held out her hand. "I am Mrs. Hunt."

Athena took the woman in, from her messy, brown hair to the spots on her yellow dress and matching slippers, wondering if, in addition to the other purported crimes of which Athena suspected her, could she be a killer as well? "It is a pleasure to meet you."

They shook hands.

Mrs. Hunt gestured to an available chair. "Please have a seat." As they both sat down, she added, "I admit I was surprised to hear from you, Miss Taylor. How do you know my cousin Albert?"

"I met him on the grounds of Woodcroft House," Athena replied truthfully.

"We don't correspond often. How is it that he came to speak of me?"

Athena now launched into her prepared story. "I'm writing a history of my house, Thorndale Manor. Just for my own personal records, you understand. Mr. Leighton said you were once on staff there and might be able to share some stories with me."

Mrs. Hunt's brown eyes grew wary. "I only worked at Thorndale Manor for a few months, and it was a long time ago."

"Yes, nine years ago, I think he said?"

"Something like that."

"Do you have any special memories of the place?"

Mrs. Hunt fidgeted with her hands in her lap. "Not really. I got married soon after. I just came and went."

"A rather notorious incident occurred around that time." Athena leaned forward in her chair. "I'm sure you know the story. Miss Caroline Vernon was convicted of murdering the man to whom she was engaged, Mr. Harold Sinclair."

Mrs. Hunt paused as if in reflection. "Oh. Yes, I do recall."

"What else do you remember of that time?"

"Nothing much. I was just a housemaid. I did my work, and I didn't mix with the family."

"I understand. But I was hoping you might know more." Athena lowered her voice. "Between you and me, I heard the most horrendous things about Miss Vernon's father, Mr. Arthur Vernon? It's said that he was forcing Miss Vernon into a marriage against her will. Was that true?"

"That's what I heard."

"Did you ever meet Harold Sinclair?"

"No." The woman's answer was simple but direct.

Athena had been hoping for a different reply—that there had been some heretofore unknown relationship between the two that might have given this woman a motive for murder. "Never? You had no interaction with Harold Sinclair whatsoever?"

Mrs. Hunt shook her head. "No. Mr. Sinclair wasn't a churchgoer, and I worked at Thorndale Manor, not Woodcroft House, and only for a short time, as I said. But Mr. Sinclair did call on Miss Vernon a few times. The master, Mr. Arthur Vernon, ordered us to leave them alone in the drawing room—shocking business, that! But I snuck a peek at him once when he arrived. Didn't like the look of him. He had hard eyes."

Athena believed her. *Well, then. That's that.* But Mrs. Hunt could still be guilty of thievery and giving in to blackmail. "What was your impression of Arthur Vernon? Did he treat you well?"

Mrs. Hunt frowned. "No. He was always short with me. 'Fetch this,' 'do that.' Never a smile or a kind word."

"I'm sorry," Athena said with sympathy.

"He kept telling me to clean out the fireplaces and lay new fires, even though that wasn't my job." Mrs. Hunt picked at the fabric of her skirts. "He kept complaining that I hadn't made the corners of his bedsheets tight enough. He shorted me on my pay on account of that, said he'd make up for it when I had 'learned to do my job properly.' I tried harder. No one could have made a bed with tighter corners than me, but it made no difference. He never paid me what I was owed."

Athena was beginning to understand Ethel better by the minute. "I imagine that must have made you angry."

"It did. But a servant is nothing. We have to be grateful for room and board and a salary, however pitiful."

Athena gave Mrs. Hunt a direct and encouraging look. "Had I been you, I would have found a way to get the money that was owed to me."

Something dark flickered in Mrs. Hunt's eyes. "Maybe I did."

Athena smiled confidentially. "Oh? I'm dying to know! What did you do?"

Mrs. Hunt squirmed and shook her head. "I shouldn't say."

"I won't write it down. This will just be between you and me."

Mrs. Hunt hesitated but then took the bait. "Well. I knew where the master kept his cash box, and where he hid the key. I took the money that was owed to me. And *between you and me*," she added, with a smile and a distant gleam in her eyes, "a great deal more."

Athena gave a gasp of feigned amazement. "How clever."

"I think so. I had met my Albert by then, you see, and we were engaged to be married. But we didn't have a penny to start our new life together. The master was so rich, he'd never miss that money." Mrs. Hunt looked highly pleased with herself.

"I hope no one found out what you had done?" Athena asked in a worried tone.

"I beg your pardon?"

"Darkmoor Bridge is a small village. Did anyone find out you had stolen that money?"

Mrs. Hunt's smile fled. She picked at her skirts again. "Well, the housekeeper made a fuss about it at the time, but she could never prove anything."

"Did anyone else suspect you and threaten you about it?"

Mrs. Hunt stirred restlessly. "No. Of course not."

"I know you gave testimony at Caroline Vernon's trial. You said you had found rat poison in her bedchamber."

The woman's brow furrowed over eyes that grew testy. "You asked me if I even recalled that, but you knew I testified?"

Athena's chest tightened. Somehow, she had to smooth this over. "Yes. Forgive me. It was just a way to bring up the subject. I was hoping you would admit to it freely."

"It's not something I like to talk about," Mrs. Hunt replied sharply.

"I understand." Athena took a breath. "I don't blame you for stealing that money, Mrs. Hunt. Nor would I blame you if someone had found out and put you in a difficult position—perhaps blackmailed you into saying something on the witness stand that wasn't true?"

Mrs. Hunt's gaze focused on the carpet. She seemed to be deep in thought. Suddenly, her mouth dropped open and with a gasp, she stared at Athena. "You're not really here to write a history of Thorndale Manor, are you?"

Athena's pulse skittered. "I've come a long way to learn the truth," she admitted. "It must be very hard to carry a secret like that for so many years. To have no one in whom to confide."

Mrs. Hunt's face went scarlet, but she remained mute.

Athena said quietly, "Did you really find rat poison in Miss Vernon's chamber?"

Mrs. Hunt waved an impatient hand. "What does it matter now? The woman is long since dead!"

"It matters to me, ma'am. I'm trying to run a school. As it turns out, parents aren't keen to send their daughters to live at a manor that once housed a convicted murderess. You have six children. Surely, you can understand my plight."

Mrs. Hunt glanced down at her shoes. "I see what you're getting at, Miss Taylor. But I don't see what can be done about it now."

"You can start by telling me the truth."

"I can't!" Mrs. Hunt cried in a shrill voice, the color draining from her face. "I can't!"

"Please, Mrs. Hunt. What really happened?"

A moment passed. Mrs. Hunt slumped in her seat and gave a long, reluctant sigh. "All right. But you must promise this will not go any farther than these four walls."

"Very well," Athena replied. She listened eagerly as Mrs. Hunt began her tale.

CHAPTER TWENTY

T HE ONLY SOUNDS that broke the stillness in Mrs. Hunt's cozy front parlor were the ticking of the old, wooden clock on the mantel and the crackling of the fire in the hearth. Athena struggled to sit patiently as Mrs. Hunt fidgeted in the chair across from her. At last, the woman spoke.

"A few weeks before Albert and I were to wed, we were in the pub one night and talking about the stolen money." Mrs. Hunt blinked rapidly. "Someone must have overheard. Soon after, I got a note from someone threatening to tell the parish constable. Unless I met him at midnight on the riverbank, by the bridge."

The same place where Sally Osborn had been found dead— and where she had presumably met her killer. "Did you meet him?"

"Yes."

"Did you recognize him?"

"No. He wore a mask."

"Otherwise, what did he look like? Was he tall or short? Thin or fat? What color hair did he have?"

"He was of medium height, I'd say, with broad shoulders, and he had blond hair."

Blond hair. It was a perfect description of Mr. Carson—if he had killed Harold Sinclair out of revenge for his friend George Osborn.

It was also a perfect description of Edward Ackroyd.

And Athena realized suddenly, of Mr. Neville Sinclair.

Something else occurred to Athena. Margaret Quince was also a blonde. "Is there any chance it could have been a woman disguised as a man?"

Mrs. Hunt paused. "I suppose. I remember he spoke very low and seemed to be disguising his voice. He—or she—said all I had to do to buy their silence was to say I had found rat poison in Miss Vernon's bedroom." Mrs. Hunt's lips quivered. "What choice did I have? Theft is a hanging offense, Miss Taylor."

"It doesn't excuse telling such a horrific lie, does it?"

A tear formed in Mrs. Hunt's eye, and she dashed it away. "Be careful whom you judge, Miss Taylor. I pray you are never put in the position I was. You can't know what decision *you* might make in such a circumstance."

I can, Athena thought. *I would never lie to save my own skin, if it caused an innocent person to die.* Quietly, she said, "I see that you have a good heart, Mrs. Hunt. And I believe your conscience has been troubling you for a long time. Please. Won't you come forward? Tell your story to the authorities and unburden yourself."

"I cannot!" Mrs. Hunt cried. "I'm a married woman with six young children! What would happen to them if I were to speak of this? I'd be sent to prison and hanged!" Mrs. Hunt stood, her eyes flashing. "If you breathe a word of this to anyone, I'll deny it. This conversation is over. Goodbye, Miss Taylor."

Athena left the house, deeply frustrated. At last, she was in possession of the truth, but she had no power to use it.

THE FOLLOWING AFTERNOON, Mr. Chapman found Athena in a quiet corridor at Thorndale Manor and informed her with chagrin that his inquiries about the runaway carriage had proven unsuccessful.

"I visited every inn within a ten-mile radius," he said, keeping his voice low. "They all hire out a great many post chaises and horses. As I had no way to name or describe the person we are looking for, I didn't get very far. I'm so sorry."

"Don't be." Athena matched his discreet tone to ensure that they would not be overheard. "I appreciate your efforts. I suppose it was too much to hope that you could learn anything by that means." She gave him a brief overview of her visit to York Prison and her talk with Mrs. Hunt.

His brow furrowed. "It sounds as though Miss Vernon might indeed have been innocent. But if Mrs. Hunt won't come forward, her admission is useless."

"I know. And yet it was helpful. Her blackmailer was a person of medium height with blond hair. Edward Ackroyd, Neville Sinclair, and Mr. Carson are all blond and of medium height. So is Margaret Quince. But Mr. Vernon repudiated every one of them. I've been thinking it over and I agree that if Edward Ackroyd *had* murdered Harold Sinclair, even if he didn't return to sea when he claimed, he would never have blackmailed Ethel Leighton into framing the woman he loved. And you said yourself, it couldn't have been Neville Sinclair. Which only leaves Mr. Carson and Miss Quince." She sighed. "Mr. Vernon wants me to give up my search."

"You should listen to him."

"I cannot."

Mr. Chapman placed his hat on his head. "So be it. But I still worry about you. If whoever killed Harold Sinclair is still out there, he—or she—won't want you looking into it. I fear you are putting yourself in danger, Miss Taylor, with every step you take." With a deep frown, he strode away.

Athena watched him go, unmoved by his warning. It was a risk she felt compelled to take.

"WHAT A GLORIOUS adventure Lydia is having on the high seas," Mrs. Hillman said, looking up with a smile from the wooly scarf she was knitting.

Athena had just read several chapters aloud from *The Wind Pirate* in the comfort of the drawing room at Darkmoor Park. "I have long dreamt of visiting foreign places," she admitted. "But I have never even left England. Have you done much traveling, Mrs. Hillman?"

"I have done my share. My husband and I used to tour all over. After he passed away, I kept it up. I have wonderful memories of holidays in the capitals of Europe and by the seaside."

"Did it ever get lonely, traveling by yourself?"

"It did at first. But when you travel, you meet so many people. A couple of years ago, I made some dear friends while staying at a seaside inn in West Sussex. We still write to each other. I've been meaning to invite them to visit me someday and host a house party—a reunion of sorts."

"How lovey that sounds. You should do it."

"Perhaps I shall. We all love music, so I could engage a singer or musician to perform here." Mrs. Hillman gave a happy sigh. "Speaking of which. Are your pupils excited about the upcoming concert?"

"They can speak of almost nothing else." A celebrated soprano from Edinburgh was due to perform in the village hall the following night. "Thank you so much, Mrs. Hillman, for providing the tickets. You have already been so generous. The books arrived yesterday, and they have made such a difference. And I cannot tell you how excited Selena and I and the girls are to be attending tomorrow's performance."

"I'm glad. I have given all the servants the night off and purchased tickets for them as well."

"How kind of you."

"This is a special event, and I can afford it." Mrs. Hillman glanced down at her work basket. "Oh, bother. I've run out of yarn." She gestured towards the bell pull on the wall. "Miss Taylor, please ring for the maid. I'll have her fetch a few more skeins."

"I'd be happy to fetch them for you, ma'am," Athena offered, rising.

"Oh? Thank you. They're in my work basket in my bedroom, up on the second floor—at the north end of the north hall, the one with a blue-and-gold coverlet on the bed. Take the servants' stairs; it's the most expeditious route."

"I'm on my way." Athena exited through a door at the far end of the room, which she had seen many a servant use in the past.

The narrow, winding staircase was gently lit by a small window at every landing. As Athena ascended, she heard the sound of footsteps heading down from above. She had just reached the small, second-floor landing when a gentleman rounded a turn in the stairs and came to an abrupt halt in front of her.

"Miss Taylor!" Mr. Vernon froze, and his cheeks colored slightly.

"Mr. Vernon." Athena's heart began to thud. She told herself it was due to surprise, not to the fact that he was standing barely two feet away from her.

Except for a brief *hello* at church, she had neither seen nor spoken to Mr. Vernon in over a week, since their conversation in the conservatory at Thorndale Manor. When he had taken her hands in his and implored her to give up her quest.

When she had responded to his touch like a candlewick to a flame.

The same exact response she was feeling now.

"What brings you to Darkmoor Park?" He rubbed his jaw, as if attempting to make sense of the moment. "Oh, that's right. You read to Mrs. Hillman on Wednesday afternoons?"

"I do." To Athena's dismay, the words came out sounding

rather breathless.

"What are you doing on the servants' stairs?"

"I … I'm fetching something for Mrs. Hillman from … from her bedchamber." Why was she stammering? Quickly she added, "What about you?"

He hesitated. "I … I was told by Mrs. Hillman that … that one of the servants had heard mice in the attic. I went up to check."

Why was he stammering as well?

"And are there mice?"

"I found no evidence of any. But I shall lay traps just in case."

Athena sensed that he wasn't being entirely truthful. Which was odd. She didn't think of Mr. Vernon as a secretive man.

Athena wondered suddenly, did his unease come from a very different source? Could it have anything to do with the same sensations she was feeling—a tightening of the lungs and a rapidly beating heart? All due to the fact that they were standing in such close proximity to each other in a small, confined space?

Athena found herself staring at his lips.

The memory of the kiss they had shared pervaded her mind.

A kiss she had told him must never be repeated. Now she regretted saying those words. Because despite all the promises she had made to herself, she longed for the feel of his lips on hers again. Even though she knew that if she kissed him again, she would never want to stop. She swallowed hard, trying to remember what they'd been talking about. *Oh, yes. Mice.*

"How nice of you. To help the mice."

"'Help the mice'?" he repeated. His voice was teasing.

Flustered, she replied quickly, "To help *with* the mice, I mean."

His lips were twitching, as if holding back a smile. Lips that she still couldn't take her eyes off of.

"I like to be of assistance when I can." He paused and seemed to be searching for something else to say. "How are … your readings going?"

"Very well. Mrs. Hillman and I both love Pryor Corbett's novels."

"How wonderful that you share common ground with regard to … that author."

Athena wanted to scream in frustration. Here they were, alone together, out of sight from the rest of the world. The perfect place for a stolen kiss. Why were they engaging in such ridiculous small talk?

"You have such a large library," Athena heard herself reply. "And you … you are fond of reading as well. You ought to give Pryor Corbett a try."

He lowered his gaze to hers. Those vivid, blue eyes were suffused with heat. "Perhaps I shall."

Athena swallowed hard. "Perhaps we could … discuss the book afterward."

"I would like that."

With every fiber of her being, Athena longed for him to take her in his arms. Could she convey her want with her eyes? Would he be able to read what she couldn't bring herself to say aloud? He seemed to do exactly that, for he leaned in close, and with his index finger, he traced her bottom lip, a movement that felt sinfully intimate.

"I haven't forgotten what you said about marriage and freedom," he breathed against her lips. "Something about friendship? No romantic entanglement? *No kissing.*" His eyes glittered. "However, the last time we tried this, I got the impression that you quite *like* kissing." Without further preamble, he brought his mouth to hers.

Athena melted into his kiss. It was utterly delectable, at first soft and questing and then filled with need on his part as well as hers. His arms enveloped her as he brought her tightly against him, until their bodies met and clung. She returned the embrace, wrapping her arms around his shoulders, one hand sliding up his neck to thread through his sleek, dark hair.

Their lips met and parted and melded together again with a

heat that threatened to consume her. As she kissed him, an unbidden thought resounded in her brain.

I love this man.

She had fought so hard to ignore her feelings, but they could no longer be denied. *I love him. I love him.* It was a revelation.

Far too soon, with a soft moan of pleasure, he released her mouth. Athena was still in the circle of his embrace, her hands resting along the curves of his neck and back, and her pulse was racing out of control.

"Now *that* was a fine kiss," he said quietly.

Their eyes met and Athena returned his smile, which seemed to be filled with affection. She longed to tell him how she felt. But her mind whirred with sudden confusion. Should she reveal her heart? Where could it lead?

Just then, Athena heard the door to the stairwell opening from a floor above and the sound of footsteps descending. Mr. Vernon let her go.

"I shall see you soon, I hope?" he asked under his breath before disappearing down the stairs.

Athena grabbed the handrail and stood quaking in his wake. A maid, carrying an armful of used linens, clomped down the stairs and stopped at the landing, jerking in surprise when she saw Athena. Gathering her wits, Athena yanked open the door to the second floor and sped through it.

She found Mrs. Hillman's bedchamber and completed her errand, struggling to banish all thoughts of the kiss, and what it might mean, from her mind. Her heart was still racing when she returned to the drawing room and gave Mrs. Hillman the skeins of yarn she required.

As Mrs. Hillman thanked Athena and picked up her knitting, she said casually, "Ian dropped by. Unfortunately, he had to leave, but he said he ran into you on the stairs?"

Athena's face grew warm as she resumed her seat. "He did."

Mrs. Hillman gave her a knowing look. "You seem flushed, my dear."

"Do I?" Athena touched her cheeks self-consciously.

"Ian's a very attractive man, isn't he?" Mrs. Hillman's lips twitched.

"Yes. Very attractive."

"And so kind and attentive. I've always thought it a shame that he never married and settled down."

"Perhaps he will one day." Once again, an image presented itself to her, of Mr. Vernon sitting with his bride, intimately conversing by candlelight. But this time, it wasn't Athena sitting at his side. It was a woman she didn't recognize.

A cold wave of envy washed over her. The idea of Mr. Vernon marrying someone else cut Athena to the quick. *Why does she get to have him?* Athena thought, upset. *I love him. If he marries anyone, it should be me.* But she was still against the idea of marriage. Wasn't she?

"He is as you say, kind and … thoughtful." Athena sensed she was babbling but couldn't stop herself. "It was good of him to check your attic for the mice."

"I beg your pardon?" Mrs. Hillman glanced up from her needlework. "What mice?"

Athena squinted at her. "He said one of your servants … heard mice up there?"

Mrs. Hillman gave her a blank look, but then with a little gasp and a quick nod, she said, "Oh, yes. The mice. That's right. I had forgotten."

For the second time that day, Athena sensed that the person with whom she was speaking was hiding something.

But what?

"HE KISSED YOU?" Selena clasped her hands with undisguised delight.

She and Athena were sitting on high stools at the kitchen

table at Thorndale Manor, enjoying a midnight feast of cheddar cheese, brown bread, sliced apples, and hot tea. Athena had tried to keep her liaison with Mr. Vernon a secret, but Selena had ferreted it out of her, insisting that Athena had a new glow in her cheeks.

Athena set down her teacup and covered her face with her hands. "And I kissed him back. Twice."

"*Twice?*"

"Yes. Once at the dower house—"

"I *knew* something had happened between you that day!" Selena interjected triumphantly.

"—and again, this afternoon. In a stairwell. At Darkmoor Park."

Selena breathed a joyful sigh. "How was it? Kissing him?"

"They were the best kisses I've ever had." Not that she'd had that many. Until recently, she had only been kissed twice in her entire life. Once, at age fourteen—a brief peck behind the village hall after a dance lesson, by a boy who had moved away soon after. And once by Giles Shaw, a kiss that she had considered quite nice at the time. But Mr. Vernon's embraces had given her an entirely new perspective on the kissing experience. *His* kisses had been tender, body-shaking, and thrillingly intimate.

"Oh, Athena! I'm so happy for you!" Selena stood and hugged Athena with fervor. "I will be so glad to call Mr. Vernon my brother!"

"Wait, wait! Don't get ahead of yourself." Athena withdrew from her sister's embrace. "They were just kisses. Not a proposal."

"Perhaps, but a kiss often leads to a proposal." Selena sat down again and took a bite of apple topped with cheese. "You can't fool me. I have seen this coming. I've noticed how you look at Mr. Vernon, and how he looks at you."

"What do you mean, *how he looks at me?*" But Athena could guess the answer; she had glimpsed it in his eyes.

"The man adores you."

"Does he?"

"Yes! Anyone could see it. And you're just as much in love with him, aren't you?"

Athena took a long, deep breath before admitting, "Yes! Oh, Selena! He's the most fascinating, intelligent, and wonderful man I've ever met. I think I've loved him for a while now but couldn't admit it to myself."

"He's going to ask for your hand. I'm sure of it."

"But—I can't *marry him!*" Athena's heart sank. "You know my position on marriage."

Selena crossed her arms over her chest. "And you know that for years, *I* have felt the same way. I love our work here as much as you do. But I am starting to think that the wedded state might actually be advantageous for some women, if they are careful about whom they choose. Look at Diana. She is so happy! Look at Mother and Father. It's sad that Mama became ill, but they were so well-suited. Don't you want to have children of your own?"

"I do," Athena admitted. "But I've accepted that, if I want to continue our work, I will have to give up that pleasure."

"Perhaps you won't have to give it up. I have a suspicion that Mr. Vernon is more open-minded and forward-thinking than many gentlemen. He said he is very much in favor of girls' education, after all."

Athena hesitated, recalling something else he had said to her, the day they had walked to the dower house. *"But if you met a man who felt as you do? Who allowed you to keep your freedoms?"*

Had he been talking about himself? *If* Mr. Vernon was truly thinking of proposing to her, was it possible that he would accept her desire for a kind of independence, and to continue working and running the school?

It still bothered Athena that if she married, the law would instantly turn over everything she possessed to her husband, including this very house. But perhaps Mr. Vernon was the kind of man she could trust to do the right thing with that kind of control. After all, he had loved Thorndale Manor all his life. It *had* been his birthright long before she had acquired it.

Athena smiled. *If Mr. Vernon loved her as she loved him*—the idea of marrying him was becoming quite appealing. More than appealing. It was absolutely intoxicating.

IT RAINED THAT night, a torrential downpour that continued until the wee hours of the morning. Although Mr. Vernon had checked the attic once for leaks after fixing the roof, this was a much heavier rainfall. Athena decided to check it herself one more time. She quickly ventured upstairs while Selena was teaching period two.

A dim light filtered in through the row of attic windows, enabling Athena to make her way across the cluttered space without the benefit of a candle. To her relief, there was no sign of dampness in the problem spot. She was about to leave when a rustling made her pause in her tracks. It was coming from the far end of the attic, which she had never explored. Was it mice?

Mr. Vernon had warned her not to explore up here on her own. *"This attic is old and not particularly safe,"* he had said. *"The floor is not sound in places."* But Athena had seen no evidence of an unsound floor. She didn't like the idea of rodents nesting in her attic. Once you let them breed, they would be even more difficult to eradicate. She must—she *would*—investigate.

Athena pressed on, past several red-brick chimney stacks that shot up to the roof, finally reaching one last chimney at the far end of the house. She heard the rustling sound again and realized it was just a pair of pigeons flapping their wings outside one of the attic windows.

She was about to turn back when her attention was drawn to the last chimney stack in front of her. Something about it felt odd. It was much larger than any of the other chimneys. Moreover,

Athena seemed to recall that there were no fireplaces on this side of the house. What was a chimney doing here?

After studying the brick expanse, she deduced that it wasn't a chimney stack at all. *It's a wall.* All the other attic walls were made of rough, unfinished timbers. Why was there a finished brick wall at this end?

It appeared to be an ordinary brick wall with a typical running bond pattern. Some instinct compelled Athena to inspect the wall more closely. She detected a hairline crack that ran along the edge of the mortar in a more or less rectangular shape. It almost resembled a door, except that it was edged on the right side by the pattern of the staggered bricks.

Doors don't belong in brick walls. Unless …

Athena recalled, at the Darkmoor Park dower house, Mr. Vernon pointing out a hidden door that opened by a spring mechanism. *Could this be a hidden door as well?* If so, it was a clever spot for it. Anyone inspecting the attic would simply think this wall to be the end of the building.

Fascinated, Athena pressed hard on the wall. Nothing happened. She tried again, pressing with all her might as close as she could to the edge of the door-shaped pattern.

A soft *click* pierced the silence of the attic.

To Athena's fascination, a heavy door, edged on the right by the alternating bricks of the running bond pattern, swung open on unseen hinges.

CHAPTER TWENTY-ONE

Athena's heart seemed to trip over itself. The brick door had only opened a few inches. What lay inside? Cautiously, she pulled the door fully open.

Her breath caught.

Beyond lay a hidden room, about the size of a modest parlor. No one appeared to be within. Athena guardedly entered the concealed space. Light filtered in through the lace curtains covering three windows, enabling Athena to take in the chamber at a glance.

Her first thought was that this might have been a priest's hole, a secret hiding place built into old houses like Thorndale Manor during the sixteenth and seventeenth centuries, when Catholics had been persecuted and discovery could mean torture and execution. If so, it had been updated since then, for the furnishings in this room were of a much more recent vintage.

The walls and ceiling were plastered. A faint shadow on the finished oak floor suggested that there might have once been a throw rug. The furnishings were similar to Thorndale Manor's guest bedrooms, fine-quality mahogany pieces that included a single bed, a narrow wardrobe, a dresser, a table, two chairs, and a small desk. Someone, Athena reasoned, had once spent a great deal of time here and had done their best to make it comfortable.

When had this room last been occupied, and by whom? There was a fine layer of dust upon the furniture, an accumulation that Athena guessed must have gathered since she and her sister had taken possession of the house. *Did its previous owner know about this room's existence? Of course he did,* Athena reasoned. That must have been why Mr. Vernon had cautioned Athena not to venture in this direction in the attic. He had hoped she wouldn't discover this place.

But why? Why was it important to keep an empty room a secret?

The mattress was stripped and there wasn't a single personal item in evidence. *Perhaps,* Athena thought, *Mr. Vernon removed all such things when he sold the house.* But if so, why had he left the furniture in place?

An idea began to form in Athena's mind. To test her theory, she tried to slide out the chair from the desk, but it wouldn't budge. She knelt down and discovered that the desk chair had been bolted to the floor. Indeed, every piece of furniture had been similarly bolted down.

Athena could think of only one reason for doing that. *Someone wanted to make sure the furniture never moved, to help ensure that whoever was up here was not overheard.*

Perhaps, when Mr. Vernon moved out, he hadn't had time to unbolt all the furniture. Or perhaps he hadn't cared. After all, he had left everything else in the attic.

But who had used this room, and when, and for what purpose?

From her kneeling position on the floor, Athena noticed a tiny gap between the floorboards in an area that might have once been covered by a throw rug. One of the boards was smaller and looser than the others. Could it be the cover for a hidey-hole? She fiddled with the board until she succeeded in prying it up.

There was indeed a shallow, open space beneath it. It seemed to be empty. But was it?

Athena reached her hand down inside the hole as far as she could go. Nothing. Suddenly, her fingers touched what felt like the edge of a piece paper. She picked at it until at last, she was able to maneuver the page out from the hole.

It was a piece of good-quality paper, covered with writing in black ink in a bold hand. Athena rose, moved to the desk chair, sat down, and began to read.

> *Lydia pierced him with a direct look and a stern smile. "John Brandon," she warned. "Pray do not underestimate me or my skills with a blade."*
>
> *The man laughed. "My darling, I know better than that. Ever since the day we met, when you held your blade to my throat, I have learned to never underestimate you. And I have no wish to argue with my better half."*

Athena froze. *Lydia. John Brandon.* They were the heroine and hero from the novels of Pryor Corbett.

She perused the entire page, then read it again. Athena had devoured every novel Pryor Corbett had ever written, many times, and *this* was a scene that had never been published.

What was it doing here, in a secret room in the Thorndale Manor attic, hidden beneath the floorboards?

Was this, Athena wondered, *an homage to Pryor Corbett's series of beloved stories? If so, who had written it?* Might it have been one of the servants? If that proved to be the case, it would be rather extraordinary. Many of the servants at Thorndale Manor couldn't read or write, other than the top ones. And those who could worked long hours and had little if any time for reading, much less writing.

Might it have been one of her students? Miss Russell was a good writer, for example, despite her youth. But no. Athena knew her pupils' handwriting well and this was a different, far more polished hand. In fact, there was something about it that seemed familiar, but she didn't know why.

It suddenly occurred to Athena that this room, and the house it stood in, had once—and not so long ago—belonged to Ian Vernon.

With a gasp, she made the connection in her brain. She had seen Mr. Vernon's architectural drawings of the Darkmoor Park dower house. The handwriting on those drawings, and Mr. Vernon's signature, had been similar to the writing on the page she was holding.

The truth struck her with the force of a thunderbolt. Athena's hand went to her mouth in shock. *Mr. Vernon must have written this!*

Despite his insistence that he wasn't acquainted with Pryor Corbett's work, could he be a devoted admirer in secret?

Or was this page a brand-new effort from the pen of Pryor Corbett himself?

THAT NIGHT, AFTER the girls were snug in their beds, Athena showed Selena the page she had found and then took her sister up to the attic to see the secret room for herself.

As they took in the chamber by candlelight, Selena shook her head in wonder. "*Are you serious? You really think Mr. Vernon is our favorite author?*"

"I think it's possible," Athena replied, equally amazed. "I knew Mr. Vernon loved books. He brought so many from Thorndale Manor's library to his cottage, he is practically swimming in them. But it never occurred to me that he was a *writer*—much less such a celebrated one."

"Your other theory might be more accurate, though," Selena pointed out. "Even though you think the handwriting was his, he might simply be a secret enthusiast. Perhaps he had dashed off a little scene in imitation of the author as a surprise gift for Mrs. Hillman."

"But if so, why would he have stashed that page beneath the floorboards?"

"I have no idea."

"The *author* option makes more sense and is far more exciting," Athena insisted.

"I agree." Selena laughed.

Athena slid her hand in awe across the desk. "If he really is Pryor Corbett, I wonder if he wrote all his novels here? It's the perfect hideaway, don't you think? A place where no one on staff would come upon him and discover his secret."

"He could sneak up here to write any time the mood struck him. He probably napped in that bed."

"But he's an architect as well. Why two professions, do you think?"

"It could be that even though his books are popular, they only provided a modest income," Selena suggested.

Athena nodded. "When his father began gambling away the family fortune, Mr. Vernon may have realized he needed to earn a living by some more profitable means."

"So, he followed another dream to become an architect."

"Yet he kept on writing."

"If he's Pryor Corbett, he has certainly been prolific! Seven novels over the past eight years!"

"Indeed." Athena closed the secret door and she and Selena made their way back across the attic. "Remember that day we had tea with Mrs. Hillman—when he claimed he had never read any of Corbett's novels?"

"Yes. How cleverly he deflected suspicion!"

"I understand now why he seemed so strange and awkward, the day he accompanied me up here to check for a leak in the roof. That hidden room must have once been his private and protected space, and he wanted to keep it that way."

"But—oh! How upset Mr. Vernon must have been, when he was obliged to give up this house and move elsewhere."

"I've been thinking about that, too. No wonder he was so antagonistic to me when we first met."

"After selling Thorndale Manor, he would have had to find a new place to write."

"I've seen his cottage. I doubt there is any private space in that small house, with a full-time housekeeper in command."

"Where do you suppose he is writing now?"

"An excellent question." As they descended the staircase, Athena's mind veered to the previous afternoon when she had encountered Mr. Vernon on the stairs at Darkmoor Park. Her face grew warm.

"You're thinking about Mr. Vernon's kisses, aren't you?"

Athena's cheeks flamed even more heatedly. "How do you do that?"

"Do what?"

"Always know what I'm thinking?"

"Your face is an open book."

They had reached the ground floor now. Athena stopped and cast her mind to something else. "All right, what am I thinking now?"

Selena held up her candle and studied Athena's expression. "Something is troubling you. Is it about Mr. Vernon?"

"Oh! You are so annoying. You're right. When I first ran into Mr. Vernon on the servants' stairs at Darkmoor Park, he was acting strange. He *said* he'd gone up to the attic to check for mice for Mrs. Hillman. But she seemed to be completely unaware of the situation at first. I couldn't help wondering if the mice had been a total fabrication and he was hiding something." Something occurred to Athena. "What if Mr. Vernon's true reason for coming down those stairs was that he had just come down from the attic because—"

"—his secret writing place is now established in the attic of Darkmoor Park!" Selena finished for her.

"Yes!"

"That makes perfect sense."

"It does." Excitedly, Athena added, "Mr. Vernon and Mrs. Hillman have been close ever since he was a boy. She must know all about his authorship. She has made no secret of the fact that she's a huge Pryor Corbett fan."

"She would no doubt have been only too happy to give Mr. Vernon shelter in her home to continue his work."

"And to think this has been going on right under our noses!"

Selena fell briefly silent. "On the other hand," she said cautiously, "we may be wrong about all of this. Even though the handwriting resembled Mr. Vernon's, there could be a completely different explanation for that page you found."

"There could be." Athena sighed. "But it would be so much fun if it's true! Somehow, I have to prove it."

"What will you do? Show Mr. Vernon the page? Get him to admit his secret?"

Athena shook her head. "A single page doesn't prove anything—it's not from a published work. And he could claim no knowledge of it."

"But what about the secret room?"

"He could make up some story about its history. No, I would rather have irrefutable evidence before I confront him."

"How do you propose to get that?"

Athena's mind hummed. "By going to Darkmoor Park and proving that he really *is* writing there in secret."

"An excellent notion." Selena nodded, grinning. "And I've just thought of the perfect opportunity."

"So have I." In unison, they cried, "The concert! Tomorrow night!"

"I CAN HARDLY wait to hear Mrs. Augustus sing," exclaimed Lucy Russell.

"My parents heard her once in London and said she is magnificent," remarked Miss Weaver.

All five pupils were dressed in their finest frocks, capes, and bonnets, and as they made their way up the crowded street towards the village hall, their excitement was unmistakable.

"Promise me you will be on your best behavior," Selena warned the girls. "You must stay with us at all times, and no talking during the concert."

"Yes, Miss Selena," the girls chorused.

It was a blustery evening. Clouds obscured the moon. The street was lined with lanterns in honor of the event, their dancing flames piercing the darkness. Athena spotted Edward Ackroyd arriving on horseback. Miss Quince and her father hovered outside the hall along with Bridget and George Osborn, Mr. Carson, and dozens of other people who were waiting for the doors to open. She looked hopefully for Mr. Vernon but saw no sign of him.

A carriage arrived, delivering Neville Sinclair and his wife. Moments later, Mrs. Hillman's carriage drew up. She and Mr. Chapman descended and exchanged greetings with Athena, Selena, and their pupils.

This is the moment, Athena decided. She yawned and said quietly, "Oh, dear."

"What's the matter?" Selena asked.

"I feel so tired all of sudden," Athena responded. "I fear I stayed up too late last night planning lessons."

"If you're too tired to stay," Selena told her, just as they had rehearsed, "I can chaperone the girls on my own."

"Are you sure you don't mind?"

"Not at all."

"Oh, but Miss Taylor! To miss the concert!" Miss Russell sounded aghast.

"It is a shame, but I think it's best that I go home and have an early night." Guilt stabbed Athena in the chest. She valued the truth above almost anything else in life. But it was just a little, white lie, and it wouldn't harm anyone. "I'll look forward to hearing all about it afterwards."

"Would you like me to walk you home?" Mr. Chapman proposed.

"No, thank you," Athena replied quickly. "I'll be fine. And I wouldn't want you to miss a moment of the concert."

"If you're weary, I won't have you *walking* home," Mrs. Hillman insisted. "You must take my carriage."

Athena hadn't expected this offer and was about to refuse. But on second thought, she realized, taking Mrs. Hillman's carriage would be far more expeditious than walking. "Thank you, ma'am. I would be most grateful. But now that you mention it—if you and your coachman don't mind—is it possible for him to take me to Darkmoor Park first? A good book always helps me to relax and fall asleep, and there is a novel in your library that I have been dying to read. If I could begin it tonight, it would help make up for missing the concert."

"Of course. I'm afraid there's not a soul at home, but you are welcome to stop in." Mrs. Hillman turned to her coachman. "Sam, please take Miss Taylor to the house, wait for her while she fetches a book, and then drive her to Thorndale Manor."

"Yes, ma'am," the coachman responded with a bow.

Athena said her goodbyes and climbed into the carriage, which whisked her away.

The road was dark, lit only by the gleam from the carriage lamps. Athena guessed they were about a quarter mile from Darkmoor Park when one of the horses gave a sharp, anguished whinny and the coachman uttered, "Whoa there!"

The carriage lurched to a halt. Athena heard the driver descend from his high seat, followed by some bustle, and then the carriage door was pulled open.

"What happened?" Athena asked.

"One of the horses threw a shoe and stepped on a nail," the coachman replied. "I'm sorry, miss, but I can't continue. I have to walk back to the village and fetch the farrier. You can wait here if you like, but it may take a couple of hours to set this right."

"It's quite all right. I'll walk the rest of the way—it's not far. The night air will do me good." Athena grabbed her reticule and accepted his help stepping down from the vehicle.

The man handed her a lantern. "Take this. I have a spare."

"Thank you."

While the driver unhitched the horses and tethered them to a tree, Athena set off on foot. As she walked down the road, the wind set her bonnet ribbons flying and made her shiver despite the protection of her woolen cloak. Thankfully, the candle inside the lantern's glass casing remained lit all the way to Darkmoor Park.

As promised, the manor house was dark and looked deserted. As she approached the front door, Athena was once again assailed by a stab of guilt. It bothered her that she had lied to Mrs. Hillman and the girls. What kind of person was she becoming? To utter a falsehood like that to people she cared about! It was so out of character.

And it wasn't the first time she had stretched the truth of late. Before, however, it had always been in the service of *solving the case*. This time, she didn't have as valid an excuse. She was only here to satisfy her curiosity about Mr. Vernon's secret identity. *This will take no more than a few minutes*, she reassured herself. *I'll be in and out of the house in no time.*

With the lantern to light her way, Athena made a beeline for the servants' stairs, which led to the attic on the northern side. Athena thrust open the old, wooden door on the top landing and stepped inside.

The attic was dark and musty and, from what Athena could discern in the feeble light, filled with distant piles of accumulated possessions. But this area at the top of the stairs was an open, uncluttered space with several cobwebby windows.

Athena raised her lantern. Her heart skittered.

Before her stood a large, brick wall very much like the one in Thorndale Manor's attic. *Did the building end here? Or did this wall also contain a secret door?*

"Pryor Corbett," she murmured, "is this your new secret writing place?"

By the light of her lantern, Athena searched for any evidence of hairline cracks in the mortar that would indicate the entry point to a hidden room. But she saw nothing unusual. It appeared to just be a solid, brick wall.

Athena was so certain there was a secret door, she started

pressing on the brick wall here, there, and everywhere, hoping she might come upon it by accident. All at once, to her excitement, the wall moved, and a door sprang open!

But in so doing, it smashed into Athena's lantern, which crashed to the floor, extinguishing the candle and plunging the room into pitch blackness.

Athena gasped in dismay. "Oh, no!" At that moment, she heard a new and unexpected sound.

Footfalls. Heading this way from the other side of the attic.

Her blood froze. She couldn't see a single thing.

"Hello?" Athena called out to the darkness. "Who's there?"

No one answered. *Who could it be?* Everyone she knew, including Mrs. Hillman's servants, was at the concert. Whoever it was, they didn't appear to be carrying a light. The sound of footsteps continued.

"Who's there? Declare yourself!"

There was no reply. Athena's pulse leapt with alarm. Who would come up here without a lantern or candle? Instinct told her that she was in danger. *I must hide.* But where? In this open area, there was no means of concealment.

Except for the secret room behind her. If it was indeed a secret room.

The darkness was so complete and so disorienting. Athena took three steps, and then three more, crunching on the broken glass from her lantern. Where was the door?

The footfalls were louder now, marching ever closer.

Another sound: that of a window being thrust open. *Why?* A rush of wind blew into the attic but did not admit a speck of light.

Athena reached out in the blackness but felt absolutely nothing. What had happened to the wall? Had she moved in the wrong direction?

All at once, someone grabbed her. Athena screamed. "Let me go!" She struggled, but strong arms held her firmly in their grip, pinning her arms against her body. She was being half-dragged, half-carried … where? By whom?

It was all happening so fast. She screamed again at the top of her lungs. Suddenly, a jolt of pain dashed through her body as she was thrust up against something hard. Wind rushed in her ears. Where was she? It felt like the frame of an open window.

Dear lord. Did her unseen assailant intend to throw her out an attic window?

Athena screamed again and fought back with all her might, trying to brace herself with her feet against what she presumed was a windowsill. But her attacker pressed on with unwavering force.

Is this the end? Am I going to be hurled to my death?

Just then, a crash rent the air, akin to shattering glass or crockery. Her attacker cried out and lost their hold on Athena, who tumbled to the floor.

Athena heard but could not see a scuffle taking place beside her in the pitch darkness. Someone else was there. Who had come to her defense? A shout. A scream. A gasp. The sounds of pummeling. Ragged breathing. Athena rose to her knees, shaking, desperate to help. But how? She could see nothing.

There came a sharp cry. A *thud*, as of a body falling to the floor. And then a new and distant exclamation, from the opposite side of the attic—a deep, masculine voice crying, "Is someone up here?"

Athena heard the pounding of racing feet. A nearby door slammed. Someone had fled. Was it her attacker? Or the person who had tried to save her?

"I heard screams!" called out the newcomer, who seemed to be headed this way. "Is anyone up here?"

Athena had heard that voice before, but she was too overcome to identify it or to reply. She had almost *died* just now. She didn't know who had tried to kill her, but she could guess why. In her investigation into Harold Sinclair's murder, she was getting too close for their comfort.

Her eyes, she realized, must have been getting used to the dark, for she was able, at last, to perceive a hint of the scene before her. Someone lay on the floor a few feet away. Athena crawled to the slender, unmoving form. It was a woman. She lay face up and wore a simple, cotton frock. She looked too slight to be Athena's attacker. A shattered crockery pitcher lay beside her. Was she alive or dead?

Athena touched the woman's chest, confirming that it rose and fell. She was just unconscious. Was it she who had come to Athena's defense? The assailant must have knocked her out and fled.

The approach of a light and continued footfalls indicated that the newcomer was trudging in her direction. Athena's mind buzzed with confusion. What on Earth was this woman doing in the Darkmoor Park attic? She appeared to be in her late twenties. Even in the dim light, Athena could see that she was pretty. Beautiful, in fact. Her hair was raven black and her complexion was as pale as snow. It struck Athena that the young woman's features were familiar. Why?

With a gasp of recognition, Athena understood where she had seen her before. They had never met in person. Athena had only seen her in portraits.

She was staring at a ghost in living form.

It was Caroline Vernon.

CHAPTER TWENTY-TWO

A THENA STRUGGLED TO make sense of what she was seeing.

How could Caroline Vernon be here—alive and breathing? It was impossible. The woman had been hanged for murder nine years ago. Hadn't she?

A voice again. "I say, is anyone there?"

Lantern light pierced the darkness. A man strode into the open attic space.

It was Neville Sinclair.

Athena started in horror. If this woman really *was* Caroline Vernon, then the worst possible person to discover her alive was Neville Sinclair. For he was the parish constable who had sent her to prison all those years ago and had rejoiced in her death.

Athena sprang to her feet. Wrapping her arms around herself as if in terror, she stood in front of Miss Vernon, to shield her from Sinclair's view. "Mr. Sinclair! I'm so frightened!" She blinked rapidly as he shone his lantern directly into her eyes.

"Miss Taylor?"

"Yes and thank heavens you're here. But how did you know to come?"

He looked confused. "I didn't know. Mrs. Hillman had a headache and wished to leave the concert early, but her coach had never returned. We spotted it at the side of the road on the way here, when I brought her home. We heard screaming. It seemed to come from up here. Was that you?"

"Yes."

"What happened?"

Thinking fast, Athena replied, "I came to fetch a book from Mrs. Hillman's library. Like you, I heard strange sounds coming from the attic. When I got up here, I was attacked."

"Attacked? By whom?"

"I don't know. My lantern fell and smashed. I couldn't see a thing. But someone tried to kill me."

"*Kill you?*"

"He tried to throw me out that window!" Athena could finally see the open window nearby and nodded towards it.

"Good heavens. Why?"

"I couldn't say," Athena lied. She needed to get this man out of here, and fast, before he noticed the woman on the floor behind her. "I am too distressed to speak further, sir. I'll explain more once we are downstairs."

"Very well." Mr. Sinclair turned as if to go, when a small moan broke the stillness. He paused. "What was that?"

Athena's pulse pounded in alarm. *Caroline Vernon must be waking up.* "I didn't hear anything. Please sir, let us go."

"Wait. There's someone else up here." Sinclair strode towards her, lantern in hand.

Athena turned, desperately trying to think of some way to protect Miss Vernon—but it was too late. Sinclair's lantern beam had already found her.

With another moan, Miss Vernon slowly sat up, her eyes still closed.

"Who's this?" Sinclair demanded.

Miss Vernon's eyes blinked open. She squinted at Athena in the lantern's glare, a look that seemed to be filled with recognition and wonder—feelings that Athena shared but was too terrified to express.

"Good God!" Sinclair exclaimed, starting violently. "Is it …? No! It cannot be!"

Miss Vernon took in the man before her and gasped in horror. She tried to rise but then cried out in pain and crumpled back to the floor.

"It cannot be!" Neville Sinclair exclaimed again with an incredulous stare. *"Caroline Vernon?* Impossible. I saw you die. I saw you hang!"

A tense silence reigned, and then Miss Vernon heaved a deep, resigned sigh. "No. You saw Harriet Fowler hang."

"Who?" Sinclair demanded, his eyes bulging.

"Harriet Fowler. She was dying of consumption. She went to the gallows in my stead."

Athena's jaw dropped. She recalled now the story of another inmate whom Caroline Vernon had befriended in prison, and whom Mr. Vernon had said had later passed away from illness. She recalled, too, what the apple seller had said that day at York Prison, about Miss Vernon's hanging.

"Skinny, pale young thing, as I recall. Might have used to be pretty, but who could tell with that shaved head and sickly complexion?"

"I took Harriet's place in her cell," Caroline was saying. "We looked so much alike, no one knew the difference. When they thought me dead from consumption, I snuck away from the burial site, unnoticed."

Athena sensed that a lot of details were missing from that story. Did Mr. Vernon know that Caroline had escaped all those years ago? *He must. No doubt, he helped coordinate the entire thing. No wonder he was so determined to keep that piece of history in the shadows.*

Athena had no time to process that notion further, however, for Mr. Sinclair's face was blazing with fury as he cried, "And where have you been all this time? Hiding in Rose Hillman's attic?" He strode to the open door in the brick wall and glanced inside. "By God, I shall charge her and everyone else involved in this scheme with harboring a criminal!"

"I've had no accomplices, sir!" Miss Vernon shot back insistently. "Mrs. Hillman knows nothing about my being here. For the past nine years, I've been living in another country. But I've been so homesick. I had to come home or die. I used to play up here in that secret room when I visited Mrs. Hillman as a child. It was a priest's hole centuries ago."

Athena listened to this speech in wonder as she glanced into the hidden room, which was illuminated by the beam from Mr. Sinclair's lantern. The chamber was eerily similar to the one in Thorndale Manor's attic, except that this room's furnishings did indeed look as if they dated back a couple of centuries or more.

"I only returned to England a few days ago," Miss Vernon continued. "I informed no one that I was coming. I snuck up here with food and water to last a week while I figured out what to do next." Tears pooled in Miss Vernon's blue eyes. "But it seems my luck has run out."

Athena knew in her bones that all this was a lie. Miss Vernon hadn't been living in another country. She was only saying that to protect her brother and Mrs. Hillman. Mr. Vernon must have built the secret room at Thorndale Manor, based on this one, to house and conceal his sister after her escape from prison. Caroline had no doubt lived there until Mr. Vernon had had to sell Thorndale Manor—when he'd been obliged to find her another place to hide.

Neville Sinclair seemed to have bought Miss Vernon's story, however. He marched up to confront her, his voice harsh and ugly. "You devil. You may have escaped the law until now, Miss Vernon, but so help me, you'll hang for my brother's murder before the week is over."

"Wait. Wait!" Athena knelt down at Caroline Vernon's side and wrapped her arms around her. "Don't do this, sir. Miss Vernon is innocent. She didn't kill your brother." Athena felt Miss Vernon's hand squeeze her arm—was it to signify gratitude or resignation?—as she continued. "A witness lied on the stand at her trial. I have proof!"

"What proof?" Mr. Sinclair spat venomously. "Can you furnish that proof to me here and now?"

"Well, no," Athena began helplessly, "but—"

"It is my duty to see that this woman pays for her crime, however overdue that payment might be." Mr. Sinclair wrenched Miss Vernon from Athena's grasp and hauled her to her feet.

"No! Don't!" Athena cried, but Mr. Sinclair dragged Miss Vernon off. Limping and in obvious pain, Caroline Vernon glanced back and met Athena's gaze, her eyes filled with sorrow and regret but not a hint of recrimination.

Athena burst into tears of shame.

She owed Caroline Vernon her life. The young woman had just saved Athena from a horrific fate at the hands of a determined killer.

And yet, if Athena hadn't come here tonight to satisfy an idle curiosity, Caroline Vernon would still have been safe in hiding, as she had been for years.

Now she was going to die.

And it was all Athena's fault.

THE NEWS OF Caroline Vernon's discovery somehow traveled far and wide that same evening.

By ten o'clock the pupils at Thorndale Manor, having returned from the concert, were all gathered in the second-floor corridor, clad in their nightgowns and chattering about it.

"To think that Caroline Vernon has been alive all this time and living on the Continent!" exclaimed Miss Weaver in wonder.

"France, they said it was!" cried Miss Gilbert.

"I heard it was Egypt!" declared Miss Jones.

"What will happen to her now?" asked Miss Cecilia.

"Why, she'll hang, of course," replied Miss Russell matter-of-factly.

"Girls! There will be no gossiping in the halls," reprimanded Selena.

"It's late. Go to bed at once!" Athena insisted, struggling to keep tears at bay. She had never been more miserable or filled with self-recrimination in her life.

Later, in a private conversation with Athena and Selena in their study, Mrs. Lloyd wept as she admitted that she'd been one of the few people privy to Caroline Vernon's secret from the start.

"It was Mr. Vernon's idea to have that other prisoner take Miss Vernon's place at the gallows," the housekeeper confided in between sobs. "The woman had no objection. She was going to die soon, anyway. No one guessed a thing. Miss Vernon pretended to be dead in her cell from consumption. Mr. Vernon paid a guard at York Prison who allowed him to take her 'body' to a doctor, he said, for medical study. He built that secret room for his sister, like the one at Darkmoor Park. At first, it was only meant to be a temporary stopping place. He planned to remove her to some safer place in Scotland to live under an assumed name. But no sooner had she got here than it turned out Miss Vernon was with child."

Athena's breath caught in her throat. "With child?"

Mrs. Lloyd nodded. "She was madly in love with Edward Ackroyd, you know. It was his child. But by the time Miss Vernon realized she was pregnant, he was away at sea and later told that she had died on the gallows. That poor young man!" She wiped her eyes. "He loved her so. I'll never forget the look on his face when he saw Harold Sinclair berating Miss Vernon at that party!"

Athena stared at Mrs. Lloyd. "Are you saying that Edward Ackroyd was at the garden party where Harold Sinclair died?"

"He was. I've never seen a man so angry."

Athena shot her sister a glance and Selena nodded silently. *So Ackroyd lied, after all, about being at that party.*

"Did Mr. Ackroyd approach Harold Sinclair or do anything suspicious? Did he put something into Harold Sinclair's drink?"

"I don't know. I was so upset, I had to walk away."

Athena frowned. They had dismissed Edward Ackroyd as a suspect, due to their belief that even if he *had* killed Harold

Sinclair, he wouldn't have blackmailed Ethel Leighton into framing Miss Vernon, the woman he adored. But he *had* been at that party. If he was innocent, why had he lied about it?

She decided to move on. "Mrs. Lloyd, as I understand it, George Osborn couldn't attend that party because he was bedridden after his accident. But do you remember if Mr. Carson was there?"

"He was. And in a foul mood too, as I recall, for he despised Harold Sinclair after what had happened to his friend."

She'd been right. Mr. Carson had also had the opportunity to poison Sinclair. "But back to what you were saying. Did Miss Vernon ever go to Scotland?"

"No. Her pregnancy made her so ill, she couldn't travel. She had no choice but to stay here, but it all had to be done with the utmost secrecy. You see, Mr. Arthur Vernon, the father, had disowned his daughter, believing her guilty of murder. If he'd found out Miss Vernon was being sheltered in his own attic, he would have cast her to the wolves."

Athena winced in sympathy.

"Who took care of Miss Vernon?" Selena asked in a quiet, sad voice.

"I did. Brought up all her meals, did anything that needed doing, all the years that she lived in our attic. It was my honor to do so. I have loved that girl since the day she was born."

Athena dabbed her eyes with her handkerchief. "What happened to the baby?"

"The baby." Mrs. Lloyd began weeping again and it was a moment before she could continue. "Mr. Vernon has a doctor friend in York, who delivered the infant and vowed to keep silent. Miss Vernon gave birth to a beautiful baby girl. But it was impossible to keep a newborn baby a secret. Mr. Vernon planned to smuggle them out of the house to another county, where she could pretend to be a sailor's widow. But the birth nearly killed Miss Vernon. She lost so much blood and got a fever. The doctor feared she was going to die. The infant needed nourishment at once, and a home. Mr. Vernon told me to pretend I'd discovered the abandoned baby in a basket on the riverbank—like Moses on the Nile. I found her a home with a good family. Thanks be to God, Miss Vernon recovered. When she learned that her daughter had been given away, she was absolutely heartbroken. But she remained weak for months and would have been unable to go anywhere else, much less care for that baby on her own. In time, Miss Vernon said she preferred to remain here at home, in the same county as her daughter, where her brother could visit her regularly."

Athena shook her head, still stunned. "Did Mr. Vernon ever plan to tell Edward Ackroyd that Miss Vernon was alive, and about the baby?"

"He considered it but decided against it. It was too risky. A sailor's mail, he had learned, could be opened before delivery. If anyone else learned about Miss Vernon, it would spell her death. And Mr. Vernon worried, too, that if the young man—who is a rather rash and impulsive individual—discovered the truth, he would rush home and not be discreet about it, which would prove just as dangerous for Miss Vernon. It was safer to just keep quiet about the whole thing." Mrs. Lloyd blew her nose on her handkerchief. "Mr. Vernon hoped—and Miss Vernon did as well—that Edward Ackroyd would move on and marry someone else, for his own sake. But he never did."

Selena let go a long, unhappy sigh. "She was truly shut up in that attic for *nine years?*"

"Yes. Sometimes, though, she so longed to breathe fresh air, she disregarded Mr. Vernon's orders, disguised herself, and slipped out late at night."

"Ah. That would account for the rumors about a 'ghost' at Thorndale Manor and in the village," Athena remarked.

"They weren't just figments of people's imaginations," Selena put in.

"All went well for years. Until Arthur Vernon started drinking and running up bills. After he died, it broke my heart that young

Mr. Vernon had to sell Thorndale Manor. His biggest worry was, where to move his sister? He finally told Mrs. Hillman the truth. He said she was so shocked and happy, she didn't stop crying for days. She was only too glad to take in Miss Vernon and continue the deception. But how I miss my girl! I miss her every single day. I hear she was content and well-cared for at Darkmoor Park until this horrible turn of events. But oh! *This* will be the end of her!" Mrs. Lloyd's voice broke as she turned to Athena. "Miss Taylor! How did Miss Vernon come to be discovered? I heard you were there at Darkmoor Park when it happened, but that can't be right, can it?"

Athena couldn't bring herself to admit to her real reason for being at Darkmoor Park that night—not yet. She repeated the same story she had told Neville Sinclair about going to the house to fetch a book, hearing a sound in the attic, and being attacked by an unknown assailant.

Mrs. Lloyd's eyes widened. "Dear Lord! How frightening. But why should someone have attacked you, Miss Taylor?"

"I have no idea," Athena lied. "Miss Vernon risked her life to save mine. I can never repay her. Oh! If only I hadn't gone there."

"How could you have known?" Mrs. Lloyd replied with a tearful sniff. "It wasn't your fault."

But Athena knew differently. Her foolish errand had put Caroline Vernon in mortal danger, and Athena could never forgive herself.

ATHENA AND SELENA didn't sleep a wink that night. They spent every moment going over what had occurred and trembling at the thought that Athena had, once again, nearly lost her life. This terrifying reality, however, paled in Athena's mind in comparison to the dilemma in which she had placed Miss Vernon.

Selena kept insisting that Athena must stop her investigation, but Athena rejected the notion. A killer was still out there. She couldn't stop now, no matter what the risk. And somehow, she had to help Miss Vernon. Selena reluctantly acceded and they struggled to think of a solution. They'd heard that Miss Vernon was being held in the lock-up in the village square but would soon be transported to York Prison. Their only recourse, they decided, was for Athena to speak to Neville Sinclair without delay—to do everything within her power to convince him that Miss Vernon was innocent.

Selena took over the day's classes. Athena hastened to the village, wrapping her cloak around her against the chill, grateful that the paths and roads were dry and that a bleak sun peeked between the clouds.

As she passed the apothecary shop, she saw Miss Quince outside, engrossed in conversation with George Osborn and Mr. Carson. Had one of them been responsible for Harold Sinclair's death? If only she could prove it. Athena heard one of them say *Caroline Vernon*. The group gave Athena a look that seemed to be half-confusion and half-censure.

Athena's stomach clenched. So, they had heard. Of course they had. Everyone had heard by now. If they were to learn of Athena's true purpose for being in that attic, would she become the village pariah? If so, she wouldn't blame them.

Upon reaching the village square, Athena paused outside the lock-up, a small, round building of grey stone that featured a domed roof, a heavy, arched and studded wooden door, and one tiny, barred window too high up to see in or out of. It horrified her to think that Caroline Vernon was incarcerated in that place.

Tears hovered at the back of Athena's eyes. If only there were a way to speak to Miss Vernon. To let her know how mortified and deeply regretful Athena was, that she blamed herself for everything and was going to try her best to help.

A young man appeared from around the building. Athena stifled a gasp. It was Edward Ackroyd. He seemed to be perambulating the circumference of the structure, his arms crossed over his chest and his features tense as if with anxiety. He saw Athena and stopped in his tracks.

"You!" he thundered. "How dare you show your face here?"

Athena froze with guilt and shame. "I'm sorry. So sorry."

"What good does it do to be sorry?" Mr. Ackroyd came straight for her and stopped a yard away, his eyes flashing with pain and fury. "To learn that Caroline is still alive after all this time. Alive! I had no idea until a couple of hours ago, when her brother told me. But how long does she have? What were you doing in that attic last night?"

"I … I …" Athena faltered.

"Did you lead Sinclair to her on purpose?"

"Of course not! I knew nothing about this, either."

"Vernon hoped I'd move on and marry someone else, but I couldn't imagine being with any woman other than Caroline. I would have rather died alone." He ran agitated fingers through his blond hair. "If only Vernon had trusted me enough to tell me. Caroline and I might have been able to steal away someplace and be together. But any hope of that is gone now." He gestured to the impenetrable stone jail behind him. "She is locked up in that infernal cell. They won't even let me see or speak to her. In a week, she'll be dead. Thanks to *you!* If I could, I would kill you now with my own bare hands," Ackroyd hurled at her before stalking away.

All the way to Woodcroft House, Athena's eyes burned with unshed tears, and a new thought pounded in her brain. Was Edward Ackroyd's show of pain and bravado genuine, or was it just an act? If he had indeed committed the murder that had doomed Caroline Vernon, why didn't he come forward now? Perhaps, after nine long years apart, he didn't love her as much as he claimed … or as much as his own life and freedom.

But then again, what about Mrs. Hunt's admission that she had been blackmailed by a blond person wearing a mask? That couldn't have been Edward Ackroyd. Even if he had still been in England at the time, Athena couldn't reconcile the idea of his having framed his true love for murder.

It was all such a conundrum.

Athena entered through the rear gate of Woodcroft House and was halfway across the grounds when she spied Mr. Vernon walking in her direction, as if he had just come from the mansion.

Normally, Athena was steeped in joy at the sight of him. But she felt no joy today. Her heart seemed to be made of lead. All night long, she'd been thinking and worrying about Mr. Vernon, aware that last night's events would bring him unspeakable pain.

Indeed, his shoulders sagged, and every step seemed to require great effort. Even at this distance, Athena could discern his downcast eyes and haggard expression. Had he come to Woodcroft House on a mission similar to hers, to plead with Mr. Sinclair for mercy on Caroline Vernon's behalf? If so, she guessed it had not gone well.

Anxiety and grief rose again as if to choke her. She loved him, although she had never told him. And how could she tell him now?

He crossed the stretch of lawn to her and removed his hat. "Miss Taylor."

"Mr. Vernon. This is all so shocking and … I'm so very, very sorry." She offered him her hand.

He took her hand and squeezed it, meeting her gaze with anguished, red-rimmed eyes. "It is a calamity. I visited Caroline at the lock-up this morning but was only allowed to stay five minutes."

"How is she?"

"She put on a brave face for my sake. She says she is resigned to her fate, that I must be prepared to let her go. But I cannot!" He paused. "I know bad news travels fast, but I'm not sure how much you know about the circumstances?"

Athena spoke frankly. "I know how hard you have worked all these years, Mr. Vernon, to keep your sister safe. I discovered the secret room in the attic at Thorndale Manor."

"Ah." He frowned. "I figured you would find it sooner or

later."

"Last night, Mrs. Lloyd told me and Selena the history of Miss Vernon's escape from the gallows, and that she had a child who was given away."

"Ah," he said again.

"I know Miss Vernon was very ill for a time and chose to remain at Thorndale Manor. Until you were obliged to remove her to the attic at Darkmoor Park."

He nodded slowly. "Well, then. I suppose as they say, the jig is up. Thankfully, however, Neville Sinclair has not got wind of Caroline's actual whereabouts for the past nine years. He bought my sister's story that she's been living out of the country. I cannot admit the truth—I can't allow any blame to fall on Mrs. Hillman. Although I don't care so much about myself, I must remain free if I'm to have any hope of helping my sister. I pray that you and Miss Selena will keep this knowledge to yourselves?"

"You may be assured of our discretion."

"Thank you." He shook his head. "I've just spent the past hour pleading with Sinclair to set my sister free, but the man won't see reason." Mr. Vernon's brow furrowed. "One thing puzzles me. He said *you* were at Darkmoor Park last night when my sister was discovered? That you were *attacked* by someone, and it was your screams that drew him to the attic?"

Athena's stomach tightened with shame, and it was all she could do to look him in the eye. "Yes. Someone must have followed me up there—but my lantern was extinguished. They grabbed me in the dark and tried to throw me out an open window."

His jaw dropped. "Dear lord!"

"Your sister fought him off. How she managed it in the pitch darkness is beyond me."

He frowned at that. "Caroline has lived in the dark for so long, she has developed excellent night vision. She never dared to light a candle, you see, for fear it would be noticed that someone was residing in the attic."

"Oh. I hadn't thought of that."

"But why on Earth would someone want to kill you?" His breath caught. "Oh. It's because you've been looking into the murder of Harold Sinclair, isn't it?"

"I think so. If your sister hadn't come to my rescue, I would have surely died."

"Oh, Miss Taylor." He heaved another ragged sigh. "I warned you not to pursue that. Perhaps now you understand why?"

"Yes." Athena's guilty conscience reared its head again. "You feared that an investigation into your sister's history would lead to her exposure."

"Yes. But I also worried that you might put yourself in danger. Which has proven to be the case."

Athena nodded, her pulse beating erratically. Any minute now, he was going to ask what she'd been doing in that attic. She owed him the truth but dreaded how he might react. "I'm going to tell Neville Sinclair everything I've learned."

"What have you learned? You have a lot of theories but no proof and not a single viable suspect."

"That remains to be seen," she replied, desperate to defend herself. "Someone just tried to kill me for looking into this. *That* has to mean something. Plus, I found the woman who lied on the witness stand."

"Ethel Leighton?"

"Her married name is Hunt. She lives in Duxley-on-Green. I paid her a visit."

His brows arched. "What did she say?"

"She admitted what she'd done and why." Athena described the meeting. "Unfortunately, I couldn't persuade her to come forward. But when Mr. Sinclair hears about this, he'll surely reopen the case against your sister."

"I wouldn't count on it. I doubt he will listen to you any more than he did to me." He hesitated, his expression tensing. "There's still something about all this that I don't understand. What were you doing in the attic at Darkmoor Park last night in the first place?"

There it is. Athena swallowed hard. There was no putting it off any longer. Twisting her hands, she admitted, "I feel so foolish about this now. But I went to Darkmoor Park to satisfy my curiosity."

"About what?"

"I had hoped to discover—or rather to prove—the identity of Pryor Corbett."

"Pryor Corbett?" He stared at her. "The author?"

She told him about the page she had found beneath the floorboards. "It was a scene that I knew had not yet been published. I cannot account for how that page came to be there. I know it sounds mad now, but I became convinced that *you* were Pryor Corbett."

"Me?" A short laugh escaped Mr. Vernon's chest.

"I thought the hidden room had been your private writing getaway, until you sold Thorndale Manor. I got it into my head that your new writing lair was at Darkmoor Park. While everyone was at the concert, I snuck up to the attic to see if there was indeed a hidden room."

Silence fell as Mr. Vernon digested this. "*That* was your purpose in going there? To unmask *me* as a reclusive author?"

A fresh wave of hot guilt impaled Athena's chest. "Forgive me. It was the most innocent of pretexts. I could never have foreseen how it would all play out."

"How it would *all play out*?" He gave her a cold, hard stare. "This *innocent pretext* of yours exposed my sister to the very man who had arrested her in the first place, and who will now send her to her death."

"I'm so sorry." Tears started again in Athena's eyes. "I blame myself entirely. If only I could undo it, I would."

"It's too late to undo it, Miss Taylor. I fear the die has been cast. My sister will hang this time. I see no way to prevent it." Anger and resentment simmered in every syllable he uttered. "But there is an irony of all of this."

Athena choked back a sob. "What irony?"

"That manuscript page you found? It did indeed come from the pen of Pryor Corbett."

"How?"

"Pryor Corbett is none other than my sister, Caroline."

With that, Mr. Vernon stalked away, leaving a dumbfounded and wretched Athena in his wake.

CHAPTER TWENTY-THREE

A FEW MINUTES' walk brought Athena to Woodcroft House, giving her little time to reflect on Mr. Vernon's revelation— and barely time to dry her tears.

As the butler answered the door, Athena squared her shoulders and requested a meeting with the master of the house.

Neville Sinclair was dressed for riding and about to leave for the stables, but he grudgingly granted Athena an interview in his study. When she admitted that this was an appeal to release Caroline Vernon, he rolled his eyes and insisted that Athena keep it brief.

Mr. Sinclair's face remained expressionless as Athena went through her list of suspects and their possible motives. She finished by explaining that Mrs. Ethel Hunt, nee Leighton, had admitted to giving false testimony at Miss Vernon's trial. "She never found rat poison in Miss Vernon's room, sir. She made up the entire story."

"Is that so?" He tugged at his blond mustache, his eyes narrowing. "And what reason does this Mrs. Hunt give for falsifying her testimony?"

"She was blackmailed into it, for reasons she prefers not to disclose."

"'*Prefers not to disclose*,'" Mr. Sinclair repeated. "And you come here, expecting me to accept this as proof of …what?"

"It proves, sir, that someone else murdered Harold Sinclair

and framed Caroline Vernon for it. Mrs. Hunt said her blackmailer wore a mask but was of medium height and build and had blond hair. Every one of the suspects I named meets that description."

He blinked at that and then let out a harsh laugh. "Miss Taylor. You must take me for a fool, but I assure you I am *not*. I considered all the people you have named *nine years ago*. None of them murdered my brother, I assure you."

"But, sir—"

"Enough, Miss Taylor. Enough!" He sliced his hand through the air like a swordsman wielding his blade. "You have tried my patience to the breaking point. Why do you feel so strongly about this subject, I wonder? Is it because you are keen to redeem the reputation of Thorndale Manor, by somehow mitigating Miss Vernon's guilt? Or is it *your own guilt* that drives you? For let us be frank: it was *you* who led me to the attic at Darkmoor Park last night, and in so doing exposed Miss Vernon and sealed her fate."

Athena felt her cheeks flame and could make no reply.

"Either way, I have given you more than enough chances to plead your case, and I am *done*, do you hear me? *Done*." He leaned forward across his desk, his eyes flashing. "Caroline Vernon is a convicted murderer. She will be transported to York Prison tomorrow morning. Make no mistake about it, *she will hang for her crime this time*. I shall see to it." He rang the servants' bell and rose. "Make this the last time you approach me about this matter. Now if you will forgive me, I must take my leave."

As Athena headed back across the Woodcroft House grounds, every step seemed to require a monumental effort. All her efforts on Miss Vernon's behalf had been in vain. Mr. Sinclair would do nothing. Mr. Vernon blamed Athena for everything, and she could only agree with him.

As she passed the dog kennel, dozens of hunting hounds eagerly leapt up and down behind the bars of their cages and barked their heads off. Their yapping had begun to ebb when she suddenly heard the approaching sound of even deeper, more furious barking.

Athena whirled in alarm to see two huge mastiffs racing in her direction, teeth bared in their snarling, black-masked faces. Athena screamed in horror and started to run but then stopped herself. She had been attacked by a dog once as a child and recalled what she'd been told, should it ever happen again.

"You cannot outrun an angry dog. It will awaken their prey instinct. Instead, drop and curl."

Athena plunged to the grass and rolled up in a ball. The dogs hurled themselves at her. Their vicious growls roared in her ears as they snapped their slobbering jaws. Fabric ripped. One painful bite after another dug into her arm, a leg, her ankle. Terrified, she recalled something else she had been told about dog attacks. *"Distract them with an object."*

Athena managed to wriggle her handbag up between her fists and shoved it at one of the dogs. The angry beast clamped down on the bag but was only distracted for a few seconds before renewing its attack.

"Get off her!" came a man's voice.

"Samson! Brutus! Down boys, down!" More shouts followed.

At last, the dogs were pulled off of her. Athena peered up at her rescuers, who were holding back the growling dogs by their collars. She recognized the first man as the groundskeeper, Mr. Leighton.

"Are you all right, miss?" he asked worriedly.

Athena's mind refused to focus. She couldn't speak. One of her arms, she noticed, was covered in gore. Her gown looked to be hopelessly ripped.

"I'm so sorry, miss," said the second man. "I'm Barnes, the Master of the Hounds. The dogs are always locked up. I don't know how they got loose."

While the dogs' keeper took them to their kennel, Mr. Leighton helped Athena to walk back to the house. Her arm and leg were bleeding, and she was in so much pain, she could barely think.

Mr. Sinclair was out riding. Mrs. Sinclair sent a servant to fetch the apothecary and ordered a maid to protect a sofa in the drawing room with sheets and towels before allowing Athena to lie down upon it. The maid tried to staunch Athena's wounds until Mr. Quince arrived. The apothecary cleaned and stitched up Athena, gave her pain medicine, and insisted on driving her home.

"I did my best to clean the wounds, Miss Taylor, but I'm not satisfied," Mr. Quince said as they neared Thorndale Manor in his carriage. "You must send for me at once if you develop a fever, for it could prove deadly."

Athena nodded dully, her mind focused on other things. How had the guard dogs gotten loose? Had the gate been left open by accident? Or had it been yet another deliberate attack by someone who wanted her out of the way?

As she and Mr. Quince pulled up in the drive outside Thorndale Manor, her attention was diverted by an entirely different problem. Mr. and Mrs. Russell and Mr. and Mrs. Jones were standing beside two waiting vehicles and arguing with Selena.

Athena threw open the door of Mr. Quince's coach and stepped down.

"It was bad enough that a murderer once inhabited this house, but to discover her *still living!*" Mrs. Jones was saying, her face red.

"To know that she had been *hiding here for years* and had never paid for her crime! It is unconscionable!" declared Mrs. Russell.

"Miss Vernon was not found here," Selena began, but she wasn't allowed to continue.

"Only because she was moved, which excuses nothing," declared Mr. Jones.

"A maid died here only weeks ago!" proclaimed Mrs. Jones. "My own daughter wrote to say that *she* had discovered the body in the river!"

Alarmed, Athena thanked Mr. Quince and said *goodbye*. As his vehicle departed, she painfully made her way towards the arguing group.

"Dear lord!" Mr. Russell stared at Athena. "Is that your headmistress?"

"Athena!" Selena gaped. "What happened?"

"I was attacked by dogs. But never mind that. What is happening here?"

Selena's frown deepened and she spoke into Athena's ear. "Word has got out about Miss Vernon."

"*Attacked by dogs?*" exclaimed Mr. Jones, without a shred of sympathy. "Is there no end to the horrific misadventures at this institution?"

"Sir," Athena interjected. "I assure you that—" But no one was listening.

"I told you this house has a *history!*" Mrs. Russell hurled at her husband. "It is said to *breed evil.* You made light of it, but now we have the proof of it!" Turning to Selena, she added, "Tell Lucy to pack up her things at once. We are removing her from this school."

Mr. Jones repeated the same order with regard to his daughter. "And I expect a full refund for this month's tuition."

"As do I," insisted Mr. Russell.

Athena could only watch in dismay as, in short order, two trunks were brought out and loaded into the waiting vehicles, and the pupils in question were marched out of the building.

Selena hugged Miss Russell goodbye. The little girl's eyes grew wide at the sight of Athena's tattered dress and bandaged arm and leg. "Miss Taylor! Are you all right?"

"I'll be fine. Don't you worry about me."

"I don't want to go." Miss Russell began to cry. "Mama and Papa are making me."

Athena winced in pain as she embraced the girl. "You must do as your parents wish."

"I'll never forget you, Miss Taylor."

"I'll never forget you. Promise me you'll keep writing wonderful stories."

"I promise."

Athena and Selena said heartfelt goodbyes to Miss Jones, who was also weeping. Both girls and their parents entered their respective coaches and drove away.

As she watched them go with a sinking heart, Athena realized that only three students remained at the school.

It could hardly be called a school anymore.

THAT NIGHT, ATHENA dreamt again of Caroline Vernon. This time, she wasn't a bald wraith trapped in a prison cell. She was the picture of health and beauty—and she was being led to the gallows.

In the dream, an icy wind blew as Miss Vernon stopped before the noose. Her head held high, she proclaimed in a strong, clear voice, "I vow that I am innocent. But I will bravely meet my fate. I bear no ill will against those who have wrongly accused me. My heart is filled only with love."

Athena awoke to find that dawn had broken, and her eyes were full of tears. The wounds on her arm, leg, and ankle ached. She was freezing cold and shivering violently.

"Athena? Why are your teeth chattering?" Selena crossed to Athena's bedside and pressed a hand to her forehead. "Oh, no, you're burning up with fever."

Selena quit the room and hastily returned with Tabitha and Mrs. Lloyd, who took turns bathing Athena's forehead with a cool, wet cloth. Mr. Quince came and diagnosed an infection. He cleaned and rebound Athena's wounds, gave her another dose of pain medication, and did a round of bloodletting, which only left her feeling weak and listless.

"I will stop by again this evening," the apothecary said in a low, worried tone. "In the meantime, keep the fire going and the windows shut. We cannot risk a bad humor entering her lungs, or she could perish."

Athena, on the edge of sleep, heard this dire pronouncement but felt too tired and ill to care. If she were to die, so be it. It seemed a proper punishment for what she had done.

That afternoon, as Mrs. Lloyd tended her, Athena roused herself enough to ask what was going on with Caroline Vernon.

"Oh, Miss Taylor." The housekeeper struggled not to cry. "I didn't want to tell you. But I heard they took Miss Vernon to York Prison this morning, and that she'll hang next week."

Athena's heart was in her mouth. *Next week.* "And what of Mr. Vernon?"

"He and Mrs. Hillman plan to go to York. They hope to visit Miss Vernon and plead her case to the magistrate."

Athena knew that would be a futile effort. *The new magistrate is Neville Sinclair.*

The day wore on. Athena drifted in and out of sleep. She heard carriages arriving. An ominous foreboding took hold of her. She dragged herself to the window and opened it. In the drive below, Mrs. Gilbert and Mr. and Mrs. Weaver were alighting from separate vehicles.

Athena listened as they, too, voiced their discontent to Selena and demanded that their daughters be packed up for immediate removal from the premises.

How desperately Athena wanted to run downstairs and try to talk sense into these people, but she didn't have the strength. She could only watch as the last pupils in the school were driven away. Athena sank down on her bed in misery. She had never felt so lost or low in her entire life.

The school was a failure and would have to close.

She had pledged to solve the mysteries of Sally Osborn's and Harold Sinclair's deaths, but other than unproven theories about a handful of suspects, she had nothing to show for her efforts.

She had only just opened her mind to the idea of marriage. But it was too late.

She loved Mr. Vernon with all her heart. But he would never

know it, nor would he care. He would surely never forgive her for her part in his sister's discovery and apprehension. He must hate her now. She'd lost him forever.

If there *was* a forever.

She was ill. So ill that she might die. *Which is only what you deserve*, Athena told herself.

But worse, far worse: Caroline Vernon was going to die in less than a week. And Athena was entirely to blame.

If only she had just minded her own business. If only she had not been so determined to solve these mysteries, especially the one about Pryor Corbett, which was so unimportant. Why was she driven to do things like this? *Why, why, why?*

Athena buried herself beneath the covers and gave vent to an onslaught of tears.

It was the end of everything.

CHAPTER TWENTY-FOUR

THAT EVENING, ATHENA was awakened from a feverish and fitful sleep by the arrival of a young physician who introduced himself as Dr. Harris.

"I've come from York at the behest of Ian Vernon," he explained, gracefully removing his top hat from his head of light-brown hair.

Athena blinked up at the doctor in surprise. "How did Mr. Vernon know that I am ill?" Her mouth was dry and her voice so low and scratchy, she hardly recognized it.

"I told him first thing this morning, before he and Mrs. Hillman left for York," Selena admitted. "I thought they should know."

"Vernon and I met in school," the doctor explained. "I treated his sister while she was in hiding and delivered her child. He insisted that I attend you without delay."

Athena was astonished that Mr. Vernon had sent a physician to help her. Did it mean he had forgiven her? "Thank you for coming, sir." She took a sip of water from a tumbler, adding, "Did Mr. Vernon send a note?"

"He did not," Dr. Harris admitted.

Athena frowned. Of course there was no note. How could she ever hope for his forgiveness, when she could never forgive herself? Mr. Vernon hated her, but he had done the gentlemanly thing and had sent a doctor. For that, she was grateful.

Dr. Harris dedicated the next few hours to Athena's care, employing new and unfamiliar techniques. He began by throwing open all the windows in the room, saying that fresh air was a necessary inducement to healing. He promised that there would be no bloodletting, a practice he decried as being antiquated and barbaric.

He demanded every last fragment of ice from the icehouse and had Athena immersed in a cold bath—"to help reduce her fever," he said—an experience which was a shock to Athena's system at first but then felt better than she'd expected. He brought with him a variety of medicines that he said had come from herbs, some of which he applied to her wounds, and others which he administered orally.

"I believe these remedies will reduce your fever and help to cure your infections," Dr. Harris explained. "If I'm right, you should be well on the way to healing in two days' time."

When Athena awoke on the second morning, her fever was indeed gone. She required a few more days' bed rest, the doctor said, and plenty of fluids. Her wounds still ached and needed to be redressed daily. But she was no longer in mortal danger. Her staff could take over her care from there.

Selena saw the doctor out. Athena's spirits were still at an all-time low. Apparently, she wasn't going to die. But the prospect gave her no joy. Nothing else had changed. Their school had failed. Harold Sinclair's killer was still free. Mr. Vernon would never speak to her again. And Caroline Vernon was going to hang. Athena curled up in bed and wept until her throat was raw.

SOMETIME LATER, SELENA reappeared and sat on one of the chairs beside Athena's bed. "Dearest," she said softly, handing Athena a handkerchief. "The mail has come. There's a letter for you from Damon."

They hadn't heard from their brother in months. But Athena was too wretched to care. Wiping her eyes and nose, she said tonelessly, "Leave it."

"I was hoping you would read it now."

"I'll read it later."

"Please, Athena?" Selena gazed at her with pleading eyes. "Sit up, won't you, and read the letter?"

With a disgruntled sigh, Athena sat up in bed and opened the letter.

Brick Lane
Spitalfields, London

My dearest Athena,

Selena wrote and said you are ill—that you were attacked by dogs and suffered many injuries. I am so sorry to hear this and I am praying for your speedy recovery.

I'm sorry as well to hear about your troubles with the school. But, Athena—nothing worth doing ever happens without great effort and some bumps along the way. You have hit a setback, and a very distressing one at that. But things will improve if you stick to your goals and try again. It's a philosophy I have learned to embrace in recent years. Keep trying and never give up. It's the only route to success.

Selena mentioned something else that is quite distressing—a murder that has cast a shadow over Thorndale Manor. I know I used to criticize you when we were children, about all those little mysteries you and Diana and Selena were so determined to solve, missing jewelry and people and such. I believed, back then, that such pursuits were unworthy of the effort you put in—that you had more important things to do with your time. You were all certain that there was wickedness afoot that must be rooted out. I thought you were wrong in that, too. I believed then—and I still believe—that most people are inherently good.

In my work here over the past decade, however, I have discovered that there is also real evil in the world. I understand now that when confronted by malevolence, it is indeed a worthy endeavor to try to find and stop the perpetrator. If that fails—if nothing we say or do can make a difference—if the criminal keeps offending and the law does nothing to prevent them—the only recourse is to protect the people in danger as best we can.

Are you still intent on solving a crime? If so, I applaud your bravery and determination. The truth, I believe now, is worth seeking. And yet you must also consider the risk. Selena may be right. The dogs who mauled you may well have been set loose by someone who wants you out of the way.

Please proceed with caution, sister dear. Think of your safety. I shudder to think what might happen if the villain attempts another such attack.

With best regards,
Your brother,
Damon

Athena handed the letter to Selena and waited while she read it. When her sister had finished, Athena said, "You wrote and told him everything?"

"Not everything. Just enough, apparently, to grab his interest."

Athena sighed. "It doesn't matter. It's too late. Trying to solve this mystery has gotten us nowhere. Caroline Vernon is going to die." She glanced listlessly at her sister. "Did I tell you that she is Pryor Corbett?"

Selena stared at her. "What? Who is Pryor Corbett?"

"Caroline Vernon. Mr. Vernon told me, that day the dogs got me. That's why I found that manuscript page in the attic."

Selena's eyes widened. "You don't say! Caroline Vernon? Oh! It makes so much sense now. We should have guessed that Pryor Corbett was a woman. All those stories about heroines who ride and shoot and do good deeds and fall in love and have adventures—she was living out her fantasy life."

"I think she was. She found a way to deal with her forced confinement and was very successful at it." Fresh tears pooled in

Athena's eyes. "And now, thanks to me, there will never be another Pryor Corbett novel."

"I wish you wouldn't blame yourself."

"How can I not? It was so stupid of me to go up into that attic."

Selena seemed to be about to reply when Mrs. Lloyd entered the room. "Miss Taylor, Mr. Chapman is downstairs, hoping to see you. What shall I tell him?"

Athena frowned. The last thing she wanted was to make small talk with a visitor. "Tell him I'm not up to receiving anyone."

"Athena, this is the third time he's come," Selena told her. "You've been so ill, I sent him away. But I think it'd be good for you to have a visitor. He's been such a good friend to us."

"I don't want anyone to see me like this."

"Like what? You just survived an attack by malicious dogs and nearly died. Considering all that, you look like the belle of the ball."

"He brought flowers, miss," Mrs. Lloyd remarked with a persuasive nod.

Athena heaved a sigh. "Fine. Show him up."

A few minutes later, the housekeeper returned and presented Mr. Chapman. He hesitantly entered, carrying a bouquet that looked like it came from a hothouse. "Miss Taylor. I have been so worried."

It took all of Athena's willpower to muster a small smile. "Thank you for coming, Mr. Chapman."

He offered Athena the flowers. She thanked him and gave them to Mrs. Lloyd, who withdrew. Mr. Chapman removed his hat and took a seat in the second chair by Athena's bedside. "Are you feeling better, I hope?"

"Physically, yes. Mentally, I have never felt so wretched in my life."

"Miss Selena told me that all your pupils have been withdrawn from the school?"

"They have. I'm sorry to say that we no longer require your services, Mr. Chapman."

His brow furrowed. "Surely, you don't mean to close your doors? Can't you find other students?"

"Under the present circumstances? I sincerely doubt it." Athena shook her head. "We must face facts. No one will send their daughters here now. There can be no girls' school at Thorndale Manor."

"What an appalling state of affairs! And not just about the school. Miss Selena told me that you were mauled by dogs on the Woodcroft House grounds? I don't understand. Don't they lock up their animals?"

"The Master of the Hounds assured me that they do."

"It's our belief that someone let the dogs out on purpose," Selena put in.

Mr. Chapman stared at Selena. "You think this was another attempt on Athena's life?"

"I do."

He frowned. "Just like the runaway carriage."

"And the attack in the attic at Darkmoor Park. Someone deliberately tried to defenestrate me."

"'Defenestrate' you?" He stared blankly at Athena.

"He grabbed me and tried to throw me out a window."

He gasped. "Dear Lord! I had no idea. Are you certain it was a man?"

"No. It was pitch black. I couldn't see. Whoever it was, they were very strong." Athena recalled something else. "Margaret Quince is as tall and broad-shouldered as a man. I've seen her lift heavy boxes."

They all exchanged a glance.

"Who knew that you were going to Darkmoor Park that night?" Mr. Chapman asked.

Athena paused to think. "It could have been anyone. I— foolishly as it turns out—announced it to Mrs. Hillman's coachman outside the town hall, while the crowd was waiting to attend the concert."

"Who knew you were going to Woodcroft House the day you were mauled?"

"I told no one, but I passed several people in the village. George Osborn. Mr. Carson. Miss Quince. Their stares weren't friendly. I ran into Edward Ackroyd outside the village lock-up. He'd just heard that Caroline Vernon had been alive all this time." She glanced at Mr. Chapman. "Did you know Miss Vernon was living in the attic at Darkmoor Park?"

"Not until the other night. I never heard nor suspected anything. What a shocking turn of events. Mrs. Hillman is devastated that Miss Vernon was found."

"It's my fault." Athena flinched as she said it and waved away his look of inquiry. "Don't ask me to explain. But I should never have been in that attic. Mr. Ackroyd knew it, and he gave me a piece of his mind. I didn't tell you this, Selena, for fear you'd worry. But he said he would kill me if he could."

"Oh, no," Selena exclaimed.

"I'm sure he didn't mean it," Athena said quickly.

"Didn't he?" Mr. Chapman's lips pressed together in a frown.

"We learned recently that Mr. Ackroyd and Mr. Carson both attended the garden party where Harold Sinclair died," Selena told Mr. Chapman.

He nodded slowly. "So Ackroyd lied about that. Why would he have lied unless he had something to hide?" Grimly, Mr. Chapman added, "He might have followed you to Woodcroft House, Miss Taylor."

"He might have," Athena acknowledged, "but Edward Ackroyd now seems to me an unlikely suspect. He doesn't fit with Mrs. Hunt's story. He would never have framed Miss Vernon for murder."

"I see what you mean." Mr. Chapman paused. "If not Ackroyd ... did you meet anyone else along the way to Sinclair's estate?"

"Just Mr. Vernon, but he couldn't possibly be at fault."

Mr. Chapman shot Athena a questioning glance. "How can you be so certain? Vernon was at the helm of the entire charade to hide his sister, wasn't he? If, as you say, you were somehow culpable in Caroline Vernon's discovery, Mr. Vernon may harbor some resentment against you."

Selena inhaled sharply. "He could have waited while you spoke to Mr. Sinclair and let the dogs loose when you left the house."

Athena hesitated for only the briefest of seconds and then shook her head. "No!" *It couldn't be.* She loved Mr. Vernon. She had once hoped that he might return those feelings. That was over now. She had ruined it. But a man's nature did not change.

She shook her head firmly. "Mr. Vernon would never harm me or anyone. He is not that kind of man. He sent a doctor to tend me. If he wanted me to die, would he have done so?"

"Probably not," Selena acceded.

"Well, then, I go back to Margaret Quince and Mr. Carson," Mr. Chapman said.

Selena nodded. "Mr. Carson may have worked on his own or in collusion with Mr. Osborn."

Athena let out a long sigh. "They are all possibilities. But what does it matter now? Caroline Vernon will hang in a few days. And I can do nothing to stop it."

Selena took one of Athena's hands in hers. "You must not think that way. Things are dire, yes, but remember what our brother said. *'Keep trying and never give up.'* He urged us to *'protect the people in danger as best we can.'* We owe it to Miss Vernon to help her."

"Help her? How? I've seen York Prison. Miss Vernon may have managed a prison break years ago, but I very much doubt she can do so again."

"I wasn't thinking of a prison break. We must find a way to prove Miss Vernon's innocence before it's too late."

"What do you think I've been trying to do all these weeks?" Athena threw her hands up in despair. "I've gotten nowhere!"

"That's not true," Mr. Chapman responded. "You have identified several suspects, each of whom had motive and opportunity."

Selena nodded. "We have to flush out the killer and get them to incriminate themselves."

"Easier said than done," Athena countered.

"Since when have you ever sought the easy route?" Selena cried.

"You're right. *You're right.* But at this point, I don't know what to do. It's all still so muddled," Athena returned with a sigh.

"We can't let that stop us," Selena countered. "We *can* solve this, and we will. You know what Mama always said—*two heads are better than one.* And now there are three of us."

Athena blinked at her sister. "What did you just say?"

"I said … now there are three of us."

"No, before that. You said *two heads are better than one.*" Athena paused in thought. "That phrase implies the value of two people working together. But it could also apply to two people *working apart.*"

"What do you mean?" asked Mr. Chapman.

"I've been so puzzled by the 'Ethel Leighton' angle. But I wonder if we've been looking at it all wrong. We've been assuming that there was one person behind both Sinclair's murder and the blackmail. But what if it was *two* people with completely different reasons?" Athena's heart began to beat faster. "Take Edward Ackroyd. He had a strong motive to kill Harold Sinclair. Miss Quince hated Miss Vernon with a vengeance. She might be guilty of both the murder and the blackmail. But on the other hand, Ackroyd may have murdered Sinclair, after which Miss Quince saw her chance to take revenge on Caroline Vernon—by blackmailing Ethel Leighton into lying in court."

Selena gave a little gasp. "Oh! That's brilliant thinking, Athena."

Mr. Chapman nodded, wide-eyed. "Well done, Miss Taylor. I agree—that's entirely possible. And it puts Edward Ackroyd back in the running as a suspect for murder."

"Now we just have to—what did you say?" Athena asked her sister. "*Flush out* whoever is complicit? The question is: how?"

They all went quiet for a moment.

"I keep thinking that this all goes back to Sally Osborn," Selena murmured. "That she was murdered because she knew who Harold Sinclair's killer was. There must be a way to use that connection."

"If only Sally had kept a diary," Athena mused, "and named the killer of Harold Sinclair, it would make this all so simple."

"If only," Selena agreed.

"Wait," Athena said as another idea came to her. "That's it!"

"What's it?" Mr. Chapman asked.

"The way to flush the killer out! As far as we know, Sally didn't keep a diary. But the killer can't know that." A flame of hope kindled within Athena's breast. "What if we *pretend* that Sally Osborn's secret diary has been found here at Thorndale Manor, and that it incriminates the person who murdered Harold Sinclair?"

"Do we know if Sally could read and write?" Selena asked. "It's not common for someone in her profession."

"Yes, she could," Athena responded. "I recall giving her a list once of duties to perform, and she read it and commented on it in front of me."

Mr. Chapman's eyes narrowed. "Wait, I don't follow. What, exactly, are you suggesting?"

Athena knew that what she was about to propose was risky. She might be putting herself in danger. But if it worked, it could save Caroline Vernon's life. "I'll set up a kind of blackmail scheme. I'll write anonymous letters to everyone we suspect, saying that Sally's diary has been found and unless they want it turned over to the authorities, they must meet me at a specific time and place, with a particular sum of money."

Mr. Chapman's face creased with worry. "I don't know …"

"What a clever idea," Selena enthused. "The guilty party will never want that diary to fall into the wrong hands. It would mean they'd hang." She paused. "Just keep in mind, if we're wrong about the perpetrator, the entire exercise will be for naught."

"Well, then, let's cast the net a little wider." Athena chewed her lip, thinking hard. "Let's 'covertly' spread the word at the pub that Sally's diary has been found, with all the particulars about the meeting. If we're lucky, even if the letters don't work, word will reach the perpetrator."

"Miss Taylor." Mr. Chapman shook his head. "There have already been several attempts on your life. You're dealing with a known killer who may not hesitate to kill again. You're effectively using yourself as bait."

"I understand. I'll take steps to mitigate the risk. I'll have a witness there with me, a man with authority who can apprehend the villain on the spot."

"Who?" Selena asked.

"Neville Sinclair would never help. I'll ask Mr. Johnson. He is to be the next parish constable, after all."

Selena nodded. "Excellent plan. And whatever happens, it will be three against one. Because I'm going with you as well."

"You are not!" A flush of panic engulfed Athena. "I told you I don't want you involved."

"I couldn't bear it if anything happened to you, Athena, when I could be there to assist. We're doing this together or not at all," Selena insisted.

Athena heaved a long breath, too tired to fight. "Fine."

"Ladies, ladies! This plan of yours worries me." Mr. Chapman rubbed his chin and frowned. "Too many things could go wrong. Even if the vicar is present, you might all be in danger. And if the culprit gets away, he might harm you at a future date. May I suggest that Mr. Johnson and I meet with the perpetrator and leave you out of this?"

"It's my idea, my plan," Athena insisted. "You're not doing it without me."

"And me," Selena declared.

"All right," Mr. Chapman acquiesced with a sigh. "But I must insist that I be allowed to join you as another witness and means of protection, and to take on any other roles that are within my power, to keep you safe."

Athena considered that. They might benefit from another man's help. "Very well. Thank you, Mr. Chapman."

"Now, when and where do you propose to hold this meeting?" he asked.

"It can't be soon enough. Without this evidence, Caroline Vernon will hang. I say we schedule it for tomorrow night."

"Will you be well enough by then?" Selena asked.

"I feel better already just knowing that we have a plan," Athena replied. "As for where—it must be someplace out of the way." She paused in thought. "How about the dower house at Darkmoor Park? It is remote and quiet. Renovations are still in progress, so no one's living there. Mrs. Hillman is in York at present, right?"

"She is," Mr. Chapman replied. "And I believe she would approve any enterprise that might save her beloved Caroline."

"Good." Athena considered. "How much should we ask for our fictitious diary? Do you think twenty pounds is appropriate?"

"I'd say fifteen," Mr. Chapman suggested. "That's a lot of money, but a sum the killer might be able to come up with in a short time."

Athena threw back the bed covers. "The clock is ticking. We have not a moment lose." She moved to the desk and wrote four letters—to Edward Ackroyd, Miss Quince, and both Mr. Osborn and Mr. Carson—describing the diary and terms and instructing them to meet at the Darkmoor Park dower house the following night at 8:30 P.M.

Mr. Chapman offered to post the letters and to call on the vicar to inform him of their plans.

"I'll go to the pub and start the rumor," Selena said.

"A lady will be conspicuous at the pub," Mr. Chapman cautioned. "I'll do it."

A few hours later, Mr. Chapman returned and confirmed that

everything was in place. "The letters should be delivered in this afternoon's post," he explained. "The vicar is on board, and I mentioned the rumor about the diary and the upcoming meeting to Mr. Barnes, the Master of the Hounds at Woodcroft House, one of the biggest gossips in the village."

"I didn't realize Mr. Barnes was a gossip," Athena said, surprised. "I only met him once, when I was attacked by those dogs. But he seemed rather staid to me."

"He's a different man when women aren't around," Mr. Chapman assured her. "I have faith that he will spread the word."

There was only one more night and day to get through. Athena alternated between resting, tending to her wounds, and taking walks to regain her strength while engaged in clandestine conversation with Selena.

"The killer will be walking into a trap," Selena said as they strode together in the garden the following morning.

"We'll get our proof and save Caroline Vernon from the gallows," Athena enthused.

Selena squeezed Athena's hand with excitement and affection. "Once the word gets out that Miss Vernon was innocent, the taint will be removed from Thorndale Manor."

"We'll get all our pupils back."

"And new pupils besides." Selena eyes sparkled.

"Yes!" For the first time in days, Athena felt a ray of hope. She had a team to help her. *We'll pull this thing off,* she told herself.

Another added outcome also occupied her thoughts. If this all went as they hoped, then maybe, just maybe, Mr. Vernon would forgive her for the grievous mistake she'd made.

And maybe he wouldn't hate her any longer.

CHAPTER TWENTY-FIVE

ATHENA SHIVERED BENEATH her cloak as she and Selena strode down the road to Darkmoor Park, with only their lanterns to light the way.

They had told Mrs. Lloyd they were going for a long evening walk. Athena's cheeks and nose felt frozen by the time they'd reached the dower house. A glowing lantern hung outside the front door, a dim light emanated from the windows, and smoke was coming from one of the chimneys.

"Mr. Chapman must already be here," Athena noted. Despite the chilliness of the night, Athena was perspiring with nervous anticipation. Her stomach clenched, and every muscle in her body seemed to twitch. In twenty minutes, the vicar was due to arrive. A half hour later, if their plan worked, whoever had murdered Harold Sinclair would show up to buy the blank journal Athena carried in her cloak pocket.

If their plan worked.

Their partner in the plot was indeed waiting for them. The house was freezing inside. Athena noticed that improvements had been made since the last time she had been there. The walls were plastered and painted, and the floor was partially laid, but a maze of piled-up construction materials still took up residence.

"I made tea—the construction crew left a kettle and teapot— and I lit a fire upstairs for warmth and light," Mr. Chapman said as he led them up to the vestibule on the second floor. "There's a good view from the window up here, where we can sit and keep watch."

The fire in the atrium hearth upstairs did little to dispel the chill. Athena recognized the makeshift table from her previous visit. She had stood just here, admiring Mr. Vernon's drawings, when he had come up behind her and touched her neck and …

"Tea?" Selena asked, pouring Athena a cup from a steaming teapot.

Athena blinked to clear her head. "Thank you."

They sat down on mismatched chairs. Selena offered Mr. Chapman a cup.

"Thank you," he said, "but I finished mine just before you arrived."

Athena blew on the hot, fragrant brew and took a sip. "You said Mr. Johnson will be here at eight?"

"Yes," Mr. Chapman confirmed.

"What if he's late?" Selena shivered as she drank her tea.

"You'll still have me as a witness," Mr. Chapman assured them. "But don't worry. The vicar assured me he would be on time."

"Who else do you think will show up?" Selena mused wonderingly.

"My money is on Edward Ackroyd," Mr. Chapman responded.

"I think George Osborn got Mr. Carson to kill Harold Sinclair, and to stage all those attacks on you, Athena." Selena took another sip.

"Maybe," Athena replied, enjoying the tea. "But you didn't hear the venom in Miss Quince's voice when she described Harold Sinclair and Caroline Vernon. You know what they say. 'A woman scorned …'"

"We'll just have to wait and see." Mr. Chapman sat back in his chair.

"Will they come on foot or horseback, do you think?"

"On horseback, I'd wager. To make a fast getaway." Athena

stared out the window, hoping for the sound of hoofbeats or footfalls that would signal the approach of Mr. Johnson. But all was silent. Strangely, her head began to feel light, as if she'd had too many glasses of wine.

"Are you all right, Miss Taylor?" Mr. Chapman had a peculiar expression on his face.

"I don't know. I feel weird all of a sudden."

"So do I," Selena admitted. "My head is spinning."

"I'm suddenly very tired. I don't know why," Athena said.

"I can barely keep my eyes open," Selena murmured.

"Indeed?" remarked Mr. Chapman. He'd spoken only a single word, but his tone and expression had shifted to something dark and seemingly self-satisfied.

Athena stared at him, suddenly wary. "Mr. Chapman? What is going on?"

He just smiled. An eerie smile that spread a chill through Athena's bones.

All at once, it occurred to her that there was no empty, used teacup in the room. The awful truth dawned upon her. Mr. Chapman had not drunk any tea at all. The vicar wasn't on his way. And they weren't waiting for a villain to arrive.

The villain was sitting across from them. He had drugged them—put something in their tea.

Selena was sagging in her chair, but her wide-eyed expression suggested that she had reached the same conclusion. "You never mailed those letters, did you, Mr. Chapman?" she asked softly.

A deep lethargy seemed to be wrapping itself around Athena's mind and body. "And you never spoke to Mr. Johnson or anyone at the pub."

He shrugged. "Why would I? You have been a thorn in my side, Miss Taylor, ever since we met, the day I arrived at Darkmoor Bridge. Or should I say, the day *after* I arrived. In fact, I came a day earlier than I had planned or led you to believe I would."

Although exhaustion and newfound dread were creeping into

her every pore, the pieces of the puzzle began to fall into place in Athena's mind. *Why didn't I see it before?* "You ran into Sally Osborn that day."

"Right after I stepped off the coach." He frowned in annoyance. "I'd never thought to see *her* again."

Athena remembered now—Mr. Chapman had said he'd been in the neighborhood a month or two before Harold Sinclair's death. "And Sally recognized you."

"Very inconveniently." He stood and, from a box nearby, withdrew a coil of rope and a knife.

Athena's pulse jumped in fear. "Wait, wait." What was he planning to do to them? She needed to stand up, grab Selena by the hand, and flee. But she couldn't move.

"What are you saying, Mr. Chapman?" Selena's eyelids were drooping. "Did you kill Sally Osborn and Harold Sinclair?"

"Not Sinclair. I got Sally to do it." He chuckled. "Sally would have done anything for me."

Athena, her heart pounding with alarm, struggled to process this remark. *Could it be true? Did Sally Osborn murder Harold Sinclair? If so, why?* "Why kill Harold Sinclair?"

"He was a bully. He was three years ahead of me at Eton and he tormented me every single day."

Athena's breath hitched. She recalled Mr. Chapman mentioning that as a young man, he had met Harold Sinclair. He had also described his school days with great distaste. *"Boys' schools in England are a place of torture, Miss Taylor."* But she'd had no idea that they'd gone to school together.

He began wrapping the rope around Athena's upper body. She realized in horror that he was tying her to the chair. She tried to fight back, but she was too weak, and he was so much stronger. Instinct told her to take a deep breath and hold it, to expand her ribcage as much as possible despite the binds of her corset.

"Nine years ago, when I came to Darkmoor Park to visit Mrs. Hillman, we had dinner at Woodcroft House," Mr. Chapman went on as he worked with the rope.

Athena cried out in pain as the cord pressed against her dog bite wounds.

"Harold Sinclair hadn't changed a bit," Mr. Chapman went on, impervious to her distress. "He was still the same arrogant, conceited swine who had tried to drown me and bury me alive and … trust me, you ladies don't want to know what goes on at a boys' school. I'd wished Sinclair dead for years and when we were invited to that garden party, I knew it would be my chance. But I didn't want to put myself at risk. I made it known that I was returning to my tutoring position in southern England, but instead, I got a room in Harrowfield in secret, and I spent a few weeks romancing the parlor maid."

"Sally," Selena murmured before she slid from her chair in a heap.

Selena must have drunk more tea than I did, Athena thought, but even so, she was incapacitated and in a frightened daze. She winced at the tug of the rope as Mr. Chapman tied a knot beneath her ribcage and she watched him cut off the rope end with the knife. At last, she slowly let out the breath she'd been holding. She had to keep Mr. Chapman talking, if only to help her stay conscious. "You courted Sally Osborn?"

"She fell for me like a ton of bricks. That is, the man she *thought* me to be. It's amazing how easily one can change their appearance by dying their hair blond and adopting a false mustache."

All this time, they'd been looking for a blond. "What did you do? Tell her what a villain Mr. Sinclair was and promise to marry her?" Athena's voice sounded so sluggish now, she didn't recognize it.

"Something like that." Chapman brought the remaining length of rope over to Selena, who lay on the floor, passed out cold. "Sally hated Harold Sinclair—he had been cruel to her. It was child's play to convince her to poison his drink. But I worried she'd talk. I should have killed her the day after the party, but I was afraid that suspicion might fall on me."

With a gasp, Athena realized that her theory about two suspects instead of one had been correct. She'd just had the wrong two people. It had been Sally and Mr. Chapman. "So, you blackmailed Ethel Leighton into … lying at Caroline Vernon's trial."

"Again, not hard. I'd overheard her at the pub, telling her beau about the money she had stolen from Arthur Vernon. She was terrified about going to prison." Mr. Chapman began tying Selena's hands behind her back. "I stayed away for nine years and thought that was long enough. I needed to rekindle my relationship with Mrs. Hillman so that stupid woman would finally name me in her will as her heir. But the minute I got here, I ran into Sally. She recognized me even with my natural hair color."

"Did she threaten to … turn you in? And herself?" Sally must have felt so guilty. She had become obsessed with the Bible, after all.

He chuckled again. "How did you guess? I had to think fast. I said I had never stopped thinking about her—that I'd come back to ask her to marry me. I told her to meet me at our usual spot down by the river."

That's why Sally wore the blue shoes, Athena thought. *She still had feelings for Mr. Chapman, and she bought his lie.* "And that's where you killed her."

Chapman wagged a finger at her. "You see, it's saying things like that that have gotten you into trouble. For weeks now, you've been sticking your nose in where it's not wanted, insisting on 'finding out what really happened.' I had to silence you. I tried several times, in fact."

The room seemed to be tilting at a peculiar angle. It was all Athena could do to stay awake. "The carriage? The attic? The dogs?" Her voice had dropped to a whisper. "It was all you?"

"You proved to be more difficult to dispatch than I'd expected." From a nearby crate, he withdrew a large tin can labeled in bold, black letters:

WHALE OIL. DANGER. FLAMMABLE.

Athena gasped in horror. He uncapped the can. The strong, fishy fumes invaded her nostrils as her chin drooped to her chest.

"I thought it was just you I had to get rid of," Mr. Chapman went on as he poured the amber liquid over the wooden floor and the crates around them. "But yesterday, your sister made it clear that she's just as determined to solve the mystery as you are. I have to say, you're very clever, the both of you. You've helped me to stage the perfect circumstances of your own deaths."

They were the last words Athena heard before she felt herself slipping into oblivion.

THE FIRST THING Athena became aware of was the sound of crackling. The second sensation was smell. *Smoke. And a disagreeable fishy odor.* Then touch. *Hot.* She was so incredibly hot. And her lungs felt scratchy.

Athena coughed and opened her eyes. She gasped in terror. The dower house was on fire! Flames were consuming the crates of construction materials around her, and the blaze danced along the floor. She tried to move but discovered she was still tied to the chair. Smoke stung her eyes and lungs and made her cough again. She saw Selena lying on the floor a few feet away, her hands tied behind her back.

Athena still felt woozy and commanded herself to focus. Somehow, she had to free herself. Because she'd held her breath while Mr. Chapman had tied her up, the rope that bound her had some give. It took some doing, but she finally managed to snake one arm up and out of the bonds and then to free her other arm.

She tried to wriggle out beneath the loosened ropes, but it was impossible. With fevered fingers, Athena picked at the knot around her midsection. It wouldn't budge. Tears burned her irritated eyes. She blinked in frustration. The fire roared and crackled. She felt time ticking away as she tugged and pulled at the knot. *Come on! Come loose or we're going to die!*

At last, the knot began to give, and it came free. With relief, she yanked off the rope and stood. Her mind reeled. Smoke continued to tickle her lungs and the strong, fishy odor caused bile to rise in her throat. She was overtaken by a long coughing fit that made her retch.

At last, she rushed to Selena's side, knelt down beside her, and shook her hard. "Selena! Wake up!"

Her sister stirred and started coughing. "Leave me alone. I'm so hot. I want to sleep."

"Selena, the house is on fire! We have to get out of here!"

Selena opened her eyes, made a face, and squinted groggily. "What is that smell?"

"The dower house is on fire! Mr. Chapman doused the place with whale oil."

Selena gasped. Athena helped her sister up. Selena wavered on her feet. She seemed to still be fighting the effects of the drug, and she struggled against the ropes that bound her wrists.

"There's no time to free you." The fire had spread, and smoke was gathering thicker by the second.

Selena's eyes darkened in terror. "And no way to reach the window or stairs. We're trapped."

A memory came back to Athena. "Maybe not. This room has a hidden door that opens by a spring mechanism. Mr. Vernon said it was a secret exit from the house."

"I don't see any door."

"Me, neither, but it was on the architectural drawing. It's over there." Athena pointed to a corner of the room, where flames were starting to lick the wall. Before her eyes, the wallpaper curled and melted, until the edges of a hidden door were revealed. "There it is."

"I see it." Selena coughed agitatedly. "But how do we get there?"

In between them and the secret door, the floor was on fire.

The area was impassable.

Athena's throat burned and it was becoming more difficult to breathe. Coughing, she glanced around in desperation. The makeshift table where they'd been sitting wasn't on fire. Springing into action, she slid the door off the sawhorses beneath it, cantilevered it to the ground, and shoved it forward towards the opposite wall. The door fell with a crash, creating a path between the flames.

"Run!" Athena exclaimed.

They raced in tandem across the fallen door to the spot where the hidden door was now completely revealed. Parts of the wall were on fire. Holding up her long skirts, Athena raised one booted foot and smashed it against the door. It sprang open.

Athena peered within. A narrow staircase led downward. "Let's go."

Athena held on to Selena to steady her as, both coughing, they cautiously navigated their way down the dark stairs, which twisted and turned. Athena soon became aware of heat searing her leg.

"Athena! Your skirts are on fire!"

They had reached a small landing. Athena gasped, too terrified to think.

"Drop down!" Selena cried.

Athena—recalling now a scientific principle they had both read about—followed her sister's advice. Curling up in a ball on the landing, Athena rolled back and forth until the flames were extinguished. With relief, they resumed their descent, both of them wheezing now. The smoke lessened, and it became increasingly cold. At last, they reached the end of the stairs, a spooky, dark area with a dirt floor pervaded by the smell of must and coal.

"We're in the cellar." Selena was still struggling futilely to free her hands.

"There must be a way out of here."

Holding tightly to Selena's arm, Athena felt her way through the blackness, stumbling and crying out when she stubbed her foot against something sharp. At length, she spied a dim light ahead and they made their way to it. It turned out to be a window in a small door set high up in the wall. Steps led up to it. Moonlight streamed in through the filthy glass.

Athena wrestled with the door's latch until it opened. She helped Selena to snake her way through and then followed, bursting out with relief onto the damp, cold grass beneath the night sky. They were on the side lawn of the house. As she inhaled the fresh air, Athena was so grateful to be free and alive, she gasped with joy.

For a moment, they just stood there, taking in the sight of the burning house from which they had escaped. A great cracking and popping rent the air, as angry, red and yellow flames shot up through the windows and from beneath the eaves. A dark cloud of smoke hung over the house and billowed upwards, blending with the blackness of the night sky.

"Let's get out of here," Athena said.

They ran around the house to the front drive, where they paused to catch their breath. Athena's eyes still smarted and she and her sister both erupted into coughing fits. Athena heard the distant clang of the church bell. A moment later came the rattle of a carriage traveling at a rapid speed. Up the road, she perceived two pinpoints of light, which she guessed to be the lamps of an approaching vehicle. "Who can that be?"

Selena stared at the vehicle but didn't reply.

In short order, a carriage drew up, the door was flung open, and a man leapt out. In the reflected glow from the burning house, Athena was able to make out his face.

It was Mr. Vernon.

"What is he doing here?" Athena asked in wonder. She'd thought Mr. Vernon was in York. To her further astonishment, two more people stepped down from the carriage. Was her mind playing tricks on her? Was that Neville Sinclair? And Mrs. Ethel Hunt?

She'd swear there was yet another person inside the carriage. *Who?*

Mr. Vernon dashed up to Athena and Selena, a wild-eyed look on his face. "Are you all right?"

Athena replied with the first thing on her mind. "Would you please untie my sister's hands?"

"I will," Mr. Vernon began. "But ..." Glancing down at Athena's skirts he added, "Dear lord."

Athena followed his gaze, surprised to note that one side of her dress and the petticoat beneath it had been charred and shredded by the flames, revealing her calf, which was as red as a lobster and beginning to blister.

"What happened?" he cried.

"Peter Chapman tried to kill us," Athena answered before collapsing in Mr. Vernon's arms and fainting dead away.

CHAPTER TWENTY-SIX

THE PEAL OF the clock in the hall brought Athena back to consciousness from a deep, troubled sleep. It took her a few blinking seconds to realize that she was in her own bed at Thorndale Manor. Why that filled her with relief, she couldn't say.

Sunlight filtered in around the edges of the drawn curtains. A fire burned in the hearth. She was alone in the room. Her throat hurt, her lungs felt irritated, and she was wracked by a cough. Athena counted as the clock's tolls reverberated through the air. Nine. Ten. Eleven. Twelve. *Twelve!* How could it be noon? Why hadn't someone woken her? Oddly, Athena couldn't recall coming to bed last night.

She did, however, recall her dreams. Or rather, her nightmares. They had been filled with images of a fire and a heart-pounding need to escape from a burning building. Why did her left leg smart so painfully? Athena sat up, shrugged the coverlet aside, pulled up her long nightgown, and studied her leg. Her right shin and ankle were still bandaged from the dog attack. But her left leg was now also wrapped in gauze up to her thigh. She noted smudges of soot on her skin and detected the scent of smoke clinging to her hair. What had happened?

All at once, the events of the previous night flooded her brain.

The plan that had gone so horribly wrong.

Mr. Chapman's smug assertions as he had tied her and Selena

up.

The dower house on fire. The secret door to the hidden staircase. How fortunate they had been to escape!

Athena remembered making it to the front drive. The building engulfed in flames. Then Mr. Vernon had arrived out of nowhere. Had Mr. Sinclair been with him? And Mrs. Hunt as well? Everything after that was fuzzy.

The door quietly opened, and Selena entered. "At last you're awake." Selena crossed to Athena's bed where she paused, coughing. "Forgive me. I can't seem to stop coughing. How do you feel?"

Athena couldn't prevent her own answering cough. "My lungs and throat feel raw, my leg hurts, and my head aches, but otherwise, I think I'm all right."

"Mr. Quince said the cough is from smoke inhalation. It may take weeks to resolve. And my head hurts too. Apparently, that's from the drug Mr. Chapman gave us. Mr. Quince suspects it was chloral hydrate, a sleeping aid he had prescribed for Mrs. Hillman."

"When was Mr. Quince here?"

"He tended you at Darkmoor Park. Your leg was badly burned."

"I don't remember a thing about it."

"You passed out. Mr. Quince applied a salve and said you will heal in time. He gave you a sleeping draft and I have pain medicine, if you need it."

They both coughed again in tandem. Athena noticed that Selena's wrists were marked with red abrasions, no doubt from the rope that had bound them. "Apart from the cough and headache, are *you* all right?"

"I'm fine." Selena sat on the bed beside her and caressed Athena's cheek. "Sister dear. There are no words to express my gratitude to you. You were so brave last night." Tears studded her hazel eyes. "If not for you, we both would have died."

"There was no time to think. I just did what I had to do."

Athena struggled to recall more about the previous night. "I remember everything up till the fire, and our escape. But after that, it's mostly a blank. Has Mr. Chapman been apprehended?"

"He has. Mr. Neville Sinclair arrested him last night."

"Thank heavens." Athena breathed a sigh of relief, then coughed again. "Having experienced Mr. Chapman's charms myself, it's not surprising that Sally was infatuated by him."

"What a rogue he is." Selena's jaw set. "We were all taken in by him. I hope I'll know better than to trust such a charismatic man in future."

"Me too. How did we get home, Selena?"

"I'll tell you, but first things first. You need to bathe. Mr. Quince said we must keep your leg dry, so I'll call for a sponge bath."

Tabitha and Laura soon arrived with pitchers of hot water and an empty round, tin tub, which Selena positioned by the hearth. Once the maids had quit the room, Selena helped Athena to undress and sit on a chair in front of the tub.

"Am I remembering correctly?" Athena asked as she lay her head back against a rolled-up towel atop the chair. "Did Mr. Vernon come to the dower house last night?"

"He did."

Athena enjoyed the relaxing sensations of hot water being poured onto her hair and heard it rain down into the tub below. "Were Mr. Sinclair and Mrs. Hunt there, too?"

"Yes. Mr. Vernon brought them."

"Why? And how did he know to come?"

Selena struggled to stifle a cough as she lathered her hands with soap. "I wrote to him."

"You wrote to Mr. Vernon again?" Athena closed her eyes as her sister massaged soap into her hair. "Why?" she repeated.

"I knew your feelings for Mr. Vernon, and that you despaired of him ever forgiving you for your part in Caroline Vernon's discovery. I wanted him to know the lengths to which we were going, to seek the truth and try to free his sister. I found out where he was staying in York and sent him a letter, informing him of our rendezvous last night."

"I can't believe you did that." But Athena was glad she had.

"I felt that bold measures were required."

"That still doesn't explain why he came."

"Mr. Vernon said that when he received my letter, he was concerned that we might be putting ourselves in danger. He was far more prescient than we were."

"Did he suspect Mr. Chapman?"

"No." Selena rinsed Athena's hair with fresh, warm water. "But he convinced Mr. Sinclair to return to Darkmoor Bridge with him."

"How is it that he brought Mrs. Hunt as well?"

"I'll let him tell you about *that* himself." Selena poured more warm water onto Athena's hair.

"When?"

"He promised to visit this afternoon."

Athena opened her eyes and sat up straight in the chair, coughing and dripping water all over the floor. "Mr. Vernon is coming *here*? *Today*?"

"Yes. Why do you think I'm trying to make you presentable? As I understand it, he had to go back to York early this morning, but he hoped to return this afternoon at three o'clock." Selena smiled as she nudged Athena to lie back again. "Now relax and let me give you that promised sponge bath."

A few hours later, Athena, dressed and fed and feeling much more like herself, waited with Selena for the sounds of an arriving carriage.

Mr. Vernon arrived, as promised, shortly after three. When Mrs. Lloyd showed him into the drawing room, Athena and Selena rose from the sofa to greet him. He was dapperly dressed in his charcoal-grey suit and top hat.

And he had brought someone with him.

Caroline Vernon.

Athena positively gaped.

Miss Vernon strode in on Mr. Vernon's arm, her lavender frock a perfect complement to her raven-black hair and cornflower-blue eyes. It was the first time Athena had seen her in broad daylight, and she was even more beautiful than Athena had presumed from her portraits.

"Miss Taylor. Miss Selena," Mr. Vernon said in greeting as the twosome crossed the room. His eyes blazed with some emotion she couldn't quite define—but it was a look that set her heart aflutter. With an affectionate nod to Miss Vernon, he added, "May I present my sister, Miss Caroline Vernon?"

The courtesies were exchanged. Miss Vernon's face sparkled with warmth and happiness. "It is such a pleasure to meet you both properly."

"And you, Miss Vernon," Athena and Selena returned in unison. Selena was beaming.

As they all sat down, Athena offered tea, but they declined, explaining that they were due to have tea at Darkmoor Park with Mrs. Hillman, who had returned on the same train from York.

Athena hid a long cough behind her hand, and Selena did the same.

Mr. Vernon's brow knitted. "I fear last night's harrowing adventures have taken their toll on you both."

"I've read that smoke inhalation can have lasting ill effects," Miss Vernon put in, her smile fading.

"Don't worry, the apothecary said that we will be well in time," Selena assured them.

"I'm glad to hear it," Miss Vernon responded softly.

"How is your leg, Miss Taylor?" Mr. Vernon persisted, worry still clouding his features.

"It hurts," Athena told him, "but I consider it a small price to pay for having survived with all my limbs intact."

"Perhaps," he replied. "But I am very sorry that you were injured."

Athena was beset by two strong emotions. Overwhelming relief that Mr. Vernon was not looking at her with antipathy.

And gratitude that Miss Vernon sat beside him, looking hale and healthy.

"How is it that you are here, Miss Vernon?" Athena asked, fighting back sudden tears. "I hope this means you are free at last?"

"I am." Miss Vernon's lower lip trembled. "I don't know how to thank you both for all that you've done."

Athena struggled for words. "Please don't speak of what *I* did, Miss Vernon. I feel so guilty. You were only arrested again and sent back to prison because of me."

"Pray, think no more about it. It is *because* of you and your sister that I have finally been acquitted."

Athena withdrew a handkerchief and dried her eyes. "I'm glad to hear it. But there's so much that I still don't understand. Please tell me everything." She turned to Mr. Vernon. "My sister said she wrote to you?"

"Yes. The moment I received that letter yesterday, I sensed you were in danger. Neville Sinclair was in York as well. I called on him and explained the situation. He expressed regret, Miss Taylor, that you had been hurt by his dogs. And he agreed that we must stop you from holding that meeting. By then, it was already late afternoon. We boarded the first train. As it left the station, I recalled something you had mentioned, Miss Taylor, that now seemed important."

"What was that?" Athena and her sister both coughed discreetly into their handkerchiefs at intervals as he continued.

"You said you had met Mrs. Hunt, and that she had admitted to lying on the witness stand. The day you told me, I was too angry to see the value of what you had discovered—and also at the time, afraid to reveal Caroline's survival, even if it might mean her acquittal. But now that Caroline had been discovered and was in prison again, I realized that Mrs. Hunt was the key—if she reversed her testimony, Sinclair might reopen the case. He waited in the carriage when I stopped at Duxley-on-Green. Thankfully, I persuaded Mrs. Hunt to come with us."

"How? When I asked, she refused to help me."

"I suggested that Mrs. Hunt amend her story slightly—to say the reason she gave in to the blackmailer is that he threatened to inform her betrothed about an 'affair' she'd had with him. A complete lie, but one which was believable and not a criminal offense."

Athena took that in with a nod. "Quick thinking, Mr. Vernon."

"It did the trick. She returned with us to Darkmoor Bridge and told Sinclair her story on the way. When we disembarked from the train, I noticed Mr. Chapman on the platform, apparently waiting to board—to place himself away from the scene of his crimes, I believe, and in view of witnesses. He was talking to a porter. Mrs. Hunt overheard him and shrieked, *'I know that voice! It's him! The blackmailer! He was masked and had blond hair, but that's definitely him!'*"

Athena gasped. "Did he try to run?"

"Yes. Sinclair and I managed to grab Chapman and with brute force we shoved him into a waiting cab. That was when we noticed a plume of smoke in the sky in the direction of Darkmoor Park. I feared the worst. A man came racing up the street, shouting for someone to ring the church bell and summon the fire brigade—and we made a mad dash over there."

"What happened to the dower house?" Athena asked. "Did the fire brigade come?"

"Yes, but I'm afraid it was too late." His lips thinned. "When I saw the building early this morning, it was a smoldering ruin."

Athena pressed her hand to her throat. "Oh, no."

"I am so sorry for Mrs. Hillman—to lose that house," Selena said sadly.

"So am I." Athena's eyes watered. "And I know how hard you worked, Mr. Vernon, to renovate the place."

"Don't worry about me or Mrs. Hillman," Mr. Vernon insisted. "We can always rebuild the dower house. We are both grateful that you ladies are safe."

"Tell me about Mr. Chapman. Selena said he's been arrested?"

"Yes." Mr. Vernon leaned forward in his seat and clasped his hands. "When we confronted him with everything Miss Selena told us and Mrs. Hunt's new testimony, he finally broke down and confessed to his part in the murder of Harold Sinclair, and to killing Sally Osborn. Neville Sinclair delivered Chapman to York Prison this morning, where he will stand trial. As the new magistrate, Sinclair dropped all charges against my sister and insisted that she be released at once."

Athena's heart felt lighter than it had for months. "Oh, Miss Vernon, this verdict is nine years overdue, but I'm so relieved and happy for you!"

"Thank you." Miss Vernon's mouth curved into a smile. "Relief and happiness barely scratch the surface of what *I* feel right now. To walk out of that prison, a free woman at last—there are no words to describe it."

"Agreed," Mr. Vernon put in. "However, ladies," he added, directing an admonishing look at Athena and Selena, "I cannot help but point out that your scheme was totally mad. You do realize that you both could have been killed—and very nearly were?"

"I knew that it was risky," Athena admitted. "But I told myself we'd be fine. We thought we had two men working on our side, after all."

"I wasn't even thinking of risk when I wrote to you," Selena told Mr. Vernon. "I just wanted you to know how hard Athena was working to find the truth."

"Mr. Vernon, if you hadn't convinced Mrs. Hunt to retract her testimony, Mr. Chapman might still be free," Athena noted. "How can we ever thank you?"

"That's the wrong question," Mr. Vernon replied.

Miss Vernon nodded. "It is *we* who owe deep thanks to both of you. Miss Taylor, if you hadn't forced me out into the open, I might have spent the rest of my life hidden away—and I must admit I couldn't stand the isolation anymore."

"If you hadn't written to me, Miss Selena, we wouldn't be sitting here right now," Mr. Vernon pointed out. "And, Miss Taylor, if not for your discovery of Mrs. Hunt, Chapman might never have confessed. For that, my sister and I are grateful beyond expression. And I owe *you* an apology."

"An apology?" Athena glanced at him, surprised. "What for?"

"Every time you came to me with your theories, I shot them down."

"I understand why. I was wrong about so many things."

"Yet you were right about many others, and about what mattered most: that the deaths of Sally Osborn and Harold Sinclair were connected. You have excellent instincts, Miss Taylor. I should have listened. Can you ever forgive me?"

"Of course I can, and I do."

His eyes gleamed with a look that set Athena's heart singing, a look that seemed to convey gratitude and something else—was it affection?

A shiver of happiness ran up her spine. She had done it—albeit with help—but due to her efforts, a great mystery had been solved, a good woman had been set free, and the villain behind it all had been incarcerated. Any lingering doubts she may have had about being less capable than her older sister were put to bed at last.

All too soon, it was time for Mr. and Miss Vernon to go. The young lady extended an invitation from Mrs. Hillman to join them for dinner at Darkmoor Park later that week, which Athena and Selena accepted with enthusiasm.

At the door, Mr. Vernon asked if he might call on Athena the following day—to "reassure himself that she was indeed recovering," he said. She happily agreed and counted the minutes until she would see him again.

"WHEN I THINK what that villain tried to do to you, it makes my blood run cold," Mr. Vernon said as he and Athena strolled together the following morning on the Thorndale Manor grounds.

Orange, red, and yellow leaves flung themselves from the ancient oaks onto the dancing breeze before fluttering to the autumnal carpet below. Athena's leg and other wounds still hurt, and she limped a little, but it was good to be outside. The air was so cool and crisp that she could feel the roses blooming in her cheeks.

"Mine, too. But what he did to your sister is so much worse. All those years that she had to remain in hiding. It is too awful to contemplate."

"Caroline made the best of it. She came up with a vocation that kept her mind and heart occupied."

"She did, indeed." In all the excitement, Athena had given little thought to Miss Vernon's authorship. "To know that she is the author of so many of my favorite novels! I am so impressed. I can hardly wait to quiz her at dinner tomorrow night, to learn what plot developments she has in store for Lydia and John Brandon."

Mr. Vernon grinned. "Good luck getting that out of her. Caroline never discusses her work with me and has never let me read a manuscript until it's finished."

"Selena and I will try to wrangle it out of her." They laughed, which made Athena cough. His brows drew together, but she waved away his concern, insisting, "I'm fine, I'm fine. Or I will be soon."

"I hope so." His eyes still looked troubled, but he gave her a slight nod as they strolled on. "I've been meaning to tell you. Remember that manuscript page you found here in the attic?"

"Of course."

"Caroline noticed it missing, not long after I relocated her to the attic at Darkmoor Park. I came back looking for it the night after you moved in but couldn't find it. I was on my way down the servants' stairs when I heard you and your sister in the hall, and I froze, worried that you'd find me."

Athena touched her cheek with her hand. "We *did* sense something strange that night. We thought it was a ghost!"

"I must have waited in that stairwell for an hour, hoping you had both gone to bed, before I fled the house."

"Was that the only time you snuck in?"

"It was. I didn't dare return."

"Well, you're welcome to return any time you wish," Athena told him. "I hope by the front door." They laughed again. She coughed again. "Where will your sister live now?" she asked.

"Mrs. Hillman insists that Caroline reside at Darkmoor Park, and she has happily accepted. At least for now."

"'For now'?"

Mr. Vernon turned to gaze at Athena as they walked along. "Edward Ackroyd came to see Caroline last night."

Athena drew in an anxious breath. "Oh? That man hates me."

"He does not. In fact, it is quite the reverse. He shares my sense of gratitude for all that you and your sister did to secure Caroline's release. He plans to call on you and Miss Selena and say as much."

"That's a relief."

"Ackroyd still loves my sister, even after all these years. It was apparent that Caroline has never gotten over her attachment to him, either. He asked for permission to court her. Of course I said *yes*."

Athena smiled. "I can think of no better outcome." Something occurred to her, but she hesitated. It was a subject she had never discussed with Mr. Vernon. "Mrs. Lloyd told me about your sister's relationship with Mr. Ackroyd," she said quietly. "I was wondering … but perhaps it is inappropriate to speak of it?"

"Miss Taylor, I have lived with the secret about my sister's life for so long, it is a relief to finally be able to discuss it. Caroline gave me leave to tell you and your sister anything you wish to know—with the request that you remain discreet."

"Of course."

"I think I can guess the question that's on your mind. You know Caroline had a child by Mr. Ackroyd. But are you aware of the identity of that child?"

"Mrs. Lloyd just said it was a girl who had been adopted by a good family."

"The girl doesn't know who her real mother is, and neither do her parents." Mr. Vernon gave her a lopsided grin. "But you and Miss Selena are both closely acquainted with the child."

"Are we?" Athena hadn't expected that. "Who is it?"

"Miss Lucy Russell."

Athena was so startled, she gasped. "Miss Russell! Oh—that explains so much. Miss Russell looks nothing like her parents. She is so clever. She has a talent for storytelling. And she spoke of nocturnal visits, when she was very little, from a woman in white—a ghost, she had presumed."

"That was my sister. Despite my warnings, Caroline crept out at times to see her little girl. She was thrilled when the Russells enrolled Lucy in your school. It felt to her as if Thorndale Manor was calling her daughter back home, where she belonged."

"What a lovely thought."

He stopped and turned to her. "Speaking of which. I hope you know how delighted I am that *you* are the owner of Thorndale Manor."

"Have you forgiven me, then, for stealing it away from you?"

"You have stolen nothing, my dearest Athena. Except my heart."

It was the first time he had uttered her given name. Athena's own heart jumped with hope and wonder at the tender look on his face. "Have I?"

"How could you doubt it?" He closed the gap between them. "All these years, I have remained alone, the keeper of secrets, looking for a woman whom I could love and trust completely. I had despaired of ever finding her. And then I met you. For weeks, I have been wanting to tell you how I feel—that from almost the first moment we met, even if I was too proud to show it, I have felt a connection to you, as though our minds and hearts are a perfect match. I have been dreaming of a life with you at my side. You made your feelings clear on the idea of marriage, but—" He swallowed hard, and in a hushed tone, continued. "Would you reconsider your position if I promise you that you'll retain all the freedoms that are so important to you?"

"That depends on what you mean by 'freedoms,'" Athena answered breathlessly.

He cupped her cheek in his hand. "I mean the freedom—if we were to become husband and wife—to voice your every wish and opinion and to know that I will honor and respect your choices, even if I disagree. The freedom to make decisions where our children are concerned, which I believe is every mother's right. The freedom to work if you wish to, in the profession that gives you joy. It is my hope that we will be a unified force, in agreement on the most important things, but when that varies, you needn't feel beholden to what I think. I respect you and your brilliant mind. I love you, Athena."

Athena's chest swelled with happiness. "And I love and respect you, Ian. With all my heart." How wonderful it was to finally express the feelings she had been harboring for this man. "You are so very dear to me."

He knelt down on the leaf-strewn path and took her hands in his. "Will you marry me, my darling?"

"I will!"

He rose again, bringing Athena with him. Wrapping their arms around each other, their lips met in a wondrous kiss, a kiss filled with emotion. Athena knew that she had met her perfect other half. And with this man, she realized all at once, Thorndale Manor, the house that she had come to love so much, would feel even more like home.

CHAPTER TWENTY-SEVEN

A THENA TAYLOR AND Ian Vernon were married three months later, on a blustery day in late January when the snow covering the ground matched Athena's gown of pure, white silk.

The bride, fit to burst with happiness, wore a veil of Belgian lace that Mrs. Hillman had worn in her own wedding. Athena carried a bouquet of sage, pine, hellebores, and snowdrops that had pushed their way up through the frosty terrain as if determined to share in the couple's bounty.

The ceremony was held in the village church. To Athena's delight, her brother, Damon, tall and handsome in his white, linen surplice and cassock, had taken leave from his parish in London to officiate as she and her new husband exchanged their vows.

They had kept the guest list to a minimum, including only close family and Mrs. Hillman, Bridget and George Osborn, Edward Ackroyd, the servants at Thorndale Manor, and the school's pupils. Ever since Caroline Vernon's full pardon, all their former students had returned, and they had received applications for several more.

Selena was the maid of honor. Caroline Vernon—or rather, the newly married Mrs. Edward Ackroyd—was a bridesmaid. Both young women beamed as they walked down the aisle, pictures of perfection in their pale-pink satin gowns.

Athena's wounds had long since healed and she and her sister—both fully recovered from the effects of the fire at the dower house—were grateful to feel in perfect health and able to enjoy every moment of this special day.

To Athena's regret, her sister Diana and her husband had been unable to attend. Captain Fallbrook was away at sea and Diana was in her ninth month of pregnancy, expected to deliver in a week or two. She had sent a thoughtful and generous gift—the funds to renovate the master suite at Thorndale Manor for the newly wedded couple—and a promise to visit as soon as she and her new child were allowed to travel.

After the service, the merry guests gathered in the Thorndale Manor dining room for the wedding breakfast.

"May I have your attention?" Ian called out, standing up beside his seated bride at the head table. "Thank you all for coming today and sharing the happiest day of my life. I should like to propose a toast to my new bride." He raised his wineglass. When their guests had all followed suit, he continued. "I wouldn't blame Athena if she—and all of you—think I only married her to regain the chance to live at Thorndale Manor. But I promise you, that's not the case."

The crowd chuckled. Athena's laugh was filled with empathy, for she understood how much this old house meant to Ian. As an example of his gallantry and forward thinking, Ian was working with an attorney to have Thorndale Manor put in both his wife's name and his own—*a remarkable concept*, Athena thought. It felt *right* to Athena, to know that the estate that had been Ian's birthright had been returned to him. It was as if the universe were righting a terrible wrong.

"I asked Athena to be my wife," her husband went on, "because I had the wisdom to recognize her as the kindest, cleverest, most thoughtful, hardworking, and truly extraordinary woman I had ever met. A woman who, when she gets an idea into her head, will not give it up for anything." He gazed down at Athena, his eyes lit with such affection, it made her heart turn over. "I cannot tell you how grateful I am to you, my darling, for not only rescuing my sister from a lifetime of imprisonment, but for rescuing me as well, from a lifetime of despair and loneliness. I am the luckiest man on Earth that you consented to share your life with me and I love you more than words can say. To my new bride!"

"Hear, hear!" cried the assembled guests.

Athena stood and kissed her husband, which resulted in a volley of hoots and cheers.

"Words cannot express how happy and grateful I am to have reached this day," she told the crowd. "My dear husband's many fine qualities are too innumerable to recount here. So, I shall be brief and simply say: I love him dearly and I look forward to our life together."

More cheers followed.

Selena stood next and proposed a toast. "Athena and I have been so close since childhood, it is difficult to conceive that I must make room in our lives for someone new—that she will be not only my sister, but someone's wife and no doubt, one day soon, someone's mother as well." As the group hooted at this, Selena continued. "But I couldn't be happier for my sister in her choice of husband. Athena and Ian, you are both remarkable human beings and I believe you are perfectly suited to one another. I wish you the greatest happiness in all the years to come. And don't forget, Ian, I am right here, watching, lest you make any missteps."

Laughter met this declaration. Damon gave the next tribute. "I could not willingly let my sister Athena go, had she chosen anyone less worthy as a life partner. But I have gotten to know Ian Vernon over the past few days, and I deem him to be the best of men. I won't be a stranger, you two. I plan to visit more often in future—and not just for a wedding."

"You are always welcome," Ian said, smiling, and Athena echoed the sentiment.

Raising his glass, Damon added, "May thy life be long and happy, thy cares and sorrows few, and the many friends around thee prove faithful, fond, and true."

Following the applause, Caroline Ackroyd stood and raised her glass. "I wish to thank my brother, who has so devotedly looked after me all these years, and my new sisters-in-law, two remarkable women who put their own lives at risk to free me from a deadly fate. I am only here today because of these three wonderful people. Thank you, thank you, thank you. I should also like to thank my dear husband, for never wavering in his love for me, even after nine years apart. More than that—he thought he would never see me again, and still, he didn't move on." Her voice cracked, and she paused as if to gather herself, exchanging an adoring look with her husband. "Those nine years were the hardest years of my life—and his too, or so he tells me—and yet the moment we were reunited, it was as if no time at all had passed between us."

The room burst into happy applause. Caroline resumed her seat and was met with a kiss from Edward Ackroyd, whose joyful expression matched her own.

Athena was touched by the obvious affection between the two—and profoundly glad that they were at last united.

"If only they weren't moving so far away," Selena whispered in Athena's ear.

"Yes, it's sad for us, but I'm happy for *them*," Athena whispered in return. Edward had balked at the idea of spending any more time at sea, away from his new wife, and had instead taken a position as an instructor at the Royal Naval Academy at Portsmouth. The couple was moving soon to that southern coastal city, where Athena suspected they would be very happy.

She gave Mr. Ackroyd a smile across the table, which he returned in kind. He had explained to Athena why he'd lied about being at the garden party. He'd been embarrassed for not trying to rescue Miss Vernon that night from the hands of Harold Sinclair. "*I should have punched the man and run off with her that very moment,*" he'd told Athena, "*even though we probably wouldn't have made it as far as the front door, and I would have been thrown in the brig."*

Athena couldn't help but glance at a nearby table, where Lucy Russell sat giggling with her schoolmates. Miss Russell and her mother and father were still unaware of her true parentage. Caroline had said she might never tell them. Edward had been shocked to learn he'd had a daughter who'd had to be given up and dismayed by the part that Caroline's pregnancy had played in forcing her secret internment. But he was grateful their daughter had found a good home, and happy that they could see her now and then and to know that she was thriving.

Mrs. Hillman was the next to propose a toast. "I see you two together and it reminds me of the way my husband and I felt about each other when we met and fell in love. Ian, you joked about marrying Athena to reclaim Thorndale Manor. I know that was not your reason, but I also know how happy you will be to live here again, and to raise your family here. Which brings me to my next point. Thorndale Manor has served well as the home for the Darkmoor Bridge School for Girls. But now that you are married, I think you may wish for more privacy."

Athena wondered where Mrs. Hillman was going with this. Mrs. Hillman darted a questioning look towards Ian, which he returned with an affirming nod. Glancing down at the young woman seated beside her, Mrs. Hillman continued. "Miss Selena. Although your sister is the headmistress of your school, I know how hard you have worked to help keep it afloat and what a talented and dedicated teacher you are. I was not blessed with children, but during the afternoons we have spent together, reading our favorite novels, I have come to feel as close to you as if you were my own daughter."

Selena squeezed the older woman's hand, and their eyes met with affection. "I feel the same way about you, my dearest Mrs. Hillman. As if you have come into my life to replace the mother I lost so long ago."

Mrs. Hillman smiled. "Which leads me to this announcement, my dear. It has long been a dilemma to decide to whom to bequeath my estate. But it is a dilemma no longer." Addressing the group at large, she added, "I have revised my will, and I am leaving Darkmoor Park to Miss Selena."

A gasp erupted from all assembled, the loudest exclamation coming from Selena herself. "Mrs. Hillman! You cannot mean it!"

"Oh, but I do. For many years, I had considered leaving my property to Ian. But as you know, he is already well provided for."

"I am, indeed." Ian smiled at Athena, his blue eyes twinkling.

Athena was too overwhelmed by Mrs. Hillman's generosity to speak.

"But back to you, Miss Selena. My bequest comes with two provisions. The first: that you be allowed to move in at any time you like, even while I am still living. I need time to teach you how to manage the estate, and I would love for you to reside with me."

Selena shook her head as if in wonder. "It would be an honor."

Mrs. Hillman turned to address Athena. "My second provision is this—or perhaps it is not a provision at all but rather a hope. It is my dearest wish that Darkmoor Park will, one day, become the new home for the Darkmoor Bridge School for Girls. For I am tired of living alone. I was a schoolmistress once, in my early years. The idea of being surrounded by young people again is very appealing."

Ian gripped Athena's hand and whispered in her ear, "What do you think, my love?"

"I don't know," she murmured, pondering the notion. Did she want to move the school to Darkmoor Park? "Mrs. Hillman does make a good point," Athena admitted. "About retaining our privacy, while the school continues at an even larger property. Perhaps we can consider it."

He nodded, his eyes bright.

Selena rose and wrapped her arms around Mrs. Hillman. "I don't know what to say. I don't deserve such munificence. How can I ever thank you?"

Mrs. Hillman returned the embrace as a hush fell on the room. "There is no need to thank me, my dear. This gift comes with strings attached, after all. You will be obliged to live with me for the rest of my life."

"A privilege for which I shall always be grateful," Selena responded.

That afternoon, after the guests had left, Athena and her husband escaped outdoors, where sunlight sparkled on the snow-covered lawns and trees.

"A fine wedding, Mrs. Vernon," he pronounced as they wandered hand in hand along paths that had been recently cleared of snow.

"It was like a dream." In the frigid air, their breath came out in misty clouds.

They had agreed to postpone a honeymoon trip—destination as yet undecided—until the summer, when school was not in session. Athena's cheeks grew warm at the thrilling thought of the wedding night ahead, as well as the few days to follow, which they would spend in privacy at Thorndale Cottage.

"A dream from which I never wish to wake." He stopped and took Athena in his arms. "You are my heart and my life, my darling Athena. I love you so."

"And I love you, my dearest."

They kissed, a kiss filled with all the affection that rang in their hearts. Athena knew how fortunate she was, to have survived to see this day and to have found her champion and soulmate. This wonderful man understood her and loved her, and she loved him with every breath she took.

They would be each other's other half and greatest support in the ups and downs of life.

Whatever lay ahead, they would face it happily together.

I am a lifelong fan of Gothic suspense, mystery, and historical romance, and I have thoroughly enjoyed exploring the splendors of these fine genres in the Audacious Sisterhood of Smoke & Fire series.

One of my favorite books is *Jane Eyre*, a page-turning and romantic story filled with dark secrets. I included many homages to that beloved Brontë novel in both this book and *The Mysteries of Pendowar Hall*, the first installment of the series. Charlotte Brontë was a feminist who, despite the backward views of the Victorian era, knew that women were equal to men, and her fiery monologues on the subject inspired my heroines' thinking. I've had such fun writing about the Taylor sisters, their life-changing romances, and their hardheaded determination to uncover the truth, come what may.

My passion for All Things Brontë also had a deep influence on the setting of this novel. For one thing, I love ancient, English mansions and estates, and it has been a delight to set each of the novels in this series at a different country manor house. For another, I've long been fascinated by the setting of a school in historical fiction. Perhaps that enthrallment began with Charlotte Brontë's heartbreakingly true description of Lowood School in *Jane Eyre*, which was based on her own experiences.

While researching and writing *The Secret Diaries of Charlotte Brontë*, which tells the story of Charlotte's scandalous passion and tempestuous romance en route to writing her famous novels, I was intrigued to discover the enormous role that her years at three different schools played in shaping the woman she became and the books she wrote. Charlotte and her sisters Emily and Anne hated being governesses and longed to open a girls' school of their own. But although they placed advertisements, they were unable to persuade a single parent to send their daughter to the remote Haworth Parsonage in Yorkshire. I felt bad for the Brontë sisters and at the same time I thought, what a wonderful concept for a novel!

In this series, just like the Brontës, I gave all three Taylor sisters the desire to open a school for girls, with an advanced curriculum that would teach the same subjects that were taught to boys—a rare concept at the time. I set it up so that they would have the ideal manor home in which to host the enterprise and achieve their dream. However, a story cannot operate without conflict! I had to throw a wrench in the works.

In *The Secrets of Thorndale Manor,* I gave Athena and Selena a similar problem to that which the Brontës had faced—an issue with enrollment. This being a murder mystery, though, their problem is due to the manor house's connection to a long-ago murder, and the convicted murderess who once lived there. To start things off with a bang, so to speak, a maid is found dead in chapter one. It was great fun to bring to life the Darkmoor Bridge School for Girls, with its intimate group of students, teachers, and staff, as well as the nearby village full of suspects—and to let the mysteries and secrets unfold!

A few other things added to the inspiration for this novel. The romantic pirate stories from the novelist Pryor Corbett are inspired in part by my adoration for the first historical romance I ever read, *The Wind Flower* by Laura London, about a young woman who is kidnapped and taken aboard a pirate ship.

The name of the house, Thorndale Manor, is a tribute to the memory of my beloved and deeply missed Aunt Leila and Uncle Neil Handelman, who were devoted supporters of me and my books, and who lived for many decades in a beautiful home on Thorndale Avenue in Chicago.

One last thing I can't help but mention—there is an act of attempted defenestration in this novel. (Defenestration = the act of throwing a person or thing out of a window.) This is due to a long conversation I had last year with my dear cousins, Maxine and Jacob Handelman, about the book I had in progress. Somehow, the term defenestration came up, and they challenged me to include it in my next novel. It took some effort to figure out how to make that happen, both to advance the plot, and so that my heroine would be unable to identify her attacker—but I hope I pulled it off in a thrilling and believable manner!

ACKNOWLEDGMENTS

I wish to express my heartfelt gratitude to the following people for their help in shepherding this novel into the world:

Kathryn Le Veque, the brilliant, kind, hardworking President and CEO of Dragonblade Publishing—and on top of that, an unbelievably prolific author. I am in awe, and I am honored to be included in the impressive roster of Dragonblade authors.

Tamar Rydzinski, my wonderful and supportive agent, Monica Rodriguez, and Celsie Moseley at Context Literary Agency, for everything they do on my behalf. Thank you!

Amy McNulty, my extraordinary editor, for her thorough and perceptive assessment of my books, helpful and uplifting comments, and for noticing all the tiny things that might have slipped through the cracks. She's the best!

Natalie Sowa, Shawn Morrison, and the entire team at Dragonblade Publishing for all their hard work and dedication. I'm so appreciative!

Kim Killion, graphic designer, for the amazingly gorgeous covers. I love them!

Many thanks to my son, Ryan James, for brainstorming with me and suggesting such interesting and diabolical ways for a villain to attempt to murder my heroine. ☺

I would also like to give huge thanks to my English friend David Doré for helping with the factual terminology and construction details in this novel. David is a second-generation builder from South Yorkshire with over fifty years in the construction industry. He accumulated his knowledge of building practices from his father and the many skilled tradesmen who taught him his trade. He patiently answered my many questions about the construction methods in England and explained in detail how repair jobs to a roof would have been carried out, especially on some of the grander houses of the landed gentry. This included supplying hand-drawn illustrations showing rudimentary details of how scaffolding and ladders would have been lashed together before the appropriate tradesmen did any repairs. Thank you so much, David!

And a huge, heartfelt thank you to all my readers everywhere. Writing novels is my passion. This book is for you! If you enjoyed it, please tell your friends, and don't miss the other books in the Audacious Sisterhood of Smoke & Fire series. I am so grateful for your support!

SYRIE JAMES is the *USA Today*, Amazon, and international bestselling author of fifteen critically acclaimed novels of historical mystery, historical fiction, and romance. Syrie loves All Things English and is obsessed with the Victorian and Regency eras. (Fabulous gowns! Men in cravats and on horseback! Country manor houses! Tea and finger sandwiches! Scones and jam! Sign me up, please!)

Syrie loves to write about strong, brilliant, adventurous women who are ahead of their time and will stop at nothing to achieve their dreams, and the bold, irresistible men who crash headlong into their lives and turn everything upside down forever. A research and story-structure maven, Syrie is committed to writing page-turning books and taking her characters on challenging journeys of growth and discovery.

After writing several romantic novels about Jane Austen and the Brontës (Syrie's favorite classic authors), a passionate version of *Dracula*, and a sizzling-hot Victorian romance trilogy, she has gleefully turned her pen (okay, her computer) to writing historical murder mysteries set in the English countryside. This requires many research trips to England, the best perk on Earth.

A member of the Writers Guild of America, Sisters in Crime, Dramatists Guild, Jane Austen Society of North America, and Historical Novel Society, Syrie has sold numerous scripts to film and television and her work as a playwright and director has been nominated for Broadway World awards and produced across North America, off-Broadway in New York City, and in Australia.

You will often find Syrie dressing up in one of her many Regency or Victorian frocks and dancing the night away at a ball—or performing on stage as Jane Austen herself. When she's not writing or reading, Syrie loves to take long walks, eat delicious food, attend movies and the theatre, direct stage plays, design and create historic costumes, dabble in photography, and play board games and celebrate holidays with family and friends. Syrie lives in Los Angeles a stone's throw from her grown children and grandson. She loves to hear from readers and can be contacted at www.syriejames.com.

Social media links:
Website: www.syriejames.com
Facebook: facebook.com / syriejames
Facebook Author page: facebook.com / AuthorSyrieJames
Instagram: instagram.com / syriejames
Goodreads: goodreads.com / author / show / .806500 / Syrie_James